MW00886658

SIN AND MISTLETOE

A CHRISTMAS ANTHOLOGY

AMANDA HOLLY   ERICA JADEN

JADE MARSHALL

ALISON MACKENZIE   M KAY NOIR

Contents

Stolen Vows
Amanda Holly

Serment au Noel
Erica Jaden

DARKEST OBSESSION
JADE MARSHALL

A RED CHRISTMAS
ALISON MACKENZIE

COVERT DESIRES
M KAY NOIR

Stolen Vows

Amanda Holly

CW's, TW's and Kinks

For a detailed trigger warning list please visit:
https://storytellerbookbox.co.za/sin-and-mistletoe-warning

ONE
NIKOLAI

Moscow

I FUCKING HATE CHRISTMAS, HAVE DONE FOR AS long as I can remember, but this year, it's worse.

The band hired to play at this evening's party is thrashing out one Christmas tune after the other, and why does this bloody music always have the sound of bells ringing in it? It's so damn aggravating I'm having visions of grabbing their instruments, smashing them to smithereens, and then ripping into the musicians until all that's left are broken body parts and blood strewn across the temporary stage.

Everywhere I look, there are Christmas trees decorated with gold ornaments, the theme for the evening, except for the holly and mistletoe which line the chimney mantels and is spread across tables laden with overflowing platters of finger foods for the elite, all prepared by our host's master chef.

I shove a slice of toast with Beluga caviar into my mouth to give my teeth something to grind on, but my fists remain clenched from being forced to mix and mingle when all I want to do is get the hell out of here. Fast. Every year, this shit they call silly season, rubs me up the wrong way and with two days to go, I'm ready to kill the next person to wish me a Merry Christmas.

Have they forgotten already?

It's been just six weeks since I buried my parents.

In hindsight, I should've made more of an effort to reconnect with them before they passed, but with everything that's happened recently, I'm barely able to shift blood through the useless organ beating inside my chest. I can't say I mourn for either of them—it's the others I can't get out of my mind.

I glance up, spot Mikhail Melnichenko trying to attract my attention on the other side of the vast ballroom inside his home, and my irritation ratchets up another notch. He wants me to follow him to his office. Under normal circumstances I'd ignore him, but my need to get the hell away from this seasonal shit wins out, so I slip away from my girlfriend Anna and the hangers-on surrounding her who have failed to hold my attention. I've politely declined the white powder clinging to the inside of her nose but gladly accepted the ridiculously expensive vodka shots being dished out so royally.

I stride through the ballroom, avoiding conversations with people desperately seeking my attention, giving them a less than friendly nod when necessary as I keep moving towards Mikhail's office.

Vodka and work have been my steady companions since resigning my commission in the Spetsnaz. Not a day goes past without me missing being part of a brotherhood like that, but after witnessing my team being massacred during our last assignment, I don't have the stomach for it anymore. According to Anna, I'm going through the motions of living by breathing, eating when I have to, and exercising until I crash, no more space or energy left for even the idea of sex, let alone desire, for her or anyone else. She's accused me of having shut down all my feelings and she's right, but I don't think I had many of them before that event either. PTSD is what the army called it. *Dead man walking* is what it feels like.

And because of that, I'm stuck running my father's empire. The old man got one over on me there, forcing my hand from beyond the grave. His aerospace company will never feel like it's mine but at least I've begun to make changes —starting with assigning a new CEO.

The company develops, manufactures, and deploys equipment for the Russian special forces, and my father used to brag he owned the biggest warfare manufacturing enterprise within the largest country in the world. That's not what I want my legacy to be. Especially not after they delivered the faulty stealth bombers which killed my team, and many more. Knowing I'm partially responsible for these deaths, even though it's only through shared DNA, is going to cost me dearly in equal measures of guilt and atonement for the rest of my life.

So, what am I doing meeting with another father-figure devil? Halting outside Mikhail's den, I watch him preparing to talk to me while my thoughts linger in Moldova.

If it weren't for the distraction of the orphan kids playing soccer on that particular day, I would have been up front, leading, instead of lagging behind, forced to bear witness to the missile instantly killing my team of eight in front of my eyes. The image of that massive crater, filled with debris and body parts, and the smell of charred flesh, claws at my sanity twenty-four seven, without respite.

I should have died that day.

"Nikolai, come in. Sit and have a drink with me."

Mikhail, Anna's father, beckons me to sit in one of the two dark green leather wingback chairs while he drops into the other. He leans forward, a bottle of the expensive vodka in his outstretched hand. I grab two crystal tumblers from the side table between us, and he pours a liberal amount of the clear liquid into each glass. This much alcohol would push me over my personal limit, and I have no intention of drinking at the rate he guzzles it down.

I take a small sip and let the ice-cold beverage trickle into my gut.

"How long have you been dating my Anna now, eh? It's high time you put a ring on her finger."

His smile doesn't reach his piercing blue eyes, fixed on my face with laser-like precision.

My stomach churns at the thought of being trapped in a marriage to the *Pakhan*'s daughter. I would not survive such a fate. She's a beautiful woman, but she's been groomed not to move without her father's permission, and after my stint in the military, I'm done following orders.

He leans forward, using his bulk as a subliminal threat. "Let me announce your engagement tonight."

I use the only excuse he cannot refute. "You know it would reflect badly on Anna. People would say it shows a lack of respect for my parents, who I have just buried. They may even assume my parents didn't approve of her, and now they're gone... It won't look good announcing anything now. It's too soon, Mikhail Yvanovich."

I used his patronymic name here as a show of deference, nevertheless, he glares at me over the rim of his glass, analysing me, the situation, before slowly nodding with a barely contained scowl. I'll bet it's not often he's out-manoeuvred.

"My apologies." He tips the contents of his glass down his throat. "You're right, of course. We'll wait until after Christmas. Sometime in the early new year."

At last, a reason to be grateful for the season. I will have to disappear for a while, until he's found another target to foist his daughter on. This so-called relationship between his daughter and I is one of mutual convenience, her presence saves me from being harassed by women intent on snaring a wealthy husband, and for her I'm a body that prevents her father from shackling her to one of his cronies. It's a win-win. At least it was.

"In that case, go dance with my Anna. And start thinking about the role I've offered you in our organisation."

A shiver dances down my spine. Nothing on Earth could entice me to join the Bratva. The organisation he's referring to has a cute name—brotherhood, ha!—for a mafia that's responsible for a litany of heinous crimes.

Eager to escape the claws of the Bratva's most feared *Pakhan*, I take my leave, and rather than heading to the dance floor as instructed, I grab my long leather coat from the coat rack in the entrance hall and walk out of the party through the back terrace.

Instead of being unseen, as I'd anticipated, I run into a small pack of drunk, entitled sons of the Moscow elite, huddled in the corner. They turn my way at the sound of my soles crunching on the snow covering the paving stones. Their fresh faces and fake smiles remind me of myself in my previous life, before I witnessed the worst atrocities committed by mankind and became Moscow's most eligible billionaire.

"Good evening, Nikolai," they chant in unison, shuffling closer together with a look of 'walk on by, dude, there's nothing to see here' on their faces.

Curious to find what they could possibly be trying to hide at a party where alcohol and drugs are freely available, I step closer. A ripple of sparkly turquoise briefly catches my eye before it's hidden behind a wall of black tuxedos. I instantly make the connection between the colourful material and the person wearing that exact hue this evening.

Victoria. Anna's younger step-sister. They're not related by blood, but they're closer than most siblings, despite being polar opposites in every way imaginable.

On the outside, Anna is tall, blond, and beautiful in that skin and bones fashionable sense. She could have graced the cover of international women's magazines if her father wasn't the leader of Russia's most powerful and dangerous crime ring.

Victoria, on the other hand, is shorter, curvaceous, and has long dark curly hair that makes a man long to run his fingers through it. Not to mention how her breasts are plump and perky on a body that's all in curves and dips, exactly what has men thinking very indecent thoughts of what they'd like to be doing to her. I'm not blind.

Then there's Mikhail, who seems to think Anna and I are a perfect match. No prizes for guessing where he thinks my perfection as a prospective son-in-law lies. I'll bet he dreams about all the things he could do with my inheritance once he thinks it's at his disposal.

But right now, it's not Anna I'm concerned about.

"What're you up to?" I ask, advancing towards the young men at a leisurely pace, eager to forget the bullet I've already dodged this evening. One way or another it looks like trouble's going to find me tonight.

"Oh, you know, just guy stuff," one of the youngsters answers with a cocky grin on his face. The condensation of his breath leaves a trail rising above him while his companions snigger, high-fiving each other behind his back.

"Yeah?" Their pupils are dilated, and the residue of this evening's drug of choice dusts their tuxes. "Care to share?"

Clearly they weren't expecting the interruption, but their leader looks me up and down before he shrugs and answers for them all. "Why not? You're not that much older than us."

The black wall parts, revealing the luscious creature in turquoise. Her back is turned towards me, giving me a full view of the perfect curves currently being hugged by a skin-tight, glittery dress crafted by a mastermind who knows exactly how to turn the female form into a delicious, irresistible treat.

"Victoria?" My voice sounds stern and cranky while I soak up the vision of the little temptress as she slowly turns round to face me.

My vision fills with her. Only her. Everything else fades into the background as I scan her face, looking for a sign she's sniffed one of the missing white lines of powder cut onto the round mirror currently being held by the guy directly behind her. It's as if her dark brown eyes, with normal-sized pupils, zap me through my own pale blue, singeing the back of my retinas.

"It's Vika," she answers, challenging me with her gaze while she plants a hand on her hip, giving me the sass I'm used to from her. "Shouldn't you be out there dancing with my sister?"

I'll take the flak from her step-father because we travel in similar circles and I have to, but not from her. Cheeky brat. She loves playing with fire, it seems.

"Did you take cocaine?" I grab her by the wrist, pulling her away from the men who are clearly out to get her intoxicated enough she doesn't put up a fight for their evening's planned entertainment. What the hell is she thinking, getting involved in such silly games?

She smirks. "What's it to you if I did? I'm an adult. I can do what I like."

Her breasts, a sturdy handful if I were to cup them in the palms of my hands, quiver in the cold air. The dress is cut so low, her chest is covered in goosebumps. She's going to freeze to death if she stays outside in these sub-zero temperatures. Her nipples are pebbling against the fabric and begging for a mouth or some fingers to fondle them. The way they pucker, a clamp would fit just right on that turgid point.

Damn her. What's she got me thinking about now?

"If you were an adult, you'd know better." I fume, dragging her behind me as I take the steps down into the garden.

"Hey, Niko. What are you doing? We were about to have ourselves a good time! I invited you to join us, man."

The nameless young leader begins to follow me, clearly outraged at the thought of being denied access to their little toy.

Halfway down, I settle Victoria against the concrete banister of the frosted stone steps before removing my coat and wrapping it around her shoulders. "Stay right here."

Her eyes flash as if she's about to fight me, until she sees the look on my face and shrinks back down, breathing warmth into my coat to increase her body temperature while I trot up the four steps back to the terrace.

I crowd into the personal space of the young man who's assigned himself the role of mouthpiece for this band of degenerates. Someone needs to take this kid down before he fucks up the rest of his life.

"You were about to have a good time, were you? With the daughter of the *Pakhan*. How do you think that's going to work out for you when he finds out you got his step-daughter high and then had yourselves a little gang bang?"

Full of chemically-induced bravado, the whippersnapper takes a swing at my face. I dodge his fist with ease before landing two of my own in his soft belly. He drops to the floor, curling into himself, moaning as the rest of his friends decide it's a good time to play a disappearing act and scarper inside the mansion where they're instantly swallowed up by the crowd.

"Get back inside before I rip your eyes out for even thinking you can lay a finger on that girl."

Realising he's on his own, and my temper is on a very short fuse, he ducks his face into his bent elbow, mutters his excuses, and scrambles to his feet before fleeing the scene.

I watch him go, wondering if I was ever an asshole like him as I take the steps down, ready to give Victoria a piece of my mind. But as my eyes settle on the step where I left her, I find it empty.

Where the fuck did she go? Blast the little hellion!

I stand at the bottom of the steps, my chest heaving. Why

do I care? Like she said, she's an adult. She can do what she wants, and I don't have to stick around to watch her do it. Then why the hell am I scrutinising the garden, searching for a glimpse of the temptress in turquoise?

I follow the trail of dainty white footprints into the garden. The deeper I go, the quieter it gets, plunging me straight back into combat mode. I force myself to regulate my breathing while I pause, filter through the sounds of nature until my ears fill with the rapid panting of my prey.

She's close.

"You can come out now, Victoria." She can't stay out here much longer in those shoes without becoming hypothermic.

I don't expect her to appear immediately—she's the type of woman who will keep a man on his toes, waiting. Savouring the moment, I smile, exercising an amount of patience I didn't know I was capable of as my gaze latches onto the evidence of her scattered breathing.

She holds out for less than two minutes, huffing and stomping her feet as she reappears between two snow-covered bushes.

"What do you want from me?" she hisses like a kitty cat.

Good question, but not one I want to consider while she freezes to death.

"I want your assurance you're not going back up there," I point towards the house where she lives, "and hooking up with those assholes who are set on getting you high and then taking turns fucking you."

She recoils.

"*Mierda*. What do you care? You're Anna's boyfriend, not mine. I can fuck anyone I want." With a hip cocked and her hands splayed, fingers touching, she manages to emphasize her hourglass figure, stirring the embers of my libido. "Now run along and go do whatever it was you were going to do."

Her words leave little clouds of vapour in the air between us, pulling an unexpected laugh from the depth of my stomach. Dismissal coming from her, it's funny. The tiny mouse trying to stand up to the big cat. She doesn't stand a chance.

"Nice try, Victoria." I emphasize each one of the syllables of her name. "But I'm not going anywhere until I've made sure you understand the danger you're in."

She scoffs. "You're not my father. You can't make me do anything I don't want to."

I smirk, knowing full well I can make her do anything with the right motivation. I can make any woman bow to me. Guess she doesn't know it. This unresolved energy that's been sparking between us has lit a fuse I am not inclined to extinguish. Now, I want to push, see how long it takes for her to spark, and then, inevitably, combust under my control.

To my left is the brick shed used to house the garden equipment, and something tells me I'll find exactly what I need to carry out an idea forming in my mind while she continues to give me sass.

I take a step towards her.

"If you come any closer, I'll scream."

"Go ahead, scream if you want."

I know she won't. Her chocolate-brown eyes have

devoured me every time she's been close, but just in case she surprises me, I grab her wrist and drag her inside the modern version of a garden shed, slamming the door behind me.

It's dark inside, the only light coming through the windows is that of the quarter-moon reflected off the snow. It's also surprisingly warm, and as I turn to find the source, I'm surprised to see the gardener is using the structure to grow plants. But more than that, I'm gratified by the orange glow of an overhead heater being used to prevent them from freezing.

She's silent now, her sassiness curtailed as she watches me closely with a little fear in her eyes. She likes watching me, little Victoria. I've seen her ogling me when she thinks I or Anna aren't looking. But it's not only trepidation I see there today. It's time to test that theory, the one which states she desires a man's touch on her, and not just any man's. Mine. Her pupils dilate as my hands slide beneath the coat to rub up and down the length of her arms, bringing warmth to her skin.

Those goose bumps have nothing to do with the cold. Same for the little pant falling from her plump lips.

The fabric of her dress is slippery, and my hands roam across her back as she glides hers in the space between our chests with a half-hearted attempt to push me away. She won't, I know it. I stifle a smile when she leans in and her fists curl into the lapels of my jacket.

Her whisper cracks through the silence. "W-what are you doing?"

Losing my mind, if truth be told. Gone is the sass, in its place is a girl with a voice made tremulous by unexplored desire. And damn, I want to be the one who explores the virgin territory of her need, the first one to claim this uncharted path. What would it feel like? My mouth on her skin, her pussy. My cock buried inside her warm, tight body...

I grip the material of her dress around her hips, pulling it up until the hem is bunched in my hands around her waist.

"Turn around," I growl into her ear.

"Why?"

There's a hint of panic in her voice, and she's back to fighting me, moving her hands to her dress, trying to lower it.

She's not getting away so easily, the little tease.

My right hand releases the dress as I pull back, then land an open-handed slap onto her nicely rounded ass, barely covered by the slip of lace I feel beneath my palm. She gasps as the blow lands on her cold skin.

"*Qué estás haciendo?* What the hell do you think you're doing?" she exclaims as she baulks.

I love hearing her revert to her native tongue, but the more she protests, the more determined I become to continue dishing out the lesson she clearly needs to learn. Men are not to be trusted. That naivety of hers needs to be dealt with. And if she's going to tease cock, she better learn there are consequences. Best it comes from me than those pricks who were going to fuck her every hole and cum all over her like a two-bit whore from a seedy brothel.

My gaze falls on a bundle of hemp rope, and I seize it

without thinking things through. Taking advantage of Victoria's confusion, I tug at her wrists, binding them together in front of her. Once she's restrained, I slip my finger between the rope and her hands, making sure it's not so tight it will damage her skin before I tie it off with a slipknot.

My cock weeps at the sight of her. She's caught her bottom lip between her teeth, and her gaze is full of questions as she wrestles with her bound hands, shifting her weight from foot to foot. I should reassure her, but I want her on edge for this next part, and my selfish need has come out to play.

One way or the other, Victoria is going to learn to submit tonight.

Two

VICTORIA

How did I end up like this? Helpless as Niko pulls on the rope, lifting my hands upward, the other end of the rope now flung around a steel rafter above.

"I'm going to teach you a lesson," he growls into my ear, making the skin along my neck come alive as if kissed by an electric current.

I should be horrified, but honestly, there's nothing this man could ever do to make me not want him. There's something about his aloof confidence that makes me hot all over. Those boys back at the party don't stand a chance again a real man like Niko, not even when I'm shaking in my shoes, wondering what the hell's got into him. Tingles are coursing all over my body, my core clenching with need, my panties already soaked and sticking to my folds.

I was only going to try a little cocaine. Where's the harm

in that? He's completely over-reacting. It was only going to be the one time. Those boys, I could fend them off. They're so far gone, I'd have had control the whole time. I did think this through. Why does he insist on treating me like a child? I'm almost twenty-one already.

Looking up, my gaze lands on the binding around my wrists. Thick strands of twisted rope keeping my hands raised, useless. The rough material is chafing at my skin when I try to move, and every scrape makes me wetter, it seems. Why does this turn me on? Or is it all about the man doing this to me?

Niko ties the tail end of the rope around a hook bolted into the wall, the shovel he took down now standing against the brick wall. It's almost as if it's there taunting me, letting me know why it's down there and my hands are thrust high above me.

Should I be trying to get hold of the tool? Swing my feet towards the handle so I can use it to beat Niko off? It's a nice idea, thinking I can get the better of him, but is it what I want right now? As much as this situation of being at the mercy of a man is one I've been warned about avoiding by several father figures in my life, instead of being afraid, it's making me feel all sorts of tingles inside my body. I mean...this is Niko, my sister's boyfriend, and he is absolutely drop dead gorgeous with his high cheekbones and square jawline covered in rough stubble, the dark hair that's just a tad too long and brushes his eyelashes, and that tall, muscular, overpowering physique which makes my mouth water.

Is he going to fuck me? His girlfriend's little sister? Do I want him to cheat on her with *me*? What is he thinking? Unless he's going to kill me. I stop breathing for a fraction of a beat. Am I going to die?

I roll onto my toes, clenching the muscles along my arms, legs, and abdomen while trying to lean into the stretch and ignore the little voice inside my head wanting me to ask for more. More what, though? I'm no angel, I read all the raunchy books, but I have zero experience with men, and I am so out of my depth here.

He's lifting my dress again, securing it around my waist with more of the rope inside the shed. My exposed ass cheeks feel the chill in the air, except the skin where his hand surely left a red mark. I twist my head back, but the bunched-up dress is in the way and I don't know whether he's left a real mark, or if it's all in my head.

Finally satisfied with his knot, he turns back toward me, raking his gaze from my feet up my legs. He pauses at the sight of my garter belt, savouring the view, and by the way he's licking his lips and his eyes light up, he either likes what he sees, a lot, or he's furious with me, again.

But then his lips slide into a grin, and my heart beats faster, knowing I'm finally being seen. By him. All this time of wondering what it would be like with a man such as him, and now the exhilaration of my initiation into this whole new world is bubbling inside me like a runaway freight train. Thrilling, and terrifying all at once. What will he do? How far will he go?

My nipples, pebbled from the cold, now pucker and

tingle some more for a whole host of other reasons when he steps closer, my breasts heavy, almost painful in their over-sensitivity now. His warm breath spreads across my cheeks, his heat chasing the cold, and I so wish he'd rip my dress off and put his hands all over my desperate body to warm me up. But no, he'll make me wait. Blood hums through my veins in anticipation of what he'll do next.

I thought he was inebriated when I saw him at the party, but there's no smell of alcohol on his breath, and his eyes are razor-sharp, making me wonder if he's got X-ray vision that can cut through fibre. I smirk. That's wishful thinking, probably on both our parts.

Time seems to stop as he stands there, watching me, making me squirm. But fuck this, I can't let him see me squirm. This is what he wants, and I've never given a man, any man, the satisfaction of getting what he wants from me.

"Is that all you've got?" That crazy voice inside me can't help itself—it's clamouring to come out, goading him into doing something, anything, to alleviate this burning need inside me. And the crazy is drowning out the fear, making me act like I know what I'm doing with a man like Niko.

His top lip curls as his eyes bore into mine, leaving me in no doubt he's on to my game.

I run my tongue across my lips. I can't help it. I'm dying here, waiting, wanting.

"Naughty girls don't get what they want. Didn't your mother teach you that?"

I gulp. So, I'm naughty now. What will it take for him to call me a good girl?

His hands slide up my arms, eliciting goose bumps all the way, and his gaze follows before he checks the rope binding my wrists once more. The warmth of his skin against mine nearly has me moan out loud, but I know better than to give him what he wants. I'm completely out of my depth here, on the one hand trying to make him fuck me, when I don't know what a man like him needs, and on the other, as much as I'm desperate to feel him inside me, I'm scared. It's too much..

"My mother taught me everything I need to know. I don't need you to replace her, now let me down this instant."

I've learned my lesson—he can cut this bullshit now and let me go.

My words have no impact on him at all. He merely carries on, running his fingertips down the inside of my arms, teasing me, making me squirm as I dance to his tune. Then, the bastard smiles.

"Not until you've learned your lesson."

What? No. But at the same time, a part of me is going, 'Yes, please.' He's so close, his breath is giving me goosebumps along my neck, and they seem to spread down my chest, along my abdomen, through my bellybutton all the way to my ovaries, making my pussy drip into my panties. My pelvic floor muscles clench as a shiver runs down my spine. I'm so inside my head, I don't notice him step back until he pivots me round and lands two quick swats on my backside.

I lift my feet, one by one, prancing on the spot. "Oww."

Damn it, that hurts.

"I'm going to make sure you feel this for a long time, little girl," he growls in my ear before he lets loose, landing slaps on my ass, peppering each cheek with a harsh, loud spanking until my skin feels like it's on fire and my feet can't keep up with his relentless rhythm. "That's it, dance for me. Show me how you take your punishment, that you want my discipline."

"*Mi-errr-daaa.*" His voice alone is enough to make my body blow apart like a hooker on crack. Add to that the constant feel of his palm rubbing my ass in between blows, his hand warm against the hot, sensitive cheeks, and I'm ready to crawl out of my skin for him.

When he starts swatting again, it's painful until it's not. There's only heat, sensation, warmth, the cold breath of the air whispering along the sensitized skin in between his swats.

"Yesss," I hiss as he continues to push me way beyond my normal pain threshold. My head drops back between my upstretched arms, and my eyes close in oblivion. I've got it bad. I've lost my mind. More. More. More. "Niko," I groan, desperate for him to give me something, anything, as long as it's more.

Suddenly, he's in front of me again, curling a finger under my chin, lowering my head until my vision is filled with him. "It's not Niko, it's Sir."

"W-why?" My voice is soft as a whisper, all the energy I possess concentrated on keeping me on my feet.

"Because you submit to me, and that's your way of signalling to me you really want this."

His pupils are fixed on my gaze, daring me to deny him.

Dare I deny him? Do I even want this?

I close my eyes, but he won't allow it, shaking my head from his grip on my chin.

"Eyes on me, little one."

His intense ice-blue gaze hasn't subsided, and it's driving me crazy, making me wish we were naked and I could rub myself against him until he can't resist me and fucks me until I pass out. I want to be in control, to own him, but who am I kidding? That's never going to happen. Not with a man like him.

"Now, tell me you won't ever be trying any of those drugs anyone tries to make you take."

His voice is stern, leaving me in no doubt he'll carry on dishing out his punishment until I agree to his demands.

"Okay, I won't." I smile, telling him what he wants to hear. I don't know if I can do this, never mind how much I'm creaming my panties with desire. This...it's not something I ever signed up for.

He lowers his head, shaking it. "It looks like someone hasn't learned their lesson."

What? But...I thought—

He swings me back round with such force, I wince at the pull of the rope against my skin until he has me foxtrotting on my toes once more, desperately trying to avoid his discipline. He dishes out several biting open-handed slaps to both my ass cheeks and thighs. I've lost count of how many times he's spanked me and, exhausted from holding myself up, I finally relent.

"Okay, Sir." Tears stream down my face, and my chest heaves, drowning in an emotion so big, I can no longer contain it. "I won't take their drugs. I promise. Just please stop punishing me, Sir. I beg you."

I sob, and it's ugly. Snot dribbles from my nose, mixing with my tears as it pools in my neck. My mascara must've left a mess on my cheeks.

"Sshhhh, little one. I've got you." He hauls me into an embrace, curling his arm around my back, taking my weight off my feet while his soft, white handkerchief wipes my face, soaking up my outburst. "Let it all out."

I feel him stretch behind me, and seconds later, my hands lower, coming down around his neck as my head drops onto his shoulder and I burrow my nose into his skin, breathing in his cologne in-between the hiccups brought on by the tears.

He smells of sandalwood and citrus fruits, vaguely reminding me of a home I used to have, back in the days I lived in Colombia and both my parents were alive. I wish I could stay here forever, but something tells me he's going to leave soon, and I'm desperate for more of him before he does. His hands on me, his mouth, his cock...

Fighting my exhaustion, I raise my legs until I'm hugging his waist and his hard length presses into my panties. They're thoroughly soaked, and there's no doubt he can feel it through his pants.

His hands lift to cradle my ass, his fingers digging into my battered skin, pressing my weeping core against him. I raise my forehead to rest it against his, wishing he'd take off his shirt so I could feel his skin against mine.

He takes two strides until he's got me pushed back, half-seated on the wooden table lined up against the wall. The second my ass lands on top of the rough, icy wood, I hiss, feeling the cold seep through my scorching skin.

He leans back, and with my wrists still bound and around his neck, my upper body moves forward, leaving me plastered against him, chest to thighs. There's a wire inside me, coiling up into a tight spring, ready to be released, urging me to rub my core against the bulge in his pants as my tongue slides across his chiselled jawline, now covered in stubble and giving him that roguish look of a pirate. I don't know what exactly I want anymore, just that it has to be him.

"Please, Sir." The soft texture of his lips succumbs to my probing tongue, and I lean in, pulling his bottom lip between my teeth before releasing it and breathing into his mouth. "I beg you...Sir, make me feel better."

My sixth sense is completely in tune with him. It's as if something inside him unfurls and melts, giving in to my desperate pleas. Or perhaps it's the way I'm grinding my soft curves into his hard torso, speaking the age-old language of sexual desire to a chosen mate. I don't know where this wisdom comes from—all I know is I'll die if he leaves me hanging.

I've laid it all out on the line. For weeks, I've watched him with Anna, wishing it was me he was courting, me he would dance with, me he would take out on dates. And now, there's nothing I can do to make it any clearer. I want him to fuck me. Will he give me what I need, knowing I'm the little stepsister of the woman he's been dating for six months? Or will he call a halt to this lava of lust winding and bubbling between us?

He cups my face between his palms, rubbing his thumbs across my lips, spreading my lipstick onto my skin.

"Fuck, I can't get enough of this look on you."

What is it he sees on my face?

"What—" He doesn't let me finish the question.

His lips descend to mine without mercy, bruising them until I open and his tongue slides into my mouth, doing the tango with mine, flicking my teeth while his hands wrap around my throat, slowly squeezing. The combination of his touches leaves me breathless, even more desperate for relief from this insane fire that's raging out of control.

Air rushes into my lungs as he lowers his hands to my breasts, pinching my nipples through the thin material of my dress.

"Do you know what you're doing to me?" he rasps.

I thought I did, but the way his hands are pulling at my lace thong, ripping it away from my body in tatters, makes me wonder whether I had any idea what this man is capable of. He fumbles with his belt, and I wish my hands were free so I could help him get his cock out and guide him to my entrance before I wake up and find out this has all been a dream.

His mouth is back on mine, gentler this time, dropping

kisses across the seam of my lips before his tongue plunders back inside.

I squeeze my arms around his neck, keeping him in place as his cock rubs along my lower lips, pushing into my clit, forcing the hood up where his cool fingers take hold of my little nub, making it pulse as I moan into his mouth. He keeps the pressure on his fingers as his thick girth pushes into my entrance and stalls.

I hold my breath, curling my legs tight around his hips. *Please, please, please don't pull away from me now.*

Then he surges inside me with a single hard thrust, and the world around me spins as my thighs clench around him. He holds still.

I hurt. It feels like he's tearing me apart with that enormous cock of his.

My breath comes out in short bursts, and I thread my fingers through his hair, gripping the soft strands between my fingers. He slowly pulls out, but it's no more than an inch before he thrusts back inside, repeating the process until I'm gushing, pushing back, searching for his rhythm, the pain long forgotten.

His cock pulses inside me like a beating heart. He's so deep, I can feel him thickening more as my body adjusts to his full length and girth. I feel him everywhere, wrapped around me, penetrated within, but there's no time to think as his fingers pull on my clit while his cock slides in and out. My muscles spasm, making me shake as I try to hold him inside, squeezing him for all I'm worth.

He groans. A sense of power engulfs me when it dawns on me I can make him lose control. He's all mine, even if it's only for a moment.

He squeezes my nipple between his other thumb and index finger, sending lightning bolts of desire through me, making my internal muscles clench around his length, pulling him deeper inside. The back of my stilettos push against his ass, locking him in place inside me, where it feels like he belongs.

This moment is nothing like I thought it could ever be. No naughty books have prepared me for this feeling of utter abandon. Nothing in the world matters except reaching the high I feel rising inside me, urging me to keep moving until I've reached that peak. And that's exactly what I do, ride him, wrap myself around him, leaving him nowhere to go until he finally ruts like a man possessed, pushing me over the edge with his magnificent cock and demanding fingers pulling and stretching my clit and nipple.

And then it happens. The world disappears for a brief moment while my body recalibrates, searching for a new state of being and my mind fizzles in a pool of sated lust.

"Yes... More... No. Yes! Ooohhhhhh," I pant, incoherent, incapable of making sense or forming a sentence. My mind and body are out of sync, no longer communicating.

It takes me a while to feel the silence settling around us.

As I open my eyes, Niko pulls out, tucks his half-engorged cock inside his pants and zips up, all the while refusing to make eye contact with me.

The chill in the air seeps into my bones as he takes my hands, pulls them over his head and begins to untie the rope. It's quick, his slipknots doing the job they're supposed to, releasing on his tug.

He rubs my wrists, bringing warmth back into my tingling flesh. His movements are slow, controlled, as if he's working his way through a check-list.

He's aloof, disconnected, done with me, his regret a living entity creeping into the shed. It wraps around me, tightens like a noose around my neck, taking away my ability to breathe, leaving me unable to utter a word as I watch him pick up his coat from the floor. He cloaks it around me, holding onto the collar as he looks into my eyes.

It's like being sucked into a black hole that's swallowed him up, and I can't bear to watch.

I lower my gaze, staring at the shoes strangling my feet.

He steps back, ready to disappear, but before he does, he utters his parting words.

"This was a mistake."

THREE
NIKOLAI

Malta

WHAT THE FUCK AM I DOING?

It's been five years since I left this life behind, yet, here I am, parked down the street from a house I've been watching since that phone call with Anna. All because my ex-girlfriend thinks her father is about to marry her step-sister off to one of his cronies. Then there's the fact Victoria's been on the run for almost two years. How did I not know this?

I shouldn't care about any of it, except I've been keeping an eye on both women, on and off, since I left Moscow. I'm here mostly because of the guilt I still feel about taking Victoria's virginity before disappearing from both their lives. At least, that's what I've been telling myself. There's no way I would have answered that phone call, let alone agreed to keep an eye on Victoria, if I had managed to get her out of my mind.

The reality is, Victoria haunts my waking moments and invades my dreams at night. She's my little secret, unless she's told anyone about what I did to her, taking her without a care that night, thinking only of my need to be buried inside her hot, dripping-wet pussy. Somehow, I don't think she did. It's not like I've gone to any effort to hide from Mikhail's Bratva, nor have I changed my identity. Unlike the little vixen I'm stalking. Mikhail would have had me found and executed if he knew I'd taken the girl's virginity.

It's a warm mid-winter day here on the small island of Malta, but because of its location in the Mediterranean, there's a balmy sea breeze running through the streets of the coastal town of Sliema. If I hadn't been in such a hurry to locate Victoria, I could have popped over to Gozo to fetch a car from Luca's uncle, Lorenzo, instead of renting this small electric piece of shit I've had to squeeze myself into. It lacks all creature comforts, including air conditioning, but the moment that bright red front door opens, I forget everything and focus on her.

Victoria.

Seeing her again after all this time is like receiving a punch to my stomach, robbing me of all breath instantly.

She's all smiles and double handblown kisses for the woman and toddler who wave her off, and I've never seen anything like it. Not the loving gaze of the little boy reaching out for her, nor the look on her face as she smiles down at him.

She's got roots here, people she knows. And that look of contentment on her features, waving at the toddler—she'll make a fantastic mother...

That's the moment I realise how much trouble I'm in. This isn't going to be a quick extraction, one where I give her a new identity, set her up in a new country, and walk away again. No, this is going to be a very different type of operation. It's going to be torture.

Fuck.

She's changed her look. She used to be a brunette, but now her hair has the sun-kissed look of island life, and her skin exudes the same healthy glow. She's a vision of beauty in a bright yellow, strapless sundress that's got come-get-me vibes written all over it.

I readjust my pants, thanking my lucky stars she's clueless what seeing her again is doing to me. She'd probably slap me senseless if she knew, and she'd have every right to do so.

She slips an open-face helmet over her hair and slides a pair of sunglasses onto her nose before stepping over the bright blue scooter parked in the front and driving away.

As I start the cookie tin I'm driving, I notice a black SUV immediately pulls out to follow her in the traffic. Two things hit me at once: one, I can no longer see Victoria, and two, her sister was right. She's being followed.

I take a picture of the number plate of the vehicle and send it to one of the only men I trust back in Moscow.

Me: *Image sent*

Me: *please check for driver id*

My phone vibrates two seconds later.

Vlad: *k*

I shove the device back into my pocket and concentrate on maintaining a reasonable distance from the car tailing Victoria. We drive for another ten minutes before the black SUV slows down and passes her.

Victoria has parked her scooter in front of a women's clothing boutique.

I dip into an empty parking spot two cars away and watch her step off the scooter. My mouth drops at the view of her ass as the wind picks up the back of her dress. She quickly smooths the material back in place, but not before my lower extremity makes it known he likes the white boyshort panties she's wearing.

Those shorts emphasize the round curves of her ass, reminding me how much I enjoyed punishing it when I last saw her.

When did my taste in women's lingerie change from racy red lace to a virginal white cotton that hides so much more than it should? Since right now, my cock throbs in response.

Up ahead, a man dressed in black jeans and a black T-shirt climbs out of the SUV before the car drives off, hiding it from view. He's of slim build and his eyes are hidden behind shades, but he's clearly checking out the street, and I'll have to be careful to avoid being spotted.

I whip out my phone again. No feedback from Vlad yet,

so I open an internet browser and search for Mikhail Melnichenko's current whereabouts. If he's got men following Victoria, he'll be making sure he's got an alibi for whatever it is these men are here to do.

The search results explode onto my screen, and I scroll through the copious images of him escorting various women to the opera and charity events all over Moscow. There are also quite a few of him dining with Igor Antonov, the man hand-picked to become Victoria's husband and a well-known associate of his. From the images alone, it's clear to see they are more than passing business acquaintances, despite Victoria running away from her arranged marriage to Igor. Mikhail's intentions are clear, and by the look of it Igor is completely on board. Why wouldn't he be? He gets Victoria and gains more power through his tighter association with her step-father.

The man dressed in black casually saunters across the road and leans back against the side wall of an alley between the shops which gives him a perfect view of the boutique. And Victoria.

I take a picture of him and send it through to Vlad with another message.

Me: *Who is he*

I get a response almost immediately.

Vlad: *rental - contract name a front - still busy*

Two seconds later, my phone vibrates again.

Vlad: *blyad - MM man - insulting*

I snort. Yeah, yeah, I know I'm taking advantage of my

friend's insane hacking abilities and making him search for stuff I could have easily found myself, but I don't want to take my eyes off that shop for a second unless I have to.

Me: *iou*

Vlad: *u alrdy o me*

I chuckle, knowing full well he's pissed off now. Not only have I forced him to use vowels in his messages, something he avoids like the plague, but now, I'm asking him for information I could easily look up myself.

Vlad's been my finger on the pulse in Moscow since I left, keeping an eye on my aerospace company and other inheritances. At some point, I'm going to have to go back home, or sell everything and disappear for good. Either way, I will keep him on the payroll. He's worth his weight in bitcoins, which has been a higher performing investment for me than gold over the last few years.

Victoria's still browsing the clothing racks inside the shop, although I'm glad to notice her gaze dart out through the window sporadically. Someone has trained her to keep her wits about her as her eyes occasionally swing back to the window, and I'd put money on it she's spotted her stalker. The other one.

Once she's engaged with a shop assistant, and they make their way to the back of the shop with an armful of clothing, I slip out of the tin can unnoticed and walk around the corner, searching for the back entrance to the alley.

It doesn't take me long to locate the back end, and I'm in luck—the entire alley is filled with various types of metal dustbins and black bags of trash from the shops and restaurants in the area. The smell of rotting food is overpowering, and I breathe through my mouth until I've pulled a thin black balaclava over my face and don a pair of rubber gloves. I'm not leaving any DNA behind here, nor am I picking up unwanted diseases.

I edge along the walls, quickly ducking behind a large dumpster when my target leans back to take a perfunctory look into the alley behind him. By the time I glance back, he's facing the shop again.

Before the guy decides to take another look back, I engage all my special forces training and sneak up behind him, with my footfall side-to-side, silent as can be to untrained ears. I cover his mouth and pinch his nose, robbing him of breath with my gloved hand, then pull his right arm behind him, hiking his hand up to the point where I easily pop his shoulder before he realises what's happening and puts up any resistance, which he wisely doesn't.

I drag him behind the dumpster and slam his body into the wall, making sure his head takes the brunt of the hit, then land blow after blow along his jaw, chest, and stomach, using him as a punching bag until he collapses in a heap at my feet. His lip and nose are a bleeding mess, and his cheekbones are already sprouting the evidence of my attack. He's pathetic for a Bratva henchman. I won't need to kill him—his boss will undoubtedly take care of that as soon as he returns home, having failed so epically.

But not before I get what I need out of him.

"Let's not waste each other's time. I know you're Bratva and work for Mikhail Melnichenko." My hand wraps around his throat. "The only words I want to hear out of your mouth are why you're following his step-daughter Victoria."

He coughs the moment I release my tight hold, but I'm not interested in stalling or dramatics, so I squeeze harder, showing him I have no reason to let him live if he doesn't give me the information I've requested.

He wheezes before answering. "We're to take her to the wedding."

"What wedding?"

My mind fills with dread. Am I too late? I risk a quick look across the street. Spotting the bright blue scooter, I breathe a sigh of relief before turning my attention back to the man in front of me.

"Hers."

It's as Anna suspected. Her father has found Victoria and is planning on dragging her back to Moscow to marry a man who will double the extent of Mikhail's power the moment she says 'I do.'

Something spurs me on to ask, "Where is the wedding taking place?"

The second he answers, I thank my instincts.

"Gozo."

Fuck.

I should have realised they'd pull a stunt like this, leaving me no time to get anything organised. What they don't know is that I think best on my feet, and right now, the only element of surprise I have is if I kill this idiot.

The decision is easily made, and I haul him onto his feet, wrap my arm around his neck, and squeeze until I hear the snap of his vertebrae. Lifting the lid on the dumpster, I haul his lifeless body over my shoulder, into the metal container, and close the lid on the trash before I head out the of alley in the same direction I arrived.

Before I walk back into the sunny street, I pull the mask and gloves off, shoving them into my pocket, satisfied there's nothing that will allow anybody to track my presence here today.

Casually rolling up the sleeves of my white shirt, I blend in with the tourists now milling through the streets. By the time I reach my car, only the front bumper of the black SUV is visible from its parking spot down the side street past the shop where Victoria's blue scooter is still parked out front.

Bending myself back into a pretzel, I squeeze my body back behind the steering wheel of the rental car, not a hair out of place, outwardly completely in control of myself and the situation. For now. Inside my chest, my heart is beating out morse code for the thoughts bouncing through my mind. *She's so close, yet still so far away.*

Victoria's in danger of being grabbed any moment now. The second the other occupant of the black SUV realises something's happened to his companion, he'll be calling for backup, and their operation grab-Victoria-to-get-her-to-the-altar will be escalated.

I need to act now, but I can't storm inside that shop and take her without raising a riot, and that would involve the police, and Mikhail would know someone was trying to prevent this wedding he so desperately seeks, from taking place. This knowledge would make him take it out on Anna despite the fact he's already married her off to another of his so-called friends. And as soon as he gets hold of Victoria, he'll make her life unbearable.

The second he finds out it's me he's after, which he surely will, he'll put a huge bounty on my head, one no hitman in the world will be able to turn down.

FOUR
VICTORIA

Is someone following me, or am I being paranoid again?

It's been two years since I found out my step-father had plans to marry me off to one of his gangster buddies, and I had no intention of waiting to find out who, what, when or where. Instead, I ran.

Somehow, I managed to climb into the back of a truck. In hindsight, it might not have been the best plan I've ever had, but at least I ended up in Finland, where it was easy to stow away on a ship. Of course, it didn't take the crew long to find me, after I stole into the pantry to grab something to eat, and they put me to work in the ship's galley. The captain took one look at me, instantly realised I was on the run, and forced me to sit down to explain my sticky situation to him. I will be forever in his debt for the new identity he provided. The ease with which he did it makes me suspect I wasn't the first girl he helped get out of a bad situation.

Thinking about Captain Edvin makes me miss my dad, the real one, not that savage Russian asshole. Growing up in Colombia and having the Escobar surname was bad, but not as devastating as watching the leader of the Bratva assassinate my father, then kidnap my mother and me. He took us to a country where we didn't know anyone or speak the local language, then married my mother. As a former Miss Colombia, she was his trophy wife. He physically abused her on a regular basis and made sure the Colombian cartel found out about it to beat them back into submission every time they voiced their dissatisfaction with him.

I shake my head, ridding myself of the memories which keep flooding back with the adrenalin rush of knowing I'm in danger. Always being on the lookout and living with the fear of being found is exhausting.

Laden with an armful of clothing I have no intention of buying, I duck inside the changing room, biding my time inside the boutique. If anyone out there is following me, they'll still be there by the time I'm done. Hopefully, it is all in my imagination.

Living in Malta has given me the time I needed to thaw out, both from the incessant cold Russian weather, and emotionally. The only thing I've held onto from a phase of my life I'd rather forget, is my close connection with a step-sister who took on the role of my protector when Mama passed away. Bloody cancer, as if she hadn't had enough to deal with in her short life.

The love between Anna and me is real. She's the only person in the world I care about now, and because I do, I can never go back to living in Russia, where I have to see her every day, knowing I betrayed her in a way a real sister never would have.

The familiar tune playing through the sound system inside the store forces my thoughts away from snow, Christmas, and a tall man who stole into my heart in the middle of the night before leaving it, and me, in tatters.

Nikolai.

My sister's boyfriend. The man I decided to give my virginity to in return for the best fuck I've ever had. I can't call it anything other than that. Hurt he'd treated me like a child, I goaded him, and what I got in return was a fast, brutal spanking and then a fuck. Without a doubt, the dumbest thing I've ever done in my life. Then why can't I forget it?

It was savage, and at the same time, it was everything I never knew I wanted. Needed. Craved. It was the best experience of my life. And the worst.

I was lucky to walk away from that moment of insanity without the lifelong consequences of having unprotected sex, yet I still wonder what my life would've looked like if I'd had his child. Instead, I'm left with the memories of a man, and a first sexual encounter that no other could live up to. So I've never tried.

Niko is all man. He's fierce, dominant. He didn't hold

back on giving me a thorough spanking because he thought I deserved it, and all the while, he still managed to make me feel cared for, safe. A combination of rough and gentle, like in my favourite books. Nothing in real life can compare.

Mierda. Why can't I outrun these obsessive memories of him? No matter what I do, the yearning never goes away. From the moment he walked away from me that night, I've done everything within my power to make sure I never see him again. My step-father is not the only reason I want nothing to do with Russian men ever again. Those boys Niko saved me from was only the beginning of a string of old, lecherous men I had to perform for, appearing in my best clothes, acting demure, when inside I wanted to stab each one through the heart and run.

The white summer dress the shop assistant insisted I try on is soft and flowy, and it breezes around my knees as I turn in front of the mirror. The cotton is sheer enough to see the outline of the bikini I tried on beneath it. Satisfied with the sexy yet virginal look of the outfit and the drastically reduced sale price, I decide to leave both on. Time to abandon the shopping expedition and spend the rest of the day on the beach while I still can.

At the payment counter, I look across the street. The man I'd thought was following me earlier has disappeared. I breathe a sigh of relief as the shop assistant appears.

"How did you do?"

"I don't want to take these off, as you can see." I smile brightly at her. "So I'll take them."

She looks me up and down, beaming. "That combination looks like it was made for you. The burnt orange bikini hasn't looked this good on anyone else who's tried it on. Good choice."

After I've handed over the cash, she cuts the labels off the bikini top and bottom as well as the dress. Closing the shop door behind me, I find my trusty scooter, the perfect island runaround, right where I left it. With my old dress and underwear safely tucked inside the top box on the back, I drive the eight minutes to the private beach club my employers signed me up for.

With the temperatures cooling down to around twenty degrees centigrade, it's quiet on the beach in the weeks leading up to Christmas, which is exactly what I need. I pick up a sun lounger and drag it closer to the surf before pulling the white dress over my head and settling down to soak up the mid-morning sun. I let my thoughts wander while my toes are caressed by the ebb and flow of the cool sea water.

The chirp of my ringtone wakes me up, and I turn onto my stomach to grab my phone from my bag.

"Vika?"

Hearing the strain in my sister's voice, I sit up, straddling the lounger with my back to the sun. "Anna, what's wrong?"

"It's time for you to move again. I'm pretty sure my father knows you're in Malta."

"What?" I jump up, scanning the empty beach for any sign of the Bratva. "Are you sure?"

"Why else would he have organised a family holiday in Malta, of all places?"

Shit. I've only been working as an au-pair for the Thompson's three-year-old son for five months, and I've already grown attached to the little guy. "It could just be a coincidence."

Who am I kidding? I don't believe in coincidences, especially not with a man like Mikhail Melnichenko. There's nothing he loves more than taking people by surprise and making them suffer. I watched it happen to my mother. As soon as she was no longer there to hold his attention, he turned his venom on Anna and me.

It's her I feel sorry for. He's all she's ever known as a father.

"I thought I saw someone following me earlier this morning," I confess. "But then, after a few minutes he disappeared, so I figured I was wrong."

"You need to leave Malta before we get there."

As ever, my sister is the voice of reason. How else do you survive being the daughter of the *Pakhan*? But while she puts on the pretence of being cold and heartless, to me, she's the exact opposite. She's putting herself at great risk by phoning me. If he ever finds out, he'll make sure she never forgets what happens when you go against his wishes. The man is pure evil.

"What if I stay inside the entire time you're on the island? I could tell Mrs Thompson I'm not feeling well and stay in my room," I reason with her, knowing full well I'm delaying the inevitable.

It's time to pack my bag. Again.

"Vika, I got hold of Niko. He's living in Sicily. He promised me he'd come find you."

She keeps quiet after dropping that bombshell. She doesn't know what happened between him and me, but she witnessed how I went from adoring him to avoiding him like the plague. He dumped her shortly after our encounter, and I've always wondered if she suspected something happened between the two of us.

"Could it have been Niko you saw earlier?" Anna asks.

"No." Absolutely no way. I'd recognise Nikolai anywhere. I lusted after him for months before I finally got a taste of what I wanted, only to have him rip my heart to shreds and leave my self-confidence in tatters.

"He should be there already." The angst in Anna's voice is clear even as a seagull above squawks loudly. "Where are you?"

"At the beach."

"OK, good. You'll be safer out in the open where there are people around."

She clearly doesn't know what it's like here on a workday morning. A couple with three kids are the only other people around, except for the wait staff at the clubhouse who glance towards the beach on occasion.

Anna's reasoning spurs me on to drag the sun lounger back up the beach where I'll be closer to the family. It's safer to be around people until Niko finds me.

That's if he's looking for me, which I'm not altogether convinced he is. Why would he, after the way he left?

Dumped me, more like. But I refuse to let that sting hurt me again. Not today. Not now.

I check the time on my phone. Lunchtime. At least the restaurant will fill up with business people coming for a bite to eat soon. I can give Niko until then to find me here. After all, he was in the Russian army doing covert missions. If he is looking, he'll find me. And if he's not, I still have enough time to decide where to go next.

The little voice inside my head tells me to start packing, but my heart, held together with barbed wire, just wants another glimpse of the man I can't get out of my mind. Just one look, and then I'll go. Anywhere in the world, just not with him.

He's more lethal to my wellbeing than all the mafias in the world combined.

FIVE
NIKOLAI

WHAT THE HELL IS SHE DOING? JUST BECAUSE THE winter in Malta is exceptionally mild this year, there's no need for her to be lying on the beach in that itty-bitty bikini which looks like it shrank in the wash. We're a mere six weeks away from Christmas. She shouldn't be here by herself, flaunting that body without a care in the world. If she were mine, I'd give her a solid spanking for showing those curves to anyone when I'm not around to keep prying eyes and roaming hands off her. But she's not mine, and I have no right to discipline her.

Fuck. Just one damn look at her, and she's got me wanting things that are not for me, like her in my bed every night, and my babies suckling at her breast; a happy ever after where she submits to me and I make sure she has everything she could ever need. I run a hand down my face, feeling the stubble threatening to grow into a beard if I go without shaving for another day, reminding me I've forsaken my daily routine from the moment I received Anna's call.

The man on the beach doesn't even know he should thank his lucky stars he's accompanied by his wife and kid. If he'd been by himself, I'd be over there making sure he keeps his eyes off Victoria in that sinful beachwear. My inner caveman has been ripped out of the cobwebs for the first time in years, and I'm at war with my burning need to grab her by her long ponytail and drag her into my cave.

My jaw is clenched so hard, I'm a whisper away from cracking a molar as I turn to survey the rocky shoreline on the other side of the bay, following the road to where I am. There's no sign of the black SUV from earlier, but I suspect he's here somewhere. My guys should have been here for this. Keeping an eye on a hellcat like Victoria is at least a two-man job. Then again, the idea of another man watching her lithe body as she walks back up the beach, dragging the sun lounger with her hips swaying from side to side...

Hell no. I'd have to gouge his damn eyes out, and he'd be no good to me afterwards.

I'm fucked. I've been on keep-an-eye-on-Anna's-sister duty for all of two hours, and short of thumping my chest, I've been reduced to acting like a primate. I should have flung her over my shoulder and taken her for myself when I fucked her at that Christmas party five years ago. That woman is fucking mine.

Instead, I'm waiting for that shithead Mikhail to marry

her off to someone else. Why? As I shake my head, trying to make sense of my actions, she saunters over to the outside bar of the beach club. It has a grass roof and looks like something that's been transported from Hawaii.

She perches that perfect ass of hers on a barstool as she chats to the barman. Is she flirting with him? The way he's smiling at her, I think she must be. My blood pumps through my veins, and my fingers curl into a fist, once again wanting to commit murder, or at the very least knock his pearly white teeth out. This woman, I want her more than I've ever wanted anything or anyone in my entire life. I want to sink my teeth into her neck, marking her while I shove my fingers up her tight channel and take her breath away right before she comes, screaming out my name for all the world to hear.

Using my phone's camera, I zoom in on the guy. He's a typical surfer, shaggy blond hair, every inch of his skin tanned. He's even got that arrogant swagger as he reaches for a glass and ingredients to make whatever she's ordered. Most women would probably fall at his feet.

You're in for a sound spanking if I catch you succumbing to his act, Victoria.

As the thought ricochets through my mind, I have visions of spanking her ass until it's burning hot and her juices are running down her legs. Then when she begs me to let her come, I'll make her wait, plugging her ass with a fat dildo, getting her ready to take my cock there while I torture her nipples with clamps and lick her pussy until she's incapable of anything but lying in my arms, fully satisfied.

By the time the barman slides a red concoction in a cocktail glass with a blue umbrella across the bar, I'm seething. Spending her teenage years living under the *Pakhan*'s roof, I would have imagined she'd be better trained not to consume alcohol while there's a threat out there. My palm aches with the need to connect to her barely covered backside. She won't be able to sit without wincing for a week.

But I can't do what I want to do. Instead, I'm hiding behind a palm tree. It's not something I've ever done for anyone else.

I need a distraction. Anything to get away from this feeling she's lit a fuse inside me. The coffee shop across the street is going to have to do. Jogging across the tarmac, I enter the shop, checking she remains in sight before I order a double shot Americano from the barista. Minutes later, with the bitter black brew in the take-away cup, I saunter back across the road, making sure to keep my face partially hidden behind the thick trunk of the palm tree.

Victoria is back on the sunbed, her cocktail glass beside her in the sand. She's only taken a few sips of what's probably a strawberry daiquiri. My mood has instantly improved since she didn't react to the surfer dude.

Maybe I'll reward her by going easy on her ass the moment I have her in my grasp.

I take a large sip of what's now a surprisingly tasty coffee and settle back into a slouch against the tree.

She remains in the same position, lying there without a care in the world, oblivious to the fact she's being stalked while I finish my coffee, pretending she's not messing with my head. I scrunch up the paper cup.

A woman screams behind me, and I turn to see her little boy step into the busy traffic. She's frantic, about to go after him. My protective instinct takes over, and I shout to her, "Stay there. I'll get him."

Sprinting into the traffic, I run to the kid, scooping him up before dropping him into his mother's arms.

"Thank you," she sobs as she smothers her little boy with kisses.

I wait for the stream of cars winding through the road to ease off before I go back to my position. Once there, I glance in the direction I expect to find Victoria, only to find the sunbed empty. Her beach towel is still there, but her bag is missing. Did she leave without me noticing?

Son of a bitch! Two fucking minutes I turn my attention away and they grabbed her. If they harm a single hair on her head I'll rip them apart, seek out their entire family tree and obliterate their name from the world forever.

I sprint towards the beach, clamber over the fence meant to keep non-members out, and run to her spot. The sand slows me down as it slips into my shoes and then seeps through my socks to scratch and irritate my skin.

Her cocktail glass has been knocked over, and the sand around the sunbed looks like two people walked away with one between them being dragged. My heart thumps inside my chest as I scan the clubhouse area, then move my gaze farther out to the street. There, on the opposite side of bend in the road, is a white van, door open, and two men dragging what looks like an unconscious Victoria between them. That burnt orange bikini is the beacon of proof as they haul her body into the unmarked van.

Chest pounding, I rid myself of the shoes and sprint back to the fence, leaping over it to get to the rental car before the van drives off. I fumble with the keys before the electric car bleeps as it comes to life, and I floor the little car into the traffic amid the squeal of brakes and hooting from drivers not enamoured with the move.

I make it past the entrance to the club just in time to see the van disappear around the corner, and I keep the accelerator pedal pushed up against the floor of the tin can, hoping like hell it has enough power for me to keep up with the van that's also speeding through the streets, well on its way to Manoel Island. The way I'm driving, I'll be lucky if this piece of shit doesn't roll over, but I can't lose sight of them.

I'm an idiot. If anything happens to Victoria, I will never forgive myself.

They're heading out to a boat—it's the only reason why they'd go to the marina. Holding onto the steering wheel with one hand, I pull my phone out of my pocket and place a call to Vlad.

Come on, pick up.

"You need to drop everything and find Mikhail Melnichenko's yacht for me. Now!" I bark down the line as soon as the connection is made. My voice sounds terse, warning him I'm in no mood to be messed with.

He immediately asks, "Name of the vessel?"

"Celestine Angel." Adrenalin pumps through my veins as I imagine the worst. I can't let them get away with her.

I should've grabbed her off the street myself, without worrying about how she'd react. What's more, I should never have taken my fucking eyes off her. *It's too fucking late now,* the devil inside me whispers back.

"She's at anchor in the Manoel Island yacht marina," Vlad calmly informs me before ending the call with a quick, "Whatever you're doing, be careful."

I hang up. No point in telling him I'll do whatever it takes to get her out of her step-father's clutches.

I slam on the brakes as the white van slows and comes to a stop at the entrance boom. Pulling into the street parking, I wait for the driver of the van to sign into the marina while my heartrate finally begins to slow down again. By some miracle, it looks like they haven't seen me following them, and I climb out of the car to continue my pursuit in my socks after I hop over yet another fence.

I should be grateful I haven't been electrocuted today with the number of fences I'm jumping over, especially seeing as I'm missing the rubber-soled shoes I left behind at the beach.

The white van idles at the mooring area for tenders. There's a stack of them belonging to the owners of the yachts anchored in the bay. The two men who kidnapped Victoria manhandle her into the rubber duck where a deckhand sits at the engine, keeping it running while they climb on board and throw a blanket over her sleeping form.

Fuck, she'd better be unconscious. If those fuckers have killed her, I'll tear them to pieces with my bare hands. But Mikhail needs her alive to get what he wants—control over Igor Antonov's network—and I hold onto that thought as the tender sets off towards the line of superyachts anchored in the bay.

It isn't until they pull up beside the light blue Celestine Angel, a fifty-meter-long superyacht, that I edge closer to the marina office and turn my attention to how I'm going to board that ship and kidnap Victoria right back from them.

My best bet for getting onto the yacht is trying to find someone at the marina who will take me out to her, and the marina office is my most likely chance of success, so I step inside the office to see who I need to chat up.

There's not a soul inside here as I make my way to the counter, looking for information on boat rentals or tenders. While digging around, I overhear the conversation of a young man pacing around outside.

"...I'm sorry I'm late, Captain..." he runs his fingers through his hair, clearly nervous. "No, Captain. My flight got in an hour ago, and I got here as fast as I could." His pacing slows down. "No problem, I'll wait for the tender. Thank you, Captain."

The computer behind the counter is locked, and there's not enough time for me to try hack into it.

Looking at the young man now slouched on the wooden

bench outside the office, I decide on a second plan of action and head outside to join him.

We nod at each other as I sit next to him. "You joining a crew?"

He clearly assumes I work at the marina as he answers. "Yes, sir. It's my first job as a deck hand."

I lean forward, placing my elbows on my knees as I make eye contact. "That's great, man. Congratulations. Which yacht?"

I hold my breath as he answers.

"Celestine Angel."

Not one to turn away a gift, I pounce.

Six

VICTORIA

"Wake up, you fucking whore."

The verbal abuse is swiftly followed by a downpour of cold water which leaves me gasping for breath and covered in goosebumps.

Where the hell am I? How did I get here? The ground is moving beneath me, and I'm struggling to open my eyes. My brain feels like it's been wrapped in cotton wool, and there's no stopping the confusing string of thoughts fading in and out.

"I know you're awake, so open your fucking eyes and stop wasting my time."

A shiver runs down my spine at the sound of my step-father's voice, followed by an immediate sense of impending doom. He's found me, and he's angry. Mikhail doesn't know the meaning of a good mood on the best of days, and I'm guessing today is not a great day for him. At least, we have that in common.

There's no putting off the inevitable. Slowly, I open my eyes. It takes a while for me to get my bearings and realise I'm on his yacht. I recognise it from the number of times my mother and I holidayed on board to get away from him for a while.

My arms are stretched above my head, and when I tug on them, they won't come down. I've been in this situation before, but it's not the same at all. As I turn my blurry gaze up, I see my wrists are tied together with a thick plastic tie wrap, which in turn is bound to the shower tap.

A dark shadow steps into the shower cabin, and before I know it, a foot connects with my midriff, leaving me gasping in pain and out of breath.

"That's for running away." My step-father's voice booms through the small enclosure before he follows the first brutal kick with a second. "And that's for making me chase you all over Europe, you ungrateful bitch."

My hair, wet from the burst of cold water, clings to my cheeks as I tighten my core muscles, readying myself for the next blow when his face slowly comes into focus. Typical Mikhail. He had me drugged to get me here.

Pure, unadulterated hatred flows through my gut, settling in my solar plexus like the weight of an elephant pressing down on my chest. One day, I'm going to kill this miserable son of a bitch. I will get my revenge for the death of my father and again for the way he treated my mother after he forced her to marry him.

His foot connects with my stomach for the third time.

"Now that you're finally back with your family where you belong, we will go ahead with your marriage to Igor. We can do this the hard way, or the easy way, your choice. If you promise to behave, I'll untie you. If you don't, I will drag you down the aisle by your hair, kicking and screaming until the vows have been said and you become Igor's problem." But Mikhail is sadistic and takes great relish in colouring in the picture. "He'll likely rape you every day for the rest of your miserable life, and once he's sick of looking at you, he'll give you to his men and let them do what they will with you."

He chuckles at the thought, leaving me in no doubt what he believes my future will look like, but he doesn't know me. Even after all these years of being under his roof and rule. I refuse to surrender. While he holds my body prisoner, my mind will find a way to get out until my dying breath, but I'll wait for that opportunity and until then, let them think they've won.

"Fine. You win." The words float in the air, and I refuse to let them take on any weight. This is not my truth.

Mikhail turns into the cabin, instructing one of his henchmen to cut me loose.

My arms drop into my lap, and my fingers tingle with pins and needles as blood flows back into them. I'm hauled onto my feet and dragged into the cabin where I collapse onto the bed, leaning forward to take the edge off the sharp pain radiating through my abdomen.

"Just in case you're thinking of trying to jump overboard or run away again, here's a little incentive for you." Mikhail nods at his bodyguard who opens the cabin door to let Anna in.

For a fraction of a second, my spirits lift at the sight of my sister. We've been communicating on the sly whenever it was safe, which hasn't been often over the last few years. As she steps closer to the bed, it becomes obvious her father has been using her as a punching bag, too. She's tried to cover up the shiner on her right cheekbone, but no amount of makeup can hide an egg-shaped bruise, and she's walking towards me with a limp. Our eyes connect and hold an entire conversation without a single word passing between us.

Clambering off the bed, I stand to receive her heartfelt hug. Shared pain has woven us together and made us sisters in every sense of the word.

"You try anything, Victoria, your sister will suffer."

"I won't," I answer, keeping my eyes lowered. This time, I know there's nothing I will do to give him an excuse to hurt the only person in the world I still give a damn about.

"The windows in this cabin are bulletproof and sealed shut. There are two guards outside this room in case you try to get out that way," Mikhail adds unnecessarily, completely unaware of the deep love I have for my sister. "Anna, you know what to do. Make her look like a bride for Igor." He looks me up and down before snorting. "I doubt the wedding dress will fit, but you'll have to make do."

Finally, he leaves, locking the door behind him, leaving Anna and me to sink onto the floor, tears flowing freely.

"What did they do to you?" I ask after I catch my breath. "And more to the point, who did it? Mikhail? Or the husband he picked for you?"

Anna wipes the tears away before answering.

"It's nothing. I don't want you to worry about me. Mikhail wants to control you by threatening me." She grabs my hands in hers and drops a kiss to my knuckles before continuing. "But I don't want to live with the knowledge you're miserable because of me. Promise me you will do what you can to get away again. Please, I beg you."

I look into her eyes, the same piercing blue as those of her father. "I couldn't live with myself if anyone hurts you because of me."

At this stage, I haven't ruled out the possibility that Anna's husband is also an abuser, and this thought kills any desire I have of escaping the clutches of these Bratva bastards.

She shakes her head, revealing the bruises around her neck. "No, Vika, please. You must promise me you will get out if you can."

Pulling her into an embrace is easier to do than lie to her, and I cling onto her as the yacht begins to move. "Where are we going? What do you know?"

"We're sailing to Gozo, the island right next to Malta. Igor is waiting for you at a local church there."

Shit. I really am out of options.

"I guess I'd better get dressed, then." If I don't, heaven only knows what will become of Anna and me.

There had been many times during my mother's marriage to Mikhail when I thought death a better option than living this life. Today, that thought is stronger than ever.

SEVEN

NIKOLAI

"DEAN, PICK UP THE PACE. THOSE WINDOWS AREN'T going to clean themselves."

Steve, the bosun on board the Celestine Angel, has taken an instant dislike to me. I hope it doesn't affect the real Dean, who I left unconscious behind the office at the marina. If it does, I vow to get him a job on the yacht my boss's uncle owns. I stole his identity documents when I took his clothes so it won't be hard to trace him once I've rescued Victoria.

There's been no sign of her since I watched her being hauled on board. At least I've managed to get the crew talking and found out she is most definitely alive. I can't walk around freely and have kept the dark blue cap of the boat uniform drawn low over my eyes to make sure none of Mikhail's men recognise me. Not that I've seen much of them as they've been inside the cabins, keeping out of sight.

As soon as the bosun moves to the top deck, Alice, the deckhand working next to me whispers, "Did you hear there's a bride on board?"

My heart rate accelerates. "A bride? Is someone getting married on board?"

She looks around before leaning in closer. "No. Apparently, we're on our way to Gozo to deliver the bride. Isn't it romantic?" She closes her eyes and sighs, clearly imagining herself as the bride-to-be. If she only knew.

"Mmm," I answer, wondering how I can make my way below deck.

"Someone said it's the owner's daughter who's getting married." The girl fans her face and sighs some more while I grind my teeth. "Can you imagine growing up with this much wealth?"

I'm not about to burst the girl's bubble and let her in on the atrocities that take place behind these particular doors.

"So I guess the bride's being pampered in the stateroom?" I volunteer a guess hoping she'll quickly counteract with information on where Victoria is, although getting to her before we reach Gozo is unlikely on several counts.

Mikhail would never take the risk of her disappearing again now he's finally tracked her down. She won't be this lucky twice. It's up to me to get her out of this marriage before it's too late.

"Apparently, the bride and her sister are in one of the other cabins. Not sure which one, but I hear there are guards posted outside her room." She bends to rinse her rag in the bucket at her feet. "It's sweet that her father loves her so much he wants to make sure she's safe. Although what he thinks is going to happen to her on board..."

"Mmm." She's making it damn near impossible for me to bite the words back. When did young women become such idiots? Have they always been like this?

Victoria is no fool. She recognised the dangerous situation she was in and took off. My chest fills with pride. Was I partially responsible for teaching her this lesson? And if I was, how will she react when she sees me again?

I quickly lower my cap as Mikhail walks onto the bridge and mutter a quick excuse about needing to use the bathroom before he spots me cleaning the windows outside. After slipping inside, I make my way to the crew quarters below deck. The cabin I've been allocated with one of the engineers is empty, and he's left his laptop open on the bed.

Luck continues to be on my side today. The device is linked to the on-board satellite connection, and after inserting my flash drive and a few keystrokes I find my way onto the dark web chat room with my team.

User 2: Need crew. Celestine Angel docking Gozo. 3 0 mikes.

User 1: K

Knowing Vlad, he's already got a team there after I asked him about Mikhail's yacht.

Voices outside my cabin warn me the crew are about to change shifts, and before I log off, I wipe all traces of my use from the laptop memory and pull out my drive before locking the laptop's screen and diving into the head. I flush the toilet and wash my hands before stepping out of the bathroom as the engineer grabs his laptop, gives me a quick nod, and leaves.

I leave the crew quarters and make my way up one level to the guest cabins. There are several men posted in the passage.

"Hey, you! This area is off limits," one of them shouts out.

"Sorry, mate." I put on the same Australian accent I used to get on board with my false identity. "I'm new. Wrong floor."

For once, I'm grateful Mikhail has a habit of dealing with his staff by issuing a bullet between the eyes if they make a single mistake. Sprinting up the stairs in case any of these men decide to let him know I dared to set foot in an area that's off-limits, I make my way back on deck where I see we're already heading into port.

Fifteen minutes later, we dock alongside another superyacht, and I'm assigned the task of securing the passerelle for passengers to step off the yacht onto dry land. With the gangplank in place, I run back to the crew quarters to fetch Dean's backpack containing my clothes. I make it back before anyone has got off and quickly hop onto the pier while no one is around to witness it.

There's nothing I'd love more than to make sure the plank collapses as soon as Mikhail steps onto it, but I can't take the chance Victoria will be carried off first, so I'm forced to leave it intact. Retaliation will have to wait as I have more pressing matters to attend to. Victoria is still in their clutches, and I need to meet up with my crew to get her back.

With the imminent arrival of two black SUVs with tinted windows at the yacht, likely to pick up Victoria, Mikhail, and whoever else is going to the wedding, I trot out of sight, ducking behind other parked vehicles to head towards the marina entrance.

As expected, my team is there in two white, inconspicuous panel vans. I reach them in time to watch Mikhail walk off his yacht, closely followed by Anna and Victoria, who in turn are ushered along by four of his armed guards.

They're not fighting their father or his men, and that alone makes this a dangerous predicament. We could try to take them out here, but we're out in the open, and the chance of Victoria being hit by a stray bullet is too great.

The sight of her in a voluminous white wedding gown seizes my chest, and in that moment I know there is no way in hell I will let her marry anyone today. Ever, in fact. Unless it's me. It's taken me five years, in which I've tried every trick in the book to forget about her, to come to the realisation—this woman is mine.

I'm coming to get you, Victoria, and you'd better not fight me when I do.

Of course I wouldn't mind if she did, but before I get side-tracked with images of all the things I want to do to her if or when she does fight me, I slip out of the uniform I stole in order to get on board the yacht and don my black suit once again. Pulling my jacket on is as if I'm sliding back into the role of enforcer, ready to take on the battle and fight to the bitter end.

"Luca says he'll send reinforcements if you need them."

I recognised Gio as soon as I stepped into the vehicle, but my brain could only focus on Victoria. Now she's safely inside the SUV, I turn to my driver and thank him.

"I see he sent five of you. Things must be quiet in Sicily."

"Running smoothly, Niko. You trained us well, and now we're here to help you. Anything you need, brother."

"Just make sure you don't lose them." I point to the black SUVs leaving the marina.

"We won't," Gio promises.

We follow the two-car convoy at a safe distance, and while we do, the men hand me two loaded pistols which I tuck into the shoulder holsters beneath my jacket.

The traffic in Gozo is light, forcing us to hang much farther back than I would have preferred. "Did Vlad give you any info on where they could be headed?"

"He narrowed it down to a couple of Roman Catholic churches and thinks it's most likely going to be Saint Lawrence's based on the fact that the bright red interior would appeal to Mikhail's Russian heritage."

I cannot imagine the interior of a church in bright red, but if Vlad thinks that's where they're headed I'd stake my life on it.

It's no great surprise when the SUVs turn off the road at San Lawrenz and stop in front of the massive dark wooden doors of the church in question.

We drive past Mikhail's vehicles and park on the side of the church, where we quietly exit the van and find the back entrance which takes us straight into the vestry where the priest and his deacons are in the process of putting on their robes.

"Good afternoon, Father. I'm sorry to intrude, but there will be a slight change to the proceedings today," I announce, startling the men of faith as they freeze at the sight of six armed men entering their holy terrain. "We're not going to harm any of you, but we are here to prevent this wedding from taking place. The only question that remains is, will you allow us to do so without violence?"

The priest looks at each of his deacons before answering for all of them. "This is the house of God. Will you please put your weapons away and explain yourselves?"

I nod at my men to do as he says. I'm the last to holster my weapons, and as I do, I give him the bare necessities to convince him to cooperate. "The woman being married today has been kidnapped and is doing so against her will. The man she's marrying is part of a massive crime organisation, and he's already murdered his two previous wives."

The priest's hand moves to sign the symbol of the cross. "May God our saviour protect her soul."

"It's more than her soul we're here to rescue, Father."

"What do you need, son?"

It's been a long time since anyone has addressed me as such. I'd forgotten what it feels like to be part of a real family.

"I need you to get me and two of my men inside the church, by your side, so we can grab the bride as soon as my other men have created a distraction."

"Then you'd best dress as my deacons and follow my lead."

I nod my thanks as Gio, Rocco, and I don the robes with help from the deacons who appear only too relieved not to have to enter the church surrounded by armed men. Hiding our weapons requires a bit of manoeuvring to keep the holsters out of sight, but we manage it before the organ music begins to play and the priest gives us the nod. It's time for us to step onto the altar.

"Don't fail me," I whisper to the men. "All that matters is we get Victoria out in one piece."

I don't need to add *at all costs*. They know.

We follow the priest, birettas on our bowed heads, as he makes his way behind the altar and begins to arrange his bible and paperwork for a marriage that will not be taking place. Our costumes and the unexpected setting should be enough to keep our identities hidden. If not, there will be a shoot-out at the altar, but I won't let it come to that.

EIGHT
VICTORIA

MY KNEES WOBBLE BENEATH THE MONSTROSITY OF A wedding dress. It's a tasteless, over the top concoction of lace and pearls, the complete opposite to anything I would have chosen myself. The veil attached to the top knot on my head is long at the back and hangs to beneath my chin at the front. It's so thick I almost feel hidden, yet not so far to be invisible enough to slip out of here. But that's not an option. It never was. All I've done for the past years is delay the inevitable.

So here I am, hyperventilating at the back of a church decorated with all the red and green hues of Christmas while the bouquet thrust into my hands containing sprigs of holly and mistletoe, digs into my fingers. Any minute now and Mikhail's carefully chosen dress will be blotted with the red stains of my blood. I'll fit right in with the general theme of the day.

The music echoes around the church, and before I can gather my wits, Mikhail pulls me down the aisle, towards my future husband.

Igor The Pig, as I've referred to him in my mind since the day I ran, looks at his watch as I'm marched to meet my fate. He glances up once more, tapping his foot as if he wants Mikhail to speed it up. He leans towards his best man, whispering something I can't hear but which leaves me in no doubt it's about me as the two of them laugh and leer at my approach.

A stern glance from the man beside me has them straightening up and wiping the mirth off their faces. Mikhail is the only man Igor listens to now, and I wonder how long that will last once he's married me. Am I his power play to taking on the role of *Pakhan*? Mikhail has no male heirs, and he's made it clear from the day I arrived in his home that both his own daughter, Anna, and I had one role in life—we're brood mares to give him grandsons who will one day take over from him. I can only hope I'm barren. I can't bear the thought of bringing this type of suffering to a child of my own.

My eyes scan the people inside the church. One guard is posted at the doors behind us, and there are two on the left and right of the church. That's at least five armed men inside. I turn to look at Mikhail's stern face. Is he expecting trouble? Why does he have guards at a wedding nobody except him and the groom knew was taking place today?

If he's worried, I probably should be, too...only I don't know what he's worried about, so my mind goes through the list of potential threats as my feet drag, trying to slow the time it takes for me to reach the altar.

Niko didn't bother to try to rescue me, so I can rule him out. That leaves...Igor. Suppressing the gasp stuck in my throat, I stall, mere footsteps away from my future. Mikhail is merrily leading me to marry a man he doesn't even trust himself...

I can't do this.

Shaking my head, I turn towards Mikhail. "No. Please don't make me do this."

Of course, it's a waste of my breath and energy. All it does is spur him on to tighten his hold on my upper arm to the extent that he's adding to the bruising he's leaving behind. It's evidence I could use against him if I could find my way to a police station and lay a charge against him. Not that I'd be able to stick around long enough to see if they actually do anything about it. In all the years I've had the misfortune of knowing this man, he's got away with every single thing he did to my mother, me, and his own daughter. His reach goes beyond that of the Pope.

And on this final thought, I'm out of time. We've reached the altar, and Mikhail lifts my veil, making me feel vulnerable and exposed to the imminent threat I feel all around me. There's nowhere to hide, no place to run to.

"Your job is to marry Igor and produce sons, unlike Anna over there who's failed to produce anything at all. Give me heirs, and you'll live. But if she beats you to it, your life is worthless." He grabs hold of my chin, shifting my gaze up to meet his eyes. "Are you listening?"

My gaze drops. "Yes."

He's finally realised how deep the bond is between Anna and me, so now he's pitting us up against each other. There is nothing this man won't stoop to in order to get what he wants. He's the devil personified.

I turn to face the altar as he steps away and leaves me standing beside the man who is about to become my husband. The stench of garlic permeates the air around him, making me want to gag. Before I do, I close off the airflow from my nose and open my mouth a fraction to breathe. If I throw up now, Igor and Mikhail will come up with ways to punish me for embarrassing them in front of the priest. And this punishment won't be pleasurable, at all.

The man of God raises his arms and begins to address us and the scattered few witnesses in the pews behind us.

I turn back to look at my sister, the bruises on her face highlighted by the stream of sunrays shining through the altar's colourful mosaic windows. She refuses to make eye contact with me, keeping her gaze lowered while she fiddles with her hands in her lap until her husband lowers his meaty fist over them and stops her. I don't know who he is. She never told me his name, only that he beats her.

What the fuck am I doing standing here about to join the Bratva Abused Wives Club?

The altar is covered in the same holly and mistletoe as the bouquet I'm holding, and I wonder who stole the decorations to turn them into the torture device that's making my fingers bleed all over the dress.

Behind the priest are three other men, their heads bent as they press their hands together in prayer. I've zoned out. What is the prayer for? I wish it was for more time. Is there an escape route behind the altar? Perhaps these men in their robes would help me, but it's more likely they've been promised enough riches to turn a blind eye to the fact the bride has no desire to get married today.

The man standing to the right of the priest reminds me a little of Niko with his height and dark hair. I can't believe he didn't come to rescue me. Clearly, our kinky fucking in the garden shed wasn't to his liking. Was I such a disappointment? I refuse to waste my last few seconds as a single woman thinking about a man who didn't even bother to stick around to check if I was okay after he found out I was a virgin. I'm not that desperate.

Igor squeezes my fingers in his hand. Is he trying to break them or merely forcing me to look away from the man who reminds me of someone I once idolised? Does it even matter?

Yet the thought of Niko won't let me go. Would he have stuck around if he'd met me before he started dating Anna? Perhaps I should have stayed in Russia, waited for him to come back for me. Did he ever reach out to Anna to try to find me, or did he simply disappear, much like I did? At least, I had a reason to. What's his excuse?

Igor pulls me closer to whisper in my ear. "Pay attention, bitch. You're about to commit your obedience to me. You won't like what happens to you if you don't. I'm not like Mikhail. He's soft. He's allowed you to run free all over Europe, making a fool of him. You won't be doing that to me."

He ends his threat on a grunt. The hard butt of his weapon digs into my upper arm as his right hand slides into his closed jacket. Does he think I'm not fully aware what he's capable of? His reputation in Russia as a feared Bratva leader is not one to be underestimated. He's made more people disappear in the last two years than the Federal Security Service has in a decade.

Once I'm married to him my life will be over. Looking up at the sun pouring in through the stained-glass window at the back of the church, I wonder if I'll be allowed into heaven if I take my own life. Is it worth taking the risk? If I've survived living in Mikhail's household, then surely I'll survive an eternity of hell. How bad could it be? At least I'll never feel cold again.

Smirking to myself, I turn my attention back to the priest. He's reaching for his holy book.

Time's up. One way or another, I'm sinking into the pits of hell right now.

NINE

NIKOLAI

IF THAT PIG GLANCES AT VICTORIA'S CHEST ONE more time, I'm going to gut him like a fish. Slice him open, remove his spine, and leave him flapping on the floor like a jellyfish until his brain catches up to the fact his heart is lying next to his body and he's already dead.

That white dress is too tight around her breasts, pushing them up, nearly baring her nipples to the poor priest, who, unlike Igor, tries his best to look anywhere but there. I can't wait to get her out of here and cover her up. She's mine. Nobody gets to look at her breasts but me.

She's trying very hard to be brave, my girl, but I see the fear in her eyes. Especially when she stares at the window behind me, the soft glow of the tinted glass reflected on her face. She's like a kaleidoscope of emotion, beckoning to me.

We're nearly there, Victoria. As soon as we have the distrac-

tion of the priest looking for the rings, we'll strike, and you'll be in my arms, right where you belong.

"... turn to face one another and hold each other's right hand." The priest has finally got to the part where we've planned our strike. "Do you have the rings?"

Igor turns to look at Mikhail who shakes his head.

"Let's see if she's packing them in here." Igor smirks before his filthy paws grab Victoria's breasts through her dress.

The men beside him grin. The look on their faces a dead giveaway this behaviour is not uncommon from their boss.

The priest, sensing the rage building inside me, turns to look my way. I nod for him to step aside. I cannot hold back any longer. I roar.

My team grabs their weapons at the same time I reach for mine, and as we do, something completely unexpected happens.

The church doors are flung open, and men wearing black balaclavas storm inside the building. Their automatic rifles fire rounds into the church, desecrating the pews as wood splinters fly through the air like projectile missiles. Holy, ivy, mistletoe, and a variety of red and green flowers are shredded by ammunition fired in all directions.

The priest, my men, and I duck behind the altar. I crawl through the space below, lifting the white cloth to search for Victoria. Her screams reach me before my eyes settle on her terrified face. She's right in front of me, on the floor, her hands raised above her head in surrender. Her body is rigid, frozen in fear. She puts up no resistance as I grab her wrists and drag her through the gap, pulling her safely behind me. The material of her dress makes it easy for me to slide her across the ancient marble flooring.

I lift the white cloth once more and find Igor lying in front of the altar. His clothing is riddled with bullets, but he's still breathing and stretches his hand out to me. I point my weapon to his throat and fire.

"That one's for touching my woman."

Blood gurgles from his throat as he tries to breathe. He covers the wound with his hands, but the blood seeps between his fingers. I raise my gun to the narrow space between his eyes.

"And that one's for having the audacity to think you're worthy of marrying her."

His face lies flat against the marble tiles, brain matter on the floor around him, filling me with satisfaction until I feel Victoria's fingers on my shoulder, reminding me to get her to safety.

These guys are definitely not Bratva, unless they're Mikhail's men and this is another one of his underhanded ways of gaining control over another man's wealth.

The rain of bullets eases up.

"Keep her safe!" I bellow at my men.

Who the hell are these guys? They have more money than sense, wasting so many bullets to kill a handful of men. Mikhail's guards on the left side of the church are dead, or close to it, judging by the amount of blood pooling around their unmoving bodies. The guys on the right are on top of Mikhail, Anna, and her husband, shielding them with their bodies. I can't tell if they're dead or not. Either way, those men are big enough to stop bullets. For now.

The sound of footsteps at the church entrance makes me look up. More men are coming in, and they're surrounding another man. He's short, not as fit as his army. At a guess, he's their leader, because they've formed a tight circle around him.

"Mikhail Melnichenko, show your face," someone screams.

He has an accent I can't place. It's not Russian, or European. It could be South American, or Middle Eastern.

Their weapons are high grade, and they're here on a mission. Whoever they are, they planned this operation, and now I know they're not after me, or Victoria, I have no intention of sticking around to find out how this ends.

"Let's go." I whisper to my men. "I'm taking her out. Cover us."

I haul Victoria into my arms, grateful to feel her slide her hands around my neck. At least she's not fighting me. She knows I'm her safe passage out of here.

The priest is shivering on the floor, holding onto the large gold cross he grabbed from the altar.

"Father, I suggest you stick to my back like glue if you want to make it out of here alive."

He may be a lofty man of the church, but he recognises salvation in the form of my offer and does just that. I feel his heavy breathing behind me as we stay crouched and edge back to the vestry while the footsteps at the back of the church come ever closer to the front pew where Mikhail remains huddled on the floor, cowering like a lone wolf ensnared in a trap.

More shots are fired, and another body drops to the ground. There's no time to worry or wonder who it is. My mission is to get Victoria safely out of here, and that's what I'll do.

Inside the vestry once more, my men barricade the door with the furniture in the room. It's not enough to keep those guys out for long, but it gives me the time I need to strip Victoria out of the hideous dress she's wearing.

I freeze at the sight of her standing before me in her white lace bra and matching thong. Damnation. This woman has the power to slay me, and all she has to do is stand there, like she is right now.

She's in shock. Her eyes are glazed over, unfocussed, but there's no time to speak to her, calm her down, reassure her everything will be all right until I've put as much distance between us and this unknown danger as possible.

Grabbing my discarded black shirt, I pull it over Victoria's head, quickly doing up all the buttons to cover as much of her skin as possible. The top of her head barely reaches my collar bones, making my shirt look like a dress on her. I grab a gold sash from the wardrobe now blocking the entrance to this room and wrap it around her waist, cinching the shirt around her, leaving no chance of her revealing more of those toned legs than I care to let other people see.

I grab her hands in one of mine and force her chin up. She's looking at me, but at this stage, it's anyone's guess if she actually sees me. I pull her into my embrace, pressing her cheek against my chest, using valuable seconds we shouldn't be wasting.

"Listen to me carefully. We're not safe yet. We won't be until we get away from here and off this island. You need to do what I say, when I say. If you don't, more people are going to die."

She trembles in my arms. It's the only sign I need that she's aware of what I'm saying.

I strip out of the clergy robes, strap my gun holsters back in place across my shoulders, and pull my jacket back on. I might be shirtless, but I'm not about to start attracting attention to us by stepping out of a church half-naked and armed to the teeth.

The sound of a running engine at the side of the church spurs me on to grab hold of Victoria and sprint out the door, jumping into the back of the vehicle with her in my arms.

Her soft, silky hair, free of the thick lace veil, brushes against my neck, reminding me there's nothing I won't do to protect this woman. I was a fool to leave her behind when I left Moscow. No way in hell I'll be repeating that mistake.

Now these possessive feelings have been unleashed, there's nothing she can do to get away from me ever again. Especially not when there are other people out for Mikhail. His enemies are her enemies, until I can find out who they are.

Why didn't they shoot her? Igor's body was riddled with

bullets, but the bastard was wearing a bulletproof vest. Even being as close to her as he was, she remained untouched. Until I can make some sense of this, we need to lay low.

The van skids around the corner, and as we pick up speed to drive away from the church, I spot Mikhail getting into one of the black SUVs. I keep Victoria's cheek pressed to my chest, making sure she doesn't see him. There's no sign of Anna. Did they kill her?

How the fuck did Mikhail get out of there alive? And who is that with him? We're too far away now for any of us to identify whether the men in black are his guards or the crew who came into the church, guns blazing.

Victoria's trembling intensifies. I shrug out of my jacket and wrap it around her, pressing her closer to my chest in the hope my body heat will do its job and ease her nerves.

TEN

VICTORIA

THE WARMTH OF HIS BODY MAKES ME WANT TO close my eyes and fall asleep, but I'm scared if I do, I'll never wake up again.

This impenetrable wall of strength my cheek is lying against is Niko. There's no doubt about it. I'd recognise his touch in a heartbeat, and mine is thumping inside my chest as if it's trying to escape the confines of my ribcage.

He came for me.

"No. No, noooo. Wait!" I wail, pushing my palms into his chest, trying to get some distance between us, but he's like a solid wall, and I don't have the strength to move. "Where's Anna? We have to go back for my sister."

"We can't. I'm sorry, Victoria. I'm sure Anna's safe. None of the bullets were aimed at you. I'm sure they weren't aiming for her, either."

I take a shaky breath. Can I trust him to tell me the truth? "You're sure?"

"Yes," he answers without hesitation.

If he's lying because he wants to get me to safety, I'll never be able to forgive myself, so I have to assume she really is safe and stop imagining the worst that could have happened. There's a side of me that's only too happy to let him take me away and not worry about anyone else. I have to believe my sister is fine and get off this damn island before Mikhail tracks me down again.

"Did you recognise those men?" Niko asks.

"I..."

His hand rubs along the length of my spine, and I bite my tongue, enjoying the moment and wondering how much to tell him. Does he really have my best interests at heart, or is he putting up a pretence, working for the Bratva? He is Russian, so it's a distinct possibility.

He remains quiet, waiting me out, and I decide to reward his patience.

"I think they're Colombian cartel." My voice is low, almost a whisper, as if I'm afraid to even say it out loud.

"You think they came for you?"

He doesn't look like he believes me, but he's also got that contemplative look on his face. He's not dismissing the idea outright.

It probably hasn't crossed his mind my previous life has collided with my present one. He's never heard me speak about my upbringing in Colombia and probably doesn't know how my mother and I came to live with Mikhail. It's not like I go around telling people, *hey, my mother and me were stolen from my Colombian father, who was part of the drug cartel in Medellin.*

"Mikhail stole my mother from them, so perhaps the cartel heard a rumour that her daughter was about to be married off to another member of the Bratva, and they decided to take me back to Colombia before it happened?"

I can't believe I've just told him that. Have I made a mistake?

The look on Niko's face lets me know he's thinking about what I said, processing it like the intelligent man I know him to be. He knew Mikhail was bad news and took off, leaving us all behind so he could move on with his life. Is that not a sign of a bright man?

He's probably also got the same questions that have been running through my mind. Why did they wait this long to get me back? My mother's been dead for many years. They've had plenty of time to locate me and bring me back to my family, so why now?

I rub my hands together, trying to get some warmth into them. I know I'm probably suffering from shock—I mean, it's not every day I've stood in front of a priest, about to be forced into marriage, which then turns into a massacre.

The feel of Niko's hands rubbing my back is soothing, but when he instructs his men to turn the heater on, it warms me from the inside.

I can't get rid of the vision of Igor's body as he dropped to the marble floor of the church. He pulled me down with him, and I struggled to get his weight off me before Niko pulled me behind the altar.

"Was that his brain I saw on the floor?"

"Yes."

He answers without hesitation again, and I have to believe he's telling the truth.

"He's dead, then?" I need his reassurance.

"Most definitely."

The threat of being married to Igor is no more, and it's like a huge weight has been lifted off my shoulders. He's the reason I've been on the run for two years now. I'm no fool, though—I know it's no guarantee my step-father isn't going to find another candidate. But for now, he's probably trying to figure out who attacked us today. With any luck, he'll assume I've been taken by the same guys, buying us some time to disappear.

But where do I go now? I should probably consider moving to America, if it weren't so bloody difficult to get a visa. Knowing the extent of my step-father's network, it's not safe to apply for papers to go anywhere. The man has spies in places I can't even imagine.

"I'm glad he's dead." I raise my hand to Niko's chest, where I feel his heart rate speed up beneath my fingertips. "Does it make me a bad person if I'm happy he's dead?"

I drop my head to my hand, then move it out of the way so I can hear and feel his heartbeat. He smells like a real man, sweat, sea breeze, and something that's essentially Niko, reminding me of the day he took control of my body many moons ago. I want to kiss him so damn bad, but I don't know if he's remotely interested in me that way. I mean...surely if he was, he would never have left without saying a word? He just disappeared. Here one day, gone the next.

When he left, a part of me went missing, and as I sit here, in the back of a moving van, it feels like I'm whole again. Am I a fool for letting him get to me in this way? Is he going to break my heart all over again?

"There is nothing about you, or within you, that could be classified as bad by anyone, Victoria."

He tugs at my chin, lifting my face to look at him. Here, in his lap, we're nose-to-nose, and I see the fire in his eyes. This, right here, is the man I fell in love with.

His hands cradle my face, and his thumbs rub across my cheeks. "I never want to hear you doubt yourself in that way again, you hear me?"

My gaze shifts from his left eye to the right several times in succession. The way he's looking at me is as if he's trying to look into my soul, but I can't let him get to me this way.

Needing to protect my heart, I slide out of his hold and wrap my arms around him while nestling my cheek back against his chest where I feel his life blood beating within his rib cage. He's my safe place—like it or not, I'll never find another place like this.

The van begins to slow, and as I look out of the window, I realise he's taken me back to the marina where Mikhail's yacht is docked.

The door beside me is opened, and Niko climbs out, still holding me in his arms. I want to fight him. Why would he bring me back here? What's he playing at?

"Can you walk?"

I nod, dazed, as he lowers me to my feet, holding onto me until he sees I can remain upright before he slams the door shut and grabs my hand. We follow his two men back to the pier. They're on full alert, hands inside their jackets upon their concealed weapons.

I can't keep walking with them like a lamb led to slaughter, and I stop in my tracks. "What are you doing? Are you taking me back to Mikhail's yacht?"

Niko looks at me as if I've just accused him of something terrible. "Of course not. We're getting you off this island, and the quickest way to do it is to head out to sea."

"On my step-father's yacht?" I won't be pulled along until he tells me his plan.

"Look around you." He gnashes his teeth.

I've clearly pushed his buttons, but I don't care. After what I've been through, I need to know what's happening next.

"Does it look like the Celestine Angel is the only boat around here?"

I tug at his hold on my hand, but he refuses to let go, and we remain staring at each other as his men wait, scanning the area, on the lookout for danger.

I give in. He's right. "No, but could you please tell me where we're going. I need—"

He sighs before lowering his head.

"I'm sorry." His pale blue gaze shifts to my eyes. "I should have been more open with you after everything that's just happened."

He's not the type of man to discuss his plans with anyone. Power oozes off him in waves, and the way he holds himself, nobody would dare question him about anything. Except I'm the one who's been shunted around her whole life, and I can't do it anymore. I need to feel like I'm in control of my life, of myself.

The silence is killing me, and I'm about to apologise when he speaks, drawing me in effortlessly. "There's a powerboat waiting for us here. It's going to take us out to sea where a plane will pick us up and fly us to Sicily."

"Plane? One that can land in the sea?"

I've seen these things on TV shows, but the thought of getting into something that small, or taking off from the ocean waves, is making me wonder whether I'm being lifted out of one precarious situation and hurled straight into another.

He smiles before he leans in and presses his lips to mine. His touch is soft, and I melt like a marshmallow roasted over an open flame. Everything about him is intoxicating.

"You'll be perfectly safe with me." He places a hand over his heart. "I solemnly swear to keep you safe for as long as you'll let me."

What does this mean? Is he going to stick around this time?

ELEVEN
NIKOLAI

I SHOULD HAVE TAKEN HER TO THE AIRPORT. THE sea was choppy, making Victoria dry heave until we finally climbed on board the sea plane. Luckily, the flight to Sicily wasn't too bumpy, and she slept in my arms for most of it.

Now, we're back in Palermo, where I have connections and can keep her safe at my penthouse apartment. We park beneath the building, and as soon as the elevator doors open to my home, I place my hand on her back and guide her into the entrance hall, hoping she'll like what she sees.

"Is this your place?"

"Yes," I answer with a measure of pride. "Wait till you see the view."

Picking up the remote control, I press a few buttons to switch on soft yellow ambient lighting and open the curtains to reveal the view of the setting sun over the city and the Gulf of Palermo in the Tyrrhenian Sea.

Her breath hitches, and she steps closer to the windows where she's framed in the orange, pink, and yellow glow of the sunset. I could get used to this, having her in my space, watching her enjoy the life I could give her. If she'd let me.

"This is incredible." She turns to me as she's speaking, and I'm happy to notice the lines of tension have eased around her mouth and eyes. "How long have you lived here?"

"The building wasn't finished yet when I moved to Sicily, but as soon as I decided this is the place I wanted to live, I put in an offer the original purchaser couldn't refuse."

It sounds a lot better when I say it like that. He was in fact stealing from the Cosa Nostra, and I had a one-sided conversation with him which ended in his death and Luca giving me the deeds to this place as a reward.

"You're so lucky you get to live here."

This building is bricks and mortar, and this apartment has been a place for me to crash when I have some downtime, but seeing her here, finally relaxed, is what's making it feel like a home.

"Come." I take her by the hand and walk her through to my bedroom. "I'm sure you're ready to freshen up and put on some clean clothes."

"A hot shower sounds absolutely perfect."

She draws out the last word like a purring cat, and the sound goes straight to my cock, making me hard as I lead the way.

She stops in the doorway to my bedroom, taking in the massive dark wood furniture. "Is this your room?"

I nod, waiting for her to object, but she's either to tired and worn out, or she's not averse to the idea of being in here. My mind instantly fills with images of all the things I'd like to do to her now she's in my domain, and I have an arsenal of toys at my disposal to execute them all.

She sways on her feet and yawns, spurring me on to ignore my own needs and step into the wet room where I open the taps to make the shower come to life, raining down instantly warm water.

Victoria stares at me, eyes wide, her bottom lip clenched between her teeth. Is that the look of fear, or something else etched onto her face? I step closer, determined to find out.

My fingers slip into the knot I tied around my black shirt after I put it on her, and I have it unravelled within seconds. Her breathing slowly becomes more laboured as I drop my hands to the lowest button of the shirt and undo them, one by one from bottom to top. The material hangs, doggedly refusing to reveal her skin to my eyes, but once I get to chest height, her breath stalls in her throat.

Slowly raising my gaze, I take in her pouty mouth, lips partially open, and a pink tinge on her cheeks. When I get to her eyes, I find her gazing straight into mine. That fire I remember so vividly is back in her brown eyes, making the gold flecks in her irises come alive.

Her hands remain at her sides, unmoving. I take it as a sign and slip my hands under the black material, parting the shirt until the white lace of her bra fills my vision. But it's the skin barely visible beneath the stitching on the fabric that's calling out my name, and I'm a weak man. Unable to hold back, I cup her breasts, feeling their weight in the palms of my hand before I spot the clasp holding the bra in place in the valley between her perfect mounds.

Thanking my lucky stars for the easy access, I undo the hooks and lean in, taking in the scent of her skin before nestling my face between her breasts. "Your breasts are perfect."

A rush of air gushes past my cheeks as she finally exhales.

Pinching her nipples between my thumbs and forefingers, I pull her closer, relishing the sound of her soft gasp before I release one nipple to suck it into my mouth and lave it with my tongue.

Her hands fly to the back of my head, and her fingers dig into my hair, confirming she wants me to keep doing what I'm doing. I'm happy to oblige, but this is my show, and I bite down, sucking the little nub between my teeth until she pants and goes onto her tip toes.

"Niko," she moans. "Please don't stop."

The thought never crossed my mind, but there's something I need to do first. Taking the two sides of the shirt, I rip, barely taking in the sound of the remaining top three buttons hitting the floor as I pull my black shirt off her, quickly followed by her lacy white bra.

Her breasts are a perfect handful, and my hands go straight back there, lifting them up to my mouth where my tongue and teeth go on a mission to lick, bite, and suckle every single inch that's bared before me.

"Yes," she hisses. "More."

I turn her around, wrapping my arms around her until I feel her back against my chest and my fingers are on her nipples again, squeezing until she squirms and her lace-clad ass rides the hard-on behind my zipper. This will be over in seconds if I don't take control of the situation.

"Behave yourself." I bite back the rest of the phrase on the tip of my tongue. *My girl.*

"I can't help it," she whines. "You're making me feel restless. I need to feel you inside me."

Thank fuck. We're on the same page. I release my grip enough to land a firm slap against her ass cheek, then grab the abused skin and squeeze until she hisses.

"Please, Niko." She pushes back against me, rubbing her ass against my pants.

"Sir," I whisper in her ear.

The word has the desired effect, and she instantly falls into the submissive role she was always destined to have with me.

"Please, Sir. Let me feel you inside me."

I land a second hard slap to her rounded ass, choosing the other cheek this time, needing to see my marks on her skin.

Mine. The lone thought rattles around in my mind while I undo my belt buckle and slide the belt through the loops in my pants. I'm tempted to watch the leather strike her skin, but with the shower running, now's not the time, and I step out of my pants, kicking them behind me.

I drop to my haunches, sliding her lace panties beneath the round curve of her ass, pausing to take in the view of my handprints on her tawny skin, framed by white lace. This would make a beautiful photograph for me to look at whenever she's not around. I've never wanted sexy photographs of a woman before, but she brings out the savage beast within me. I want it all with her.

"Lift," I order once the white lace is around her ankles. She follows my command, raising one foot, then the other to let me remove her final piece of clothing. "Step into the shower."

She moves forward hesitantly until reassured the temperature of the water is to her liking, and she moans softly as the rainfall shower cascades down around her.

Without taking my eyes off her, I remove the shoulder strap with my weapons and leave it on the vanity beneath the mirror before reaching out for her beneath the downpour. I wrap my arms around her, holding her for a few moments until she's like putty in my hands.

Planting a kiss in the crook of her neck, I pump shower gel into my hands and begin a leisurely massage of her neck, shoulders, and back, soaping up her skin while the water sluices off the bubbled suds before disappearing down the drain. After I'm done with her back, ass, and legs, carefully avoiding the juncture between them, I suppress a chuckle when she stomps her foot, expressing her displeasure at my hands as I turn her to face me.

The displeasure slowly morphs to soft sighs of pleasure as my fingers slowly massage her breasts, lifting each one, giving them the attention they deserve. My fingers are too slippery with the foaming bubbles to get a good grip on her nipples, and they slip off again and again.

She giggles.

I want to bottle the sound so I can listen to it over and over on repeat. She's addictive.

I pump shampoo into my hands and massage her scalp before taking strands of her hair to rid her of the scent of the shampoo she used before she was forced to get into a wedding dress. I want to purge all of it from her memory. Forever. Replace it with memories of this. Of us.

I'm never letting her go. My mind's already coming up with a plan to make her mine.

She tilts her head back, rinsing the shampoo from her hair. Such a simple act, yet I'm enthralled, unable to tear my eyes away from her.

When she's done, she locks her gaze with mine, challenging me as she soaps up her hands and murmurs, "My turn."

Desperate to feel her hands on my body, I give her free reign as she slides her hands across my wet skin, threading her fingers through my chest hair, taking her time to cover me in soap, inching her way downward faster than I would normally allow. But she's in a rush to reach her destination, and I'm in no hurry to stop her.

Precum leaks from my tip as she fists my cock, her fingertips barely touching around my girth. She's so dainty, her fingers so slim as she slides them up and down my length. Beside her, I feel all powerful, a giant of a man. Her man, if she'll have me. She will. I'll make sure of it.

Her tongue brushes over my slit. I groan, grab her face between my hands, and keep her in place as she tries to move closer.

"Keep your hands around the base of my cock."

She slides them down, squeezing her hands one by one as if she wants to milk me. Fuck me, it feels so good. My woman is feisty. She's going to keep me on my toes, but at the same time, I'm going to enjoy keeping her on hers.

"Now open your mouth and stick out your tongue."

She responds instantly, eager to receive me.

I brush my thumbs across her cheeks as I tilt her head to position her at the correct angle to feed her what she wants.

Precum coats her tongue as I push forward, inching in. Her eyes widen as my girth stretches her lips. I'm only halfway in, and she's already struggling.

"Good girl," I murmur. "Look at you taking my cock."

Her nostrils flare at the praise. I slip my hands to the back of her skull, pushing my length inside her mouth until her gag reflex kicks in.

"Relax, open your throat," I order as she tries to fight me.

When she settles, I slide farther down her throat, and she leans into me, taking me in as far as she can. "That's my good girl. Your mouth feels incredible. You deserve a reward for taking me so deep."

TWELVE

VICTORIA

THE MORE HE PRAISES ME, THE MORE OF HIM I WANT to swallow down. Tears leak from my eyes, and I don't know where this emotion coming from. It's overwhelming to be with him. He's everything I want in a man. I feel safe when he's around, and knowing he'll kill anyone who tries to take me is the greatest aphrodisiac.

The temperature of the water is cooling down, making my body shiver. Niko notices it immediately and pulls out of my mouth. I don't want to let him go and try to grab onto him, to keep him in place, but he's not having it.

"Naughty girl."

He closes the tap and pulls me upright before stepping out of the shower and returning with a white fluffy bath towel. He squeezes my hair with it, getting rid of most of the water before he rubs my body dry, getting down on his knees to make sure he reaches every inch of my skin.

"I'll take care of you. You've been through a lot these past years, but now, you get to leave it all in my hands. Nobody is going to get to you ever again. You have my word."

He can't really make those kinds of promises. Someone is after me, likely my own family as well as my crazy step-father who's hell-bent on using me to fill his coffers even further.

"What about Anna?" I blurt out, assailed by guilt I could have forgotten about her even for a second.

"She's with Mikhail," Niko answers. "I got a message from my crew while we were in the car. Her husband didn't make it out alive, though."

"Good." My Colombian family look like they're finally getting on with the task of protecting me and those I love. It's a little late, but I'll take it as a win. It will go some way to eventually being able to forgive them for leaving my mother and me with the Russian Bratva all those years. "We still need to get her away from her father, though. He's a monster."

"We will. My contact is busy getting more information, and as soon as I've got that, we'll go after him, guns blazing. You and your sister will be reunited, and Mikhail will be eliminated."

I believe him. He's not the type of man to divulge details or give me a throwaway remark without following through. His word is his bond.

"There's nothing we can do until the morning, so after I've fed you, we'll get some sleep."

Sleep? Is he kidding me? My body's on fire, one big bundle of need, and it's not going to be satisfied with sleep.

He turns his back on me as he runs the towel across his back. His shoulders are much wider than his hips, and his muscles flex with the movement of his arms. I bet he looks good in the gym, lifting weights, sweat trickling down his eight-pack.

My nipples pucker at the image I've conjured up, and I rub my thighs together, looking for relief. Hell. I've got it bad.

"Somebody needs a spanking." He smirks, catching my reflection in the mirror, watching my movements as I clench my Kegels. "Keep that up, little one, and you won't be able to sit for at least a day."

"Promises, promises," I mutter, reaching for him. While my mind is screaming at me to back off in case he hurts me, my mouth hasn't caught on and is goading him once more.

He grabs my wrists in a single hand, holding them together in a steel grip without inflicting pain. He's taking control, and I love it. It's exactly what I want from him, what I need.

"Please, Sir. Make this burning ache inside me go away."

He lifts my hands, drawing me closer to him as he does. "And what is it you think I should do?"

He's going to make me say it, make me beg explicitly. I've never verbalised my sexual desires, and my cheeks burn at the thought. "I think you should fuck me, Sir."

"I think so, too, but before we fuck, I want you to understand this is not a one-night stand like the last time.

This thing between us isn't something I'll brush aside. When we do this, you're mine. Forever. I won't let you go again."

Time freezes. My lungs fill with the scent of his musk shower gel mixed with an earthy, masculine smell I will always identify as his.

"There hasn't been a single day since that evening in Moscow, when you took my virginity inside my step-father's garden shed, that I haven't thought of you or longed for your touch."

"Mine," he growls and pulls me into his chest, lowering his mouth to claim my lips. His tongue slides along mine, twisting and curling as I surrender to his assault.

Out of breath, he pulls away then lifts me into his arms to carry me to his massive four-poster bed. "You'll be wearing my ring before the sun sets tomorrow."

Marriage? To Niko? Permission to be in his bed and have him in mine for the rest of our days? There's nothing I want more.

No, I do... I love him; I want him heart, body and soul. But if his body is what I must settle for, I will. Because it's Niko. He's doing this to protect me—no one else can claim an already-married woman.

But still, being his... It makes me giddy suddenly, this prospect.

"Promises, promises," I giggle as he turns me over and peppers my ass with a solid spanking.

"You're going to be the death of me," he growls before

biting my ass cheek. "But not before you've given me at least four children and wear my mark."

I don't know if he's being serious. The children, I'm okay with that, at least the making of them. But his mark? What does that mean? Yet as he spreads my legs and latches onto my clit with his mouth and tongue, I don't care about any of it anymore, as long as he keeps doing what he's doing.

He pushes a finger inside my wet pussy as his tongue burrows into the hood protecting my clit, swirling round and round as he adds a second finger and scratches the little patch at the front of my channel that has me wailing out his name.

"Nikooo. Sir. Please, oh, please, let me come."

His fingers are ruthless in their pursuit of friction, and as he grips my clit between his teeth and pulls, I fall apart beneath him, losing myself, my mind, my sense of awareness as I tumble into a long-awaited climax. Wait, was that his permission to come? He didn't say so, but that tug, it felt like he wanted me to take the plunge...

"Such a good girl."

Relief floods me. I didn't overstep—there isn't more punishment coming my way. Can't say I would've liked another spanking, not when all I want is his cock filling me up.

His tongue swipes across my oversensitive clit, and I arch my back as he opens my legs wide.

"Now take my cock like the good girl you are."

Finally! Yes, please.

He thrusts inside, filling me up, and it's like the homecoming of a long-lost lover which I tell myself is ridiculous because I only had that one moment with him.

The feeling of loss as he left me then slides in, making me doubt his motives. I squirm beneath him. Should I stop this?

His fingers thread through mine as he pushes my hands above my head, holding them in place while he continues to slowly slide in, hold still, then pull out of me, awakening senses and yearnings I've kept suppressed. I want to believe he wants me so damn badly, but I'm scared he's going to leave me shattered like he did last time. Marrying him, it means nothing if he has no feelings for me, just like he showed me that fateful Christmas.

"Get out of your head. I see you, thinking, worrying."

His next thrust is hard, and he remains in place, getting my full attention when all I want him to do is keep up the slow burn that's taking me closer and closer to falling over the cliff of oblivion again.

"Look at me."

How can I refuse when he uses that commanding tone of voice? He's in charge, and fight as I might, I want him to be. I raise my eyes to his and am immediately assaulted with the warmth and sincerity in his gaze, and it feeds my hope that this time, it's for keeps.

"You're mine." He pulls back, and only the head of his cock remains between my lower lips.

"Sir..." I lift my hips, trying to force him back inside me.

"You feel that?" he asks as he gently rocks his cock, filling me with a mere inch before retracting once more.

"Yes, but I need more. Please, Sir. Give me more." I'm losing my mind. I was so close, and he's making me wait.

"That's for you. Only you. I haven't been with a single woman since I was with you."

What is he saying? It's been five years. How could he have been celibate for that long?

"I don't understand."

"I've been yours since that day I took your virginity, right after Mikhail told me he wanted me to get engaged to Anna."

The words hit me like a bucket of iced water poured over my face, and I try to move. "You were getting engaged to my sister?"

"No. Never. Your step-father wanted to make the match, but I didn't then, nor do I now, feel anything for your sister." He gives me a couple of inches of his cock before he continues. "From the moment I saw you, I've been haunted by visions of you. Every time I close my eyes, it's these beautiful brown eyes I see watching me, and it's your body I've longed for."

His confession brings tears to my eyes. I can't believe this big, strong, independent man wants me when he could literally have any woman on the planet.

"Don't cry, Victoria." He lowers his face towards me, lapping up the tears leaking from the corner of my eyes. "Nothing is going to get between us ever again. You're stuck with me for the rest of your life."

"You're sure?" I can't help asking. After all, I come with a host of danger, a rabid step-father, the Colombian drug cartel, and who knows what else. "I would understand if I'm too much trouble for you to take on, I mean with all that's going on."

I give him the out, but the look of outrage on his face is enough to tell me he's not interested in it. He's one-hundred percent sincere. He really does want little old me.

He flips me over, somehow keeping me rooted in place with his cock as my body rotates through the air and I'm on the bed on all fours. He moves closer behind me, ploughs back inside my channel as his hands roam down my back, slowly pushing my shoulders down to the bed.

"You are never to talk about yourself in a derogatory manner."

His lifts his hands off my shoulders, and before I know it, he's spanking me, using my ass like a set of bongo drums. The pain is instantaneous, radiating through my skin, into my muscles, heating me up inside and out. When it feels like it's too much, I edge forward, but he refuses to let me go and hauls me straight back into position, hardly breaking his rhythm in the process.

"You might need a daily spanking from now on, until you learn not to speak badly of my woman."

The way he emphasises those last two words has me rocking back against his thick, hard length. Could I be this lucky? There's no time for doubts when I feel his thumb press against my dark ring.

I clench my little hole tight at the pressure of his digit. "Niko! What are you doing?"

Of course I know what he's doing, but I've never had anything go in my ass before, and I'm scared.

"Relax. Your ass is part of you, and you belong to me now. So, who does this ass belong to?"

Oh, shit. I'm not ready for this.

He slaps my ass. "Answer the question."

Mierda.

"You, Sir. My ass belongs to you."

His hands rub against the abused skin on my ass, making me want to wiggle against him, wag my tail like a happy puppy.

"That's right. Now open up and give me this ass."

I tilt my hips and let go of the clenched muscles. Behind me, I hear him spit, before his fingers smooth his saliva around my back passage, easing the way for his thumb to slide in. It doesn't hurt. If I'm honest, it feels naughty and completely taboo, which sums up our relationship. He's like the forbidden fruit I never thought I'd be able to taste, and he's showing me a side of myself that's unexpected, and exciting.

His left hand grips my ass, and with his thumb inside my forbidden hole, and his cock building up an intoxicating rhythm, I'm panting, and groaning, and slapping my ass against his abdomen as I chase my release.

"Do you feel that, Victoria?" He grunts and grinds both his cock and thumb inside me. "I'm everywhere inside you. You're mine. Tell me."

"Yes, Sir. I feel you. I'm yours." I moan as he picks up the speed. He's set me ablaze, making me feel his thumb and his cock, letting me know he owns every inch of me, and it's so hot. "I'm going to come!"

"Not before you beg me," he roars behind me.

"Please, Sir. I beg you. I need to come, please, Sir."

"Come, now."

And I do. I come so hard, my body shakes uncontrollably as he fills me with his seed before collapsing on top of me. His warm, heavy breaths surround me on the pillow, and his body blankets me with his heat from head to toe. I'm cocooned, safe from the world as he gathers me up beneath him to protect me.

If this is what our life together looks like, I'll be exhausted and floating on ecstasy for the rest of my days.

Thirteen

Nikolai

I WAKE UP SPOONING VICTORIA'S WARM BODY, feeling like I've won the lottery. After we fell asleep, I woke in the middle of the night when she took my cock into her mouth. She pouted when I refused to come down her throat, but there's no way I'm coming anywhere but deep inside her pussy until her abdomen is round with my baby. I want it all with her. The ring on her finger, babies, growing old and grey —a lifetime.

Forcing myself off her delicious body, I head into the shower, leaving her snuggled beneath the duvet. I need her well-rested. We have a long day ahead of us today.

First thing on the agenda is her safety. Getting my ring on her finger is imperative, and I place a quick call to one of my connections to make the arrangements. They'll be here in two hours. After that, she'll be under my protection legally too.

Once I've showered, I dress quickly and quietly before I drop a soft kiss on her cheek and leave her to sleep.

With a fresh cup of coffee in my hand, I head into my office, leaving the door open in case she wakes up and looks for me. Having my woman in my bed makes my heart ache to go back to her, but I need to eliminate the threat that's out there before I can relax and enjoy simply being with her.

There's never been a time in my life I got to slow down, take a holiday, or just be, but with her, it's become the thing I crave most. I want to be with her. All the time. I'm obsessed. This could become a problem, but I'll deal with it if it happens.

I open my laptop, click on the links I need to for my open connection with Vlad, and start a new chat.

Me: *Home. Safe.*

I chuckle. He's going to have to deal with vowels today. I have things to get done.

Vlad: *K*

Me: *update on Victoria?*

Vlad: *attack Gozo Colombian*

She was right. They came for her. Fucking bastards left her to rot in Russia even after her mother's death. After three years of dodging Mikhail's attempts to marry her off, she ran away. Then they still waited another two fucking years before they made their move. I will never forgive them for leaving her defenceless against Mikhail, yet at the same time, I'll be eternally grateful they did. If they'd taken her, I would never have found her. I'll have to make it up to her every single day for the rest of her life, starting today.

Me: *so why did they come for her now*

Vlad: *the wedding*

Vlad: *they want her 2 marry 1 of their own*

Look at him, writing proper words. He usually likes to do my head in with the extremes he goes to in order to hide his identity. I guess he's cottoned on I'm not taking any risks of miscommunication when it comes to my woman.

Me: *who do they want her to marry*

Vlad: *boss man*

What the fuck?

Me: *isn't that her uncle*

Vlad: *No extended family not blood related*

I'm trying to wrap my head around the news when Victoria sidles into my office wearing one of my T-shirts. It reaches mid-thigh, leaving her shapely legs exposed.

"What are you doing?" she asks, running her fingers through her bed-tangled hair.

I love the tangles her fingers get stuck in, reminding me of our night-time activities. My cock stirs. *Yeah, buddy, I get you, but now's not the time.*

"Chatting to my contact." I push my chair back from my desk, making room for her. "Come here and give me a kiss."

She runs her finger across her top teeth and lowers her eyes as her cheeks flush. "I have morning breath, haven't brushed my teeth yet."

I growl.

She glances up. "Sorry, Sir. I forgot I wasn't supposed to say anything bad."

I smile. She'll learn. The spankings are something I will always find an excuse for, no matter how well-behaved she becomes, but I suspect she likes them as much as I do, and she'll be misbehaving on a regular basis.

She sits across my lap and leans in to give me a quick peck on the lips.

That won't do.

I lift her body, giving her the space she needs to straddle me before I slide the T-shirt up, bunching it around her waist. She's naked beneath the cotton shirt. Perfect for what I have in mind.

"Lift your hips."

She lifts onto her knees, leaving me enough space to unzip my pants and take my cock out. Facing me, she can't see what I'm doing behind her. No doubt she's got an inkling with that naughty smirk on her lips and twinkle in her eyes.

"Someone's frisky this morning."

Frisky? I woke up aching to stuff my cock inside her, and now she's come here looking for me while she's not wearing any panties, I won't deny myself any longer.

"Woman, you have no idea. Now sit down and get your-self off on my cock."

I love the way she blushes for me and make a mental note to keep coming up with outrageous statements that will redden her face as often as possible. It's quickly becoming my new favourite foreplay.

She struggles to get me inside her, not knowing it's making me harder, thicker, compounding the problem for her while my libido ramps up. Fuck, I want to push her down and ravage her like a wild beast, but she must be sore after last night, and I don't want to hurt her like this. Not right now, anyway.

Wrapping my hand around the back of her neck, I pull her into a kiss, slowly sliding my tongue across the seam of her lips until she relents and lets me inside. The feel of her tongue against mine is like pouring gasoline onto an open flame, and I plunder, devour, savour her mouth until we're both gasping for air and her lips are puffy.

"I owe you a spanking for saying something derogatory about yourself, but you'll have to wait until tonight."

I know full well she's going to worry about that for the rest of the day, and I get off on knowing she's going to be anxious, and dripping for me all day long. Well, after I've fucked her in my office, that is. I have to finish what I started.

"My contact tells me the leader of the Colombian cartel, Eduardo Escobar, has decided he wants you for a wife. Between him and Mikhail wanting to marry you off to a Russian Bratva member, you're quite the sought-after prize." I kiss her bruised lips. "But you're mine, and they're about to find out." I wrap my hands around her shoulders, impaling her on my cock. "Now ride me."

"You're so bossy," she quips, then begins to move, first rolling her hips, grinding down on me and panting to accommodate my girth. "And so...big."

I slap her ass. "Sassy girl."

"Who, me? No, Sir." She grins, then rises onto her knees slowly before sinking down on my length inch by inch, repeating the movement until she's moaning out my name and practically bouncing on my lap. "I need to come. I'm so close, Niko."

I slap her ass once more, harder this time. "You know the rules."

"Please, Sir. Oh, oh, ooooohhh," she moans. "Please, can I come?"

Burrowing my hands under the shirt, I find her nipples, then squeeze them hard, making her moan louder. "Come for me."

"Thank you. Ohhhh, thank you, Sir. Yesss!"

She hops about on my lap like an out-of-control spring coil until I pull her down and hold her there while I sink my teeth into the base of her neck. My sperm squirts into her, marking her as mine in the same manner as the bruise she will wear just above her collarbone.

Collapsing against me, she purrs like a content kitten as I wrap my arms around her, breathing her in. My mind is spinning, working through the options at my disposal to keep her safe, but the more I mull it over, the more I realise I'm going to have to do something I never dreamed I would.

But it's Victoria, and for her, I'll do whatever it takes.

When building security phones me, I pick up the call.

"We have a visitor here for you, Mr Volkov. The lady's

name is Simone Eastwood, and she has a rack of ladies clothing with her."

"Send her up," I answer before ending the call. "The clothing designer is here for you."

"What clothing designer?"

I raise my brow. Is she going to fight me on this?

"Okay, Sir." She backs down. "But I haven't even showered yet."

"Don't worry about that. She's got products with her for you to choose from. Shampoo, conditioner, perfumes, that sort of thing."

Her mouth opens as the elevator doors ping open. I lift her off my lap, zip up my pants, then head out of my office.

"Niko," Victoria squeals behind me. "I need to clean up."

I turn round to find her standing beside my desk, squeezing her knees together. Then it dawns on me, and I smirk, satisfied. My cum is leaking out of her. "Leave it there."

I'm a barbarian, but the thought of my woman walking around with her skin stained by my seed makes me want to pound my chest.

I hear her huff behind me, then follow, as I walk to the entrance hall. "Simone, thank you for coming at such short notice."

I hold out my hand, and she takes it while glancing over my shoulder.

"No problem, Mr Volkov." She steps to the side. "I take it this is the young lady in need of clothing and accessories."

"Victoria."

She stretches out her hand, and the two women immediately enter into a conversation around the clothing rack.

"I'll be in my office if you need me." I check my watch as I walk away. "You have an hour and fifteen minutes before our next guest."

"Who else is coming?" Victoria asks while holding onto a bright blue chiffon gown.

"I like that colour on you. Get that." I smile. "And whatever else you need or want."

As I walk away, she cries out, "You didn't say who's coming in an hour and a quarter."

I should keep her guessing, but I relent. "The priest." I smile before adding, "You'll need to find a wedding dress on that rack."

Fourteen

Victoria

For the second time in two days, I'm staring at myself in a mirror wearing a wedding dress. Except this time, the dress fits me as if it was made for me and is exactly what I would have chosen if I'd had one custom-made.

Instead of white, it's a pale grey which is a much better colour against my naturally tanned skin tone. It hugs my curves and accentuates my small waist, making me look like a woman who knows how to dress. Which I actually do after my visit with Simone. She pointed out how to make my shape work for me rather than trying to dress in the same style as my sister Anna who has the figure of a catwalk model.

I tuck a stray curl back into the clip holding them off my face. Simone styled my hair in a messy ponytail which allows my curly hair to bounce around my shoulders. The look is sexy and alluring, together with my smoky grey eyeshadow and soft pink lips.

I can't believe I'm marrying Niko. The man I fell in love with while he was dating my sister. The man who awakened my desire and has set it on fire ever since. He acts like he loves me, and I choose to believe his deeds. After all, his eyes come alive whenever he sees me, and the way he can't keep his hands off me is more than I ever hoped to find in a man I'm about to marry.

The knock at the door is swiftly followed by Niko stepping into the room. He comes to an abrupt halt and sweeps his eyes down my length before slowly walking towards me.

My heart pounds inside my chest. Does he like what he sees? My tongue swipes across my lips in a nervous gesture, wishing he'd say something.

"Woman—" His arm slips around my waist, and he leans forward, bending me back, "—you take my breath away."

His lips claim mine as he slides his hand behind my neck, hauling me upright. He pulls back, runs a finger over the hickey he left behind on my neck, rubbing the skin-tinted makeup away. "Don't cover this up. I want the whole world to see it and know you're mine."

Well, then... I will wear his marks with pride, now and forever more.

"The priest is here. Let's get married before I have to drag you in front of the good man with my cum dripping out of you."

Why does that turn me on? Just the thought of it makes

me want to rip him out of his black suit. When I'm with him, I forget about everything else going on around us. Perhaps it's the familiar sandalwood and citrus smell of his cologne, or the way he takes control of my every need, fulfilling my desires beyond my wildest imagination. He's the only man I have ever submitted to, and the only man who I trust.

I grin. "Yes, let's get married."

Four people await us in Niko's lounge. Two are men I recognise as they've been posted outside our front door, one is a serious-looking chap with a black briefcase, and then there's the priest, who is currently enjoying the view with a glass of red wine in his hand.

I like this guy already. "Sorry to keep you waiting, Father."

"Not at all. I've been enjoying this beautiful view and a delicious glass of your South African Merlot." He raises his glass to us. "Let's get you two married." He takes another sip before he sets the glass down and opens his bible.

The wedding ceremony is over in a heartbeat, and after we repeated our wedding vows, Niko slips a beautiful oval-shaped black diamond engagement ring on my finger as well as a clear diamond-encrusted wedding ring, both in white gold. When it's my turn to put a ring on his finger, he holds out a white gold band with a circle of small black diamonds in the centre. The priest even speaks of how my wedding band fits within Niko's and how it made us a perfect fit, which brings a lump to my throat and tears to my eyes.

It turns out the man with the suitcase is Niko's attorney who has us sign the marriage contract. I now own half of

Niko's fortune, and unless my eyes deceived me, that now makes me a billionaire alongside my husband.

My head is spinning. I knew he was a wealthy man, but had no idea of the extent of it. No wonder Mikhail chased him relentlessly. He wanted that fortune at his disposal, which it would have been had Niko married Anna.

We pose for several photographs taken by Niko's guard Gio who is an amateur photographer in his spare time. Niko also makes him take a few happy snaps with his mobile phone which he quickly shows me before sliding it back in his pocket.

He put together a wedding in a couple of hours, and looking at the images on his phone, you'd never guess this wasn't planned months in advance.

After half an hour of drinking wine and eating delicate finger foods, Niko works everyone out of his apartment before returning to me with a black bag in his hands.

"What's this?" I ask, wondering what other surprises he has up his sleeve.

"This is your new phone." He pulls the box out of the bag, opening it and taking out a slimline gold phone. "I've programmed it with my number so you can always get hold of me." He hands it over. "Let's set up the biometrics so it only unlocks with your fingerprint."

The phone does its thing, and Niko finishes it off, then sends me the pictures he has of our wedding. But the only thought swirling through my mind is that he's leaving. Why else would he want me to be able to get hold of him on his phone?

Is it happening again? I can't bite back the words and burst out, "Are you leaving me?"

He looks up, visibly horrified at the thought. "Fuck, woman. Why would you think that?"

I shake my head. Why? Seriously?

"You did it before," I whisper.

"I was a fool then." He takes my stiff fingers in his grip, rubbing his thumbs over my knuckles. "You're my wife now. Nobody's leaving. Not you, and definitely not me. I'm the guy who never wanted to get married, and yet, I've just declared my love for you in front of four witnesses."

Yes, he did. I have to stop second-guessing his motives, otherwise, this marriage will have no chance of success.

He kisses my fingers, still clenched in his hands. "But I do need to take care of something right now, and I want you to stay here where I know you'll be safe."

"Where are you going?" I just told myself to trust him, yet here I am wanting to know his every move.

"I'm going to see my boss, and then I'm paying your step-father a little visit."

"I'm coming with you," I blurt out.

"Out of the question. I don't want you anywhere near Mikhail, and you can meet Luca some other time." He takes a step back as if the physical distance will stop me from arguing with him.

"I will stay in the car while you meet with your boss if you want me to, but you are not leaving me behind while you go do whatever it is you have planned with Mikhail. That man murdered my father, made my mother's life miserable, and just tried to marry me off to one of his cronies. I deserve to be present to witness whatever it is you do there."

I have an inkling he's going to put a bullet between his eyes just like he did to Igor, and if that's the case, I want to pull the trigger, or at the very least watch him bleed out.

"Please, Niko. I won't ask for much in our marriage, but this is very important to me. I'm begging you to take me with you."

He stands with his hands on his hips, considering my request, but knowing what type of man he is, there's very little chance he will relent.

He lowers his head, shaking it.

He's not going to take me with him.

Stepping into his personal space, I lower myself to my knees before I look up at him.

"What the hell are you doing?"

"I'm on my knees, begging." I blink my eyelashes in an attempt to add a little humour to a situation which is fast becoming a defining moment in our marriage.

"Fuck, woman—" he threads his fingers through his hair, "—am I never going to be able to deny you anything?" He blows out a deep breath. "Alright, you can come with me."

I grab onto his hands, using them to pull myself upright within the restriction of my wedding dress.

"But you're not going in your wedding dress, and you're to obey my every word the second we leave this apartment."

I'm hardly listening, already halfway across the room to get changed in our bedroom.

"Are you listening to me, Victoria?" His voice booms around the lounge, bouncing off the bare walls.

I have my work cut out for me if I'm going to turn this place into a real home.

"Yes, Sir, I'm listening," I answer, appeasing him after he went against his instincts to keep me home, safe.

Once I've changed into black leggings, black boots, and a long-sleeved thin black jersey, I join him back in the kitchen where he's busy loading his weapons before slipping them into his gun holster beneath his jacket. As I stand watching him, he picks up a small revolver.

"Have you ever fired a gun?"

I look at the weapon in his hands. It looks tiny compared to his preferred pistols. "I have. Anna used to go to the shooting range and take me with her. She said it was important for us to know how to defend ourselves, but he would never allow us to have our own weapons."

"Well, that's about to change. This is yours. It comes with a holster you can strap to your belt if you're wearing a loose top like you are now, or you can put it in your handbag."

He's giving me a gun? Clearly, he's not afraid I'll ever use it against him.

"Thank you." This means more to me than the rings on

my finger. He's giving me choices I've never had before, and it makes me love him even more.

I slip the gun into the handbag as he places his hand in the small of my back. "Let's go."

He's still shaking his head in disbelief by the time we get into the basement and he escorts me into the back of yet another black SUV. The two men who have been guarding our apartment are in the front, and he raises the privacy screen before turning to me.

"Luca Sforza is the head of the Cosa Nostra. I've been working for him since I left Russia, and he has some idea of who I was in Russia, but that's about to change, and I need to bring him up to speed." He grabs my hand and squeezes it. "Seeing as you're with me, you may as well come in and meet him."

"Only if that's what you want. I don't want to get in your way."

He drops a kiss to the back of my hand. "He'll understand why I'm doing what I'm about to do as soon as he meets you."

FIFTEEN

NIKOLAI

A WISE MAN WOULD HAVE LEFT HIS WIFE AT HOME before he tells his boss he's resigning and follows it up with the murder of the man who's responsible for the death and destruction in her life, but I've never been accused of being wise, and I like having Victoria beside me.

As soon as we arrive at Luca's family home, I help my wife out of the car and guide her through to his study. The room has been freshened up in the past year, and where it was once dark and gloomy, it's now bright and airy, much like the effect Luca has had on the Cosa Nostra since he took over from his father.

"Niko." Luca moves round his desk to greet me. "And I see you've brought a guest. You should have warned me. Vivi and the kids have gone out."

"This is my wife, Victoria." My chest fills with pride as she holds out her hand to meet Luca.

Luca glances my way before he takes her hand. He covers his surprise up quickly and answers, "Congratulations. I can see why you married this lovely lady."

She gives him a shy smile before releasing his hand and slipping it back into mine.

"Let's sit down over here." He gestures towards the lounge area to the side of the room.

As soon as I'm seated beside my wife, I give him the speech I've been practicing all night. "I can no longer work for you. There are some things I need to do you won't want to have linked to you or the organisation."

He steeples his fingers as he stares at me from his well-worn leather armchair, something that's remained in place despite the upgrade of the rest of the room. "Go on."

"Victoria is the step-daughter of Mikhail Melnichenko." He knows about Anna, and what her father had envisioned my future to look like within the Bratva, and I'm grateful he remains silent. "He arranged a marriage between her and Igor Antonov two years ago, but she ran away."

"Wise woman," Luca murmurs.

"He finally caught up with her and had her kidnapped then brought to the church in Gozo." A tremor runs through Victoria, and I squeeze her hand in reassurance. "What he doesn't know is that Anna contacted me and asked me to get her sister out of there, which I did, but not before the Colombian cartel turned up and sprayed the church with bullets."

"Why the hell is the Colombian cartel getting involved in a Bratva wedding?" Luca leans his elbows on his knees, his interest piqued.

"Victoria's surname is Escobar. Her father was the cousin of Eduardo Escobar."

"The leader of the Colombian cartel?" Luca is openly staring at Victoria as if he's looking for a familial resemblance. "And what do they want with your wife?"

"Eduardo believes that with her connection to Mikhail Melnichenko, he will be able to open up a trade agreement to get his cocaine distributed in Russia."

Luca whistles. "That's quite a coup if he can get that done. Would Mikhail agree to it?"

Victoria snorts. "That man will do anything for money and power."

"That's quite a predicament you've got yourself into." Luca's staring straight at me, leaving me in no doubt his comment is for my benefit. He knows my back is up against the wall. "You're going to need some help."

I hadn't counted on his offer. In fact, I came here to make sure he wouldn't be affected by my situation. "I can't ask you—"

"You're not asking, I'm offering. In fact, I insist you accept our help." He gets up to retrieve his mobile phone from his desk. "I assume you have a meeting set up with Mikhail? What about the Colombians?"

I take a deep breath. "I set up a meeting with Mikhail at a

hotel in town, then I asked Eduardo to meet us there, too. Neither of them knows I've invited the other."

"Change the location. You could be walking into an ambush if you go to a hotel. Tell them to meet you here."

Luca picks up his phone to type out a few messages as I grab hold of mine and do the same.

"Thank you, Boss," I utter as soon as the messages have been delivered and marked as read. "I'll rustle up the team, get extra guards on perimeter duty, and make sure they're all armed to the back teeth."

"Already done, Niko. Relax. Now, while we wait, why don't we enjoy a glass of wine from my uncle's vineyard."

Luca pours two glasses of a light rosé and hands one to Victoria and me before pouring himself a glass of sparkling water. He sobered up for his wife Vivi and hasn't lapsed in all the time they've been married.

"Cheers to the happy couple!" He holds up his glass as both Victoria and I take a sip of the cool nectar.

"This is lovely," Victoria murmurs as she lowers her glass.

"My uncle Lorenzo owns and runs the family vineyard in Africo on the mainland. His wines have won several prizes, but none are as popular as this rosé." He glows with pride as he talks about his uncle.

The three of us embark on a conversation that takes us from wine, to family, to favourite holiday destinations, and as the hour strikes four, the first of my invited guests arrives.

I make the introductions between Mikhail and Luca before Mikhail turns to Victoria and scowls.

"You've been giving me quite the runaround, young lady."

It's clear he wants to say a great deal more to her, but I stop him in his tracks. "I will warn you once only before I take action. You do not speak to my wife that way."

Mikhail, his finger lifted towards me, freezes with his mouth agape. He recovers enough to utter a single word. "Wife?"

Wrapping my arm around Victoria, I raise her left hand to allow the diamonds to glitter in the glow of the light. "Yes, my wife, and as such, you will treat her with respect."

I look over Mikhail's shoulder where I'm relieved to glimpse Anna.

"You married Niko?" Anna runs into Victoria's embrace.

My wife's tears streak her cheeks as she nods and shows her sister the rings I placed on her finger a few hours ago.

Anna reaches for my hand and pulls me into the embrace with her sister. "I'm so happy for you both. I always wondered if there was something going on between you two." She slaps us both on the shoulder. "Now I know I was right."

Luca pours them both a glass of wine as Anna takes a seat next to her sister and Mikhail sits in a white wingback chair.

"So what's this all about, then?" Mikhail asks. "You think marrying Victoria would displease me? Why did you send an army into the church to kill Igor? You could have just told me you wanted to marry her, and I would have been happy to welcome you into the family."

Victoria takes a gulp of the wine, nearly choking at the

suggestion of our marriage being one to give Mikhail some sort of advantage.

"This wedding has nothing to do with you, Mikhail." Hearing the footsteps in the passage, I continue the rest of the sentence until my next guest steps into Luca's office. "I arranged this meeting so you could meet Eduardo Escobar."

Mikhail jumps to his feet. "What the fuck is this?"

"Sit down, Mikhail." I lean towards him, letting him know with my physical presence I will not be tolerating any outbursts. "Eduardo is responsible for the attack at the church, and I've invited him to our meeting so he could look into the eyes of the man who murdered his cousin and took his family."

Eduardo looks ready to kill Mikhail with his bare hands as he growls. "You tried to double-cross me. Count yourself lucky you're still breathing, *cabrón*."

"Gentlemen, I'll remind you both you're in my home, as my guests. Please remember there are ladies present and mind your language," Luca reminds them with a firm reprimand.

"He's responsible for murdering my son-in-law." Mikhail waves his hand towards Anna who clearly isn't sorry about her loss. "He nearly killed me!"

Now that would have saved us all this meeting today, not that I mind the opportunity that's suddenly occurred to me.

"Eduardo, thank you for joining us today." He bows his head as I hand him a glass of wine. "The reason I wanted you to meet is because both of you want to gain something by using Victoria, and I will not allow that to happen."

I take her hand as I sit down next to her. "Victoria is my wife." I hold up the evidence one last time for Eduardo to see before kissing her fingers over her rings. "She's mine, and if either of you tries to take her from me, you will pay for it with your life."

"Now hold on a moment," Eduardo interrupts. "Victoria is part of my family, and you will not deny me access."

"She's my step-daughter," Mikhail splutters. "How dare you keep her away from me or her sister?"

"First and foremost—" I raise my voice, "—she is my wife! You will respect that. And neither of you gets to dictate whether or not you see her. That is entirely up to Victoria, and if she never wants to see you again, then you will both stay away."

There's an eerie silence in the room, as if my words have sucked the air right out of here. I mean every word. If she doesn't want to see them, so be it. There's a rage that's been building inside me from the moment they both appeared. Neither of them cares about Victoria—all they want is what she can do for them, and that shit ended the minute she said 'I do' to me.

She's mine in every sense of the word. Mine to love and mine to protect. Forever.

The smile on Anna's face as she leans in to squeeze Victoria's shoulders lets me know she approves of my behaviour. That just leaves Mikhail and Eduardo. The ball is in their side of the court now. Will they acquiesce and leave quietly, or will they give me the satisfaction of killing one or both of them for her?

"Fine," Eduardo answers first. "I'll agree to your terms under one condition."

Mikhail scoffs at his remark. "Nobody cares about your conditions, asshole."

Luca leans forward, placing his elbows on his knees, reminding everyone of his presence as the Don of Cosa Nostra. We're in his territory, and nothing happens here without the potential of his intervention.

I bow my head towards Eduardo. "What condition do you have?"

"You give me Mikhail and your assurance that when you take over as *Pakhan*, you will grant me access to your cocaine market."

Mikhail comes to his feet, and I follow suit, standing between him and my wife.

"Sit down," I bellow, pointing to the armchair behind him.

The room pulses with my unspent rage until he sinks back into the chair, and I turn to Eduardo. "Why?"

"He murdered my cousin, then took his wife and daughter. He needs to pay for that. Taking everything he's built seems fair."

It's exactly what I'd hoped for when I set this meeting up, but I pretend to take some time to think about his proposition before I answer. "I will agree to that if his daughter consents to let you take her father and if you agree you will work with her as my second."

I glace past my wife and settle my gaze on her sister. "Anna, what do you say?"

She stiffens her spine, already transforming into the creature I knew she was all along. I've just given her the opportunity to get rid of her controlling father, and her answer doesn't disappoint me.

"Yes."

Mikhail jumps to his feet, lunging towards her. "You ungrateful fucking bitch. After all I've done for you. You will burn in hell for this."

I manhandle him away from her as she remains seated and calmly answers with a clear voice. "I've been in hell my entire life, living under your rule. It's time for you to pay for the murder of Vika's father and the way you treated her mother and her."

Sixteen
Victoria

Malta

It's been weeks since Mikhail was taken to Colombia by Eduardo and his men, and although there was nothing in the media about it, Niko told Anna and me they killed him. I hope there was torture involved before his demise.

It's a relief not to be looking over my shoulder anymore, or worrying about him finding me.

As far as my Colombian family is concerned, I haven't decided whether or not I want to go back there to meet them all. It's hard to forget they never came to find my mother and I, and their reasoning they were worried about Mikhail torturing or killing us is not something I can easily accept. Maybe one day I'll learn to forgive them, and when I do, I may go back to Medellin and show Niko where I was born. Until then, I choose to keep them at arm's length.

Marriage to Niko is like living in a dream. He's bought us a home in Malta after I refused to live in Moscow, and we've been here most of the time, although we won't be able to avoid going to Moscow now and then as he's now officially taken over as *Pakhan*. He made Anna his second in command like he said he would, and she's remained in her father's home where she's flourishing under my husband's protection.

As for me, my husband has been keeping me busy, introducing me to the people working at the various businesses he owns as well as showing me his homes. Who knew one person could own so many of them? A few he inherited and cares nothing for, such as the palatial properties in Moscow, and others he's bought with his own money, like the apartment in Palermo which he loves because of the stage of his life it represents.

But this house in Malta is the first one we chose together. It's big enough to house us and that big family he keeps telling me he wants. I've always loved children and want to have ours, but whether or not I'm up for giving birth to four or more kids like he's suggested remains to be seen.

I run my hand over my abdomen. We haven't used protection since we got back together, but so far, we haven't been blessed with a pregnancy. I'm in no rush, though, as I'm loath to give up his undivided attention, especially now he's converted the annexe to our bedroom into our very own playroom. It's nothing like the rooms I've seen in the movies, because my husband decided he liked the idea of modelling it on the toolshed where we had our first encounter, and what my husband wants, he gets. Unless I put my foot down and make him change his mind.

It suits us, the rustic interior, but more importantly, I love the implements he's collected and uses to tie me to or suspend me from. I love our time there and can't wait for him to come home.

Running my hands down the bright blue gown he had delivered for me this afternoon, I wonder what he has in store for us tonight. This time, there was no underwear that came with a dress which leaves my back exposed and has a long slit up the side of my leg.

His footsteps echo on the stairs, warning me of his presence before he calls out my name. My skin breaks out in goosebumps, and butterflies take flight in my belly. Finally, the wait is over.

"There you are, my wife." He steps towards me, carrying a bunch of long-stemmed red roses and yet another black velvet box.

"Thank you, *mi amor*." I take the roses from him. "These are beautiful, and they smell divine."

"Nothing but the best for my wife. I had them flown in from Ecuador this morning." He leans in, wrapping his arm around my waist. "Now put those down—" he takes the roses, placing them on my bedside table, "—I want to taste you."

He drops his voice for the last part of the sentence, and I know our playtime has started.

He tilts my face up to meet his, and as his lips descend to mine, his hands come up to cup my face, holding me in place as he takes his time, tasting my lips, my tongue, and the inside of my mouth.

"Who do you belong to?" he growls as soon as his lips move away from mine.

"You, Sir. I belong to you." He's so possessive, needing the constant reminder. I like to tease him about it, but truth be known, I love that about him. It makes me feel cherished. "There's nobody for me but you."

"That's right." His breath whispers over my ear, sending a rush of heat down my spine. "On your knees."

I melt at his feet, eagerly awaiting what I know will come next.

"Take out my cock." He watches my fingers as I undo his belt buckle, open his pants, and lower his zip. "Good girl, keep going. You know what to do."

I pull his briefs down and lick my lips as his cock springs free. I raise my hands, about to grab hold of his length when he commands, "Leave your hands by your side. Only your mouth."

He's challenging me. I smirk, knowing full well my ass will be suffering today. He's in the mood to spank, flog, or whip me with his belt. My nipples pebble against the cool silk of the dress, and I clench my thighs together as I run my tongue along his length before opening my mouth and sucking him in.

His hands dig into my loose curls, gathering my hair into reins he can pull to hold me steady as he slides down my throat. "Open your throat, wife."

I do as he says as he thrusts his cock in as far as it will go, pushing my nose into his skin. He rocks on his feet, and time stands still as my lungs scream for air, and my fingers dig into my thighs to distract me from the lack of oxygen.

"Such a good girl," he says before he releases me and pulls me off his cock, wiping up the drool dripping from my mouth. "Stay on your knees."

I sit back, leaning my ass on my feet, watching him take off his clothes and walk into the adjoining bathroom where he throws them into the washing basket. My husband is a neat freak, often picking up after me without complaining.

He comes back into the bedroom swinging his keys, all smiles for me as I maintain the position he left me in and wait for him to unlock our playroom. He steps inside, switches on the lights, and ensures the room is safe, as he always does, before giving me his next command. "Crawl to me."

Impatient to find out what he's got up his sleeve today, I drop to my hands and knees and make my way to him.

"Good girl." His hand caresses the top of my head as he takes the key and locks us inside the room. "Now stand up so I can see you in this beautiful gown."

I get back to my feet and watch that beautiful smirk I love so much appear on his face as he takes me in from top to toe, then returns to settle his gaze on my breasts. My husband is a breast and ass man, so it's no surprise when he steps closer and runs his fingers down from my chin to my breast bone, before he takes the neckline of the dress in both hands and tears it apart.

"I liked this one!" I whine as the dress flutters to the floor. "One day, you're going to have to let me keep the dresses you buy for me."

"But I like ripping them off you."

"Of course you do."

He slaps my ass. "Guess who's just earned herself a spanking."

That would be me. I can barely hold myself back from doing a happy dance, but I do. Last time I did one of those, he doubled my punishment and denied me an orgasm so I try to sound contrite as I utter an apology. "I'm sorry, Sir."

He opens the wardrobe running along one side of the room. Inside it, he's got his collection of rope, paddles, floggers, and a whole host of other implements created for pain and pleasure.

My breath stalls in my throat as I wait for his choice, hoping he won't come out with the flogger with knotted tails, or worse, the studded paddle. Those things hurt like a bitch, and I want my husband to fill me up with his cum without inflicting a severe punishment, but he looks to be in the mood for it.

He turns around to face me, holding a leather blindfold.

"I can hear you thinking all the way over here. So let's get you started with this tonight."

He drops the wrist and ankle restraints on the floor beside me before covering my eyes and tilting my head back to ensure the soft lining is firmly in place over my nose, leaving no gaps for me to see through.

With my sight gone, I'm hyper-aware of his movements and ready for him when he moves behind me, pulling my arms back as he whispers in my ear, "Are you ready for this, wife?"

I love the way he makes the word sound like an intimate caress every time he calls me that.

"Yes, Sir." My nipples are begging for his attention and my body is more than ready for him to twist and bend me while he fucks me breathless.

His cologne wraps around me as he leans in to nip the skin around the base of my neck. He can't resist leaving visible love bites all over me. I'm becoming quite the expert at covering them up with make-up even though he wipes it off whenever he spots it.

The soft lining of the leather wrist restraints hugs my skin as he fastens them in place one-by-one before the air shifts in front of my feet and he drops to his knees before me. He leans in, inhaling my scent as his hands caress the outside of my legs before he curls his hands around my ankles. He lifts my feet onto his knees, one at a time, securing the ankle restraints. Once they're buckled on, he twists them until the steel buckles are where he wants them.

Warm hands roam up my legs again, circle round to grip hold of my ass as he leans in to bite me above my hipbone. I gasp. This is a new move. He licks the bitemark then sucks my skin between his teeth, making sure to leave another visible sign of ownership. He's hinted at getting tattoo on my mons which says 'property of Nikolai Volkov' but I've told him 'no' in no uncertain terms. At least not until we're done having babies. I can't imagine the embarrassment of a gynaecologist having to look at that while I'm busy giving birth. But knowing my husband, he'll find a way to make it happen.

"Such a good girl." He's standing right in front of me now. I feel his warm breath spread across my breasts.

I really hope he brought nipple clamps.

As if he's tuned in to my thoughts, he grabs hold of my nipples to pull and twist until they extend for him. I hear the slight tinkle of a bell when he tightens the first one around my right nipple. I'm in luck—he's brought the weighty ones.

Crap. What is it they say? Be careful what you wish for! He's twisted the clamp tighter than ever, and it hurts like hell. I bite down on my lip to stop myself from crying out. I'll take what he gives me, knowing full well the reward will be worth it.

As soon as the second clamp is in place, he slaps my breasts, making the bells jingle.

There's a distinct hint of a smile in his voice as he tells me, "I've learned to love the sound of bells when they're on you, wife." He follows it up with another round of slaps, landing the last few directly on my nipples, making me squirm and moan. "Beautiful."

He pulls my arms up, clipping them onto the spreader bar hung from the ceiling. Without shoes, I'm forced to go onto my tip toes. My muscles stretch as I dance on my feet, trying to keep my balance.

"Sir?"

I want to know what's coming next, but he's covered my eyes, and I have no idea what the ankle restraints are for. I was expecting him to use the red leather St Andrew's cross leaning against our back wall, but he's suspended me from the ceiling, leaving me guessing. The bells jingle with each breath, pulling on my twin tips as I try to find a comfortable position, worried I won't be able to last long with this immense stretch.

Niko, ever observant, lifts my left foot and slides it into a shoe. It's one with a platform I discover as soon as my foot hits the ground and the pull on my arms becomes more bearable. He slides on the other shoe before I hear him fiddle with metal chains, and I worry what he's up to all over again.

He clips my left ankle to the chain and pulls, lifting my leg out to the side. *Mierda*. He's hoisting my leg up to the wall with the chain, leaving me standing on one leg while exposing my pussy for whatever he has in mind. My body trembles, setting both bells off as he slides his hand down my suspended leg until he gets to my weeping pussy.

"Someone's excited," my husband murmurs in my ear.

"Yessss," I purr as he slides two fingers into my weeping channel and pumps. "Please, Sir. More. Please."

"Greedy girl." He chuckles as he withdraws his fingers.

"Noooo," I whine.

"Behave, or I won't let you come at all tonight."

The first strike of the riding crop hits my ass before I realised what was coming next.

"You'll take ten because I had to speak to your Colombian family again today since you're still not picking up your phone when they call you." He rubs his hand across the welt on my ass. "Now be a good girl and count them."

"But that's not fair," I wail.

The air swishes behind me as he lands another blow right below the first one. "I'll keep going until you count them out." Another blow follows his statement.

"Three... that's three, Sir."

He chuckles. "Oh, no, you don't. You know we only start the counter when you start counting."

"Okay, one. One, Sir." Hell, he really means business tonight.

Each stroke he lands is right beneath the previous one, leaving me with the entire midsection of my ass cheeks on fire by the time we finally get to the last one.

"Ten. Thank you, Sir." I thank him like he always makes me, before he decides he's not done with me yet.

"You took those well." He steps away, lulling me into believing we're done with that horrible crop, until it strikes the inside of my raised thigh.

Fuck. I don't understand. Why am I getting more?

"And because you took them so well, I'm going to give you five more."

I daren't ask why, and he knows damn well I won't risk receiving more punishment when he's in his element like he is this evening.

"Your cousin Amalia in Medellin wants to come visit you, and if you'd answered your phone, you would have been able to tell her whether you want her to visit or not. But you didn't answer, so you left me no choice."

He lightly taps the end of the crop against my pussy, increasing the effort he puts into it until he lands a hard blow I'm completely unable to prevent from hitting my vulnerable clit.

"I'm sorry, Sir," I sob. "I forgot my phone at home when I went to the salon this afternoon." And that's when it strikes me. He's not upset because I didn't answer my phone, he's upset because I left the house without it. "I promise I won't forget it again. I know you worried about me."

He lands three blows to the inside of my thighs before he drops the crop and wraps his arms around my waist. "I do worry about you, woman. You're my responsibility. I need to know you're safe when you're not here with me."

I lean into his shoulder as the tears get caught in the blindfold. "I'm really sorry."

He drops his hands to my ass, squeezing my cheeks in a firm grip, making me wince. "I know you're sorry, now. I need you to remember to take your phone with you whenever you leave the house. Anyway, seeing as you didn't answer your phone, I told Amalia she's welcome to come visit whenever she wants."

Well shit. There's no getting out of that now.

He thinks I don't know he's put a tracker on my phone. I should stop teasing him by leaving it behind on purpose, but I do love his punishments. Well, except maybe this one. He was harsh today. Perhaps he's onto my game, as well.

He caresses my back, waiting for me to calm down before he moves away again. When he returns, I hear the flip of a plastic bottle top and know exactly what's coming next. He pours lubricant into his hand and spreads it around my back rosebud. He's been training me to take his cock, and recently, we've moved onto the widest butt plug, but something tells me it's not a toy he's going to be stuffing into my ass today.

The chain links clink as he unclicks it and drops my leg back to the floor, giving me both feet back to balance on before he lowers my arms from the spreader bar attached to the ceiling. He walks me across to where I know the spanking bench is. "Bend forward and lean over."

His instructions are short and precise. He's fully immersed in the scene, and it's happening just as he meticulously planned.

The leather feels cool against my stomach as he attaches my wrists to the bench, making the nipple clamps jangle as my breasts move with each pull on my arms. Once my wrists are attached, he pulls on the clamps, making me hiss and howl until he lets go, leaving the devious clamps to dangle and do their thing. My nipples are on fire, and the more they burn, the more my pussy weeps.

He places his hand in the centre of my back as he walks back around the bench, letting me know he's there as my body trembles. I'm so desperate for his cock, I'll do anything he wants right now.

"You're going to feel these for a few days at least," he says, running his hands across the welts on my ass, slapping them with his open palm as if they haven't taken enough abuse.

I always love the reminders after his punishments, but I have a feeling this time, it will feel a little worse.

"Spread your legs."

I move one leg, then the other, shuffling my feet farther apart to make it easier for him to attach my ankles to the bolts on the spanking bench.

As I let my head drop, the sound of the bells rings in my ears before my breasts press into the footholds on the bench. How could I forget they're at nipple height when I'm bent over like this? My already sore nipples throb some more, but I'm too out of it to lift my body and take the weight off. Instead, I let the pain take me to another place, where I float while I wait for something to happen.

The hairs on Niko's thighs scratch the back of my legs before he presses something against my butt hole. It's not a toy, or his fingers. As he continues to push, I realise it's his rock-hard cock trying to gain entry through my sphincter muscle. It's as if he's trying to split me in two, even with the addition of extra lube each time he withdraws a little.

"Bear down," he demands, slapping my ass. "This cock is going in your ass tonight, one way or the other."

"Arrrgghhh," I howl. His cock is thicker than any of the plugs he's made me wear.

I pant, bear down, try to open for him, and suddenly, he's inside, slipping into my forbidden channel with a speed that takes my breath away.

"Oh, baby, if you could see how good you look, taking my cock in your ass." He growls. "Fuck, wife, you feel so damn good."

He leans forward, biting my back as he slips a hand beneath me and zeroes in on my clit, taking it between his fingers, pulling, pinching.

"Now squeeze." He orders, and when I do he rasps in my ear, "Fuck yes!"

He doubles his efforts on my sensitive flesh.

"Oh, shit... ooohhh, Sir! I'm close, please, can I come?"

"Not yet." He grips my hair, pulling me partially upright, setting the bells off once more as I huff and puff, desperate to hold back my climax until he gives me permission. "Now," he yells, strumming my clit and pulling on my hair until the bells are jangling uncontrollably. "Come for me, wife."

And I do. I fly apart, fragment all around him as his seed spurts inside my ass and he bites the back of my neck until he's done.

I think I pass out, but as I come to, he steps away, unbuckles the restraints, and wipes away the mess we've made before pulling me into his arms and carrying me back into our bedroom.

He lays me on the bed, beneath the duvet, then gently removes the nipple clamps, sucking my buds into his mouth to alleviate the pain.

"I love you so much, Victoria. I can't bear the thought of anything happening to you." He stretches out on top of me, resting his head between my breasts.

I wrap my arms around him, threading my fingers through his hair. "I know, Niko. I'm sorry. I won't leave the house without my phone again. I know how much you worry."

"I do. You're my wife, and I love you more than life itself."

He really does mean it, and he shows me every day, in all the ways. "I love you, too, and I swear you won't have to worry about me again."

He smirks. "I doubt that very much, wife. You're a brat, but you're my brat, and nothing you can do will ever make me love you less. Now go to sleep."

And I do, safe in the knowledge that I've found the love of my life, and he's never going to let me go.

About Amanda Holly

Amanda Holly writes sizzling romance in the sub-genres of mafia, suspense and thriller. When you pick up one of her books you're guaranteed an action-packed read in every way.

Growing up as a global citizen, moving from continent to continent, Amanda is happy to call Johannesburg in sunny South Africa her home. Her suitcase is always ready to go whenever the travel bug bites, but for the moment, she's happy to travel there through the tips of her fingers so she can take her readers along with her.

You can stalk Amanda Holly Author on her website. Facebook, Instagram and TikTok.

Serment au Noel

Erica Jaden

CWs, TWs & Kinks

(*Warning: Contains Spoilers)
This book contains mature themes and is intended for adult
readers. Specific content warnings include, but are not limited to:

ON-PAGE MENTIONS

Organized Crime
Death
violence
murder
Cheating (not between
MCs)
Arranged marriage
Handnecklaces (non-sexual)
Virgin FMC
Forced public sex
Humiliation
Domestic violence (between
MCs)
Dubcon (between MCs)
Rape fantasies

OFF-PAGE MENTIONS

Killing a pet Murder of
family members

STORY WRITTEN IN
US ENGLISH

ONE
CAMILLA SANTORE AKA THE RUBY

I STOOD IN FRONT OF THE MIRROR CHECKING OUT my dress and trying to focus only on my dress. I felt beautiful wearing the off-white trumpet cut, made from satin and lace.

While it was cold outside at the California coast, since we could only be married on Christmas Eve, it was still warm and cozy inside.

Thin straps graced my shoulders as the beautiful woven fabric flared out just below my hips. The dress hugged my body in all the right places, and I couldn't imagine what Philip was going to think as I walked down the aisle.

The dress came with a long-sleeve jacket that turned this beautiful trumpet cut into a fairytale wedding gown.

I took a deep breath.

Philip.

I tensed up sometimes when I thought about him. He

was half-and-half, cut right down the middle: fifty percent so serious that you were afraid to simply look at him wrong and fifty percent playful in that he could make you laugh until your tummy hurt.

I knew he'd already killed a few who had betrayed our family, but not enough yet to carry the tiny number one beneath his left eye. That only belonged to those who'd killed a hundred or more. He wasn't to be messed with, and yet I loved to mess with him every chance I got.

This morning had been a very stressful morning. I was lucky to love my groom because this was an arranged marriage, put down in the slates since I was ten years old.

We'd worked hard at our relationship through the years while the Solomons lived in New York with us. He was my brother's age and always around. So it wasn't that hard to become friends and later on start something deeper. Not all of us were that lucky.

The Santore and Solomon families would merge with the two of us getting married, meaning that the docs and the distribution my father had grown into an empire over the past ten years would be run under one roof.

The same would happen to my sister, Emi, when she married Gustaf Davini, and my brother to his sister when she came of age at twenty-four. They owned their own empire in transport.

My father believed that this merger alone would get us up the Don-Tier. A tier that was run by one family, one very powerful family that could either annihilate you from this world or move you up to a better future.

Their members had intermingled with all of our Dons' lives, Mafia clans, from all over the world.

Some said that they remained in Italy because it was their home base to take care of the Dons, keep them in line. Every decision that we made was run by them. Or in our case at least, brought to their attention. We weren't that important or that high up in the tiers for them to have a final say, but my father had made it his oath for them to see us. If they wanted to or not. They would acknowledge our existence after this merger, and if we were lucky, maybe our children would one day merge with theirs. That was the ultimate goal.

For the past fifty years, it was all my family had lived for. Their rules, and if you followed them, made name for yourself, worked hard—they would see you.

My great grandfather Levi Santore had come from Italy. He knew some of them, and he was proud to get an opportunity to be part of the Dons. He worked hard, made a name for himself, and started the distribution that was today known as the S.A.N.T. Distribution.

My life was never mine. Since I was a little girl, I was told how to act and to keep myself intact for my husband until our wedding day.

It hadn't been easy either.

The smile that had slowly pulled my lips toward my cheeks disappeared as I remembered the consummating ceremony that Philip and I would have to perform tonight.

Even our first night wasn't ours.

It would be recorded and presented in front of a crowd wearing plague doctor uniforms. I knew my father would be there, and Philip's father would be there, among others that we had never met before. It was a ritual that the Dons lived by.

The rules were simple, but as I thought about them, terrifying too.

He needed to orgasm, I needed to orgasm, there had to be blood present, I needed to yell his name, and we couldn't stop until all of those things happened.

My friends had helped me in faking an orgasm. It had left us laughing our asses off on plenty of nights since they doubted that I would orgasm tonight, with it being my first night. It would be painful, and the stories about breaking your hymen around my age left me horrified.

It was a wonder my mother and bridesmaids had left me alone to gather my thoughts and just have a few minutes for myself.

But then, why wouldn't she? I always did everything she'd trained me to do. Jumped through all of her hoops.

I needed fresh air and slipped out of the room through a side door that was connected to this one.

I exited the hallway and paced down the passage, taking deep breathes, trying to process all of the activities that were going to happen later.

I tried to redirect my thoughts by staring at the beautiful Christmas decorations that lined the walls. White and green wreaths hung from the walls with trees standing in each corner, beautiful Christmas ornaments decorating their branches.

I turned around the corner and found myself in front of Philip's door.

I was about to knock when the door clicked open and sex noises came from inside his room. My body stiffened. Maybe it wasn't him. It could be my brother or Charlie, his idiot of a best man. I turned around and was about to close the door when I heard a woman yelling his name.

"Philip, don't stop. I'm coming. I'm coming."

My breath caught in my throat as she continued yelling and screaming her orgasm.

Philip grunted like a beast as he came. Tears welled up in my eyes as the woman laughed; I knew that laughter by heart. It belonged to my fiery best friend, Victoria.

They were both laughing now.

"Do you really have to get married?" she asked.

"You know I have no choice. I wish you were part of the Dons. I would marry you in a heartbeat."

Heat crept up my back, and I tried to take another deep breath. I couldn't ruin my beautiful dress and makeup by sweating like a pig.

I heard him zipping up his pants and them speaking about getting back to their parties before anyone noticed they were gone.

A tear ran down my cheek as I turned around and ran into the opposite direction.

I was set to marry him in less than half an hour, but I kept running. I turned around the corner just as they exited their room. My tears blurred my sight, and one rolled down my cheek. They were walking the opposite direction.

Betrayal knocked the strength from my legs, and I slid down the wall, to the ground.

I'd thought he loved me, thought he cared about me. And today of all days, I found out that it was a farce and he actually loved my best friend, who wasn't even part of the Dons. Her family was a bunch of nobodies.

I'd always known Vicky felt something for him, but never in a million years did I think she would betray me like that.

She knew I had no choice, and while I could've married a betrothed that I loved and trusted, she obviously just didn't give a fuck about that.

Her betrayal was the worst.

I wiped the tears and snot from my face. Fuck this wedding; fuck everything.

I refused to marry Philip Solomon. He didn't deserve to be a Don. None of them did.

Two
Alfonso Pontisello aka the White Rabbit

"I'm not marrying that whore." I slammed down the phone in my father's ear. Rules were rules; she'd broken them by fucking another who wasn't even a Don. I'd always known that Simi was a slut. Always known she was sexually active.

Her family was so fake, and they shouldn't even be Dons in my opinion.

Our marriage had been arranged before we were even born, to merge hotels with beachfront property. Her family owned most of the coastline in California and especially LA. I was supposed to be in New York for our wedding that would take place today, but I'd stayed in California after I'd received a video of her fucking someone else who definitely wasn't me.

I would get married. My grandfather's shares that he'd left

me would become mine, but I would marry on my terms. Who I wanted. Even if I had to pay for it.

I was done with Simi Deluca and her cheap whoring ass. She was supposed to stay intact for me. Hell, all the other woman had done that; why couldn't she?

The door opened, and Nico entered.

He was a head shorter than me, bulky with blond hair that covered his ears. He wore his two-piece suit, required of him being my right hand and going everywhere with me.

People thought he was my bodyguard, which was a joke as I was a giant compared to his size.

"Is there anything I can do for you, boss?"

"Yes, find me a bride," I spoke in Italian.

"Sorry?"

"I'm not marrying Simi. Find me a bride to marry today."

"Who?" His face painted a picture of pure horror. I'd never asked of him anything that would be woven this tightly to my life. That was how much I trusted him. Fuck, if I could marry him, I probably would.

"Anyone who looks desperate for a husband. Just find me a bride."

He nodded, and I turned back to face the ocean. This hotel had been my grandmother's favorite.

She'd loved the ocean, and when my grandfather was gifted this spot by the Delucas a long time ago, he'd built this beauty, even named it after her: Anna.

I always stayed here whenever I was in the states.

My phone buzzed, and my father's name, Rico Pontisello, flashed over the screen.

I refused to marry her, and he was going to find out just what happened to naughty little girls who broke years of tradition. I knew what this could mean for her and her family; I didn't care. I was that callous and vicious.

An entire family engraved on my body would not make any difference. They were going to learn the hard way that if you wanted to keep your spot on the top tier, play with the big guys, you had to do so by following years of traditions and rules.

But I had to admit, I'd never liked the little bitch. She was a spoiled brat and thought if you snapped your fingers, everyone would jump just because Daddy had money. It was not one of the morals on which I was raised.

My family was raised with time-honored traditions, and we all followed the rules that we couldn't break.

Simi wasn't even my type. She had no ass, and her tits were so fake and way too big for her chest.

No, I liked a round ass that I could fuck till Tuesday came, and I loved natural tits that were in proportion with a woman's body. A handful was enough, or at least that was what my father always said.

My phone vibrated again. This time it was my mother. She'd probably heard what had happened and was going to beg me to reconsider just for the merger.

She should know me better by now. There would be no reconsidering. The elders would deal with them, probably saving their lives and slapping their wrists. Either way, they weren't my problem anymore.

All I had to do now was focus on my grandfather's shares. He'd left me fifty percent of his hotels; it was all in the trust, run by my father's corporation for now. My younger brothers would get twenty-five percent each. All they had to do was live by his rules: get married, settle down, build a family to carry on the Pontisello name. It wasn't that much. Even if I had to pay someone to carry my children, I would.

In today's day and age, people were desperate, and they would find the Don's way of life extremely exciting. Invigorating.

My phone rang again. This time Nico's name flashed on the screen, and I picked it up.

He laughed and couldn't stop.

"It's not funny," a woman said.

"Sorry," he apologized and then continued in Italian, "I found you the perfect bride, ready to say her I do's."

THREE
THE RUBY

MY TEARS REFUSED TO STOP ROLLING DOWN MY cheeks, so I could only imagine what I looked like at the moment. Black mascara smeared down my face as I ran past guests giving me that wide-eyed, worried look.

The elders would probably have our heads for this, but I didn't care. At this very moment, I didn't give a flying fuck. I knew my mother would drag me down that aisle if she got her hands on me.

I rushed to the elevator and as faith was on my side, it opened. A few people walked out as I rushed into it and collided with a guy. He caught me since I was about to lose my balance, and I just sobbed.

He smelled dangerous. Cigarettes mixed with a musky, wooden undertone.

I couldn't even see his face; tears blinded my sight as my

heart shattered, and the poor guy collapsed with me to the floor. His grip never loosened; he held me tight.

"Please, get me out of here."

He simply stroked my hair and spoke in Italian. I had no idea what he said, but the tone sounded relieved. He pushed a button, and the elevator stopped. I cried harder into his chest.

I thought of all the promises I'd kept. I should just fuck this guy in the elevator, right here and now. It was stupid to keep myself a virgin for someone like Philip.

The guy was patient as I sat in his arms, ruining my beautiful wedding gown. Then when I finally found myself, I tried to wipe my eyes.

He handed me a handkerchief. Who still carried those?

I took it and wiped my eyes. Black mascara lingered on his white handkerchief. I'd ruined it too. "I'm sorry."

"Don't apologize; what happened?" he asked. A slight European accent lingered with his English one, but it was slight.

"What always happens? They fuck someone else hours before the wedding."

"Testa di cazzo," he said, and I chuckled. I didn't know Italian. The language never took with me. Still, I knew a few cuss words. I thought he said that he was a dickhead.

The guy was cute, had a big tattoo that peeked from underneath his collar, and bleach-blond hair that reached his ears.

He screamed danger, and I needed dangerous now to get out of my miserable life.

He smiled at me. "What are you going to do?"

I shrugged. "My family will force me to marry him. I have no choice."

The guy frowned. "Force, on Christmas Eve?"

I nodded. "It's arranged. Wish I could get out of it."

"You don't say..." His lips curled again. "What if I told you that I have a way, will you at least come and hear it out?" His English was impeccable. Sure, there was an Italian lilt to it, but not as bad as some of the Italians I'd met in the past.

I nodded. Everything in my body screamed not to. That I was only getting myself into more crap. This guy could be a drug lord or worse, work in the human trafficking department. I could be in a crate in an hour, just by agreeing to hear him out.

He fished his phone out of his pocket and dialed a number. He laughed.

"It's not funny."

"Sorry," and then he switched over to Italian. I'd always loved the language but hated learning new languages. I wasn't as clever as my sister. My mom always said that I was lucky to be blessed with beauty since brains were not bestowed upon me.

She was so cruel in so many ways. I had other talents, talents she'd tried to suppress. Like my art; I loved to draw and loved to express myself through drawing, being creative.

The guy put the phone down and stood up from the ground.

He gave me a hand, and I looked up at him, hesitant to take it.

His hands were covered in tattoos, and my body continued to scream that I should get away from him, but my mind was made up. So I took his hand and allowed him to help me.

He pressed the button again, and the elevator moved, this time all the way up to the top.

"My name is Nico, and I need to you be open-minded. But I really do think that I have the solution, not just for you, but for someone in a similar situation to the one you've found yourself in."

"Camilla Santore."

"Santore? That's very Italian."

"I know. My great grandfather came from there. I've struggled to learn the language. I'm not good with languages."

"I'm sure you have other talents." He ran down his eyes down my dress and licked his lips. Somehow, I felt naked as the elevator dinged and the doors opened.

I gasped as white walls and windows from floor to ceiling welcomed us.

I stepped out onto marble tiles and grabbed Nico's arm as my shoes slid. The entire loft was dressed with white furniture and tiles and carpets. It was chic, and I was used to chic, but this was on a different scale.

There was a staircase leading up to a second level. Whoever stayed here had loads of money, probably even more than Philip and his family.

Nico never left my side as I clutched onto his arm. We walked up the stairs.

"Be yourself. And tell him your story, but know this is only a business contract."

I nodded and took a deep breath.

We reached the top, and he walked us to a set of double doors that were on the second level.

He knocked on one, and a deep voice that sent tremors through my body instructed him to enter.

Nico opened the door, and I followed him inside.

He spoke immediately in Italian, and I looked up. I froze as I stared into a pair of beautiful green eyes and the darkest mop of hair I'd ever seen.

He had a neat beard and a thin-line, neatly trimmed mustache right above his kissable lips. The guy was a giant, but that was not what took my breath away.

Below his right eye was a number one, meaning he was part of the Dons. The question was, just how far up.

FOUR
THE WHITE RABBIT

"So Nico tells me that you're in the same predicament as me?" I inquired, and she simply stared at me. I knew what I looked like. The tattoo on my face was a bit scary, but if she could look beneath it, she might find my soft side. The little I owned.

"Sorry, I don't speak Italian."

I looked at Nico. I was sure he'd told me that he'd gotten a feeling that she was part of the Dons.

"I never learned the language, or more like I tried and it never took."

I switched over to English. I had to say, she was gorgeous. Even with her face smeared with running mascara, she was fucking beautiful. She had this long chestnut hair that glistened, and her messy curls were practically begging me to grab her and fuck her mouth.

Big beautiful brown doe eyes stared back at me.

"Your name?" I asked.

"Camilla Santore."

Santore? I was sure I'd heard that name before.

Nico looked up from his phone. I knew he was already Googling her family when he nodded. She was part of the Dons. Maybe a lower tier.

"What happened?" I questioned, planting my ass on the desk behind me.

She glanced around the room, playing with her hands. Her wedding dress was slightly ruined.

"I found him fucking one of my bridesmaids. My best friend." Her voice broke on the last part.

"You ran away?"

"I'm sure you understand why I ran. There's no way out of a betrothal." Her voice lowered. "I know the markings on your face. I know what that one beneath your left eye means."

"Good." I smiled. "Then I don't have to bore you with our traditions."

"Why do you need a wife?"

I lifted my ass off the surface and towered over her as I neared. She smelled fucking sweet, and I bet she tasted just as good. Her throat bobbed, but she refused to take a step back. Defiant; I loved it. Loved the thought of breaking whatever spirit she had and making her submit. I leaned closer to her, so that she could hear me. "Because the one I was betrothed to also fucked one of my groomsmen." The last part was a lie, but the girl related.

Her gaze met mine.

"You're still intact?"

She nodded.

My lips curved upward, pleased that no man had touched her that way. "Good." I stepped out of her personal space and could hear her taking a breath. I opened a drawer. Mica had dropped this off early this morning. It was a contract. I pushed it in front of her. "I'll give you time to read it, and then you tell me if you are ready to become my wife."

She looked at me and then at the contract. She stood straight, puffing her chest out and showing the perfect shape of her tits. "What's in it for me?"

"Oh, a lot more now than what's in that contract, la mia piccola fuggitiva." *My little runaway.*

Her jaw muscles pumped softly. She must hate the pet name I'd given her. My lips curved again. She walked toward the desk and picked up the contract.

"Nico, take her to the spare room; I still have some business to conduct."

He nodded and left with her.

I watched as she departed. This arrangement could turn into the best thing that had ever happened to me. She already knew the way of the Dons.

Nico returned a few minutes later. "I told you she was perfect."

"And she just ran into you?" I asked.

"If that isn't fate, I don't know what is."

"I will need all her family's details before this hour is up. Make it happen."

"Already busy. You'll have it in a few."

I indicated to him to leave me alone. I needed to think about how I was going to punish the Delucas. I was sure my father would have the last say, but if my grandfather was still alive, he would've ruled with me, overthrown his command and annihilated her family line.

Through the years, my father had become soft on all the Dons that were at the top tier. If my grandfather was still alive, none of them would be at the top anymore. Their legacies would've been wiped away from this earth.

My phone buzzed, and I saw it was a text from my mother. I read it.

Come home now. You have your wedding to attend. I'm not playing around, Alfonso. You can forgive her this once.

I chuckled. "No fucking way."

I switched off my phone and put it in the drawer. I'd let them know after I was married and after I decided what to do with the Delucas for their betrayal.

My father was going to learn the hard way, that shit was going to stop.

THIRTY MINUTES LATER, Nico dropped the file on the Santores in front of me.

It was quite big.

"Impressive."

"Oh, wait till you read it. These mergers would've gotten the elders' attention."

My gaze dropped from Nico's to the file; I opened it.

She was the oldest daughter of the Santore family. They had a son, Milo, five years older than her. Their great grandfather Levi had opened the distribution company fifty years ago in New York, and for the past fifty years, they'd worked hard. I saw it in their file. Saw it through their bank statements and financials.

They had another daughter, Emily, a few years younger than Camilla. She didn't look anything like her sister. She reminded me of Simi.

I carried on reading through her file. Nico had left as I paged through their company's details and information. How didn't we know how big S.A.N.T had gotten? This merger with the Solomons would've gotten them noticed. Their offspring could easily have merged with my offspring; that was the sort of noticing this merger would've done.

A merger Grandfather had warned Father about. The kind that could be wrong for the Pontisellos. And it was. But now that we would marry, we would merge with the distribution, and the percentage of the docs that my family already owned would chuck the Solomons to the bottom.

My lips curved. The guy was going to fume, whoever he

was. Losing to a Pontisello was not easy, and he was going to learn the hard way just how difficult losing can be.

I turned the page and found the Solomons' file.

Philip Solomon was the oldest and probably the guy that my little runway was set to marry.

The guy was handsome, that I had to give him. He was five years younger than me and had no markings whatsoever. That meant they were pussies.

I paged through their financials. I knew most of them as the Pontisellos had bought eighty percent of it to help them keep their title in the tiers. Something told me the Santores had no idea about that. This merger was everything to the Solomons. Maybe if Philip had known that, he wouldn't have fucked around on his bride.

I prayed now that she would take my offer and was even contemplating changing that ridiculous contract. I could offer her and her family so much more than the Solomons.

I hated dishonesty, and this family was only riding on the backs of the Santores to get to the top.

Her brother and sister were set to marry into another family in transport. I had to give it to her old man; he had vision. They weren't as dishonest as the Solomons, and my hand itched to force Victor's hand to buy out the entirety of the docs.

Then he would have to come clean to the Santores. Would have to tell them how he'd deceived and lied for years.

They deserved the annihilation along with the Delucas. We needed new blood. It was something my grandfather has said, and my father had promised he would look into, trying his best to get new blood into the Dons.

But my dad was a fucking pussy.

I chucked the file into my drawer. I knew everything I needed to know to make her my wife. Now the ball was in her court, and I vowed I wouldn't show her how badly I wanted this merger.

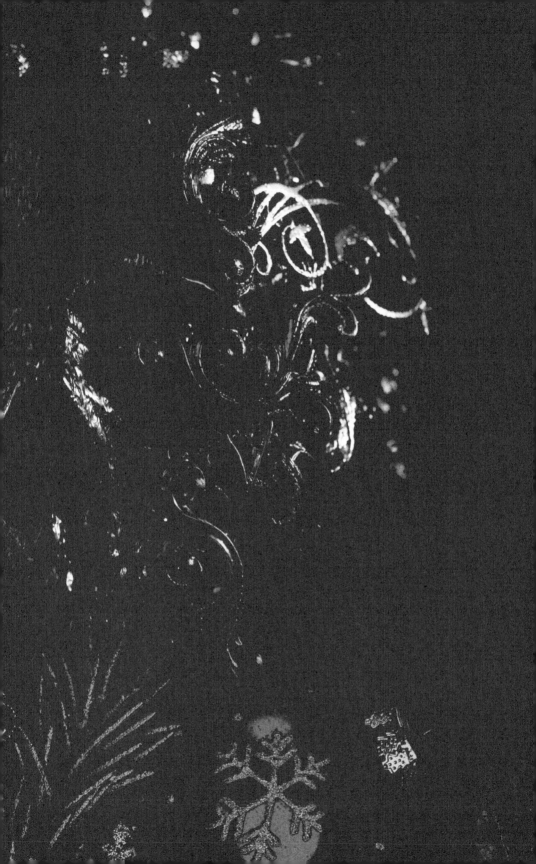

FIVE
THE RUBY

NICO TOOK ME TO THE SPARE ROOM AND CLOSED the door behind me. He didn't even ask if I wanted something to drink.

My heart was still beating like a drum. I knew whoever Alfonso was, that he was a Don. How far up the line, I had no idea. He was gorgeous though, and I was sure that if he was far up, I would've known his face. But I didn't. Meaning he couldn't be that far up, right? Then again, there were plenty of families in the Don. Plenty of them in the tiers. At least a hundred per tier.

My father was living a fantasy thinking that he could make the elders see.

I stared at the contract. He must have contemplated this for days because this was a solid contract.

It carried the date, but not the names. His name was

missing as well as mine. There were open spaces for us to write down our full names. Address information followed.

Again, his was open. But I knew he spoke Italian, meaning he could be of the Italian Dons. They were much better than the American ones, at least in father's opinion—which was a plus, I thought.

I wondered what my father was going through. He didn't really deserve this at all, me rebelling against this merger, but what else could I do? Philip had broken me. He'd shattered my soul—and who knows, maybe this new merger might make his fantasy come true even faster. Alfonso definitely gave off Don vibes; then again, the number underneath his left eye made me hesitant. The Dons rarely got their hands dirty. They had guys like Nico doing the dirty work for them, and Nico didn't have the one underneath his left eye. Was he a Don's bodyguard? My father would freak at that.

I pulled myself out of my thoughts and looked back down at the contract. Next to date of marriage ceremony, there was TBA. The location, he'd left that open as well.

Section three was the declaration. This was the only part I was interested in as it was where I would learn what he wanted and what I would get in return.

One: We were legally free to marry and understood the responsibilities and rights conferred by marriage.

That wasn't a lie. This was my choice, even if it was a business agreement.

Two: We committed to supporting each other in

marriage, sharing responsibilities and rights as outlined in this contract.

What responsibilities?

Responsibilities as followed:

The wife should be loyal to the husband in any form and place.

The wife should perform her duties as a Don's wife.

My throat closed. He was a Don.

She should give him at least one son and after, she could decide what she wanted to do.

She would be at his side at every event, whether she wanted to be or not.

She should meet his needs, whether physical, emotional, and/or sexual to the best of her abilities.

She should keep him happy to the best of her abilities.

She should stay out of his business, be submissive, and let him run his house.

That one was going to be hard. I wasn't the submissive kind, and Philip had known that. He'd understood that I would respect him in front of friends and family. Other Dons. This guy didn't.

She would sign off the rights to their child if she decided to terminate this contract.

She should understand that once they married, that he owned her, she was his and his alone to do with whatever he wanted.

I didn't like this contract at all, but then again, the one I was going to sign with Philip wasn't much different. It listed all the duties of being a Don's wife.

To submit to their need, no matter your own.

Tears pricked in my eyes. I wasn't going to get a better life by signing this, but it was the only way out of the merger my father wanted me to complete.

My gaze scanned through his responsibilities.

They weren't much. Just that he would protect her, give her whatever she wanted, and if the contract was finished after ten years and she'd given him a son, he would let her go with the equivalent of ten million, worked in on the economy's growth, and she could start anew.

Without the child, of course.

Okay, that wasn't so bad. Ten years and then I could have whatever I wanted. That was doable.

The financial agreement was all his. There was nothing about a merger or anything, and I wanted to know if he would change that.

I could get my father's assets to him. At least make him proud of this new merger. I was sure by looking at the assets on here that I couldn't touch that there would be a prenup to sign. I knew that Alfonso was wealthy.

You didn't need a degree in accounting to discover that. He'd blatantly put all of his assets in this contract, and the assets alone were like four pages long.

Fuck, how far up the tier was this guy?

Amendment and termination followed, basically repeating what I had already read.

And then it was just signatures. It was a straightforward contract stating what I would have to do and what I would have to give up. A child.

I didn't know if I could, but that was a then problem and not to be worried about now.

Father would be happy about this merger; I was sure of it.

My gaze landed on the pen on the desk in the holder, and I decided *fuck this*.

Mother would drag me down the aisle, so I filled out my name and everything else. Afterwards, I marched back to his office. Didn't even knock and opened the door.

He was on the phone and simply stared at me. Then he nodded.

I closed the door and walked toward his desk. He didn't take his eyes off me. I felt like prey being hunted by the most dangerous predator. But I was here of my own free will. He set the phone down, and I puffed up my chest.

"I want you to reconsider a merger with S.A.N.T. Distributions. It was what the Solomons were going to get if they merged with us."

He nodded. "I saw. And it would've been your father's biggest mistake."

"Excuse me?"

"First of all, I'm a businessman, Camilla. I do my research first, and I'm thorough in what I do. The Solomons are done. They own less than twenty percent of the docs, but I guess it was something they didn't share with your father."

"No, that can't be."

"You calling me a liar?"

I swallowed hard at his tone. I shook my head.

"Someone else owns eighty percent of the docs. They were tagging you for a ride; this merger would've gotten them out of their rut and probably paid to get back the eighty percent they had lost."

"How do you know this?"

"I told you, I do my research well. The merger was a mistake. The Solomons are dead weight. The merger would've pulled you under, and something tells me that's the opposite of what your father would've wanted."

My gaze flickered to his, and he smiled. "My grandfather too."

"Is he still alive?"

I shook my head as I couldn't believe Alfonso had the power to give my father exactly what he wanted. This was my way out without losing my family.

It was a shock learning the truth about Victor and Rita. They'd lied to my father for years. Dad wouldn't have done this merger if he'd known the truth.

"What is it, la mia piccola fuggitiva?"

I hated when he called me that. I didn't know what he was saying, but I wasn't going to tell him to stop. I'd tell him after we were married. "My father is doing his research constantly too. He would've picked up that this merger was the wrong deal. Why didn't he?"

Alfonso sat in thought for a minute, and then his green eyes locked with mine. "Because your father has enemies close to him that were probably paid off by the Solomons to lie to him."

My mind immediately went to Andrew Westwood. His firm was handling our affairs and accounts. My father's *research*.

"He would never believe me."

"He doesn't need to. He will believe me."

Six

The White Rabbit

She had signed the contract after I'd told her that I'd make the amendments. Her mother had trained her well. She was already putting her trust in me, and yet she didn't know me one bit. I signed too with a note to amend the assets and include the merger.

"I'll have an invitation drawn up to your family. Someone has to attend the consummating ceremony."

Her cheeks flushed, and she nodded.

I loved how shy she still was, and she was fucking stunning. The guy was a fucking idiot, a total dickhead for ever letting her go.

"I'll send the amended contract to you soon and then we'll get married."

She knew it was the only day we could get married: Christmas Eve.

"Don't bother to get undressed. It won't take long to add the amended part."

She nodded once again.

"Nico," I yelled, and the door opened. I told him to take Camilla and get someone to refresh her makeup and hair. The wedding would take place soon.

Nico nodded once and instructed Camilla to follow him.

A part of me couldn't wait for the consummating ceremony, and I considered amending her responsibilities too, but I did have my needs. I would love to have her in my dungeon, to play with her until she bled and make all of her fantasies come true—hers and mine. It was why I wanted someone who had never been touched, so that I could mold her into whatever sex slave I needed. I could make my fantasies become hers and would make her so addicted that she wouldn't be able to live without me.

I never could see this with Simi; I despised every inch of that woman.

I phoned Mica and told him to make the amendments. We'd already spoken about the merger. Her father would be glad to merge with us. We were stronger and more financially stable.

I was already fulfilling his fantasy.

After I got off the call with Mica, I phoned Fiona. Told her to get the invitations ready for my consummating ceremony.

She gasped when I told her it was to a Camilla Santore and not Simi Deluca.

"Do we have a problem?"

"No, sir. How do you spell her name?"

I gave her the spelling of her name and surname as it was on the contract.

"Who do I send the invitations to?"

"Oh, everyone who is important and needs to be at the ritual." I cut the call as Nico entered.

"It's moving fast." He brushed his hand through his hair.

"Usually when something is meant to be, that is the only pace, Nico."

He nodded.

"Thank you. She's perfect, like you said."

"I didn't do much; fate brought her to me. And I knew she was yours."

I smiled. "Reason I trust you the way I do."

He smiled and bowed then asked if I needed anything else.

"Just the priest."

"He's on his way. You need a suit."

"I have plenty in my cupboard. I'll find something to match her."

He laughed as he walked out and closed the door.

My family was not going to like this, but then again, I didn't give a flying fuck anymore.

TWO HOURS LATER, I stood in the foyer with the priest awaiting my bride.

She walked in, wearing her wedding dress. Her makeup was redone, and if she had taken away my breath before, this was taking away my very essence.

She was fucking gorgeous. Her gaze flickered to mine. She swallowed hard, and I was sure if she could run away, she would, but she kept walking toward me.

She came to a standstill next to me, and then the priest began with the ceremony.

It wasn't a big one, just formalities, and then we had to repeat what he said.

"Alfonso Matteo Ricardo Pontisello," the priest said, and Camilla gasped.

My lips threatened to curve upward. Of course, she knew our last name. Everyone knew our last name. "Will you take Camilla Elisabeth Milana Santore as your legal wife? To love and to hold, for richer and poorer, in sickness and in health, until death do you part?"

"I do."

He asked Camilla the same, and she hesitated for a moment. Silence lingered. I looked at her. She appeared frozen.

"Camilla," I whispered. She shook out of it.

"Of course, I do."

My lips curved upward once more, and the priest stated that I could kiss my bride.

I turned to her and her gaze slid up to meet mine. I had to bend down by a lot as Camilla was easily 5'2 to my 6'4 frame.

Warm breath caressed my lips as mine hovered over hers. I

love the tease, it was my ultimate game, and then when I couldn't hold my hunger anymore, my lips crushed onto hers.

My tongue delved into her, stroked her tongue, and in a few strokes hers came alive.

She cupped my neck and mimicked my tongue's rhythm. She pushed herself tighter to me. Her body was aching to be touched. Something told me she needed the fuck more than I did.

My mind grew hazy, and the priest cleared his throat. He brought me back out of my thoughts, and the kiss broke apart.

She breathed erratically, and her eyes were even wilder staring at me.

She let go of my neck, and there was a slight strain in my back muscle. What the fuck was that?

I gave a curt smile to the priest and thanked him for his time.

We signed our marriage certificate as Nico showed the priest out of the room.

"You didn't tell me your last name was Pontisello."

"Would it have made a difference?"

She thought about it before shaking her head.

"Good. There won't be a consummating ceremony tonight. The earliest I could arrange for one is tomorrow night."

She swallowed hard as her cheeks flushed once more. But she did not say a word.

"Is there a specific person you would like there?"

"It doesn't matter," she muttered.

"I'll have some clothes brought up to you and have Cartier bring a selection for you to choose from." We hadn't done this with rings. It was a bland ceremony.

It was the opposite of what she'd probably wanted. Having her wedding at Anna's told me that much.

"I'm sorry it wasn't the wedding of your dreams."

"For some reason, it doesn't matter anymore." She looked sad and distant. Betrayal washed over her features. I touched her chin and forced her gently to look at me.

Her eyes glistened.

"If you give me a chance, look beyond my markings, I'll make you forget his name in due time."

Her tears vanished immediately as the red shine on her cheeks reappeared.

Her gaze broke with mine, and she swallowed hard.

"But for now, I have plenty of phone calls to make. Order whatever you like from the kitchen and have Nico call me when Cartier arrives."

She nodded, and I left, walking back to my office. I couldn't wait for tomorrow night to find out just how sweet she was going to taste.

SEVEN
THE RUBY

OKAY, PONTISELLO WAS HUGE. THEY'D BASICALLY
started the Don tiers and were way up the food chain. I was
still struggling to process that I was married to a Pontisello.

Neither my father nor mother was going to believe me.
But then, he did ask who he could make the invitations out to
for tomorrow night's ceremony. Meaning that I was going to
be alone on my wedding night. How fucking amazing was
that.

Heat flooded to my cheeks as I replayed his comment
about how he would make me forget Philip if I just gave him a
chance.

Somehow, I doubted that he knew how beautiful he truly
was. Every time I was near him, there was this charge
happening in my body, not to mention when we'd kissed.

What was that? It felt as if everything around me simply disappeared.

I knew he wasn't a direct line of the Pontisellos.

Rico had two sons. Alfonso wasn't one of them. Maybe he was a cousin, three times removed. Had the same grandfather. But he was still up there with the rest of them.

A knock came at the door, and it opened. Nico entered with bags of clothes.

He did shopping too?

"Something for you to wear. Hope they fit."

I nodded.

"Are you hungry?"

My stomach growled. "Starving."

"Then pick up the phone and order something to eat, Camilla."

I nodded again.

He closed the door, and I did exactly that. The menu in this room was different than the ones in our rooms.

There weren't prices on this one, and my mouth watered just reading the descriptions of the food.

I dialed a number, and a lady answered.

"How can I help you?"

"Hi, I don't know which room I'm in."

"Don't worry, miss. It's the Pontisello suite. How can I assist you today?"

"Oh," a chuckle left my lips, "May I please have a burger and fries sent up? With a bottle of champagne."

"Of course. Anything else."

"No, that'll be it."

"Food will be ready in twenty minutes."

"Thank you."

I set the phone down and wondered if I should've ordered something for Alfonso too. I wanted to phone back but then realized that I had no idea what he preferred. I didn't know the man I'd married any more than the one I was supposed to marry.

That brought new tears to my eyes, and I hated them. I hated that I couldn't switch off this feeling of betrayal. It had led me to the biggest and best merger that my father couldn't even succeed in organizing. I knew my grandfather was smiling down on me. I wished he was alive to know that I'd done it. Not Dad and not my mother—but me.

I also decided that it was something I wasn't going to tell her. She was going to be livid, but at least she couldn't force me to marry that lying son of a bitch anymore.

I wondered if my father knew the truth, what he would do.

I got out of my dress and took a long shower.

The warm water made love to my body and eased the knots in my muscles.

By now, we would've said our vows and would've finished taking wedding photos. We probably would've been walking in as Mr. and Mrs. Solomon.

I didn't have that. And I wasn't Mrs. Solomon. I was Mrs. Pontisello.

My mind still struggled to process that fact. I knew Alfonso was up in the tiers, probably third or fourth tier, but never had I imagined he was way up at the top. I just needed to find out which Pontisello brother was his father.

There were three.

Rico, Marcello, and Jacob. Rico was the main Pontisello. He ran everything. He even owned the first chair of the elders. What he said, went. No questions asked.

He had two sons: Luca and Roberto. They were always in the limelight. And the dangerous one of the two had a nickname—the White Rabbit—but I didn't know which one that was.

Stories about him had always scared me. They said he was vicious. Killed without flinching, but even as the White Rabbit, none of Rico's two sons carried the mark underneath his eye like Alfonso. Maybe they were still working up to it.

I didn't know much about Marcello and Jacob. My father's sole focus was on Rico. He wanted to merge with him so badly.

He might be disappointed that it wasn't the right Pontisello, but I knew I'd done well. I didn't care what they were going to say, but then again, I wasn't going to tell them a thing. My consummating ceremony would do the job for me.

They could find out tomorrow with everyone else that I was a Pontisello now.

When I felt clean, I got out and clutched the lush towel to my body.

I got dressed in the jeans that Nico had brought and pulled a shirt over my head. It all fit like a glove. The jersey was soft and the boots a bit big, but it marked off the look so beautifully.

I dried my hair and reapplied some makeup that the makeup artist had left for me. All my things were still in my room.

A knock came at the door, and the butler pushed in a tray that probably had my food.

I thanked him, and he took out the bottle of Golden Rouge. Daddy had told me not long ago that when we moved up in the tiers, he would buy me that bottle. It was valued at 2.5 mil. Yet here, they popped it as if it was just a bottle of Pelligrino.

He poured in half a flute and hand it to me. I was literally shaking as I tried to do the math of how much I had in my hand.

He nodded, and I brought it to my lips and tasted it. It was a weird taste; somehow, I've always disliked the expensive champagnes. It wasn't sweet or delicious. You needed to develop a taste for it. It was sour and tasted like shit, not that I knew what shit tasted likes. Well, to me that was this champagne. Maybe I just wasn't a fan of expensive drinks.

I thanked the butler, and he put the black beauty back in the ice bucket. The bottle alone was beautiful with a pure gold emblem and black-as-night colored bottle.

I devoured the burger in a few bites and sipped the champagne. I wished I could share it with my dad. He would probably agree that it tasted like shit and that made me laugh out loud.

I finished my burger and switched on the TV. Put it on Netflix just to kill the silence and the war going on in my head.

A knock on the door made me sit up in bed, and Nico entered.

"Cartier is waiting for you."

I nodded as he eyed the bottle of champagne.

I looked at it. "I just asked for champagne. They brought that up. Sorry."

"Stop apologizing. It's not my taste, but Alfonso would enjoy the fact that you love it."

I didn't, but I wasn't going to tell Nico that.

I followed him to the lounge and was surprised that Alfonso was sitting on the couch, wearing a pair of jeans and a white sweater. It brought out his eyes even more. Man, this guy was truly beautiful, and I had no idea what I was going to do with him tomorrow night.

"Come sit, Camilla."

I thanked the heavens that he didn't call me that Italian name and plopped down onto the couch next to him.

He touched my back, and I had to admit, the warmth of his hand felt good. There it was again. That magnetic pull that I couldn't explain. It dried my throat instantly, and I had to clench my thighs tighter so that I didn't try to jump my husband tonight.

That was what he was: my husband.

It sucked to be a Don. I wondered why he couldn't get the crowd attending the other ceremony tonight to come to ours instead. I could ask him, but it would only make me sound desperate, and I was sure that Nico was going to tell him that I liked the Golden Rouge.

"The choice is all yours," Alfonso spoke in that husky voice of his. It would make any woman ooze between the legs.

I tried to focus on the rings. They were all beautiful but felt way too big for my taste.

I looked at Alfonso who stared at me. "What is it?" He spoke in his honey tone that made my stomach flutter. Already?

"Do you have something that would not make me drown when I swim?"

He smiled, looked at the jeweler, and asked for a less prominent piece.

The old man smiled and took the box away, placing another smaller box in front of us.

These rings were smaller in diamond size too. My gaze landed on a piece, and I wanted to reach out for it but stopped. I pulled back my hand and apologized as my mother's years of training kicked in.

"Don't apologize, Camilla." Alfonso opened the box. "Which one?"

"The one by your pinky."

He picked it up and handed me the rose gold band with a delicate design and the diamonds placed in the middle. It almost reminded me of vines.

I put it on my finger, but it didn't fit. It was a bit big, but I loved this one.

"Do you have this in her size?"

"Let's see her size." The old man reached for my hand, and I laid my hand in his. He put my finger into a ring measurer and worked to find the right size.

Once he'd confirmed my size, he said, "I'll have it send over tonight around six."

"Thank you, Pierre," Alfonso replied.

The old man bowed his head, and his assistant help clear up the boxes.

Alfonso already had a band on his ring finger. It was beautiful, plain, but I doubted the price was plain.

"I really thought this was going to take hours," Alfonso remarked.

I huffed and smiled. "Guess I always know what I want. Was it expensive?"

"I don't mind paying for a ring, just as long as you love it."

"I'm sorry none of the big ones grabbed my attention."

He tucked a strand of my hair behind my ear, and my heart instantly beat faster as his hand lingered. He smelled divine, dangerous even, and I make a mental note to Google him. I was sure he was somewhere on the net.

"You're a breath of fresh air, la mia piccola fuggitiva. That's for sure. I have work to do; thank you for keeping it short."

I nodded, and he took a sip of my champagne. He smiled.

"Finally, someone who can enjoy the expensive tastes that life has to give."

I smiled in return. If he only knew that I had to force it down my throat.

"Keep it. I have more than half a bottle left."

He raised the glass and stood, walking back up the stairs to his office.

EIGHT
THE RUBY

I DRANK THE BOTTLE UNTIL IT ACTUALLY TASTED sweet. I hated when it was finished; my head was spinning, and I fell asleep.

The next morning, I awoke still wearing my jeans and jersey. The blanket was pulled over my body, and I could only assume who had done so. The velvet black box on the bedside table grabbed my attention. Then my gaze flickered to my ring finger. The bands were already decorating my finger. Probably Alfonso.

Today was the day that I'd have to face everyone, tell them that I was already married, and hopefully spill the beans that the Solomons had lied and that my father had a double agent working for him in his company.

I hadn't decided yet if I was going to tell them who I'd married. Maybe they'd already left the hotel. Who knew? I was always seen and raised as someone or something that could advance our status.

I got up. I found another pair of pants, not jeans, but black stretchy pants in the bag.

I had to tie them up with a belt as this pair was a bit big. I pulled on the white knitted top that went with it and the black ankle boots that Nico had brought.

I tried to find something about Alfonso Pontisello online, but for some reason they kept showing me Rico, Luca, and Roberto, but never Alfonso. I doubted that he would have lied to me about who he was.

That would be seen as treason, and they could kill him for that.

It was one of the reasons I wasn't going to say that I'd married a Pontisello.

What if it was a scam and he wasn't one? It would mean that I'd just merged with someone who was even less of what the Solomons were, owned less than them, if that was even true.

I needed to know where he fit. I needed to know if he was who he'd truly said he was.

The loft was still quiet when I exited, and I planned to be back before he knew I was gone.

I took the elevator down to the seventh level that we'd booked out and walked down the lonely hallway to my room.

It was quiet inside. Nobody was waiting for me, and I started to pack.

Halfway through, a key sounded in my door, and it opened.

My mother froze when she saw me. I looked away as her eyes burned with a rage that I knew all too well.

"Where the fuck were you yesterday?"

I huffed as I chucked in my blouse. "Not marrying that cheating bastard."

"What are you talking about?"

"I had to get some air, and he was right across the hotel fucking Victoria. I saw them with my own eyes."

My mother closed her eyes and pressed the top of her nose. Like my little tantrum was just a bump in the road.

"I'm not marrying him."

"For crying out loud, Cami. Didn't you learn anything I taught you? You have to be intact. They could annihilate our family if the women are not intact."

"Upper tiers, Mom. I doubt they give a fuck about our bottom feeders."

She killed the distance with haste, and her arm pulled back so quickly, my brain didn't even register that the slap was going to follow.

It was so hard that I almost lost my balance, and my cheek burned like fire. Tears pricked it my eyes as I cupped my cheek.

"We are not bottom feeders. Your father and grandfather have worked hard to get us where we are. It's not easy moving up a tier in fifty years. It takes years and years. Be grateful that you have a betrothed."

I stared at her. She blurred in my sight. "Please tell me that you didn't know about him screwing around."

"Of course, I knew. It was part of the deal. They don't have to be intact, but you do."

"So they get everything they want and we just have to be okay with the scraps?"

"Camilla. If this merge doesn't happen, you have no idea how far you are setting us back."

"I'm setting you guys back? Thanks a lot, Mom." I zipped up my bag.

"You will marry him, so help me."

I walked to the door. I wasn't going to tell her everything, but I would tell her this. "Yeah, I'm afraid that it's too late. I'm already married, just not to that lying son of a bitch."

My mother froze, and it was the perfect time for me to leave. I pulled my bag along on its wheels behind me and rushed down the hallway. My mom was a lot like me in so many ways. She was beautiful; I shared plenty of her features. And like me, she wasn't the smartest either. She had her beauty, and she knew the power she owned behind it.

I looked back, and my door was still closed. She was still processing. I turned around the corner and smacked into someone.

"Sorry," I said, as Philip stared at me with pure rage.

"Where the fuck where you yesterday, Camilla? You made a fool out of me."

Anger took over, and I pushed him as hard as I could.

"Oh, I made a fool out of you? Where the fuck were you, Philip, before our wedding?" I yelled at the top of my lungs.

"What?"

"I saw you fucking my best friend in your room. You didn't even try locking the fucking door."

"Not this shit again."

"Stop. My mother said she knew. I'm so done with you."

Philip laughed. "You and I will never be done, Cami. We are bound for—"

"Save it for your whore."

I stormed past him. My heart pounded like a drum, and I knew he was following me. I could hear his breathing behind me, like a bull.

He grabbed my hand and twisted my wrist as he pushed me against the wall.

"This merge will happen. Even if I have to drag you down the aisle myself."

"No, it won't. Maybe now you and your father will tell mine the truth. How you needed this merge more than we did."

I saw the truth reflecting in his eyes. The fear that they had finally been discovered.

"Oh, I'm not as stupid as you think I am. I know your little scam. How you own, what, twenty percent of the docs, maybe even less?"

"I don't know what you're talking about."

"You don't fool me, Philip, and get your fucking hands off me."

"No, you are mine, and you will...." He froze as a knife pressed into his throat.

Nico appeared behind him. "I suggest you take your hands of the lady as she requested."

"Sir, this is none of your concern, and you will take your knife off my throat if you know what's good for you."

Nico chuckled. "Ooh, I'm scared." But he did take his knife from the bastard's throat. A drop of blood oozed from his neck where the knife had nicked him. Philip pressed his finger into it and then licked his own blood.

Like always, Philip was ready to fight, and in two jabs—they were so fast, I hardly saw it coming—he was on the floor, couching, trying to catch his breath.

Nico's gaze flickered from Philip to me. "And I suggest you walk."

I didn't like the warning in his tone. He grabbed my bag, and I followed him quickly to the elevator.

Inside, it was silent. I didn't know if I should speak or not. Nico wasn't.

"I just..."

"Save it for him. It's not me you need to explain your disappearance to."

He was cold, and I didn't like it. For the first time, I was afraid as my mother's words hammered against the walls of my mind. The Pontisellos had the power to annihilate all of us.

The elevator opened, and there was no sign of Alfonso. I took the first step out, and a hand suddenly grasped my elbow in a tight grip. He pushed me against the wall, and pain seared down the back of my head and along my spine.

His other hand curled around my throat as he growled at me. His eyes were wild as he ordered Nico in Italian. He sang like a little bird as Alfonso started to squeeze tighter. I struggled to breathe.

I could see the rage dancing in his green eyes. They were turning darker by the second.

I couldn't even apologize. Stars started playing at the edges of my vision. As he snarled, Nico finally finished with his report.

"I'm only going to say this once, la mia piccola fuggitiva. You better listen." He squeezed tighter. "I'm a very possessive man, and I do not share."

I tried to kick him, but my attempts were effortless.

"You will never wake up again and decide to go for a stroll without telling me or Nico, do you hear?"

I nodded.

"I don't share," he growled and then pushed his lips onto mine and his body tighter against me. I could feel his hard shaft as I tried to take in breath, but he kept on kissing me with a frightening roughness.

This guy was going to kill me.

He stopped, and I fell to the ground, crouching as I tried to take a breath. Alfonso left me there as he walked away. Tears rolled down my cheeks.

Never in a million years did I imagine my husband would ever do this to me.

After a moment, a hand appeared in my face, and I looked up. It was Nico. His eyes were soft. Something behind them told me that he didn't like it when Alfonso manhandled women.

"Don't cry; swallow your tears. I promise, if you obey him, submit to him, this business deal will be a pleasure. Please do not disobey him again," he begged.

I didn't nod. It wasn't in me to obey, to submit. I was his wife, not his fucking dog. If he touched me like that ever again, I would slice his fucking throat.

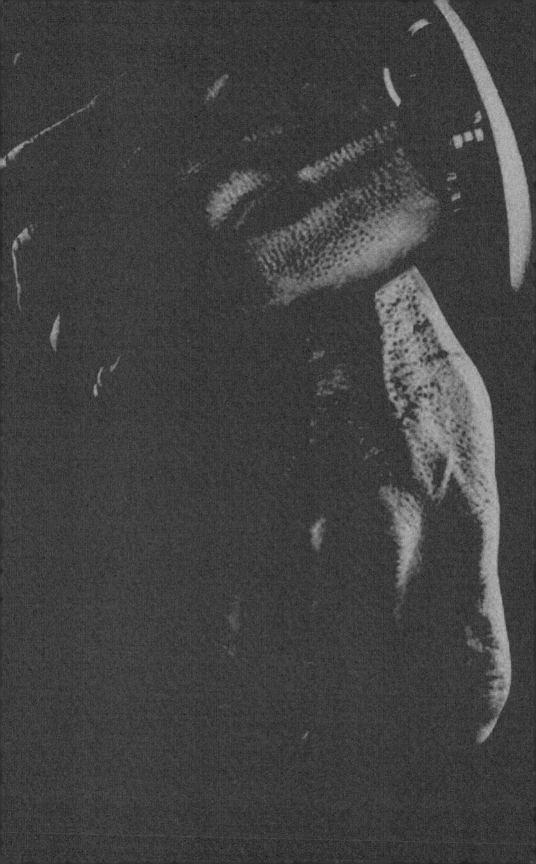

NINE
THE RUBY

NICO ENTERED THE ROOM LATER THAT AFTERNOON. He put the consummating robe on the chair. I hadn't seen my abuser yet, and for some reason, my body didn't want him like that anymore. I was still teary and looked away so that Nico didn't see.

"You know how this world is, Camilla. Your mother has taught you well."

"He didn't have to do it that way," I managed to say.

"How else are you going to learn?"

"By simply telling me not to do it again, Nico. As easy as that."

"Well, the way he grew up, the women in his life didn't always listen when someone told them nicely. His way, you won't do that again. Get ready, take a bath, do what you need to do. They are coming tonight, and you will consummate this wedding, bind your contract. The doctor will be here around three to check if you are still intact."

I shook my head as he left.

His patience was gone, as well as his compassion. There was nothing behind his amber eyes anymore. After all, he was working for Alfonso. He was his right hand or bodyguard or go fetch buddy, whatever Nico was.

I got up and examined the robe. More tears pricked as I wished I could run away from this, but something tells me that Alfonso would find me.

I took a long bath and sipped on the champagne that was brought up earlier. It tasted like shit again. I knew it was Golden Rouge.

When I got out, I froze as my mother and sister were waiting in my room. They were each sipping on a glass and giggling like little girls.

"Camilla," my mother smiled, "Why didn't you tell me that you'd married a Pontisello? How on earth did you pull this one off?"

I sighed and closed my eyes. "Leave."

"What?"

I opened my eyes and glared at her. "I said leave. I don't want you here."

"Sis?" Em started.

"Don't, Em. Just don't. Take Mom and get out. I mean it."

"Honey if I was hard on you, there was a reason."

"I said get the fuck out of my room!" I yelled, and my

mother froze. Tears blurred, and I wished I could pull them back. Not once had they ever listened to me. Never had they given me anything that I'd truly wanted. Now that I was married to a fucking Pontisello though... But I didn't even know where he fit, probably the back side of the family. He had to be the runt; it was why I couldn't find anything about him online. They were hiding him.

My mother set down the flute.

"No, please, take that with you. It tastes like shit. But I'm sure you will enjoy it."

My mother stared at me, picked up her glass, and left.

I broke down and cried my heart out. I didn't want to do this today, but I knew if I didn't do this willingly, he would force me, and it would be twenty times worse. So I had no fucking choice on the matter.

I would have to carry on with this consummating ritual, but he could bet his sweet narcissistic ass that he was going to wait good and long for his bundle of joy.

The White Rabbit

I felt bad as I signed the merger contract with her father and uncle. He'd worked hard on building S.A.N.T Distributions to the level it was at, and I could tell it was a hard pill to swallow when I revealed to him the truth about the Solomons.

But I'd also promised that if he trusted my family, they would be looked after with this merger. The man literally had tears in his eyes, and then he said it. I needed to promise him that I would look after his Camilla. She had been raised to please another, not a Pontisello.

I nodded. I hated that I'd promised to give this man what he'd asked for because I didn't know if I was going to be able to keep my word.

"Who will be at the ritual tonight?"

"It will only be me," her father replied. "Is your father coming?"

"No, but I think my cousin will be there. She has been at many of them."

Her father nodded with a grin. He was eager to sign his daughter over to me. It was such a fucked ritual to be honest, one that fathers usually did when their children were still young and not between a father and the husband.

I shouldn't have manhandled her the way I had this morning, but I did not do well with sneaking around, not knowing where my fucking wife was. I'd always had that problem. What was mine, was mine, and mine alone—I did not share.

The contracts were signed, and the door opened. The doctor emerged just in time and nodded. She was still intact.

I held my hand out, and her father was eager to shake our agreement. "We have a deal; welcome to the family."

"The honor is ours," her father stated. He was so eager to please, and maybe that was what my grandfather had meant about new blood. They were passionate about the Dons and intent on a solid arrangement.

"There are refreshments in the foyer. You will be called

when it's time," I said, and he nodded, stood up, and walked out with his brother. I could tell none of them had ever dreamed of this day.

I wanted to go to Camilla, to see if she was okay, but Nico had already motioned earlier when he'd made a round that she wasn't.

I was her head. She had to listen to me; what I wanted was all that mattered. It was how it was, and I wasn't going to grow soft on her. Even if she was everything I'd ever ached for.

I'd met her mother earlier. She'd literally fucked me with her eyes—in front of her husband. But I could see where Camilla had gotten her beauty from. It definitely wasn't her father.

Her sister looked like their father.

I'd let Camilla deal with what she was going through. She would pull herself together. I knew what was expected of me tonight, and I was going to deliver. I was going to seal this deal tonight.

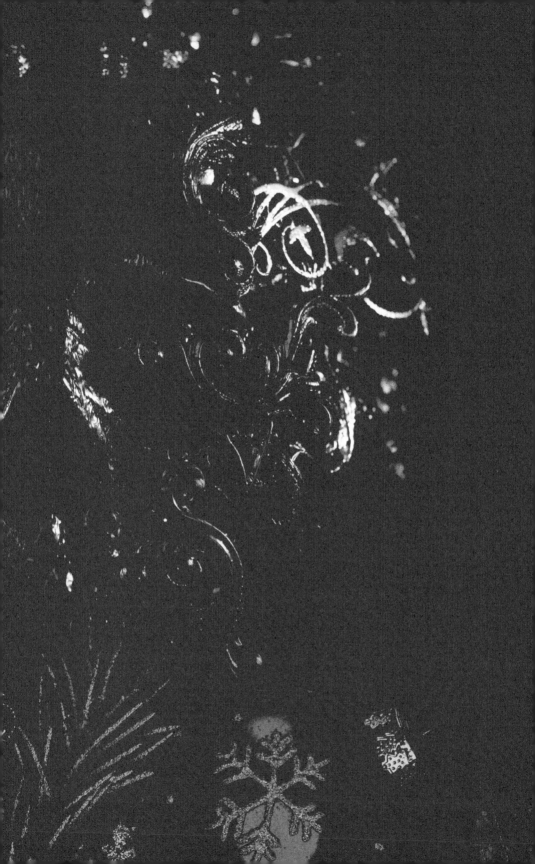

TEN
THE RUBY

I WAS ALONE THE ENTIRE DAY. THE DOCTOR CAME. He told me I could request for someone to be here with us. I said no.

He did his inspection and gave me a wink. I hated that. So creepy.

They delivered food and then I ate slowly. I really wasn't in the mood for tonight, and I couldn't stop crying. The tears just kept on flowing. I'd never felt this alone in my entire life.

I knew tonight was going to be horrible. He was big, gigantic. I'd felt it when he was getting off strangling me. He was hard, and he'd pressed his shaft right into me. The worst part was that my body had loved every second of it because I was drowning between my legs when I got to my room. My pants were soaking wet, and it wasn't because I'd peed myself. I wish I had peed myself.

This feeling I was experiencing, I'd never experienced it before. It was fear and excitement all in one, and it was clashing, starting to make me feel sick.

A knock at the door made me want to scream. Maybe it was time, but I doubted it. It was too early.

Nico entered and looked me over. I hadn't put on my robe yet, and he stared at it, hanging over the chair.

"Cami, don't do this, please."

"Do what?"

"Defy him. I begged you earlier, just do as you are told and your life will be easier. He is a good man; he just doesn't know how to handle his shit sometimes."

"No fucking kidding. I still have his fingerprints around my fucking neck, Nico."

"Just put on the fucking robe." He threw something on the bed. "And make sure you get a good amount of lube on that tight cunt of yours."

Heat seared up my cheeks and ears as I watched Nico turn around and walk out the door.

My gaze flung to the white and black bottle that was on my bed. I grabbed it. It was lube. Silicone-based. That was against the rules. Was he fucking insane? If they discovered I had lube on me... I closed my eyes. But I feared if I didn't, he would tear me open tonight, and I would be screaming, just not his name. I'd never been this scared either. It was supposed to be something invigorating, something erotic, and here I was fearing for my life.

I picked up the lube. It felt like it was the only way I was going to get through tonight. Fuck everyone.

I took off my jersey and pulled off my shirt. I took off my bra and then started working off my pants and underwear. I only had my socks on, but nobody fucks with socks on, so I pulled them off too. My wedding pedicure still looked beautiful. At least my toes looked stunning.

I grabbed the bottle off the bed where Nico had thrown it, twisted the cap open, and squirted a good amount onto my hands. It was cold, and I just slapped it on my pussy.

I sucked in breath since it was freezing, but my fingers started working the lubricant along my length and in-between my folds. I found my clit, started working the lube in good, and my eyes closed as it felt euphoric. I'd dreamed about tonight so many times. Just to get it over and then I could have explored Philip's body just the way I'd wanted to.

Now that would never be my reality, and I doubted that whatever I'd felt for Alfonso would ever return.

I was like a flower; I blossomed with gentle and died with rough. Something I doubt my new husband would ever grasp.

A moan left my lips as my finger kept circling my clit. I knew I should stop. Now wasn't the time to come. I couldn't, but I wanted to come so badly. I wanted to come hard, and I knew tonight it was just not going to happen.

I doubted that Alfonso was that type of man, that type of lover.

I'd seen a different side to him this morning that scared me shitless.

A knock on the door forced me to stop. The tingles were still there. I was aroused but hadn't come.

I covered up just as the door opened.

Nico entered, and he looked pleased when he found me in a robe. His gaze flicked to the lubricant bottle.

"You know it's against the rules to use lube. He knows that; why would he send it to me?"

"Because some families can break some rules, Camilla. You have much to learn. Here is your mask. Put it on and follow me."

I took the black lacy mask that would only cover my eyes and tied it on. The robe was closed in the front by tiny hooks. It was a beautiful robe too. The satin fell softly over my hips, and my heart pounded as I pulled the strings tighter behind my head.

Nico helped tie it into a knot. "For what it's worth, he feels like shit."

My eyes slid up to meet his.

"But you didn't hear it from me."

I FOLLOWED Nico into a room filled with members of the Dons. Tiers. I knew my father was probably somewhere among them. If my mother was here today, my father was probably with Alfonso signing a merger contract.

Everyone looked at me, and I froze. I wanted to run away.

Nico pushed me from behind, and I inched forward until I reached the bed.

"Keep your robe on," Nico whispered just as I went to take it off, and I turned to look at him.

He turned around and left the room, closing the doors behind him.

There was no sign of Alfonso, and all the hooded figures wearing their doctor plague masks were staring at me, waiting for me to take off my robe. My hands moved slowly to my robe when Alfonso entered the room. He was dressed in an elegant black robe and wore a more masculine mask. He stopped on the opposite side of the bed.

My heart stammered in my chest. My hands trembled as my fingers lingered on my robe. This was humiliating, getting undressed in front of your father.

I swallowed hard as Alfonso climbed on the bed. An eerie silence followed. Couldn't they play some music, just to drown out the silence?

I kept staring at him. His green eyes stared from behind his mask and his neatly combed hair was now a messy black mop, making him even more dangerous than earlier. He moved to the middle of the bed on his knees and stood on his kneecaps.

He motioned with his finger for me to join him. And I just stared at him. He cocked his head and gave me a threatening look. Now was not the time to defy him.

I put one knee on the bed followed by the other one. I lift

my robe a bit as I shuffled toward him. My heart felt as if it was beating in my throat.

I stopped in front of him. My throat was so dry, and I feared that I might throw up.

He leaned closer, smelled so good, and his breath caressed my neck. "You keep your eyes on me. Pretend they are not here." His voice was gentle. There wasn't a tremble. As if he had done this a million times.

I nodded and then his lips planted a soft kiss on my neck before he lifted his head. He spoke to them. "There will be no orgasm coming from her tonight, and there will be no yelling of my name leaving her lips either. I will orgasm, and I will show you the blood you need to see. We are consummating a wedding, not making a porno."

The one in front objected in Italian, and Alfonso cut him dry. I had no idea what he'd said, but the entire room fell silent.

Another spoke into the recorder that was filming the two of us. My name was spoken first. It was the first time I'd heard it without the last name I'd grown up with. I was a Ponticello now, and then they spoke his names. I'd heard it on our wedding day.

The speaker ended with another name: Coniglio Bianco. A gasp pushed past my lips as I understood that last word.

I stared into his green eyes, and he opened his robe. His entire body was draped in scars and covered in tattoos, but that was not what my eyes lingered on. Above his left breast was a tiny tattoo of a white rabbit.

Alfonso was the White Rabbit, meaning that I'd had it wrong all this time. The White Rabbit was Rico Ponticello's oldest son.

Eleven

The White Rabbit

I sat on my knees, ass resting on my heels. She was still staring at the white rabbit tattoo lingering on my left breast.

I pulled her chin up so that her eyes could meet mine and saw there were so many questions in them. Questions I didn't know if I had the answers to. She swallowed hard and went to open her robe. I stopped her and shook my head.

I could see her frown behind the mask. She didn't understand my kindness tonight. Not that I blamed her. My temper had been hot this morning, like lava, and now I was ice. It was always hard to know which one was coming.

I brought her closer to me. Mouthed that her eyes should stay on mine.

She nodded.

She was stunning, and this was probably my most anticipated day I'd ever gone through. I hated when I'd discovered her missing from bed this morning. No note, and I felt as if I was going to destroy the entire loft. Nico had left to find her. I was on edge, thinking she had already left, and then when she returned, I became like a volcano. But I wasn't one anymore.

Her body was an inch away, but her eyes never left mine. I could see the pleading behind them. She had no idea how to do this. I hadn't taken her through tonight either. She would be okay though.

My lips curved slightly as I was so fucking proud that she was a virgin.

"Focus on me," I reminded her, and she nodded.

I didn't open her robe. I wasn't going to display my wife's naked body for them to see. Her father was in this fucking room. I doubted it was something he wanted to see.

My hand pushed between the entrance of her gown, and I needed to know if she had doused her cunt with the lube that I'd given to Nico tonight. He'd even offered to put it on her, and my blood had boiled once again. Then the jerk laughed.

He knew she was becoming my weakness.

My hands curled around her thighs and back, allowing my fingers to brush against her cunt. She was dripping in the lube, and I smiled. She was a good girl. She'd listened, and it pleased me.

I stroked her length and watched her eyes threatening to close. I stopped touching her since tonight wasn't about her coming or enjoying it. I wasn't going to show the entire world how to please a woman, and I was definitely not doing it in front of them either.

I grabbed her other leg and hoisted her onto my lap. She hadn't expected that and grabbed my neck, tighter than usual. She was a bit higher than me. I wanted to kiss her so badly, but I knew if I did, I would lose my senses and fuck up tonight. So I just stared at her.

"Don't look at them," I reminded her. "And wrap your arms tighter around my neck."

She did everything I instructed. It was her first time, so I believed she would have no idea how to do any of this without my guidance.

"Squeeze my hips tighter with your thighs." She did that, and her grip around my neck also tightened as I let go of her legs. She stayed in place, and I smiled at how well she took direction.

My free hand pulled my robe open, and my fingers grip around my girth. I was already fucking hard. I smeared my fingers down her length again, and she moaned through tight lips. Her legs were already trembling around my waist.

I transferred some of the lube onto my cock, and then when I was soaked with the lube, my finger slid down her length of her folds again, finding her opening and pushing one finger into her.

I groaned. She was so fucking tight.

I kept staring at her lips. She bit them as her eyes closed.

I'm sorry, my little runaway, but this is going to hurt.

I grabbed my shaft and pressed it against her opening. We needed to get this over with as fast as possible.

She whimpered as I slowly pushed my cock inside of her. Her walls squeezed around my girth tight, and I cussed.

I couldn't remember the last time I'd felt this way inside a woman.

She tensed as I pushed in all the way. I grabbed her legs again and promised that I would do all the work tonight. She just needed to hold on.

My own eyes threatened to close as I pulled out of her and pushed into her again.

Another whimper left her mouth, and she wanted to shy away. I got a tighter hold of her legs and started moving her on top of me. She would get the momentum and help, not that it mattered. She was as light as a feather.

The momentum started to build as she buried her head beside my neck. I fucked her faster as she sat on me. She was so light, I didn't need her help with the motion.

Focus, Alfonso, fucking focus. I couldn't lose it now, but I wanted to tear this little fucking shit apart. Why had she entered my life? This wasn't normal. Whatever this was between us, it wasn't fucking normal.

I wanted to hear her scream my name, everything that I'd told them they were not going to hear. But I wanted to drown them out so badly and just fuck her hard, brand her as mine.

She whimpered more and more because her pussy was so tight around my cock.

It felt as if my cock was being strangled. I was almost

there, and it hadn't even been ten fucking minutes. So embarrassing.

I knew she wasn't going to orgasm. She was showing me too much pain. But I could, and I would. I would do anything not to cause her more pain.

My orgasm pulled from my balls, and I wanted to pull out of her, but I stopped. She was my wife. I could come deep inside of her as much as I wanted to. But at the same time, I wanted to have her all for myself for as long as I could.

I growled and pulled out as I came hard. I couldn't even jerk off as I needed to show them her blood.

I growled as it was fucking hard not to finish. I hugged her tighter, breathing through my nostrils. The orgasm was almost painful because I couldn't finish.

She was breathing fast, but didn't lift her head from my shoulder.

"I have to show them," I whispered, and she unhooked her trembling legs from around my waist.

She put her weight on my shoulder and looked the other way, down. As if she was ashamed. I hated that as I showed them my cock. It was covered in patches of her blood. Her hymen was broken, and she was a virgin no longer.

"Now get the fuck out of my room. All of you," I ordered.

As one, they all turned to the left and walked out through the doors.

Twelve
The Ruby

I couldn't keep it in any longer as the sob tore from me. That was so embarrassing. Why would they do this to us? For what reason? The doctor had been there to show them that I was intact. Why did we have to consummate our wedding in front of all of them?

Alfonso lifted my head and pulled it back onto his shoulder. "It's over. They're gone. I'm sorry for the pain."

He let me cry, and I sobbed my heart out. I felt so empty. He was patient and waited until I finally stopped.

"Let's get you cleaned up and give you something for the pain."

His voice was like honey. Gentle again. I nodded, and he took off my mask.

His was already gone as he dried my tears. His gaze was soft; the beast that had taken over this morning was gone.

"I'm sorry about this morning. My temper sometimes gets the better of me. But you can't leave me like that again, la mia piccola fuggitiva. Promise."

"I promise, if you stop calling me that."

"Where's the fun in that?"

I shook my head, knowing that he wouldn't stop. He stared at me. I could see the hunger he still had dancing inside those green irises.

He focused on my lips but didn't kiss me. Instead, he climbed off the bed, tied his robe, and lent me a hand. He didn't let me climb off; he picked me up bridal style and took me to the bathroom. He planted my ass on the toilet seat as he drew me a bath. He threw in essential oils and then opened a porcelain bowl that contained petals. He added some to the bath.

Then he left the bathroom and for the first time tonight, I felt a little like myself.

How was I ever going to enjoy having him inside of me? But that wasn't just it. No, he'd changed the rules tonight. I guessed he could. He was at the top of the tier. But I felt like an idiot for getting the brothers so wrong. Alfonso was the White Rabbit. They said that he had so much luck, that 'the cat' would not have been as suitable a nickname. The White Rabbit was all about luck.

I'd seen it tonight on his body. All his scars that he tried to cover with ink.

I wondered how many near-death experiences he'd had.

The bathroom door opened, and he reentered. He was

still in his robe. I shook myself out of my thoughts as he bent over to close the taps.

"You okay?" he asked, and tears pricked again, but I felt stupid crying over a little bit of pain. All my friends had agreed that fucking someone for the first time was painful. And the older you got, the more painful it was.

He stroked my cheek softly with his fingers, and I looked at him.

"You okay?" he repeated.

"I'm fine. I just didn't know what to expect. Thank you for being so kind tonight."

He shook his head and just stared at me. "What sort of a husband would I be if I let everyone sees my bride's perfect body?"

My lips curved into a small smile, and his lips mimicked mine.

"The water is warm; you should get in." He winked, and I stood from the toilet seat. I still felt so wet, and I had no idea if it was the lube or blood. Alfonso didn't leave, and I would have to get used to undressing in front of him. He was my husband, after all. I undid the robe from its hooks and let it fell to the ground as I settled into the bath.

It was deep, and the water was nice and warm. I sat down into the bubbles and covered myself, by hugging my legs.

He took a sponge and washed me. It felt great.

My eyes opened, and I looked at him, resting my head on the top of my knees. The water felt great against the ache between my legs and down my back.

He didn't stop, just kept on washing me.

"Would you mind if I joined you?"

I stared at him in a bit of shock. I didn't know what to say; he was being so patient with me tonight. But I knew he needed to clean himself too, so I shook my head. I didn't mind.

I was his, but I still needed to find out if he was mine.

He got up, and my eyes followed him. This guy's body was like the David sculpture, the epiphany of perfection, minus the scars and bullet holes decorating him. My gaze flickered down to his still rock-hard cock. Even that was a masterpiece. I looked away before he realized that I was staring. My pussy still ached, but I was also hungry. I'd waited for this for such a long time.

I heard him climbing in and felt him sliding down in the tub behind me. He carried on washing me, and I opened my eyes again. It felt so good.

The loofah got replaced with his soft lips, and I had to force myself not to moan. I couldn't show him that a part of me still wanted him. I was too sore tonight, and I had to be stronger than this, right?

"If you can learn to not defy me, this will be an amazing business transaction. I want you to keep that in mind, please. I hated being rough with you."

I didn't reply. I knew he was sorry, but I also knew that he'd gotten hard by handling me like that. I admit I got soaking wet being handled like that, but I despised myself for it.

His lips kept traveling down my back, soft kisses, warm kisses.

"I'm a very jealous man, Camilla, and I know I said it already, but I do not share, and finding your room empty this morning, not knowing where you had gone..." He fell silent for a moment. "I didn't like that feeling. Don't do it again. One thing I need to make clear. You are mine, and tonight I might not have branded you as mine, but I will. I promise you, my cock will be the only one you taste. Obey my rules and I will kill anyone who looks at you the wrong way. But don't give me a reason to be jealous."

I feared his warning, as I could still envision the number one tattooed underneath his eye. He would kill anyone, that I knew as much. He'd already killed a hundred.

"If you give yourself freely to me, let me explore my sexual desires with you, let me do whatever it is I want with you, give me what I need..." There was so much want in his tone, but for some reason, my heart pounded behind my ribcage. "I promise that I will take care of you and give you whatever your heart desires."

Whatever my heart desires. Nobody had ever offer me that. I turned my head to look at him. His eyes were a light green again. I stared at him and then nodded.

"Good girl." He planted his lips softly on mine, but it stayed with a juicy peck., nothing more, and then he climbed out, cock hard, and took a towel that hung over the rack and turned it around his waist.

I stared like a stalker.

When he was done and turned to look at me, I looked away. But from the corner of my eye, I saw him pulling off another towel. My heart stammered again, thinking that now the real fucking was going to start and while I was still aching.

He brought the towel closer and ordered me to stand.

I obliged, aches and all, and he wrapped the towel around my body, before picking me up and taking me to his bed.

He set me on it and covered me with his satin blankets. "Sleep tight tonight. I still have a lot of work to do." He reached over to his drawer and took out a suede box. He put it on the bed. "Merry Christmas, la mia piccola fuggitiva."

I felt bad then. I hadn't gotten him anything and had actually forgotten that today was Christmas.

He brushed my cheek with the back of his hand and turned to leave.

"What does it mean?" I asked.

"What?"

"That la mia picca thing?"

His lips curved. "La mia picolla fuggitiva?"

I nodded.

"My little runaway."

I closed my eyes at how fitting it actually was. I was a runaway. I opened my eyes watched him open his room door, still wearing the towel that hugged his hips. He had Latin writing on his back with a Catholic cross spread across the length and width. Everywhere on that man was a tattoo, and I was sure every one of them meant something.

My eyes closed quickly, and I slipped into oblivion.

Thirteen
The White Rabbit

I'D DOZED OFF IN THE LOUNGE CHAIR WHEN A knock woke me up. Father entered, and he did not look a happy man.

He glared at me and threw his jacket over the back of the chair.

"Why do you defy me? Do you know what you cost us yesterday? And you married a lower tier?"

"Stop, if Pops was still alive..."

"I'm not my father; I'm not that ruthless."

"No, you're weak, that's what you are. And it shows with our generation. I'm the only one with the number one under my cheek."

"Alfonso?"

"No, Father, it's the truth. We have traditions to live up to. Pops warned you to never loosen the ropes."

"We are not barbarians," Father roared.

"We live by codes, for generations we've lived by them, spoken their oath, and now you want to break it. Grandfather warned us that you would become too weak."

"I'm not weak; I'm just not as ruthless as your grandfather. The man never thought things through, he just pounded and killed."

"Maybe there was a reason, to keep the other Dons in line. To live by the Dons' traditions. I did. I did them all, I've lived by them all, and I got a whore as my betrothed for my efforts. I deserved a virgin; I obeyed the rules."

"Alfonso, I didn't think that she would turn out to be like that."

"No, you didn't, but you'd loosened the ropes around her father's neck. You know if grandfather was still alive, the Delucas would've been made part of the past as of last night. They would've been annihilated for what that little bitch did. The new Dons are growing weaker. He thinks it's okay to break rules and break traditions. You're only making more shit for yourself, shit that I'm afraid will fall on me to clean up. Fall on my children one day to clean up."

"You are not serious about this marriage."

I laughed. "It's done, Father; it can't be undone. She is everything I ever wanted and deserved."

"She can't even speak Italian."

"I don't care. She's worthy of the Ponticello name, and she will carry that name until the day she dies. I will put back the fear of the Dons and the Ponticellos into everyone as long as I live. Now get the fuck out of my loft and only speak to me again when you grow a pair of balls."

Father pushed me against the wall. "I'm still the head of the Ponticellos, Alfonso, and you will not speak to me like that. You might not have respect for the way I reign over the Dons, but you will obey my rules. The Delucas stay where they are. I'll draw up a new deal with Jason, let him know what Simi did was wrong, but you will not harm one hair on their heads. Is that clear?"

I could easily take my father, but what sort of a son would that make me? He was right; he was still the head of the Dons. And there would be consequences.

I nodded and watched as he departed.

FOURTEEN

THE RUBY

I WOKE UP THE NEXT MORNING WITH A BIGGER ACHE between my legs. Shit, how long was this going to last? I was still in Alfonso's bed, and his satin linen made love to my body as I stretched. He was nowhere to be seen, and I doubted that he'd slept in his bed last night.

I got out and walked naked to the bathroom, picked up the robe that I'd worn last night, and went back to my room.

I got dressed and then followed the sound of voices. I didn't like that there was a loud woman's voice coming out of the lounge. I didn't understand a word they were saying, but it sounded joyous.

I entered, and Alfonso looked elated. The woman next to him was stunning, about my age with black as night hair and the same green eyes.

"Camilla, I want you to meet my cousin, Lorette Ponticello."

The girl got up and reached out her hand to me. I shook it. She had a firm grip.

"Welcome to the family. I was just telling my cousin how your little nuptial rites caused a lot of havoc back in Italy."

"How do you feel?" Alfonso inquired before I could ask questions.

"Better, I guess."

"You guess?" His eyebrow raised.

"Fine, I'm still tender." It barely came out, and I lowered my head.

The woman spoke in Italian, and Alfonso reprimanded her. She laughed. I wished I understood this language.

"Lorette was at the ceremony last night. She was there in my father's place. He couldn't make it, and he's sent apologies."

I could tell it was a lie by the way his cousin raised her eyebrows.

My gaze flickered to his; he was being so friendly, but we were married now, and he needed to know that I wasn't as stupid as he thought.

"Don't lie to me. I know your father isn't happy about this arrangement."

His cousin laughed. She said something in Italian again, and Alfonso glared at her. She fell quiet immediately. His gaze landed back on me.

"Enjoy your breakfast." He stood, and Lorette begged him to come back before turning to me.

"You have guts, girl."

"I would appreciate it if you could speak English in my presence until I've learned how to speak Italian fluently."

"Touche. You are very bold, and I have to admit, I love it. But I don't think he does. So if you want to keep that little heart inside your chest beating, I suggest you ease up around my cousin."

"I'm not afraid of your cousin. He's my husband, and he will respect me."

"Sweetheart, you're dreaming. He's a Ponticello. The Ponticello men are taught from a young age that males get everything and females give everything."

"Yeah, well, that's not my way. If he wants, he needs to give too."

I didn't like her and so I got up and went back to my room.

I was alone the entire day again. That night, Nico dropped off a beautiful black number and said that we were going out. I put on the dress that hugged my boobs and butt perfectly. The shoes were beautiful, and it felt as if I was walking on clouds, six inches and all. But then again, my sister had always teased me that I had rubber feet. Felt nothing in them.

It came with jewelry too. Very expensive jewelry. Around eight, I met the party. My stomach growled as I'd only had a bit of fruit this morning. I was starving.

Alfonso looked delicious in a black suit that fit him like a glove. He smelled divine too. I hated that Lorette was joining us.

We greeted each other, and against my word, she spoke Italian again. She had no respect for me, that was obvious, but I wasn't the type to repeat myself. She would learn the hard way that I was just as important as her.

We went for a dinner and then afterwards, we went to a night club.

Alfonso had a meeting, and that was very boring. He ignored me. He could've left me at the hotel for all I cared. This was only a business arrangement, after all. I had to be out with him wherever he went.

At the club, I decided to go to dance. Alfonso called me back, but I refused to stay. He might be my husband, but I wasn't his little slave who was going to obey like a good pup. I was a human being with feelings and emotions.

I ditched him, and since I was tinier, I could easily slip through the crowd of people.

He was a giant, and his growls scared people huddling tightly in front of him. He was going to learn the hard way that gentle was more powerful than aggression.

I danced my heart out but wished I had some friends here. His cousin was a snob, and I had no time for people who refused to respect me.

I partied with strangers, having a fun time. I couldn't even tell where the VIP club with Alfonso and his fucking snobbish family was anymore.

I took one shot after another and just enjoyed myself.

And then shit rolled into my path in the form of a drunken idiot who refused to keep his hands off me.

He pulled and tugged at me on the dance floor.

"You do not want to do this, buddy. I'm married and married to your worst fucking nightmare."

He laughed. "Yeah, were is your little nightmare?"

"I promise you, he is everything but little."

The guy laughed, thought I was joking and kept tugging me, rubbing himself against me. He assaulted me with his breath, and I had to push him away so that he couldn't kiss me. Suddenly, a gun cocked, and Alfonso stood right next to him with his gun against the idiot's head. He pissed himself, and I froze, staring at both fucking fools.

I shook my head and rushed away from this crap.

"Camilla!" Alfonso yelled, but thank heavens, no shot went off. A hand grasped around mine, and Nico appeared out of nowhere.

"Stop toying with him."

"I'm not toying with him. He's out of his fucking mind."

"You married him. I've told you, if you stop defying him, your life will be amazing."

"Defying him, Nico? He treats me like I'm a fucking idiot. Lying to me. I won't have that kind of marriage." Tears welled up in my eyes.

The bear of a man appeared behind me and lifted me over his shoulder, walking toward the exit.

"Put me down, you bastard!" I hit his back but doubted

he felt anything. A hand slapped me hard across my ass, and I cried out. It burned, and yet my body absolutely loved it. He manhandled me into the SUV and climbed in behind me. I couldn't even sit on my ass because it stung. Lorette and the extra she'd picked up laughed and spoke in Italian again. Tears blurred my eyes. If this was how he was going to treat me, fuck submitting to him.

He yelled at her in Italian and when I refused to acknowledge it, I realized that he was yelling at me.

"I don't understand Italian," I shouted back, and he grabbed me around the throat again. Nobody said anything in response.

He growled in Italian again as tears built up in my eyes. My entire body ached. We were not going to be a great match. He was going to kill me one of these days.

"Alfonso," Nico yelled from the front, and he shoved me against the car door. My body slammed into it as I coughed, trying to get my breathing under control. I kept coughing and when I finally had it under control, the SUV stopped in front of the hotel. I got out of the car and darted for the doors.

"Camilla," Alfonso snarled behind me again. I didn't stop. I continued defying him. Tears rolled freely down my face as I could still feel his fingers around my neck and his palm on my ass. He was a monster, but the worst part was that my body absolutely loved every second he was manhandling me. I was soaking wet between my thighs.

What did this mean, that I loved his sadistic side, that it

got me turned on? It was sick, and I didn't understand any of it.

I pressed the elevator button as I saw the giant of a man rushing toward me. I contemplated standing my ground or running for the stairs, just hiding before he really killed me tonight. I decided too late though, and he grabbed me as I went to make a run for it. I fought him by assaulting him with words, and he tossed me over his shoulder again and walked into the elevator as it opened. He commanded the others to wait as they tried to enter, and the doors closed with only the two of us inside. My heart thumped faster, and my fear heightened as adrenaline shot through my body.

He pulled me off his shoulder, and I slid in front of him. He pinned me like a bug against the wall. "Why do you keep on defying me after I told you not to?" he screamed in my face.

"Oh, but you can treat me the way you want? Is that it? Is that how this business arrangement is going to be, Alfonso? You going to take and take until I'm dry and have nothing more to give? Is that right?"

"Yes, it's my right."

"Your fucking right. What about my right? You are not the only one who got raised by a tight hand, you fucking bastard. Ever since I was born, it's been how to sit, how to please a fucking Don. And this is what I get? Manhandled when I don't listen? I'm not a fucking dog."

He roared and punched the wall of the elevator. The elevator shook with us in it. He spoke again in Italian.

"English!" I insisted, and he grabbed my mouth with his fingers.

"Stop yelling at me."

"Stop treating me like a fucking idiot."

He planted his lips on me and kissed me hard. I punched him and pushed him away. When he didn't budge, I bit him, and when he still didn't budge, I made sure my leg connected as hard as I could with his balls.

That made him stop and release me. He doubled over, and thank heavens, the elevator stopped.

"Camilla," he grunted as I rushed toward my room.

I could hear his panting behind me as he tried to catch up with me. As I reached my door, he pulled me back and slammed me into the wall.

"You are such an ungrateful little bitch," he hissed. "You will submit, one way or another." He was taking off his belt and unbuttoning his pants.

"Oh wow, Alfonso, you are such a fucking man," I countered as I knew what his last method of getting me to submit was—raping me.

He growled as I taunted him more to rape me. Prove what a big man he was, and then he tore my panties from my body. His hand cupped my mound, and he gasped. His eyes stilled as he stared at me. I closed mine in embarrassment as I knew what he was feeling.

"You getting off on this?" he asked, shock lacing his voice.

"Let go of me!" I pushed at him, and his hand disappeared from between my legs. My feet touched the ground, and I pushed him away and rushed to my room. I opened the door and then locked it behind me.

He didn't follow, and I thanked my lucky stars that something had stopped that man's fury he'd had for me tonight.

The adrenaline washed away, and my legs and everything shook. My throat and ass still hurt as shame washed over me like a tidal wave. Why was my body reacting toward him like this? I didn't understand, but I knew tonight, it had saved my life.

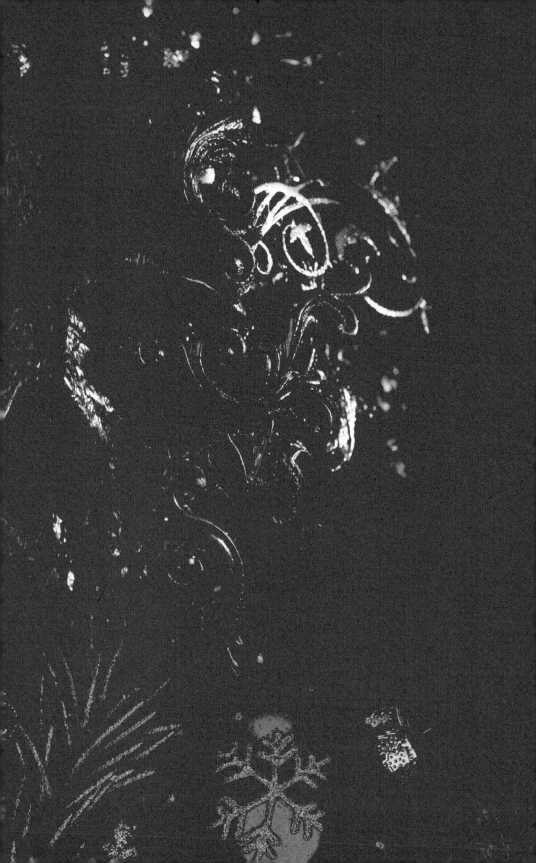

FIFTEEN
THE WHITE RABBIT

THE DOOR OPENED, AND NICO RUSHED IN.

"Where is she?" he asked. "Alfonso, where is Camilla?"

"In her room," I answered him. The little cunt was getting off on me manhandling her.

"Is she still alive?" he questioned, and I burst out laughing. Nico stared at me as I stood there still in a daze. "Alfonso, is she still alive?"

Chuckles that turned into laughter poured from me as he looked at the belt in my hand.

"Oh fuck, he's losing it," my cousin sang.

"Lorette, go the fuck home. Please," I begged.

She stared at me and walked into the room. "Your bride still alive, cousin."

"Yes, she's in her room. I do have some sort of restraint." I kept chuckling though as Nico continued to stare at me. I walked to my room.

Camilla was getting turned on by the way I handled her. Nico had no idea just how well he had chosen my bride-to-be, and I wanted her now more than ever.

I closed my office door and locked it. I was still furious, but feeling the wetness around her opening, glistening her up for my cock, was the last thing I thought would happen tonight. Shame sprawled over me as I finally realized what I was about to do. I was going to rape my wife. But she was mine. It wouldn't have been rape. Sure, in another household, another tier, it would've been rape, but she wasn't an ordinary woman. She was a Don, and the Dons had rules and traditions. Still, shame washed over me. It was the last thing I wanted to do. I'd treated her like shit today since this morning when she'd spoken out, called me on the bullshit that had left my lips.

She wasn't like your ordinary Don woman. It felt as if she was truly made for me, and her defiance was something that I loved; although I hated it just as much.

But the fact that her body was reacting exactly how I wanted it to react—oh, that was my biggest fantasy come true. And I wanted her now more than ever.

I grabbed my shaft in my hand and jerked off. She'd had me hard as a rock all night, and I'd tried to cool down, but seeing her with another man, my blood boiled again, and then she'd pushed me away and defied me over and over. She was like a little Chihuahua. There was no stopping those dogs, and I'd actually killed one that belonged to my grandmother because he'd refused to stop yapping. She'd made me feel like that tonight.

But I needed to find a way to control myself, otherwise I feared my temper would end her life. And that would be a damn shame.

She would submit one way or another, and I thought I might have just found out how.

She was more like me than she would ever admit.

I came all over my hand and growled as I kept pumping my dick, imagining I was fucking her mouth. Just thinking about that made me want to go hard again. This girl was going to be the death of me; it was just a question of when.

THE NEXT MORNING, I felt like crap. I had been on a conference call the entire morning and found Camilla eating on the balcony, just staring out at the ocean.

I grabbed a plate of fruit and a pastry and joined her.

She hardly acknowledged me when I sat down at the table.

"I'm sorry about last night."

"Save it, since I know this is how it will be from now on. You love manhandling women; you are a fucking abuser, Alfonso, admit it."

She got up and walked to the entrance. She was testing me again, and I grabbed her wrist. I counted to ten and instead of hurting her, I brought her wrist to my lips and kissed it. She froze.

"I know it's hard for you to accept my apologies, but I am sorry. You are not like the other girls I've met. You're different."

"Spare me your empty words. Tonight, you'll just find another reason to chuck me against the wall and threaten to rape me."

"It's not rape if you're mine." My temper was coming out to play again.

"Yeah, who told you that? Your daddy? Rape is rape. If it's not consensual, it's rape. Last night would not have been consensual."

"You sure about that? You were dripping wet between your thighs."

She closed her eyes as embarrassment colored her features. "My body reacts the way it does. It doesn't mean I like it." She pulled her hand away and stormed back inside.

I stared after her and sighed.

I would have to make this work with her. I knew bodies, and a body wouldn't act like that if the girl didn't secretly want it. Maybe she had fantasies that she found hard to admit to. But she would. With me, there would be no shame.

SIXTEEN

THE RUBY

IT HAD BEEN FOUR DAYS SINCE ALFONSO'S LITTLE manhandling game. The most boring new year was awaiting me.

Why had my body reacted like that? Did I secretly want him to do that to me? Did I love it? It was hard to make sense of when I had no one to speak to about it.

I'd always had weird sexual fantasies with Philip, but nothing like this. Rape was wrong, and here I was, fantasizing about Alfonso raping me. It scared me to death.

His temper was something that should completely terrify me.

And yet it was the fourth day that he'd been bestowing gifts—very expensive gifts—on me.

This morning it was tickets to Italy. He wanted to take me

to Puglia. I'd been there once when I was younger, on a family vacation, and it was the best damn vacation of my life.

It was a break we'd all needed desperately.

I would've loved to see it again, but it meant that I would be taking this trip with him, and I didn't want to go anywhere with him just yet.

I picked up the phone to order breakfast when the lady on the other side apologized and told me that she'd been instructed not to bring up anything to me.

It was Alfonso; he was forcing me to eat with him.

So I figured I wouldn't eat.

I saved my energy by sleeping half of the day and watching Netflix the other half.

How long we would be staying here, I had no idea.

A knock came at my door, and I closed my eyes, pretending to be asleep. It opened, and I could feel a presence next to my bed, probably watching me. My mother had always said I was a real drama queen and faked sleeping the best.

I didn't know if it was Nico or Alfonso, but when knuckles brushed my cheek softly, I knew it was Alfonso. He left after a minute, and I waited another few minutes to make sure he was really out of the room before I opened my eyes.

Tears pricked as the other part of me wanted to make peace with my husband, but I needed him to treat me differently. I needed his respect. This was a business transaction, not a real marriage. But he wasn't keeping his side of the contract.

He wasn't giving me what I wanted, and now none of us were getting what we wanted. It was a vicious cycle.

Later that night, I sneaked off to the kitchen and tried to find something small to eat. The fridge was basically empty. There wasn't a sliver of food to be found. I was tired of alcohol. I sighed and shut the fridge door, jumping when I found the semi-giant sitting at the breakfast nook watching me.

"Why are you so stubborn?"

"Why do you have such a temper?"

"Was born with it."

"Me too."

I got ready to leave when he grabbed my wrist again. "Camilla, please. It's been five days. I said I was sorry, and I meant it."

"Some things you can't fix with a sorry, Alfonso." I stared at him. I could see the regret in his eyes. His gentle side was at the wheel, and I was a sucker for gentle Alfonso. But the beast, the rage in this man, was too much to handle.

"I only protect what is mine."

"Protect?"

"Don't start, please," he pleaded.

"Then don't push it. It's not nice being strangled all the time and slammed against a wall whenever you don't get your way. And I have the right to protect myself. If you're not going to feed me, you're going to starve me to death, and you can't force me to eat with you. You fucked up; own it." I pulled my arm out of his grasp.

"How do I fix it?"

"By starting to keep your end of our contract."

He growled, and my thighs clenched. I hated my body and the way it reacted to that man's impatience.

THE NEXT DAY I was free again to order food. I ate like a beast since I was practically starving. A knock came at the door, and Alfonso stood in the doorway.

"I have to leave on business for a couple of days. Nico is here if you need anything."

"He's not going with you?"

"No. What I have to do is for me alone." He left, and my curiosity wanted to know where he was going. The contract had clearly stated that he'd want me to go with him everywhere he went. Another part I guess he wasn't going to act on at the moment.

At twelve, I watched him leave. He climbed into his Range Rover, and the driver drove him off, probably to the airport. One thing I knew for sure: that man looked great in his suits.

Nico knocked on my door later that night. I opened it, and he just stood there staring at me. "You like this, Camilla?"

"Fuck off, I mean it." I closed the door in his face. Thank heavens Nico wasn't like Alfonso; he left me alone for the remainder of the evening.

Asshole blaming me for his temper—typical male.

But I knew what my mother would've said if we'd spoken.

She would've fought with me too for not listening to my husband. Giving him what he required. It was the way of the Dons, but it was the one thing of the Dons that I'd always rebelled against. Philip had known how I felt, and I'd thought that I'd gotten a great deal with him. That he would treat me like his equal. Now it was something I had to fight for all over again. It was draining; Alfonso was draining.

The clock on my bedside read midnight. Happy fucking new year.

THE NEXT THREE DAYS, I finally found a way to relax. Nico dropped off a phone for me on the second day, and it didn't surprise me when Alfonso texted me just a few hours later, wanting to know how my day was going.

Fuck off

I typed back and sent it.

I'm trying. Please.

I don't care. Leave me alone.

Yeah, unfortunately that's not what our contract states. You need to provide me with an heir. When can we start?

Of course, he would play that card.

> Why don't you just take it? It's the
> type of man you are, no?

I didn't get a reply. I knew I was taunting him. I shouldn't be doing it, but I loved it. Loved the little victories.

I fell asleep watching a horror movie and woke up with a giant figure watching me. I simply stared at him. I knew he knew my eyes were open.

"What are we going to do, Camilla?" he breathed. "As we both know, we can't go on like this. Is this it? Is this how you are going to treat me from now on? Do I have to take whatever I need from you?"

"You've been doing it since we got married."

"Bullshit," he spoke. "You're stubborn and hold a grudge like no other. I want to make this work, but I can't do it alone."

"It's not a marriage, Alfonso."

"It's a binding contract for ten years. I won't break it before then. I need an heir from you as I refuse to go back to Italy and tell my mother she was right about this entire ordeal. So tell me what it is you want from me, so we can move forward."

I froze. Somehow it worked. I'd never have thought in a million years that it would work on him, but it did.

"I'm waiting."

I pushed myself up and sat straight. Alfonso moved forward in his chair.

"I need you to stop treating me as if I'm an idiot and respect the fact that I do not understand Italian. I'm not like anyone you've ever met."

"Oh, I've learned that the hard way. What else?"

"Control your temper. I know what you felt that night, I don't know why my body reacted that way, and it scared me to death."

"It's nothing to be scared of," he responded. "I can help you explore it, if you want."

"Explore it? You threatened to rape me, and I..." I couldn't even say it. I was still so ashamed of it.

"It's normal, Camilla."

"No, it's not."

"Everyone is different. Your sexual desires have been suppressed for a long time. Sometimes it happens. It's what you end up with. What else?"

"I blossom with gentle, not with anger and aggravation."

He nodded. "What else?"

"Just treat me like you at least like me."

"I do like you, more than I should. In fact, I think I love you, but that's not possible since we haven't known each other that long, so it's probably something I ate and am struggling to work out of my system."

My lips threatened to twitch at the sarcasm in his tone.

"Now here's what I need. And I will give you all of the things you need only if you give me what I require."

I nodded.

"You need to learn Italian. It's nonnegotiable."

I nodded again. "What else?"

"In front of people, what I say goes. If you don't like it, you speak to me behind a closed door about it. You can throw a tantrum, do whatever you need to do to get it out of your system, but in private—not in front of my family which causes embarrassment."

I nodded my agreement once more. "What else?"

"In public, you listen. I say things because I know this world better. I'm higher up, and you were not trained to function on our status level. So I need you to learn by obeying, understood?"

I agreed.

"You want to shake on that?" he questioned.

I stared at him. Then moved forward. My face was an inch from his, and I could feel his breath on my lips. "How about we kiss on it and start fresh?"

"Sounds like a plan."

SEVENTEEN
THE WHITE RABBIT

HER LIPS TOUCHED MINE, AND THE KISS STARTED off tender but quickly turned passionate. I'd ached for Camilla for the entire past two weeks, and she'd finally given a part of herself to me.

The unknown pull that had always been there between us took over, and she climbed onto my lap and straddled me. The kiss deepened as my cock hardened inside my pants. Her hips grinded into me, enjoying my hard-on as our tongues danced the rhythm of whatever the fuck this was.

I didn't want to stop kissing her. I wanted to make love to her, to have her naked in my bed and fuck her brains out. I wanted a week with her in my room uninterrupted and then to fly her to Puglia and just enjoy the sun. Fuck some more and finally put a baby inside her belly.

I want to know her better, and a part of me even wanted to fall in love more than I already was.

She worked herself up against my hard-on as we breathed like bulls through our noses, refusing to break this kiss. She was one hell of a kisser too, that I had to give her, and I still wondered what her mouth would feel like around my cock.

I grabbed her legs and held her tight against me. She continued to move her hips, riding my cock, and I growled into the kiss. Finally, our kiss broke, and we both complained. I felt like a teenager dry fucking my first love or whoever she was; I couldn't even remember. I cupped Camilla's neck and pulled her face closer to mine.

"Stop riding me," I ordered.

She didn't obey.

"Camilla."

"We're not in front of your family; I don't have to obey you."

My lips curved. "Then I hope you're prepared to let me fuck you." I pulled her tighter against me and grabbed her lips with mine again as the kissing war resumed.

I stood up with her, and she held on around my neck. I chucked her onto the bed as laughter poured from her lips. The yoga pants she'd slept in were flimsy, and I tore them off. She gasped, and I knew it turned her on. I grabbed her leg and started worshiping her feet, sucking her toes and licking her all the way up to her ankle. Her leg jerked slightly beneath my touch, and I loved it.

She was ticklish but didn't break the moment with laughter. My lips moved from her ankle, leaving a trail of wet kisses toward her knee. And then further up the inside of her thigh. I was getting ravenous as I moved toward her cunt, and I wasn't surprised at all when I removed her thong and found that the flimsy piece of lace was soaking wet.

I grunted as I slid my finger in between her folds and felt her arousal. She gasped as my mouth was still busy with her thigh, moving toward her labia. I kept stroking her length, and she started to moan as I sucked in one of her lips. She whined and breathed harder as my mouth let go of her lip and my tongue circled her clit. She tasted divine as I licked her clit and pressed a finger into her.

More complaints left her mouth. She stuttered in a breath as I kept sweetly assaulting her pussy with my tongue, mouth, and fingers. I wanted her to come, I needed her to come, to prepare herself for my cock.

Her noises grew tighter as I pushed another finger into her opening. She was so fucking wet as I finger fucked her faster.

"Fuck, I'm going to come."

I didn't stop. I begged her to come in my head, and then her pussy contracted around my fingers. She came like a man, as her arousal dripped from her cunt. She was fucking amazing.

She cried out as she wanted to close her legs. I slowed down the thrusting of my fingers and stroked her clit with the tip of my tongue more slowly.

She shivered but started to find herself. I kissed her

mound before I lifted my head and moved toward her. She stared at me and panted faster.

"How was that?" I asked.

"Amazing," she breathed and touched my cheek.

"I'm sorry."

She touched my lips and shook her head. "It's in the past. We focus on the future now."

I nodded, and then she pushed me onto my back, climbing on top of me and straddling me again. She placed herself on my cock, and I groaned as it felt so good. I'd never for a moment thought that this was how our conversation would end. I'd thought she would fight more, as she too had a vicious temper.

But this I loved. I reached out for her face and cupped her cheek as she rubbed herself along my cock. My finger pushed into her mouth, and she sucked hard on my thumb. All her actions were turning me on, and I was sure that I would die from need if she decided to get off of me.

She pushed my arm away and lowered her head; her lips crashed on mine as she kissed me again. My hands rested on her naked ass and stroked her legs and butt cheek while she continued rubbing against my cock. I was so fucking hard and ready to fuck.

"I want to fuck," I hissed out, and she laughed.

"I don't understand Italian, Alfonso."

"Sorry, I said that I want to fuck you."

"Oh, I bet you do."

I grabbed her behind her head and sat up with her. Our

lips still kissing and sucking each other as her fingers roamed down my body. She fiddled with the bottom of my khaki pants, and the button popped open. Her hand stroked my cock that was tightly inside my trunks. She was only making things harder for herself, but I wasn't going to tell her to stop. She tugged on the hem of my pants, awkward movements, and I decided to help. I pulled my khaki pants off and down my legs. When they landed at my ankles, I kicked them off.

My trunks were next. She was already working them over my ass, but I helped her with them too.

My erection jumped free, and her grip immediately curled around my shaft and started to stroke it hard.

I groaned and cussed.

"You love that?" she husked.

"Yes," I replied. "Don't stop."

We kissed again as she kept stroking my length. Her grip was almost as tight as her pussy, and for some reason, she started fussing too. I wasn't playing with her or stroking her, and she was so busy with me, she couldn't play with herself either.

I guess she got turned on by my arousal too. She was an amazing specimen, more sexual than she could have ever known.

"Fuck, I want you so badly," she whimpered against my lips and dropped to her knees.

The beast came out in me as I pulled her hand away from my length and guided her down on to my shaft.

I had to feel for her opening again, but she helped this time and then pushed herself onto me.

A string of cusswords left my lips at how tight her cunt was, stretching her over me. The euphoria was going to be the death of me as she lowered herself down on me an inch at a time.

"You okay?"

She nodded, but I knew tomorrow she was going to be sore. She was already a bit more dry then what she had been a few minutes ago.

"Where's the lube?"

"I think it's in the drawer."

I growled. Fuck that. I spit on my hand and pulled her off my cock, smearing her cunt with my spit, and then lowered her back on top of me. It became easier, but she was still tight. I wasn't going to last long as I guided the movement.

"Fuck," I grunted as I pumped her faster. She held on to my neck as I plunged her pussy onto my cock time and time again. I rolled us over and had her on her back and rammed into her.

Her complaints turned into little yelps as I sunk deeper into her faster and faster.

My finger found her clit again, and I stroked her while I fucked her. She was becoming more wet as my dick pushed into her opening, stretching her tight entrance over and over again. My spit had helped with the friction.

I could feel my orgasm starting to build as my mind clouded, but I didn't want this to stop.

My finger circled her clit faster. "Fuck yes, don't stop. I'm going to come," she whined.

I moved faster. I was close too, but she needed to come before I would. My finger stroked her swollen nub faster as she screamed and begged me not to stop.

I obliged and didn't stop. "Fuck, you need to come; I'm close."

"Don't you dare fucking stop now." The need was in her voice, and my mind felt as if I was going to lose it.

I moved faster, and my own sounds muffled hers. My finger moved over her clit faster, and finally she screamed as her pussy convulsed around my cock, her juices poured from her, taking me over the edge with her. I pulled out and came all over her stomach.

I grunted like a bear as I spilled my sperm. She laughed but sounded satisfied.

My mind was hazy, and I rolled to my back next to her, trying to catch my breath. The entire room was hot. I needed a shower, and we probably needed to clean my seed from her body.

She laughed and rolled her head onto my shoulder. I kissed the top of her head. She was my home now. And I'd make it work somehow, I vowed to find a way to make it work.

THE INTRODUCTION PART TO THE FIRST BOOK IN THE DON SERIES BOOK I FORGIVE ME FATHER AVAILABLE ON PRE-ORDER.

https://books2read.com/u/mY2a2w

ABOUT ERICA JADEN

Erica Jaden is born and raised in South Africa where she's married to her first real love, a wonderful, supportive husband.

She adores crafting worlds and creating soulless male characters who are remorseless and relentless when it comes to love, and the unfortunate heroines who fall for them.

When she is not writing, you can find her either cuddled up on her reading chair with a good story wishing she could jump into one of her morally grey worlds, or doing something highly creative.

Her stories do come with at least two pages of CW's, TW's & kinks. Lot's and lot's of kinks, so you are warned.

♪

Darkest Obsession

Jade Marshall

CWs, TWs & Kinks

(*Warning: Contains Spoilers)
This book contains mature themes and is intended for adult
readers. Specific content warnings include, but are not limited to:

ON-PAGE MENTIONS

Violence,
Death & Murder
Organized Crime
Juvenile Violence
Step Siblings
Obsession Teenage
Infatuation
Death/ Murder of a Parent
Military Injuries
Voyeurism
Unprotected Sex
Breeding
Explicit Language
Light Spanking
Cheating (Not between
MCs)
Pregnancy
Alcohol Use

OFF-PAGE MENTIONS

Sexual Assault of a Minor

STORY WRITTEN IN
US ENGLISH

DON'T LOOK BACK!

DANTE DELUCA

Fourteen Years Old

MY FATHER BROUGHT HIS NEW WIFE HOME TODAY. She brought her little girl with her.

Blonde hair in pigtails and the widest smile I have ever seen on a kid. She's a tiny little thing and I instinctively want to protect her from the darkness of the outside world. From the darkness living inside the walls of this house. She keeps looking around, her gaze bouncing from one thing to the next, taking in everything this new house has to offer.

"Here is your bedroom," I say when my father asks me to show her around.

"It's big," she says, turning in circles. "Do you sleep here, too?"

A chuckle falls from my lips. "No. My room is across the hallway."

"What if I have a nightmare?" she asks softly, her big blue eyes staring at me.

"You can always come to me," I reply, never even considering any other response.

FIFTEEN YEARS OLD

I stare down at my crimson coated fingers. Revulsion swims through me and I want to shower more than I want to take my next breath.

"Don't look so fucking disgusted," my father says sternly. "This is what you were born to do."

I want to say something, but my throat is closed up. All I can do is wish that this entire night passes quickly. Tied to a chair in the center of an abandoned warehouse, is a man in his late thirties. My father says he is – was – an informant. He was telling family secrets to the FBI and for that he had to die.

At my hand. I slit his throat like it was the most mundane thing I have ever done.

This is how my father plans to make sure his little heir falls in line. All this moment has done is solidify my decision to never have anything to do with the godforsaken DeLuca family.

"You did well," Amos says, placing his hand on my shoulder.

I stare at him in disbelief. How can he praise me for what I did?

"I threw up the first time I killed a man," he says lowly with a soft smile.

SIXTEEN YEARS OLD

I watch like a hawk as some punk kid touches Eco's shoulder, leaning in too close. Before I can think through what I am doing, I stomp over to them. I grab his wrist and twist, bringing him to his knees.

"What the fuck man?" the kid cries out.

"Don't touch my sister," I say, my voice low and threatening. For the first time in my life I consider killing someone without my father's order.

"Stepsister," Eco corrects, glaring at me.

"Semantics. You're a DeLuca now and the riffraff need to know their fucking place."

What I really want to say is she is mine and no one gets to touch her. But those words will never pass my lips, they can't. I'm not in love with Echo. It's just a crush.

"I don't know what your problem is," Echo says, her hands planted on her hips. "But I need you to hear me. I'm a Campbell, not a damn DeLuca. And you are not in charge of me."

Twenty-One Years Old

I am the son of a monster. A man that is ruthless in everything he does, holding no prisoners and accepting no excuse. Not even from his only child. I am expected to fall in line, like a good little heir of a mafia boss.

But he made a mistake.

He brought an angel into my life.

Echo Campbell. My eighteen-year-old stepsister.

For years I have tried to convince myself that I don't love her. That what I felt was simply a childhood crush. But I know the truth, deep down in my soul. I can't seem to keep my eyes off Echo, no matter how hard I try. I have made lists in my mind, and I know every single reason why we can't be together. But that doesn't make me love, or want, her any less.

She is the only girl I have ever wanted, and she is also the only girl I can never have. Echo Campbell. My sixteen-year-old stepsister One day she was a little girl with pigtails and the next... not so much.

My stepsister.

My heaven and my hell.

My waking mind may know that what I am feeling is wrong but that doesn't matter when I fall asleep. I dream of her, of doing depraved things to her sexy body. Every morning, I fight the urge to take my cock in hand and each day I lose that battle. I have rubbed myself raw with thoughts of her running through my mind and still, I can't stop thinking of her.

That's why I am leaving. I am damaged by the life my father has thrust upon me. By the deeds that I have committed and the blood that already stains my hands. I am dirty. Unworthy. And she deserves so much more than I can ever offer.

And now, I am going to do the most cliché thing I can think of. I am joining the Marines.

I will run away from the life I have been living, the life I have been forced into. Doing this will keep me far away from her, and my asshole father, which is a bonus. She can blossom into the woman I already know she is going to be and live a happy, carefree life. Away from me and the stupid fucking feelings I can't seem to control.

Away from the darkness that thrives in me.

Away from the damn DeLuca name.

Slinging my bag into the bed of my dark blue pickup truck, I cast a glance at the house I grew up in, but I don't return. I won't say goodbye to my father because I don't feel like having that argument again. And I can't say goodbye to her. If she asks me to stay one time, only once, I know I will. And then all of this will have been for nothing.

She deserves more than me, more than darkness and death, and this is the only way I know how to give that to her. I will give up anything if it means that she can have the life she has always dreamed of. I never even had the guts to tell her how I feel. But I know in my dark heart this is for the best.

I have done my best these past two years to shelter her from my life. From what my father does for a living, from what he makes me do, but I know she is aware. After all, she isn't stupid.

There isn't a future for us together. My soul is blacker than black while she is pure, perfect light. I won't taint her. I won't drag her down to my level.

It's time for me to grow up and get over this infatuation I have with my stepsister.

Twenty-six Years Old

I am heading home.

I swore I would never return but I don't have a choice in the matter. An IED ended my career as a Marine in the blink of an eye. It has been eight years since I saw my father or Echo.

We send birthday and Christmas cards but that is the extent of our communication.

I have no idea what waits for me when I get there but I have no where else to go.

It's my birthday and I'll cry if I want to

Echo Campbell

Fourteen Years Old

I HAVE A CRUSH ON MY STEPBROTHER.

I feel like a freak but every time I am around him all I can think of is kissing him. I want him to hold my hand and watch movies with me. I want to call him my boyfriend.

I also know that isn't a good idea. I know I can never tell anyone how I feel. He is my stepbrother and can never be anything except that. So, I push the feelings down, deeper than I ever could have thought possible.

I avoid him as much as I can except for the family dinners we are both forced to attend.

———

Sixteen Years Old

I stand in the icy wind staring straight ahead. The wind whips my black dress around my calves, stinging as it slams into my wet face. I can't remember when I started crying but it feels like I will never be able to stop.

Arms wrap around my shoulder, pulling me into a warm body.

"I'm sorry, Echo," Dante says. "I know this is hard. But she is at peace now."

"I know," I hiccup. "She was in so much pain. But I miss her."

"One day, you will miss her a little less. I promise."

I trust his words. He should know. His mom died, too.

Eighteen Years Old

He came into my room.

A man I once trusted.

He took what wasn't offered.

He called it my birthday present.

I thought I was safe in this house. Now I know better.

MEN SUCK—END OF STORY.

ECHO CAMPBELL

"GLASS OF ROSÉ," I ORDER LOUDLY OVER THE ROCK music blaring in the background, my fingers thrumming on the scarred wooden bar top.

The cute bartender smiles at me as I order, but I know he isn't really flirting. He has seen all my friends at the table we snagged and is trying to work his way into one of their pants by being friendly with me. It's the same dance I have been doing since junior high, and I won't fall for his bullshit. I may not be the prettiest or skinniest girl in our group of friends, but I'm not an idiot.

If he wants to talk to one of them, he has to find a way to do it all by himself. I wouldn't be very receptive even if he were flirting with me. Men are assholes, and I have put myself on the shelf for the foreseeable future.

"Not that I mind getting drunk on a Tuesday," Hailey

says around the straw in her beer. "But why are we here?" She casts a gaze at the clientele, her disdain for the people and the venue clear for everyone to see.

Her distaste for the local watering hole isn't lost on any of us. Dixie's is a supposed biker bar - which has never actually been confirmed - on the wrong side of the tracks. I've been here many times over the years, and even though it's not the most hygienic place, I have never had any problems. The people are always friendly, and the booze is cheap, which is precisely what I need tonight.

It may also have to do with the fact that my stepfather, Thomas DeLuca, is the head of the DeLuca mafia family. Since I can remember people have avoided me. I could commit a murder and get caught red-handed in this town and no one would say a damn word. I would just walk away scott free.

"I need to be somewhere Simon won't show up. Dixie's seemed like the best bet," I answer, taking a seat.

I look around at the sparce Christmas décor and the ugly plastic Christmas tree on the bar. This place really is depressing at this time of the year, but it's better than my damn apartment.

"Why would you ever say that?" Bethany asks sarcastically drawing my attention back to the conversation.

"Don't start with this shit again," I grumble. "Yes, he isn't very manly and wouldn't be caught dead in a biker bar. That's exactly why I chose this place."

It's the same logic I used when I started dating Simon. I

went for someone exactly the opposite of my regular type. I like a muscular man with rugged good looks, broad shoulders, dark hair, and maybe even a few tattoos sprinkled in. Simon is tall and lanky, with blonde hair, and boyish good looks.

"And why are we avoiding your boyfriend?" Hailey questions with a raised brown.

"Because he isn't my boyfriend anymore," I reply after taking a sip of whatever the hell the bartender is trying to pass off as rosé. "And every time I look at his stupid face, I want to throat-punch him."

My four best friends, people I grew up with, stare at me in varying degrees of shock and confusion.

"Explain." Samantha looks ready to murder someone.

"I found another woman's blue lace panties under the bed. Our bed. In my apartment. He tried to play it off as being mine, but I'm not dumb." I lay out my mortification for my friends. "Once he finally confessed, I told him to get the fuck out of my apartment. The end."

"What a prick," Bethany proclaims to a round of nods from the others.

This is why I called them to join me. For the next two hours, we drink while berating Simon, the dickhead idiot. We laugh until we cry, and even though some of them weren't sure about being here at Dixie's, we all end up having fun.

"So," Hailey slurs, already sloppy drunk. "What you need is some rebound sex. I mean real big dick energy."

I laugh loudly. "Nope. I am done with men for the foreseeable future. I have the worst taste."

"This isn't about taste," Samantha interrupts. "This is about getting railed by a big, strong man and then walking away in the morning. It's even better if you walk with a limp afterward or can't walk at all. You know, get laid and get out."

"Oh my God," Bethany breathes.

"Don't be such a prude," Samantha bites out. "It's just a one-night stand."

"Not that. Over there." She grabs Samantha's jaw and directs her vision to the desired area.

"Sweet baby Jesus. If I weren't married, I would ride that pony all night long," Samantha moans, drawing laughter from all of us.

I can't help but laugh with them. They are some of the best, most outspoken people I have ever met. Turning around in my seat, I try to see which of these poor men they are objectifying. It only takes me a moment to spot him. My mouth dries up, and my heart rate spikes. My palms grow sweaty, and I feel like a teenager again, worried about what my clothes and hair look like to other people. To him. I hate that he can take me back to that time without even looking at me.

"Oh Shit," Pauline whisper-shouts. "We know that pony."

The entire table devolves into a fit of giggles, but I don't join. Our gazes connect, and I can't seem to rip myself away from the dark hazel gaze that traps me. His gaze seers my soul, making my heart beat triple time.

Fucking Dante DeLuca.

A Hero's Return
Dante DeLuca

I HAVE BEEN BACK IN THE TOWN OF BLACKWOOD Falls for all of an hour, and already I want to rip my hair out by the roots. My father is working on my last God-given nerve, and I have to leave before I punch him. Or maybe I'll just shoot him.

"Where are you going, Dante?" he questions as I grab my keys off the table in the foyer.

"Out." I make my way to the front door, fighting to hide my limp, my weakness, from his gaze.

"What do you mean out?" He sounds surprised. "We need to finish our conversation."

"I mean, I am leaving this house. Probably to find a bar where I can have a drink without the judgmental stare of my father drilling into the side of my fucking head," I snap at him.

"You can't keep running away from this," he replies following me. "It is time for you to take your place as the head of the DeLuca family. I won't be around forever."

"I told you then and I will tell you now, I have no fucking interest in being the head of this godforsaken family."

I don't wait for him to say another word before slamming the door behind me. Since I can remember, all he has ever done is criticize and judge me. My grades were never good enough, I didn't score the winning touchdown in the football game, and I didn't want to be the perfect little mafia son. I chose to serve my fucking country. Something that would make any other parent proud.

Except my father.

Nothing I have done in my life has ever satisfied him. And now that I have been medically discharged from the Marines, he only has another thing to lord over me. He sees it as another in a lengthy line of failures.

I can't stand being in that fucking house for another fucking minute.

Jumping into the driver's seat of my matt black Ford F250, I headed toward the only bar in town I ever frequented.

Dixie's.

It's a biker bar, run by Arch Fiends MC, an outlaw biker club, and somewhere someone like me was always welcomed. It may have been almost ten years since I stepped foot in this god-forsaken town, but I still know how to find the damn bar.

Stopping on the packed dirt, I stare at the building that has remained the same since I can remember. The red brick building has been tagged with graffiti repeatedly over the years, and the windows have been painted over to keep prying eyes out.

Chromed out motorcycles line the side of the building, and I know the crowd that has always frequented Dixies is still the same, more, or less. The faces may have changed, but I would bet a hundred dollars, the vibe is still the same.

"No weapons," the meathead at the door says when I step closer, once more trying not to show my limp to the outside world. But the man doesn't even bother to look at me. He is wearing a leather cut proclaiming him to be a prospect.

"No problem."

His gaze snaps up, and I can't help but chuckle. I know that I'm a big bastard. I always have been. But judging from the size of this guy, few people he has met are bigger than him. Until now.

"I'm not looking for any problems," I say when the bouncer looks unsure whether he should let me in.

"What a boring way to live," a female voice says from behind me.

Turning, I take in the petite frame of a pixie-like woman with fire-engine-red hair and tattoos covering almost every inch of her exposed arms. She pats me on the shoulder with a smile.

"You can let him in, Leo. This is Dante DeLuca," she explains. "He's been gone for a while, but he is one of us. Living in the underbelly and making it look easy."

"I'm a law-abiding citizen." I counter.

"And I'm the tooth fairy. We can't choose what we're born into."

"I'm not sure we have met before," I say with a frown, not happy to be judged by some strange woman.

"We actually have," she says as she walks away. "Name's Amy McIntire. We used to go to school together."

"Damn woman," I say with a quick smile. "Seems things have changed while I was away."

"Not everyone is the heir to a criminal empire," she says with a wink. "Some of us have to make our own way. And stop flirting with me, I'm not interested."

And then she is gone, and I am left staring after her. Well, shit. The little nerdy girl that sat in the front of every class, as far as I can remember, became kind of a knockout. Who would have guessed?

The bouncer begrudgingly allows me entrance with a mumbled, "Don't start any shit. We don't want any problems with the damn DeLuca's."

I want to tell him to fuck off, that I have nothing to do with my family's business, but I don't. No matter how many times I say it, no one will believe me. In this town I will always be the mafia boss's son, no matter what I do.

Walking in, memories assault me. The interior is loud, old-school rock music blaring overhead. People mill about, bodies packed close together in the smallish space. There are grocery store Christmas decorations hanging haphazardly throughout the bar. It's busy on a Tuesday night.

The crowd splits for a moment as I look for a way to make

it to the bar and the shot of bourbon I have been craving, but instead, I lock eyes with a woman. She is fucking stunning. Curvy as fuck with a hint of cleavage on display, her blonde hair up in the same customary ponytail it always has been. I don't have to be close enough to know her eyes are a stormy grey.

My cock is already hardening in my jeans at the sight of her. I should be embarrassed, disgusted, angry, anything but happy to see the object of my years' long obsession.

I may not have laid eyes on her in ten years, but I know every damn thing there is to know about the woman across the bar.

Echo Campbell.

My angel.

My own personal hell.

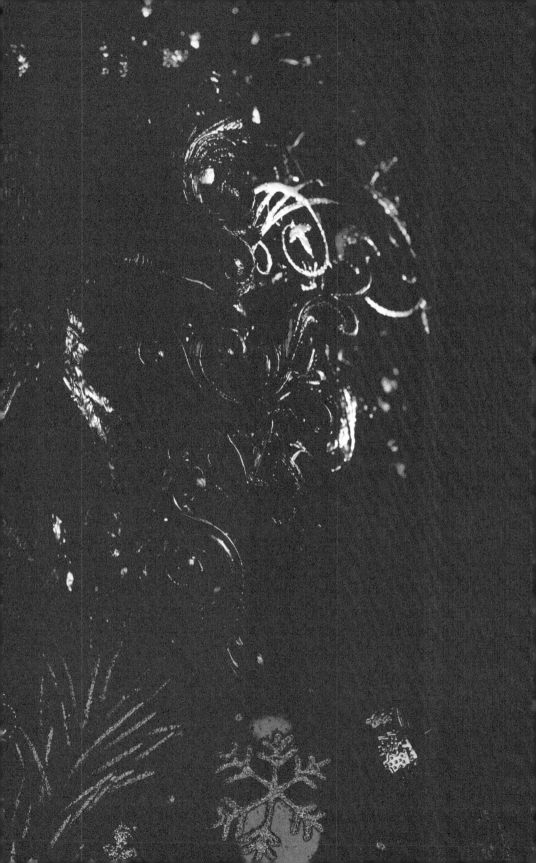

Blast from the Past

Echo Campbell

I BREAK THE CONNECTION BETWEEN US AND TURN back to my friends. I try my best to paste a smile on my face, but I don't think I actually accomplished what I was aiming for because it feels more like a grimace. Thank God they're all a little drunk. I don't think they can see the confusion and fear on my face. The last thing I needed tonight is to run into my stepbrother.

My hot Marine stepbrother. My mafioso stepbrother.

"Ladies." The deep timber of his voice washes over me as he greets us all. A shiver works its way down my spine. "Echo."

I don't look back at him. "Dante." My friends are all staring at him with stars in their eyes.

Yes, that is the Dante DeLuca effect.

He mesmerizes anyone with ovaries. Hell, even some men fall under his fucking spell. I am not too proud to say that even I am not immune to it.

His calloused right hand lands on my shoulder, squeezing it. The bared flesh exposed by my white tank top pebbles beneath his touch, along with my nipples, and I curse my traitorous body for reacting to him. Just like it always has.

Even as a teenager, I had an immense crush on him. He was all I could ever think about, all I ever wanted.

Seems not much has changed.

"When did you get back?" Hailey asks with a coy smile.

My gaze snaps to her. She is basically falling all over herself, fawning over him. I want to roar, to rage. But I can't. He isn't mine, and he never was. I cried when he left, my young heart shattered. But I never told anyone the truth, mourning the loss in private.

She has every right to flirt with him. Hell, she could even date or marry him and I wouldn't have the right to say a single fucking thing. Dante DeLuca is out of the question. Always has been, always will be.

"Not long," he answers coarsely, squeezing my shoulder once more. "I need to get a drink. I'll see you later."

What the fuck does that mean? My mind runs a mile a minute as he strides toward the bar. There is something off about his gait, something I can't quite explain.

All of my friends' gazes are stuck on him, just like mine. I wish I could say I was strong enough that I didn't check out his firm ass or the way his jeans hug his thick, muscular thighs. But you can bet your last dollar I did. Every woman in the bar did.

"Fuck," Pauline breathes. "How is it possible that he got hotter?"

"Right?" Bethany chirps in. "Isn't he almost thirty now? Like when does the decline in his looks start?"

I can't help but laugh at her disgruntled tone.

"You!" Hailey points at me accusingly. "Why didn't you tell us?"

"I didn't know," I reply with a shrug, lifting my hands in surrender. "I barely see Thomas anymore, and we rarely talk. I haven't spoken to Dante except for Christmas and birthday cards in almost ten years. We aren't really family. You know what I mean?"

"Really? I always thought you all were close?" Samantha leans forward.

"It was different when we were all living together. But then mom died, Dante joined the Marines, and I grew up and moved out. Thomas didn't really want me to start with, but he loved my mom to no end. When she died, he was stuck with me."

"That's heavy," Bethany mumbles. "Why didn't you ever tell us?"

"There was nothing to tell. Thomas was never abusive," I lie. "Actually, he was always good to me. He was just indifferent."

"I wish you had told us," Hailey drunkenly hugs me. "But we are your family. And we love you so much."

Tears burn my eyes at her words. There is a boatload of stuff I never told my friends.

"I know, sweetie. I've always known."

The Appointment

Dante DeLuca

I STARE AT THE STEEL AND GLASS DOUBLE-STORY building that houses all the medical professionals in and around Blackwood Falls. This is the last place I want to be, but if I want to live a normal life and regain the full use of my leg, I don't have a choice.

I have to keep this appointment with the physiotherapist and start the long, hard road to recovery. Stepping inside, I appreciate the cool interior while I fill out the customary paperwork. Taking a seat, I listen to the monotonous music in the waiting area, wishing I was anywhere but here.

The receptionist smiles brightly. She is one of Echo's friends, Pauline, I think. A small golden Christmas tree stands proudly on her desk beside the sign-in sheet.

"You can go through, Dante. The doctor will be with you shortly."

She gestures toward a door on the right. I enter the office and allow the door to close behind me. The room has floor-to-ceiling windows with a view of the river and the mountains behind it. There is a massive bookshelf on the left and a desk in the middle of the room. Sitting in one of the tan leather chairs, I survey the room, trying to get a feel for who this doctor may be.

In here, there isn't a single personal touch or Christmas decoration. I haven't met him before, but he comes highly recommended.

The door opens, but no one approaches or speaks. After a moment of tense silence, I turn, only to find Echo standing just inside the room.

We stare at each other for long moments before she finally rounds the desk and sits, placing a folder on the surface in front of her.

"Doctor Phillips has had a family emergency and won't be available for the next couple of weeks. You are welcome to reschedule for when he is back," she says, staring at a spot above my left shoulder.

What the hell did I ever do to deserve this kind of treatment from her? I know that I ignored her for the majority of the time we lived together, but it was better than the alternative. I never thought she would hate me for it, though. We are still family, after all.

"Echo," I say. "Look at me."

It feels like forever before her gaze finally locks on mine.

"Is there a reason why you're avoiding me?" I ask.

"Avoid is such an ugly word," she says with a blush. "I'm trying to keep this professional."

"And last night at the bar? When you wouldn't even look at me," I counter.

"What do you want from me, Dante?" The old tell-tale flush of anger that I have never forgotten blooms on her cheeks. "It's not like we have ever been close or even friendly. I'm treating you the same way I would any other man I haven't seen for ten years."

Fuck. Why does it feel like I got kicked in the nuts? Was that supposed to hurt?

"Fine," I grunt. "Then treat me."

A deep frown mars her beautiful face, and I want to rub it away with the tip of my finger.

"What?"

"You wouldn't be here if you weren't qualified. So, tell me what I need to do to get my leg back to normal, and let's get this show on the road."

I'm behaving like an asshole. But she hurt me with her words, no matter how inadvertently and now I am doing the same. I've always acted like an asshole toward her, so I can just continue the same way I always have.

I've also gotten hard – again – in the time I have been sitting here, verbally sparing with her. Something that I'm not proud of but it is what it is. She has always had this effect on me.

She stares at me with shock before she recovers.

"You had a distal femur fracture as a result of the IED

explosion. It is one of the most severe cases I have ever seen." Echo never even opens the folder, proving that she already worked through my case and memorized the details. "The surgery to implant the screws was six months ago, and it seems like you've made a steady recovery. The only thing that remains is getting your leg back into shape."

"What does that mean? Should I start running again?" I ask.

"We need to do some leg exercises and work on your range of motion before you can go running again," she counters. "I will get you a set of exercises you can do at home and the number of a therapist that can help you."

"You can't do it?"

"I don't think that's a good idea," she replies, her frown still firmly in place.

"I don't understand why you're trying to get away from me. Am I not your family? Did I do something?"

She stares at me for the longest time.

"No, Dante. You are not my family. You used to be my stepbrother, but now you are just a patient. I am busy and don't have the time for any new clients."

She has a tell. Beautiful little liar. She chews her bottom lip whenever she is being less than truthful.

"You're my still my stepsister," I say, my jaw clenching. It's the only thing that still binds us together even if I hate calling her that. "And if you wanted, you could help me after hours," I counter, trying to bait her into spending some time with me.

Anger flashes across her brow before she can mask it. She

glares at me, breathing heavily, considering all her options before answering.

"Friday, seven o'clock. Where do you want to do this?"

"I'm staying at the house with my father."

She goes pale, swallowing, before she can regain her composure. What the hell is that about?

"Fine. I'll meet you there."

Nodding, I discreetly shift my erection before standing. "Thanks, doc."

MEMORIES

ECHO CAMPBELL

I HATE THAT I LET DANTE GOAD ME INTO THIS. I have been berating myself and trying to think of a plausible excuse for the past two days. I haven't figured anything out, so I am parked in front of the house I grew up in.

I am also frustrated by the fact that it took me an extra hour to do my hair and makeup, and I changed my outfit three times. It has been this way since I can remember. I want him to think I'm pretty. How can I still be stuck on this damn crush? And how do I make it fucking stop?

Technically, I only lived here for four years after our parents got married, and only half of that was spent with Dante before he left. And I was actively avoiding him most of that time.

Today, my nerves are frayed. I don't want to spend time around Dante, much less touching him. I also don't want to go into this godforsaken house where all the memories are waiting to bombard me. Every last good memory I have of this place has been replaced by something dark.

But Dante has always brought out the worst in me. Even when I was younger, he would goad me into things I didn't want to do by baiting me.

The front door opens, and Dante stands on the top step, dressed in grey sweatpants and a fitted black t-shirt, staring at me, his gaze challenging me to put my car in reverse and drive off like a coward. Instead, I open the door, grab my bag, and step out.

Each step I take toward him has my heart stuttering, emotions threatening to overwhelm me.

Silently, Dante leads us into a downstairs living room which he has cleared of furniture. I stare at the pale walls, wishing I was anywhere but here. One of the housekeepers has taken the time to put up some Christmas decorations and I want to vomit. Nothing about this fucking place should ever pretend to be cheery or welcoming.

I always hated living in this house. It is too big and empty. It doesn't matter that the most expensive items are everywhere. This house is devoid of love and happiness. No, this beautiful shell hides the rotten core wonderfully, exactly the way Thomas DeLuca intended.

Taking a deep breath, I center myself. All I have to do is teach him the exercises and then I can get the fuck out of here. That is when the memories assault me. Birthdays, Christmases, dinners, and more, all spent with my mother. And then, all the darkness, pain, loneliness, and empty moments after she died.

This house used to be filled with love and laughter. But not for long. Then the fear and the tears took over.

"Echo," he starts, but I cut him off.

"I thought I could do this, Dante. But I was wrong," I say softly, allowing my emotions to get the better of me.

Already, I can feel the tears gathering in my eyes. This is the last place I spent any time with my mother, and her memory lives in every corner. It's too hard being back here, I lie to myself, forcing the other memories down. If I let them surface, I will almost certainly have a panic attack and then I won't be able to get away from this place.

"Shit!" Dante curses. I don't expect to feel his arms wrapped around me. "I didn't even think about how being here would affect you. I'm so sorry."

He thinks my emotions are because of my mom and I'm grateful he doesn't know the rest. My heart would break if he ever looked at me in pity. I would rather live with the indifference he has always shown me.

My skin is aflame. Being this close to him, smelling his unique masculine scent, drives me insane. I inhale deeply before pushing away from him.

"I'm sorry," I say wiping away a stray tear. "That was very unprofessional."

"Listen, I know we haven't seen each other in ages, and even then, we weren't all that close. But you don't have to treat me like a client. I'm still just me."

I stare at him. I take in his strong jaw and chiseled cheek-bones. His dark cropped hair that has started growing out, and deep hazel gaze. He is a perfect specimen. But I can't focus on that right now.

"Perhaps we can try again after the holiday season?" I ask with a small smile. "We would only have had one session anyway."

"That sounds good," Dante nods in acceptance. "We can find somewhere else to do the sessions as well."

"That sounds good." Turning, I walk back to the front door, Dante following on my heels.

"Is that you, Echo?" Thomas calls out as he descends the stairs.

Panic slams into me and I quicken my pace, walking out the door and straight to my car before sliding into the driver's seat. The need to get as far away from this place is riding me hard.

"What are your plans for the holiday?" Dante asks conversationally, dissecting me with his stare. "Spending time with your husband and extended family?"

"Just going up to the cabin mom left me," I say softly, willing him to leave me alone.

Thomas stands in the doorway watching us like a hawk and all I want to do is leave. My skin crawls beneath his gaze and I swallow down the bile rising in my throat. But Dante was right. I have no reason to treat him with anything but friendly disinterest, so I remain calm and continue to chat like the world isn't closing in on me.

"Alone?" Dante asks, prying.

I roll my eyes at his reaction. "Yes. I've been doing it for years, Dante. I'm a big girl now. I can take care of myself."

"There could be a snowstorm up in the mountains! Have you checked the weather?"

"I have. And I've been through storms before," I reply, starting my car and putting it in reverse. "Don't worry so much. You're going to get wrinkles."

I give him my best fake smile as he glares before I reverse down the driveway and make my way home. With every mile I put between myself and the house on top of the hill my heart-beat steadies. I stop at the store for some staples and a big ass bottle of wine. I'll need to be drunk to sleep tonight.

I need to drown my demons.

Here is my Truth.
Dante DeLuca

"Can I talk to you?" Amos, my father's second-in-command asks when he finds me in the kitchen.

"I'm not sure what we could possibly have to talk about," I reply, taking a sip of the coffee I just prepared.

"We need to talk about your father. And the future of the DeLuca family."

"That has nothing to do with me. You know I'm not interested in anything to do with the family."

Amos shakes his head. "You don't really get a choice. You were born to lead this family. Why do you think I spent all that time training you, showing you the ropes?"

"Because my father told you to?" I say with a roll of my eyes.

"No." He takes a breath, running his hand through his hair in agitation. "Your mother did."

"Excuse me?" My voice is filled with anger and disbelief.

"Annabelle was the DeLuca, not Thomas," he explains. "Your father took her last name and the family mantle. He has taken this family from bad to worse. And it's time for you to fix it."

I'm shocked, shaken to my core by the words a man I have known my entire life just shared with me. How much of my own life isn't what I thought?

"Tell me the truth," I demand. "Everything."

"That will take days, weeks. I will, but now..." he says shaking his head. "What I can tell you is that the enemies are at the gates. Your father has pissed off some unbelievably bad people. People that intend to harm anyone that has ever been part of his life or family to get their revenge."

My first thought is Echo. Panic envelopes me. Not for my own safety but for hers. If my father has fucked this up as badly as Amos says I can guarantee that whoever wants to take him out will know about her.

"What do you expect of me?"

"Get rid of him," Amos says with finality.

"Kill my father?" I ask, shocked.

I know that it happens, that some sons take over as the head of their families by killing the previous head. But I'm not that man. I may be a killer, but I'm not a damn sociopath.

"Well, that's one way. But I would suggest trying to talk to him first."

My nerves are shot to shit. I haven't been able to get ahold of Echo since she left. I should have said something, stopped her from leaving. It's insane for her to go up the mountain alone. And now I have the added stress of the family bullshit, my father pressuring me to take my place at his side, and someone that may or may not want to hurt Echo as an extension of our family.

"Severe weather conditions are expected for this Christmas weekend," the balding weatherman on the television rambles. "Be prepared for a lot of snow."

I switch off the living room television with a sneer before tossing the remote on the couch. My gaze drifts to the large picture window, snow already covering every available surface, the mountain white in the distance. My fists clench at my side with the need to do something.

Anything.

Slipping my phone from the back of my jeans pocket, I scroll to Echo's number - the one she didn't give me - and stare. I hit the call button for what is probably the hundredth time and listened to the ringing down the line. She hasn't answered in two days, and I doubt she will now, but I still try.

"You have reached the voicemail box for Echo Campbell."

Her recorded message drones. I end the call after listening to the rest. Restless energy thrums through my veins.

"What are you doing?" my father questions from the doorway.

I didn't even hear him come back home. I am so lost in my worry for Echo that I have all but blocked out the rest of the world. Her reactions when she was here before bother me and the fact that she all but fled, running from a place that was once her home has been driving me crazy.

"Does Echo still visit you?" I ask instead of answering his question.

He looks shocked that I would ask such a thing.

"Why would she?"

"Because she is family," I reply automatically.

"No, Dante. She was my wife's child, and my wife has been dead for many years," he says stiffly. "I fulfilled my promise. I raised her, but she isn't my child."

"You're a fucking asshole." I glare at the man who calls himself my father. "If there was ever any doubt in my mind, you just erased it."

"What are you going on about?"

He looks at me like I have lost my fucking mind.

"I left this house to get away. From you. I did the right thing so I wouldn't disappoint you again," I say, my voice clear as I lay out my truth. "I gave up the only thing I ever wanted so it wouldn't affect you."

"Dante," he starts, but I cut him off with a glare.

"For years, I have been forced to listen to you and all your ridiculous opinions. Now it's time for you to listen to me."

I wait to see if he will cut me off again. When he remains silent, I continue.

"I've been in love with Echo for as long as I can remember, and you..." I shake my head to clear the rage. "I gave her up so she could have the life she deserved, so I wouldn't disappoint you yet again. When her mom died, I left her here, knowing that you would be here for her, that she would have some form of family. And now you tell me she has been alone all this time."

"You love her?" he asks with a disbelieving chuckle, not addressing the fact that he all but abandoned her.

"Not that you would know anything about love," I sneer.

"Well, you can have her now," he replies with derision. "She's a decent lay."

"Excuse me?"

The words are barely above a whisper. He can't be serious. A haze of red clouds my vision and I know that one of us will die before the day is through.

"What? You think I lived in this house for years with that teenage pussy strutting around here, barely dressed, and I never took what was offered?"

I snap. I circle my hands around his neck and slam him against the entryway wall, sending a Christmas wreath crashing to the floor. I didn't even realize I was in front of him.

"You touched her?" I ask between gritted teeth, my anger overtaking any logical thought.

He laughs, even as his face changes color. "I did more than touch. I fucked the cherry right out of her," he boasts. He doesn't struggle or try to stop me. His arrogance and the fact that he doesn't believe I will harm him, keeping him calm in the face of my rage. He doesn't know me as well as he thinks he does. "And if you were a real man—"

The words die on his lips. His head twists at an awkward angle as I snap his neck, not needing to hear his words. His limp form slips from my grasp, landing with a thud on the polished tiles beneath my feet. It seems like I may have been wrong. I am a sociopath. He was a fucking monster, and I left her alone with him. How did I not know? What did he do to her? Dark thoughts swirl in my mind as I stare down at his dead body.

"Amos!" I call out loudly, knowing the man is still somewhere in the house.

A moment later he descends the stairs, his gaze glued to my father's body. He raises a brow in question but doesn't speak. He was my father's second-in-command. I guess he is mine now.

"You wanted him gone," I say without a speck of remorse. "I'm the head of this family now."

"Good. I will tell the men I found him here. Blame one of the many enemies he has made," Amos replies.

"You mean, start a war?"

"We are already at war," he replies darkly. "The men don't need to know you killed you father. It will only cause dissent in the ranks."

He has always been loyal to the DeLuca family, and I know he will serve me well in the future. I didn't want this life, but this is how I will be able to protect the woman I love from being hurt any more. I move toward the stairs while he speaks.

"I'm leaving for a few days," I say. "Let everyone know the

change in leadership. If they don't want to live beneath my reign they should leave before I get back."

"Where are you going?"

"I need to find Echo. If this family is going to war, she needs to be safe."

"About damn time," he replies, his phone against his face, already doing what I have decreed.

"Meaning?"

"That girl belongs here. With you."

Heading toward the room I have been using, I toss the few things I unpacked into my bag before slinging it over my shoulder. The woman I love is on this god-forsaken snow-covered mountain, and I need to find her before it's too late. I'm in charge of my own destiny now.

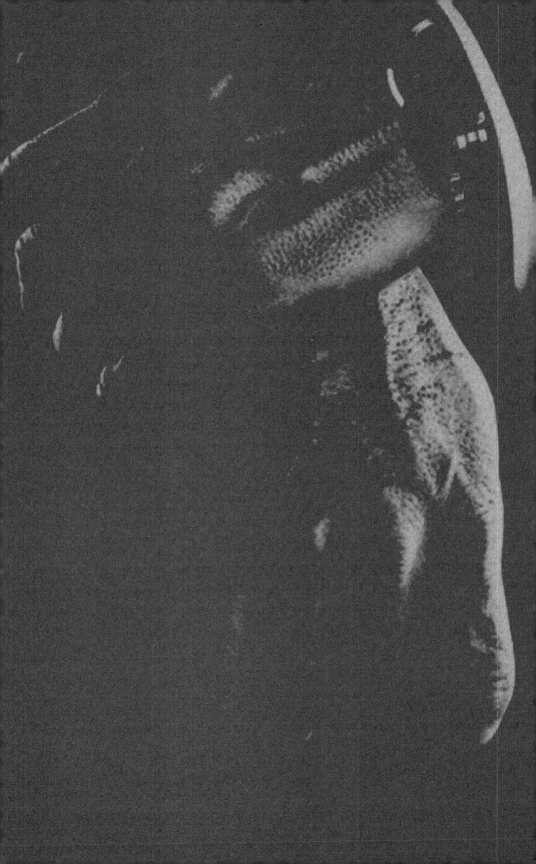

Dante to the Rescue

Echo Campbell

The wind howls outside the small cabin. I have been coming here since I found out about the property. It was a month after my eighteenth birthday when the lawyers contacted me and let me know that my mother had left me this little surprise. The first year, it wasn't livable, but I put in a lot of work, and one of the handymen in town was willing to help me out for next to no payment until we finally got my little slice of heaven livable.

I have been up here in storms but never anything like this.

It feels like the entire house is straining to remain upright as the wind and snow batter it from all sides. And for the first time in years, I regret not telling anyone that I am up here. If anything happens, no one will know to look for me and that thought has fear clawing up my throat.

Sitting in front of the fireplace, I add another log to,

fighting off the panic attack I feel bubbling up inside me. I stare at the Christmas tree I spent hours decorating. My mother would have loved it.

Loud knocking sounds on the only door of the cabin, drawing me from my thoughts.

"What the fuck," I mumble, thinking my mind has finally snapped and I am now officially imagining things.

I don't move from my spot on the floor, but I do stare at the door. Did Thomas find out about this place? Does he think I told Dante what happened all those years ago? The man is the head of the fucking DeLuca Mafia Family and will most certainly have me killed if he ever thinks I told anyone his dark, dirty secret. Especially the son he has been fighting so hard to get to accept the life he wants for him.

More banging, more insistent. "Echo!"

That can't be right. What would Dante be doing here?

"Echo!"

Lifting from my seat in front of the fire, I step up to the door, unlatch the deadbolt, and slowly open the door. I do it cautiously. If the wind slams it open, I could hurt myself or, worse, not be able to close it again.

Thankfully, I am not going crazy. Dante steps inside before slamming the door closed and relatching it. I'm at a loss for words. His being here right now just doesn't make sense.

"Thank fuck," he breathes harshly before wrapping his arms around me.

I allow him to hold me a moment, breathing in his scent

mingled with the cold, fresh smell of the storm outside before speaking. "Why are you here, Dante?"

He stares down at me, not releasing his hold. Something in his gaze has changed, but I can't put my finger on it. He smiles, and my thoughts are momentarily scattered.

"I was worried about you."

"I'm perfectly safe."

"Echo," he sighs. "It's the worst snowstorm in ten years. I couldn't just leave you up here alone."

There it is. Dante, the savior, the Marine, comes to his little stepsister's rescue. Like I can't take care of myself. It seems things really don't change. He will always see me as the little sister he never wanted. Just like his father.

"I told you I could take care of myself," I retort, pulling away from him.

"Like you did with my father?" he asks harshly.

His words dump ice in my veins.

"You don't know what you're talking about," I hiss defensively, although I can already feel the tears gathering.

"He told me," Dante announces flatly.

I need to put some space between us. I shouldn't be angry at him. He isn't at fault for how I feel. But my heart hurts, even all these years later, knowing that I will never have the one man I have always loved. I'm damaged, broken. But now he knows it. I can't stand to see the pity in his gaze.

"I don't want to talk about this," I say, walking into the kitchen area.

The lights flicker, drawing my attention.

"Fuck."

"Where's the generator?" he asks, changing the subject and taking charge of the situation.

"In the outbuilding."

He stares at me. "We'll have to wait for the storm to calm down," he says just as the lights give a last flicker and remain off.

It may only be noon, but the clouds have darkened the world around us. The only illumination in the cabin comes from the fireplace.

"Looks like I am going to be here for a while."

"I want you to leave," I demand, trying to keep my cool. "I don't want you to be here."

"And I want to know what the fuck my father did to you."

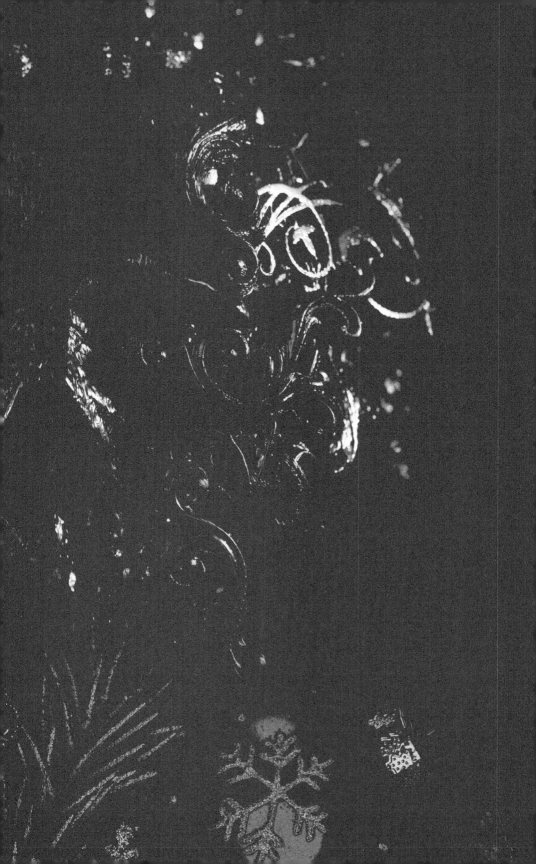

Caught in a Storm

Dante DeLuca

She acts like I'm not even here. It's been three of the longest, most tense hours of my life. Being in war is less stressful than trying to figure out this woman. I want nothing more than to go to her and wrap her in my arms, but I'm not exactly sure she would reciprocate.

The cold is also making my leg act up. It hurts like a mother fucker and I should be sitting. But I grit my teeth and push through the pain, never looking away from her for a second.

She is pissed off that my father told me what he did even if I don't know the full story. She is pissed off that I confronted her about it. I want to apologize for leaving her alone with a monster all those years ago. I want to beg for her forgiveness, but I have no idea where to start. I want to take this time we have alone together and tell her the truth, tell her I want to be with her, and I don't care what anyone says or thinks.

I know how I feel. What scares me - and I don't scare easily - is that she may not feel the same. She may see me as an extension of the monster that hurt her.

I watch her from my spot at the kitchen table. She is curled up on the couch, a thick fluffy blanket covering her knees as she reads on her Kindle. She frowns, and I know the time has come. Her battery is running low. She won't be able to ignore me forever.

Laying the device on the coffee table beside her, she rises and stomps into the kitchen, not once looking in my direction. The yoga pants she is wearing draw my gaze to her perfect ass and thick thighs, driving me crazy with need.

"Are you hungry?" she asks, opening one cupboard after another.

It takes me a moment to reply. "Sure. But I would really like to talk to you."

"It doesn't matter anymore," she says, not looking at me. "What happened, happened. I've moved on and I don't want to relive it. Why can't you just leave it alone?"

"Because he hurt you!" My anger at the situation makes me snap at her.

"That was a long time ago," she says, turning to face me with tears streaming down her face. "I don't ... I can't relive it."

Moving to her, I cup her face in my hands. Using the pad of my thumb, I swipe away her tears.

"He'll never hurt you or anyone else again," I say with finality.

"You can't say that. You don't know that." She shakes her head, stepping away from me once more.

"I can. He will never touch you again." My voice is emotionless. "He's dead."

"What?" she exclaims. "Who killed him? Is there a problem with the family? Are other families coming here? Do I need to be worried?"

"No," I say, leaning my hip against the counter. "I killed him. After he told me what he did. I'm the head of the DeLuca Family now."

"Why would you do that? You hate the family business."

"Because he hurt you."

It's as simple as that. I'm trained as a killer courtesy of Uncle Sam. Not to mention the training I was put through in my formative years. He hurt someone I love, and I took his life. There were no second thoughts on my behalf. Silence descends on us, each working through everything we just said.

"How long do you think the storm will last?" she asks, changing the subject while removing a pot and some canned soup.

"No way to tell. Could be a couple of hours, could be days," I reply cautiously. "Enough time for us to talk."

Her gaze clashes with mine, a hint of fear in the depths before she turns her back on me to continue with the food.

"As soon as it calms a bit, I'll go out to my truck and get

the extra supplies I brought and take a look at the generator."
I try to assuage some of her fears. "It will be okay."

She spins to glare at me.

"How the hell will any of this be okay?" she sneers. "I'm trapped in a cabin, in a snowstorm, with the last person on earth I want to spend time with! You just admitted to killing a man, your own father, for fuck's sake. You shouldn't have come here."

She slams a bowl of lukewarm soup in front of me before walking away, leaving her own food. I hear the door to the only bedroom slam shut.

How the hell did that go so bad?

I WAITED over an hour for her to come out of the room, but she didn't. I won't force her to be around me. Her words from earlier make it clear how she feels about me. The fact that I confessed to murder surely doesn't make her feel safe with me.

It hurts to know that she doesn't feel the same way I do, but it doesn't do anything to diminish my feelings. I will always love Echo. And that means that I will always do what is best for her. Even if that means letting her go. Even when it hurts worse than any other pain I've felt in my entire life.

Grabbing my bag from beside the door, I head to the bathroom for a shower. I need to clear my head, and I hope that there is still some warm water left with the power outage.

I listen for sounds of movement from the bedroom but hear nothing. I light a candle I found in the kitchen to illuminate the small bathroom. Inside I find nothing but a shower, basin, and toilet but Echo has tried to make it pretty. Dark red bathmats are on the floor and some plants sit on a shelf.

Opening the water, I allow it to run for a moment while I strip down before hopping under the barely warm water. I wash my hair and body before reverting to my regular habits.

Taking my hard cock in hand, I stroke from root to tip with thoughts of the woman in the room across the hall. The soft grey jersey she is wearing today left an expanse of creamy shoulder exposed to my gaze and her black tights hugged the full shape of her ass and thick thighs perfectly. I've been at half-mast since I walked through the door hours ago.

Stroking myself, I up the tempo until I can feel the tingle in my balls. My orgasm rushes down on me, thoughts of Echo slamming into my mind.

"Echo," I moan as my cum splatters against the tile wall.

My breathing is harsh in the small bathroom, my heart beating violently against my rib cage as I try to regain some semblance of composure before shutting off the water.

My attention is so consumed with thoughts of the woman I love but will never have, that I almost miss the click of the bathroom door shutting. I know I closed that door firmly.

Did my little stepsister just watch me masturbate in the shower?

After the Show

Echo Campbell

I'VE BEEN LYING HERE IN THE DARK FOR OVER AN hour feeling sorry for myself. It isn't really Dante's fault. He has been gone for so long. He knows the truth now and he wants to find out what happened. I can't keep hiding from the past. I should probably just have a simple conversation with him so that we can move on.

But I honestly don't want to relive the damn memory. I wipe away another errant tear before swinging my feet off the bed. I've cried enough. Thomas is gone and will never be able to hurt me again. I don't have to live in fear anymore. Padding across the wooden floor I open the door and walk across the hallway. I need to splash some water on my face before I face Dante once more.

Opening the bathroom door, I realize my mistake.

Fuck.

Even in the low candlelight, Dante is gorgeous beneath the spray of water. Through the glass I can see tan skin and rippling muscles. His taut ass is on show for me to ogle. His head is bowed, one hand placed on the shower wall as the water sluices down his perfect body, washing over the dark ink that swirls on his skin.

Is he...?

No, it can't be.

But I watch his ass muscles flex, the cords in his neck straining as one word falls softly from his lips.

"Echo."

I'm frozen to the spot. Dante DeLuca was just masturbating to thoughts of me. And it was hot as fuck.

Slowly, I back out and close the door, praying that he doesn't realize what I just saw. The door clicks into place and my breath stalls in my lungs, waiting to see if he heard it. When nothing happens, I tiptoe my way down the hall and into the kitchen.

My mind is torn, my hormones rampaging. Minutes ago, I was crying, feeling sorry for myself. And now, I want to run back to the room and find my little purple bullet vibrator. I must be going crazy. It isn't normal for anyone's emotions to go from one to the next in mere moments.

Entering the kitchen, I grab the soup that is now stone cold and restart the gas oven to heat it again. I listen to the man I just watched masturbate in the shower move around the other end of the cabin. By the time Dante makes it to the kitchen, I am leaning against the counter, eating lukewarm tomato soup.

I almost swallow my tongue when I see him. Why in god's name does he have to look like every woman's wet dream? Grey sweatpants that do extraordinarily little to disguise his cock, something I fight very hard not to stare at, a white wife beater that hugs every muscle in his torso, too many tattoos on display, drawing my gaze, his hair wet and disheveled having grown out a bit in the time he has been home.

His steps don't falter as he approaches me. His left hand cups the bowl, taking it from me and placing it on the countertop behind me as he cages me against the firm surface. His body is millimeters away from mine and I am finding it hard to breathe. I can feel the heat of him through the layers of our clothing, my traitorous nipples hardening.

"Did you enjoy the show?" His voice rasps in my ear as he leans down.

Shit. I really hoped he didn't know I was watching. I shake my head.

"I don't know what you're talking about." My voice is a husky whisper as the lie falls from my lips and a blush warms my face. I've never been good at lying.

His right hand grabs my hip, and I swallow the wanton moan that wants to escape me.

"So, if I put my hand down the front of these tights that have been driving me crazy for hours, I won't find your pussy wet for me?"

Oh. My. God. Why the hell is he talking to me this way? And why is it so fucking hot? I shake my head again, afraid to use my voice.

A devilish smirk crosses his handsome features. "I think you're lying, princess."

"Dante."

"I think I should find out," he continues like I didn't just say anything.

I don't do anything to stop him. We are alone in a snowstorm, on the side of a mountain. Away from everyone who knows us. This may be my only chance to have him. Yes, I know that this is a ridiculously stupid idea, but he is all I have ever wanted. I will deal with the heartbreak and the fallout once the storm clears.

"Tell me to stop," he says staring into my eyes. "I'm not him."

I shake my head. I don't want to think about Thomas now. I want to let the man I've craved for years do whatever he wants. Consequences be damned. I'm not traumatized anymore. Years of therapy helped me fix that. Now, I want to forget my past, forget that we were ever related by marriage, and just give into what I've wanted for years.

His calloused hand slips into the band of my tights before cupping my overheated sex.

"No panties. Jesus Christ, woman," he growls against my throat where his head now rests on my shoulder. "So wet."

His thick finger slips through the slickness that has gathered there before spearing me. My head tips back on a moan at the feel of him pressed against me, a single finger fucking in and out of me.

"So fucking sexy." His lips run along the column of my neck, kissing, and nipping.

"We shouldn't be doing this," I say, trying to be the voice of reason in this situation even though I don't want to. My brain is screaming that this is wrong no matter how good it feels.

Dante straightens from me and removes his fingers from between my thighs before sucking them into his mouth, his gaze locked on mine. It is the sexiest, dirtiest thing I have ever seen in my life.

"Tell me why I shouldn't take what I have always wanted?" Dante asks.

His words wrap around me. Could he really feel the way I do? Is that even possible?

"You're my stepbrother," I say weakly. "I'm damaged goods."

"I haven't been for years, as you yourself pointed out the other day. I'm honestly beyond the point of caring either way." He stares at me, looking for something before he continues. "I joined the Marines to give you a chance at a normal life. Away from me. I should have stayed, claimed you, and kept you safe. But the truth is you're the only one I've ever wanted. You're the only woman I have ever loved. I don't care what happened while I was gone, I'm here now."

"Dante..."

He cuts me off, covering my mouth with his hand. "Either tell me you don't want me or let me do what we both want."

CONFESSIONS

DANTE DELUCA

LAYING OUT MY TRUTH FOR HER ISN'T EASY BUT I have to take the chance. If I never tell her how I feel I will always wonder what could have been. It's not like I am going to fuck up a friendship between us because it doesn't exist.

I watch her process my words before she smiles softly behind my palm. I remove my hand so she can speak, praying she'll say the words I want to hear.

"I want you," she whispers. "I've always wanted you."

Instantly, I lift her in my arms and her legs automatically wrap around my hips, cradling my erection against her covered sex. Turning us, I slam her into the nearest wall before fusing my lips to hers. I kiss her with all the bottled-up passion I have in me. With every single ounce of pent-up frustration. Her hands thread through my too-long hair, scratching my scalp.

In the past ten years I haven't been a saint, but I was never able to get her out of my mind. Each woman I have ever tried being with was only a cheap imitation of her.

I press my cock against her mound and swallow the moan she releases, the sound driving me nuts. Pulling away from the wall, I walk us down the hall to the only bedroom.

"Your leg," she murmurs.

"I'm fine. And even if I wasn't, it wouldn't stop me."

Beside the bed, I slowly lower her down the front of my body.

"I have been thinking about this for years," I say lowly as I cup her cheek. "I'll be fucking you over the kitchen counter at one point or another but for this first time, I want you laid out on the bed so I can devour you."

A visible shiver works its way through her body. My hands grab the bottom of her jersey, lifting it over her head to expose her skin to my gaze. The demi cups of her bra barely contain her heaving breasts. I lightly run my index finger along the edge of the lacy cup, watching her nipple distend beautifully beneath the material.

"So sexy," I whisper, pushing her tights down her thighs.

I kneel to help her out of the constrictive garment, my face level with her bare pussy. For a moment I lose my concentration, staring at the puffy pink lips, moisture clinging to the flesh. My tongue darts out of its own volition, sweeping up the desire that is spilling from her.

"Fuck!" she moans above me, swaying slightly.

Reluctantly, I stand, remove my wife-beater, and drop it

to the floor. Her small hands work over the muscles in my chest, touching old scars and tattoos. I see the questions in her stormy gaze but now isn't the time to talk about my past.

Now is for us.

Unclipping her bra, I watch her large breasts fall free, swaying slightly as the material falls to the floor. My cock kicks behind the confines of my sweatpants, precum decorating the crown and wetting the fabric.

I push her back, allowing her to fall on the bed.

"I am going to consume you," I smirk.

Lowering my sweatpants over my hips, my cock springs forth. Wrapping my hand around the length, I stare down at her. Echo spreads her thighs wide, giving me an even better view.

"Actions speak louder than words."

The Only Man I Ever Wanted

Echo Campbell

He looks at me the same way that a predator watches its prey. Like he wants to eat me whole. My breasts are heavy, my skin feverish, my pussy dripping. This is pure torture, watching him stroke his rock-hard cock.

"I need you, Dante," I say.

"You have me. You've always had me," he murmurs.

"Prove it," I challenge.

"I will." He smirks. "But before I fuck you, you'll be begging for it, princess."

Dante drops to his knees, using his shoulders to make space for himself as he pulls my ass to the edge of the bed. There is no preamble as he dives in. His tongue works me from my asshole to my clit, laving every inch of my sex. His lips fuse to me as he sucks and nibbles, pushing my arousal higher and higher but never going where I desperately need him.

Moans fall from my lips as my body writhes beneath his ministrations. Three fingers spear into me, my body bowing off the bed.

"Please."

"Yes baby, let me hear you beg."

"Dante," I growl.

He chuckles darkly, his tongue tracing my clit lightly before he blows on it. My hand finds the back of his head, pressing him against my sex, fed up with his teasing. Dante moans against my sex before sucking harshly on the extended nub while I rub my pussy against his face.

My thighs tremble as my orgasm crashes over me, a scream tearing from my lungs. It's long moments before I can focus again.

Dante is leaning over my body, his weight braced on his forearms as he stares down at me. The crown of his cock is pressing at my entrance. He watches me with a hooded gaze, desire painting his features. Cupping his face, I lean up and kiss him, tasting myself on his lips.

"If you want me to stop, you need to tell me now," Dante says, his voice strained. "I won't force you to do anything you don't want, but I also won't give you up after this, Echo."

"Dante..."

"I'm serious. I've waited what feels like a lifetime and I won't let you go." He's as serious as I have ever seen him. "I'll fuck you deep and hard. And I will be doing it without protection."

My pussy flutters, trying to pull him into my channel and force him to keep his word.

"I'm not on birth control," I say, trying to be logical.

"That's kind of the point, princess," he says with a smirk. "I'll pump you full of cum, breed you, and bind you to me forever."

Fuck. Fuck. Fuck. Why does that sound perfect? Why is that all I want? Why does the though of being filled with his cum make me want to fall to my knees and beg him to do it over and over.

"Please, Dante," I beg, not caring how it sounds.

He bottoms out in me with one fluid stroke, his cock stretching me and filling me. And then he starts to move. At first, his strokes are long and measured, his muscles straining with the effort of holding back.

"So tight. So wet," he mumbles. "Better than I ever dreamed."

"More," I beg, scoring his back with my nails. "Harder."

"Fuck," he groans. "I want this to last."

"I don't care if it lasts. You can fuck me again whenever you want."

He speeds up, his cock spearing deeper into me than before. His thrusts become harsher and less measured, his hand wrapping in my hair and pulling my head back.

"You can bet your ass I will be fucking you whenever I

want. I'm going to flood this cunt with my cum every day until you overflow."

His dirty words only ramp up my arousal. My walls flutter with my impending orgasm. His other hand moves between us, finding my hard clit and rubbing furiously.

"I want to feel you cum on my cock," he groans, biting down on one of my nipples. "I need to feel your pussy milking me dry."

I go off like a firecracker on the Fourth of July. My orgasm consumes me, stealing my breath and my vision, leaving me a gasping mess.

"Echo." His groan is the only thing I hear as his cock kicks inside my channel, and I feel his cum paint me from the inside.

Snowed in

Dante DeLuca

THE STORM CONTINUES TO RAGE OUTSIDE AS ECHO lies sprawled across my chest in the darkness, sleeping peacefully. I can't believe I finally got the girl I always dreamed of, and it's better than I ever imagined. But we didn't discuss what this means. Things were said in the heat of the moment, but I know that doesn't mean she'll let me keep her.

I don't know where we will go from here, and quite frankly, I don't care, as long as I have her by my side. We could stay here in Blackwood Falls or move somewhere else, as long as we are together. Fuck the family. I don't care what it costs to have the woman I have always wanted.

"What are you thinking about?" Her soft voice filters into my thoughts. "I can hear your brain working over the howling wind." She presses a kiss to the skin above my heart.

"The future." I smile.

"And what does that look like?" She sounds nervous.

"Right now? Fucking you on every available surface in this cabin while hoping the storm lasts another week," I say, trying to lighten the mood. A chuckle escapes me at her gasp of mock outrage.

"I could probably live with that," she sasses, and I swat her delectable ass beneath the blanket.

Sitting upright against the headboard, I pull her into my side.

"I'm not sure about the rest," I say. "What I want may be..." My words taper off. I don't want to overwhelm her.

"What?" she asks, looking up at me through her lashes.

"I want it all," I confess. "I want to build a life with you, and I'm terrified if I push too fast, I'll lose you."

I don't look at her as I say all of this. This woman is my life, my future. And if she denies me, I don't know how I will ever recover. Echo moves away from me, and my heart sinks. Maybe I have jumped to the wrong conclusion. I could want more than she is willing to give. Maybe this time in the cabin is all I will ever have with her.

What if this is a one-time thing? A fling in the storm before she returns to her life. I won't be able to see her in town and remember what happened here without losing my mind.

She shocks me by swinging her leg over my lap, straddling me, her pussy flush with my already hardening cock. She takes my face in her hands, forcing me to look at her.

"I love you, Dante DeLuca," she says. Honesty shines

brightly in her stormy grey gaze, a beautiful smile gracing her features. "I don't care if you want to live on the moon. I want to be wherever you are."

"And the family? I'm in charge now, I can't leave it behind this time." I'm testing the waters, but if this isn't what she wants I will give it up in a heartbeat.

"Then I suppose I'll stand by your side," she replies quickly "I never thought of being a mafia wife but I'm sure it can't be that bad."

"Thank fuck." I breathe the words around the knot in my throat as my lips crash down on hers.

"HARDER!" she screams as my hips piston against her ass.

Echo's body is thrown over the back of the couch. I wrap my hand in her hair for leverage and do precisely as she demands, using all my power to thrust into her hot, wet cunt. The sounds around us are obscene, dirty, and perfect.

It's been four days of being snowed in, and I can honestly say that they have been the best days of my life. Christmas has never been something I celebrated, but this has changed my mind. Echo is the best Christmas present I could have ever received, and I will be celebrating her and the holiday every fucking year.

"Come for me, princess," I command, smacking her ass on another punishing stroke.

She goes off like a fucking rocket. Her walls gripping my length and keeping me locked inside her, milking me as my own orgasm sweeps through.

For long moments, neither of us speaks, our panting harsh in the silent cabin.

"Are you sure you want to head back to town now that the storm has passed," I ask, stroking my hand down her spine before stepping away from her. "We could stay here a little longer."

"This is where I came to be when everyone else had somewhere to go," she replies, redressing. "I didn't want to be a burden on anyone or for people to pity me."

"Baby..."

"But now, I have somewhere to go, someone to go to." Her smile is brilliant.

"And you always will."

She smiles beautifully as we redress, grabbing our bags and heading out to my truck. I will drive us home and then send someone to retrieve her car. I don't want to spend a moment away from her.

Driving down the mountain, I know we still need to have a conversation, one that neither of us is looking forward to.

"Babe," I say, drawing her attention to me. We need to talk about some stuff. "I know you don't want to, but there are things I need to know."

I see the happiness drain from her eyes. She stares straight ahead. "Fine."

"I need to know if you want to live at the DeLuca estate."

"What?"

"Whatever happened is in the past, but we are building a future. I don't want you to live in a house that will hurt you. I'll burn it to the fucking ground and build a new one if that's what you need."

"Pull over."

I stare at her for a moment before doing what she wants. There isn't much space on the single lane, but I try to get out of the way in case someone else needs to pass. The moment my truck stops moving, Echo is in my lap, kissing me like she hasn't done it in days.

When she pulls away, she smiles. "Thank you."

"My pleasure," I say confused. "But would you mind explaining what just happened."

"I thought you wanted to know about Thomas," she says softly.

"I don't care about that, babe."

"I know that now. And I love that big old house. Of course, there are a million things I would love to change, but I spent the last years of my mom's life there with her. I met you there."

I watch her closely. "So not too many bad memories."

"Sadness. Loneliness. Yes, there's lots of that but that's because I spent so much time alone," she explains. "There is only one truly bad memory there. And I moved out the next day."

"If you're sure."

"I am."

"Well then, if you get off my lap, I'll drive us home and you can start planning the remodel."

She laughs freely before kissing me once more. It lasts for long moments before she shifts off my lap and I drive us down the mountain. To our home.

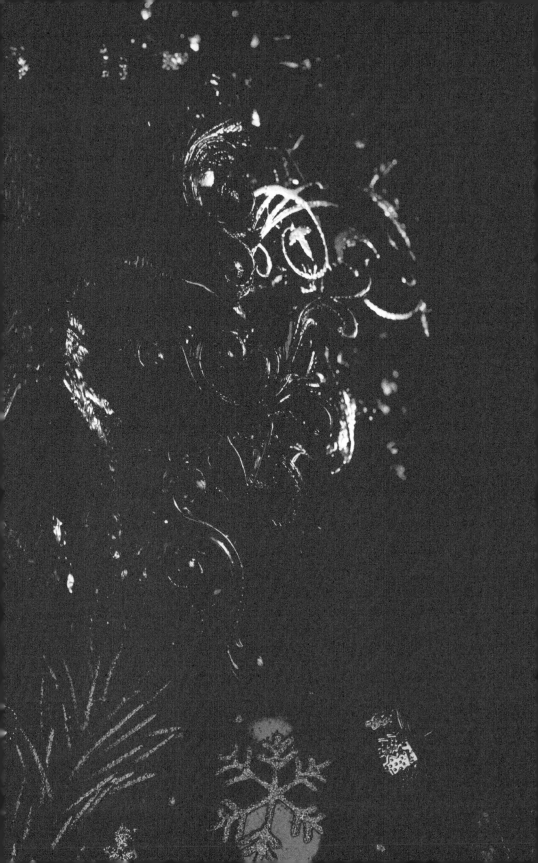

Happily, Ever After

Echo DeLuca

Three Months Later

I dance with Amos while Dante stares at me. He looks like someone stole his favorite toy and I can't help but laugh.

"What is so funny, Mrs. DeLuca?" Amos asks with a grin.

"Your boss is acting like a brat," I say casting a glance in my husband's direction.

"He is," Amos says with a chuckle. "But he has been waiting for years to claim you. And even as a child he didn't like to share."

"You knew?" I ask, shocked.

Amos winks. "I've been a member of this household for as long as I can remember. I've seen many things in my time."

"You never said anything."

"It was his choice to make. But I knew if he ever came

back, he would claim you." Amos says this last part with absolute confidence.

"What if I was already married?"

"Why do you think you've only had a handful of boyfriends in your life?" He smirks, not looking the least bit remorseful.

"You didn't," I gasp.

He says nothing as the last notes of the song play before placing a kiss on my cheek. Spinning me around, he dips me low.

"The head of the DeLuca family will always be my priority."

Bringing me back up, he releases me into Dante's arms. A new song starts, and Dante pulls me close against his body, swaying us along with the slow melody.

"So, tell me wife, what have you been discussing with Amos?"

I giggle. "Dear husband," I place a kiss on his chin. "Your man was simply explaining how he knew our love was inevitable."

"I like the sound of that," he says with a smirk. "Like nothing could ever keep us apart."

"Well, if ten years, thousands of miles, and the worst snowstorm in years couldn't keep us apart, I don't see what can."

He kisses me softly, holding me close as we dance.

"How much longer do we have to stay here?" he asks, and I know what he has in mind.

I look around at our guests. My friends and colleagues are here mingling with some of the most dangerous mafia families in the world. There are a few members of the Arch Fiends MC here as well.

It took a week for Dante to figure out what exactly his father had fucked up. It took a month more to start rebuilding relationships. The most important one being with the local MC. After all, they were the ones that wanted to wipe out anyone and everyone associated with the DeLuca family.

Now, we are on better footing. I am even friends with the president's wife, Amy. We spend time together whenever the men have business and even sometimes when they don't.

"We haven't cut the cake yet," I reply.

"I'd rather eat you."

"Fine," I sigh.

A moment later, he sweeps me off my feet, carrying me out of the ballroom. Everyone in attendance hoots and hollers. He carries me down the long hallway of the local hotel until we are in the elevator. I place kisses down his neck, working to get his baby blue tie loose.

"I need you to behave for two minutes and explain how the fuck I get you out of this dress once we're in the room."

I can't hold back my laughter. I knew when I bought it that he was going to struggle. It is fitted with a corset that laces up in the back. The skirt has a little body to it but not too much. Instead of explaining to him how to divest me of the layers, I nibble at the flesh below his ear, knowing it will drive him crazy.

"Woman," he growls, striding from the elevator to our suite.

I don't know how, but he inserts the key, kicks the door open, and strides inside without missing a beat. I find my back pressed against the closed door as Dante presses his lips against mine, kissing me until my toes curl in my heels.

"I want you out of this fucking thing," he demands. "I swear to god I am going to cut this off you with my knife."

A shiver works its way through me at the thought. "Do it."

He stares at me. "Are you sure?"

"Just cut the ribbons on my back and the dress will fall off," I explain.

Dante puts me down on my feet before turning me to face the door. I listen to him move around and I know he is retrieving his favorite blade from beneath his jacket. I press my hands against the door hoping to give him better access.

"Stay still."

I hear the ribbon give way under the sharp blade before the dress pulls away from my frame, slides down my body, and pools on the ground around my feet.

"Fuck," Dante hisses behind me. His knife lands on the floor with a thud before his hands caress my ass. "If I knew you weren't wearing any underwear you never would have made it to the reception."

I moan low as his fingers work through my folds, spreading my arousal everywhere.

"Keep your hands against the door," he murmurs in my ear. I listen as he lowers the zipper on his pants. "I'm going to fuck you against the door in nothing but those sexy-ass heels."

"Yes," I moan as he notches the head of his cock to my entrance.

Slowly, torturously, he slides his erection into me. His pace is measured, and I know that he is trying to make this last, but I don't want slow and soft. Not right now.

"Is this what sex is going to be like now that we're married?" I ask, pushing his buttons.

"Excuse me?" His voice is low and gravelly.

"I thought you wanted to fuck your wife."

"Fucking brat."

He lands a blow to my right ass cheek before upping his tempo. He pounds into me, holding my hips tightly. It only takes a few minutes until we are both tumbling headlong into our orgasms and landing in a tangled heap together on the floor.

"I love you, Mrs. DeLuca," Dante murmurs against the crown of my head.

"And I love you, Mr. DeLuca."

EPILOGUE
ECHO DELUCA

One Year Later

IT'S MY FIRST CHRISTMAS AS A MARRIED WOMAN. As the wife of a mafia Don.

Instead of putting up a Christmas tree in the house we live in, I packed my bags and left my husband a note on the fridge. I won't spend the holiday in the home we have made our own in this last year even though only good memories now reside there.

No. I will be spending it up at my cabin. Our cabin. It's where our lives started together, and I find it appropriate to start the next phase there as well.

The drive is easy. Surprisingly, only a little snow has fallen for this time of the year. My excitement is overwhelming as I unpack the groceries I bought and bring in the few items of clothing I have packed.

My cell phone rings, and I ignore it. It rings a few more times, and even though I want nothing more than to reassure him - because I know it's him calling - I don't. I leave it to ring and ring while I prepare for what is to come.

It's less than an hour later when the banging starts.

"Echo DeLuca! Open this fucking door!" Dante curses loudly from outside. "I swear I will kick it down."

I hope he doesn't. After all, it's not locked.

It takes him a moment before he realizes that. I hear the door slam open. It takes him a minute or two to check the lounge, kitchen, and bathroom before he finally finds me.

"Christ." He wipes his hand across his mouth, staring at me with crazy, lust-filled eyes.

The room is illuminated by all the candles I have placed and lit throughout. I am waiting for him in the center of our bed in a set of blood-red lingerie I ordered off the Victoria's Secret website.

"I want to be mad," he says, stepping into the room. "You damn near gave me a heart attack. But seeing my Christmas present waiting for me like this has drained most of my anger."

"Do you like the wrapping I chose?" I ask coyly, spreading my legs to give him a better view of the crotchless panties.

"You always pick out the best presents. And the wrapping is stunning," he says with a cheesy grin.

He discards his sweater and shirt on the floor as he stalks toward me, hunger burning in his gaze.

"It's not Christmas yet," I admonish when he reaches for my bra strap. "You have to wait for your present."

"Fuck no."

"Dante."

"No," he rasps, pressing my thighs further apart. "After having thought my wife, the love of my life, had decided to leave me. I deserve to open my present now."

Cupping his face, I gently kiss his lips. "I would never leave you, Dante."

He stares at me, searching for any lies in my words, but he can't find any. I love my husband and the life we have built together.

"You're also not allowed to run away from me," he grumbles, undoing his jeans and freeing his erection. Notching the crown at my entrance, he nips at my bottom lip before thrusting into me. "Even if it is to surprise me with the best Christmas present ever."

He strokes into me, long and sure, until we both reach our pinnacle, following one after the other into bliss.

After the euphoria has faded, I lie on his chest, listening to his heart beat loudly beneath my ear.

"There's another part to your Christmas present," I say softly.

"I already have everything I want, babe. You don't need to get me shit."

"It's something small. Something you don't have yet." I'm

nervous. I don't fucking know why though. "There's an envelope on the nightstand."

Dante sits upright against the headboard while I turn and sit with my back to the door. He frowns at me because I'm usually curled up against him, but I want to see his face. He grabs the envelope and opens the flap before pulling out the piece of paper inside. He stares at it for long minutes. Several emotions scroll across his features in a blur. Shock, fear, and then happiness.

"Really?" he asks, his voice a broken whisper, choked up by emotion. His gaze bounce from to the sonar photo between his fingers.

I nod, unable to speak, my own emotions clogging my throat. In a split second I am back in my husband's arms, his lips pressed to mine in a passionate kiss.

"Thank you," he murmurs between kisses.

"You did all the work," I say with a giggle.

"I meant," he says holding my face in his hands. "Thank you for giving me a chance. For accepting me, for loving me. And now for giving me a chance to be a father."

"All of those things are easy to do, Dante. We were made for each other."

About Jade Marshall

Born and raised in South Africa, I now live in the Northern Cape in a small mining community by the name of Kathu. At 35 years old I have been with my husband for 16 years, although we have only been married for nine. Together we have a beautiful 16-year-old daughter.

For years I wanted to follow my passion for writing but always doubted myself. After finding my publisher and releasing my first novel I was able to build up my confidence and move forward with my fledgling career.

Stalk Jade Marshall on her socials:
https://linktr.ee/jmarshall.author

A Red Christmas

Alison Mackenzie

(*Warning: Contains Spoilers)
This book contains mature themes and is intended for adult readers. Specific content warnings include, but are not limited to:

ON-PAGE MENTIONS

Choking kink
Murder
Bondage
Attempted suicide
Blood and gore.

OFF-PAGE MENTIONS

Mentions of suicide

STORY WRITTEN IN
US ENGLISH

ONE

ASHLEIGH

NO REMORSE, NO FACIAL EXPRESSION. I FELT nothing and had no regrets.

The trial took longer than what I expected. June Langley, the best lawyer to represent the Mafia families, had prolonged the case due to the lack of evidence,

"We have rescheduled the case of Campbell versus Volkov for the 11th of January". The mallet hit the podium where the judge sat to draw everyone's attention. The cuffs on my wrists rubbed against my fair skin, turning it red from the irritation. The two officers grabbed my arms, pulled me up, and moved me towards the holding cells, passing the Volkovs. I left the room with a faint grin. The hate I had for that family was deep. I couldn't stand their presence.

Every. Single. One of them.

The officers led me to the waiting room. I knew full well

that my father was busy discussing ways to have me at home with the family during the holidays. It of course might be the last Christmas I spend with them. My eyes roamed the dull room, waiting for the verdict. After a while, some old guy accompanied my father with keys in his hands. I couldn't help but grin as my handcuffs were being removed, only to have my ankle strapped with a black device. A tracker. They were clearly putting me under house arrest, so I could spend the holidays with my family. "You have the documents, Mr Campbell. One wrong move and she's back under our own surveillance." The man had such a coarse sound when he spoke, which indicated years of smoking. "Of course, thank you again Sir." My father looked at me with expression of hope. So naïve.

"Ready to go, bunny?." My lack of response made him sigh, and lead me out to the back of the building where he had parked his car. A Hyundai Kona, which had tinted windows and was a dark red. The red reminded me of the blood that covered my hands that night. My father was a gentleman. He opened the car door for me even though he knew his eldest daughter was a criminal psychopath. My eyes never met his as I slid in and grabbed the handle inside the door, slamming it shut. I just want this holiday to be over with. My father followed into the driver's seat, clicked his seatbelt on and started the engine. We drove off, beginning the silent car ride home. My father tried making small talk, mentioning how my mother was going to be so excited to have me for the holidays, while he kept rambling about the rest of my family. He said we were heading to the family lodge to spend Christmas there, surrounded by snow. Soon we arrived at the two-story family home. The patio brimmed with eager faces, to greet me for the first time since my conviction. How could they all be so ignorant?

As I climbed out of the car, I felt someone pull me in for a tight embrace. "Oh, My baby!" My mother's perfume was overwhelmingly sweet. "Okay Marisol, let her breathe." My father interrupted when my mother let me go. Her face had this loving look of a caring mother who has not seen her child in years. "We are so happy to have you home, bunny." My mother pressed a kiss to my forehead and sighed, before making her way inside. My grandmother scolded my siblings, all younger, to head in the house and give me some space. I forced myself to enter the family home. It had this modern-looking, filled with clovers carved into every wall.- the emblem that represents my overly superstitious family. The rooms were filled with the familiar scent of ginger and cedarwood. Walking towards the kitchen, my grandmother stood by the oven, speaking to whatever she was making in there to check if it was right.

My eyes moved around to see my siblings, Jace, Niall, and Bridget, running around. They all had the Campbell ginger hair and green eyes. They look identical, but their personalities make them completely different. My siblings were a set of triplets. I was their only oldest sister, and I have not been home for the past couple of months. In that time, they seemed to have grown. I missed their 14th birthday while sitting in that god-forsaken holding cell.

My father sure took his sweet time getting me out. Luckily, my family's name and influence allowed them to keep me in an isolated cell. Jace stopped to look at me disapprovingly, evidently still upset with my absence. Jace was the oldest of the triplets. Niall came out last and their difference was only 2 minutes and 21 seconds. He was definitely more grown-up than the other two. Bridget is carefree; she is the protected innocent child and the Campbell family favorite.

My father placed a gentle hand on my shoulder and smiled at me. As he opened his mouth to speak, I noticed that his smile never reached his eyes. "I know you've just arrived, bunny," I flinched at his pet name for me, I was never really a fan. "we're about to head up to Luca, you just need to pack some clothes for the weekend. That's no problem is it?". He didn't wait for my response as he turned to walk into the kitchen to speak with my grandmother, who was now taking a hot tray of fresh-baked cookies out of the oven. Luca is the family lodge up in the mountains, and every year the Campbells go there for the holidays. I walked up the staircase and headed to my room, which looked exactly how I left it. The curtains and bedding were changed, but the room was set up just the same as before. I sat down heavily on my bed, finally remembering the discarded phone in my pocket. I fished it out, opening it to the few messages from an unknown number that I have been ignoring–You will get what's coming to you–and placed the phone into the bag I grabbed from under the bed. I rummaged through my closet for some clothes to shove in the bag, along with shoes. I zipped it up and passed the vanity, which had pictures of the family stuck on the mirror. I stood there for a while looking at each one, remembering the real reason I was in this situation.

The ride to the family lodge took under two hours, one hour and forty-five minutes of holiday songs blasting in the car and of watching the black security SUVs driving behind and in front of our two-family cars. When the cars came to a halt, the triplets were the first to hop out of the car in front of the one I was in and run towards the welcoming coziness of the lodge. Once everyone was out of their cars I followed by grabbing my bag and dug in to find my phone. "You coming, Bunny?" My father called from the patio of the lodge. I nodded once in acknowledgement as I walked over, stealing glances at my phone as I did so. Two of my father's security agents followed promptly behind me.

The inside of the family lodge was warm, welcoming and decorated with wreaths, lights, stockings and all the necessities for the holiday. The smell of burning wood mixed with a freshly polished floor made me nauseous. While the family spoke near the fireplace, I headed to the room that was always mine when we came up to the lodge. Each door I passed had a wreath hanging on it, including mine. I sighed, taking it off and placing it on the drawer in my room.

My phone went off a couple of times on my way inside the house. I pressed the button to look at the screen. It was the same number as before, sending the same threats as my siblings used to throw at each other when they were younger and couldn't agree on something, which was almost always. I found it amusing and opened my screen to read the most recent message.

> You cannot run away from your punishment, Lisichka

Very subtle. Very Russian. Very stupid.

I switched my phone off and lay on my bed, looking up at the wooden ceiling with a grim smile on my face. I had no good feelings towards this holiday, and even worse feelings towards my sentencing resuming.

Two

Avgust

Annika's death automatically made me the heir to the Volkov Mafia. My sister was two years older than me. Before the news of her murder had reached me, I was doing some sightseeing in South Africa. Scouting out new businesses and allies for Annika. South Africa was a gold mine–literally–it has so many potentials, just a pity the Chinese Mafia have their grips on its economy and govern-ment. Annika would have loved it. Although she was murdered in cold blood by the Campbell's heir, and her motive is yet to be spoken of.

I hate that family. But hate cannot fully express the depth of my feelings towards them, nor can it describe the anger I've experienced since Annika's death. The weight of my duty grew heavier every day, as the responsibility of carrying my family's name became demanding on my own. This was the only time in my life that I resented solitude.

I could feel my muscles twitch with anger as I looked down at the screen in my hands. If I had less self-control, I would have crushed this phone in my hands, or flung it out of the moving car, or smashed it under the heel of my shoe. My messages were going through, they were read, but no reaction. Not even an attempt to block the number. I grabbed my phone from the charging port in the car and start dialling in for a favor.

"Jax," I answered, "I don't have any time for the 'How are you' and 'How's the family' bullshit." I was in a hurry.

"Damn, Gus, you really cut to the chase, huh? What's up?"

"Ashleigh Campbell, I need her exact location."

"Didn't your father insist you stay out of this for the sake of your family name in the trial?." I rolled my eyes with a grunt of frustration. "As of right now, I am higher than my father in the family's rankings. Get me her location."

"On it, Boss." The line went dead, and the car came to a halt by the warehouse. I got out along with my driver/body-guard, Sascha. His presence was not needed, but it was insisted on by my mother, especially since Ashleigh was not in a cell awaiting the verdict of her actions. I still do not understand why we could not retaliate instead of getting the law involved.

My thoughts were interrupted as we reached the inside of the warehouse. The smell of the harbor covered the lingering scent of blood. I stopped by the table that had my equipment set out neatly; I grabbed my gloves and buckled them in place on my hands as I looked over at the two men, clearly exhausted, who sat bound to the steel poles holding up the roof of the warehouse. Sascha stood by the entrance, another four of my men scattered throughout the area, keeping their distance while I approached these filthy excuses for men with a small switchblade in my left hand. "This is the svolach *(scumbags)* huh?." I glared down at them with a sinister grin. "What did you think was going to happen? Did you believe you could run away? Flee the country and live out the rest of your days with the stock and money you stole from me?" I grabbed one of their dirty faces and took his ear between my gloved fingers. He whimpered, his mouth was gagged with a cloth but I could hear his begging and pleading.

A swift flick of my wrist was all that was necessary to cut his ear away from the flesh it was attached to. It took mere seconds for his blood to soak my hands and his face, spilling to the floor with audible drops. I motioned for my men to untie him. His screaming continued through the muffling of the cloth in his mouth. His friend shook his head, also begging. Once the first one was untied, I grabbed his free hand and shoved his amputated ear into his trembling palm before I turned to his friend.

"I am not done, but I can't help but love the sound of those screams. Beautiful, wouldn't you agree? The sound of a man in pain as the consequence to his own actions." I removed the cloth from his mouth.

"P-please, I can fix this!" He pleaded continuously. "But we both know you cannot." I grinned at his pleading eyes. "I can, I swear! On my life." I clicked my tongue. "Your life..." I paused to watch the expression on his face contort into sobs, "Meaningless. I won't be taking your word on that." My bloodied glove grabbed his face between my fingers, silencing him and his begging. "Who am I?" I asked in a dark tone.

"Avgust Volkov, the head of the Volkov Mafia." He sputtered from the force of my hands around his mouth. "Good. As the head of the Volkov Mafia, I command you and your little friend to death, for theft, and simply for the disrespect you've shown me and the Volkov name." He shook his head frantically as I walked back to the table, replacing the switch blade with a shotgun.

I turned towards the two now untied men, who were on their knees, begging every divine being to save their lives. No god could help them now. Before they could say another word, I pulled the trigger of the shotgun, my bullet tearing through the eye socket of the earless one. His body fell like a domino piece. I turned my focus on the other and aimed at his chest. When I pulled the trigger a second time, my aim was just as impeccable as the first. He too fell like a domino. I approached their bodies and delivered extra shots to their heads. Their blood pooled around me. I gave the shotgun to one of the men, as well as the gloves. "Get rid of the bodies, or display them. I don't care." I said, as I took a cloth from the table and wiped my blood-stained face. I moved back towards the entrance, leaving the men to do what they were told.

Sascha handed me my phone, and I pressed it to my ear. "Talk to me."

"I have sent her coordinates via email, and her father paid off the wardens and judges so that she can be placed with an ankle tracker and kept with her family, obviously for the holidays". I clenched my jaw at the mention of Ian Campbell paying off the law just to have his daughter, a cold-blooded murderer, home for the holidays. "Thanks, Jax." I ended the call and got into the backseat of the SUV while Sasha got into the driver's seat.

"Sir?." He looked into the rear-view mirror. My eyes moved to meet his and my fingers swiped on my phone. The destination appeared on the GPS screen, replacing the radio. Sascha nodded, and the car started. My eyes moved across the screen in my hands, and with a finger, I clicked on the attached image. There she stood, emotionless, as she was surrounded by family. Her black hair was tied up, strands surrounding her pale complexion. She wore jeans, a Celtics jersey, and flats. What caught my eye was the device strapped around her left ankle. They actually fucking did it. I scoffed and switched off the screen. Ashleigh was a monster. I will not stop until she is gone.

THREE

ASHLEIGH

THE NOISE OF EXCITEMENT AND CONVERSATIONS filled the living room as I approached it. I saw my parents along with my grandmother discussing something while the triplets were decorating the white Christmas tree in the corner of the room.

"Bunny! Come over here". My father called as he grabbed another mug with his freehand. My grandmother smiled over at me as I joined the little circle they have created. "Your mother is adamant to hit the slopes tomorrow morning". My father shook his head with a grin on his thin lips that were covered by his graying mustache. "Oh please, don't make it look like I was the mastermind behind the idea". My mother laughed before taking a sip of whatever was in those mugs. My father handed me the one he grabbed. "Your mother's eggnog, we always drink it when we get to the lodge, remember Bunny?". He smiled, and so did his eyes. I wrapped my fingers around the hot mug and nodded.

"So, since we agreed together that we will hit the skiing adventure tomorrow morning, I should make some chocolate bombs". My grandmother winked. Her chocolate bombs were hot chocolate powder in a chocolate sphere with marsh-mallows. I remember the first time she made them; the triplets were five years old, and they had the biggest sugar rush to date. I sipped on the eggnog as they continued discussing tomorrow's plans, my eyes familiarized with the cozy atmosphere my family always created during outings or get-togethers. You wouldn't say we were known as the Irish Mafia. The Campbell family have dug their name deep into the roots of this country, yet they were not the only family that did so. There are the Russians, the Italians, and the Americans, all of which have their own territories. Most disagreements land upon routes to traffic illegal drugs, weapons, and so on–or the occasional business betrayals.

Funny enough, the Irish got along more with the Italians rather than the Americans. Mainly because of the strong bond between my father and the head of the Italian family. The Russians were brutes, and the Americans knew their place.

It was a long evening of settling in and trying to avoid conversations with my family. They say they love me, yet I can feel their judgment sizzling off their pale skins. My father saw me as this fragile porcelain doll that needed protection and that really irked me. Hell. I shot the rival family's heir in cold blood. Where does that scream 'Must protect at all costs?'.

The triplets had scattered to their rooms for the night, and so did my grandmother. This left me with my parents.

The silence between us could be sliced with a Swiss knife.

"Ashleigh-". My mother broke the quiet atmosphere, which made my eyes move towards her. "Honey, can we forget about what happened and what's awaiting? Can we just spend Christmas as a family?" I could feel my father's eyes on me as well, while my attention was focused on my mother. "We will try our best to help you, but-" She took a sigh, a pause. "This may be the last time we spend Christmas as a family, together." My mother spoke with a pleading voice. Her eyes were soft as she spoke of how this may be our last Christmas together.

"You speak as if I will be gone forever, but you forget we are part of the Mafia organizations. The Irish mafia to be exact, and we have control. The trial is just for show." I spoke for the first time since the court. It's true, I do not understand why this family thinks and continues as if they will never see me again. We have the power over this government like the other families. My father cleared his throat. "What we mean is, we just want you to interact and feel safe surrounded by your family." I scoffed at the mention of safety and family.

"Want me to pretend? Fine. I will." As I stood up from where I sat. "Ashleigh, please." My mother pleaded in which I looked down at her from where I stood and she sat there with her green doe eyes looking up at me. If anything, really this is her fault, the murder was her fault, the accusations all started with her. Her choices were going to ruin this family. I narrowed my eyes at her and before I could say anything, my father stood up and cleared his throat. "Very well, we can accept that". I looked over at him and he responded with a faint grin.

"Goodnight". I managed to get out before moving down the hallway towards my room at the end. I shut my door behind me as I stepped into my room. My unruly black hair was loose from the tie I had placed it into earlier. I moved to my vanity and brushed out my hair before tying up again. A quick change of my clothes into my pajama pants and a knitted jersey. I sat on my bed for a good minute thinking about everything that can go wrong tomorrow, especially with this thing on my ankle. I leaned over to switch off the bed lamp and climbed under the covers, seeing the blinking green light of the tracker slide deep under the covers.

Tomorrow was definitely going to be an interesting day out with the Campbells.

NEXT DAY

IT DIDN'T TAKE everyone long before we made our way to the Ski Adventure Park. Everyone was dressed warmly. My skiing pants were as white as the snow, but it had green accents. A matching jacket sat on my shoulders, zipped to the top. My beanie that my grandmother had knitted for me covered my ears and my goggles sat on top of the beanie. I rode alongside my parents and in the other SUV, my grandmother and the triplets followed close behind. The car ride was yet again a silent one where at a point my father switched on the radio.

"We urge residents to keep warm and safe as we announce a few tremors were felt in neighboring towns and cities. Proceed with caution and avoid the snow-' My mother clicked her tongue and switched to the next station. "Can never trust the weather warnings anymore". I shook my head and watched as we approached the Park. It looked like a winter wonderland. The car stopped and not long after, so did the SUV behind us. The triplets were yet again the first ones out and ran to go check in and take to the slopes. I couldn't help but smile as their red hair contrasted amongst the white snow and their excitement that radiated off them. My grandmother was not going to take part due to her hip replacement. She would sit inside and read the latest gossip by the fireplace in the reception. My parents got out and so did I. We too followed the triplets to the reception.

The process took less than ten minutes before we got our boards and made our way to the lifts. My mother walked alongside the triplets while my father accompanied me along the short journey to the lifts. My mother and Niall took the first one, Jace and Bridget grabbed the next one, and my father and I grabbed the next. I kept observing my surroundings since we came here. My tracker is hidden under the wide legs of the skiing gear I wore, thankfully.

We hopped off the lift, joining the rest of the Campbells. My father spoke to my siblings about the rules and safety while skiing. My mother stood not far behind him, leaving me on one side, looking at the rest of the people enjoying themselves. My father demonstrated to the triplets how to dodge objects and people, and how to slow down and speed up. I watched Jace go ahead first, and he was off with a laughter that could be heard through his mask. Bridget was next. She was eager to catch up to Jace and lastly Niall joined but almost slipped as he took off. My father insisted my mother go ahead. She loved skiing and could have been a professional if she was not involved in the life of criminals.

"You need to follow right behind me, Bunny. Otherwise, after a couple of miles, that thing will go full blast and declare your presence". My father nodded towards me and slid on his goggles. I gave him a thumbs up as he took off. I watched him for a few seconds before moving closer to the edge.

Darkness covered my eyes, and a hand covered my mouth from behind as I was pulled backwards into the snow-covered woods. I did not fight and waited till we stopped. My eyesight was restored, but the hand still covered my mouth. I recognize the brooding male in front of me.

I bit down on the hand, causing the person to pull away. "You bitch!". They kept their hold on my arms behind my back and the brooding male looked down at me. He had to be around six foot two inches, towering over my frame. I grinned menacingly. "Nice to see you, Volkov". He grabbed my face between his hands, squishing my cheeks. "I will kill you". As the words left his lips, the ground started shaking a bit. He looked down and around, seeing people move quickly with panic.

"Uh... sir, we need to take cover". His sidekick, with a deepened voice covered by the scent of cigarettes, spoke in a worried manner. "Bullsh-". I swallowed back my words as a siren went off. Not just any siren. A siren that warned only when an avalanche was taking place. "Fuck". Volkov spat out as we saw the snow and boulders coming down and closer. "Sir! This way!". His sidekick grabbed me as he moved deeper into the woods.

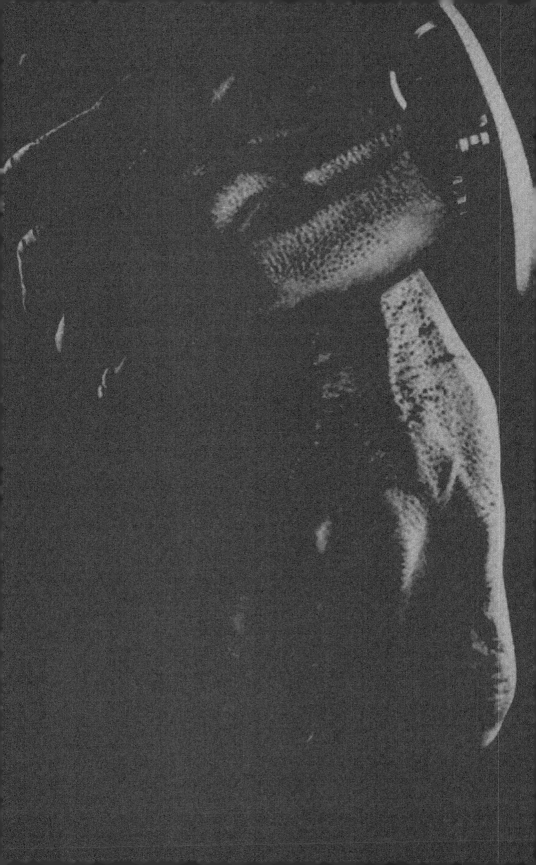

FOUR
AVGUST

FUCK. FUCK. FUCK.

I followed Sascha into the woods and running was difficult when you were surrounded by snow. Sascha had thrown Ashleigh over his shoulders. She was silent, and very rightly so. We moved as fast as we could. The ground under us shook as the avalanche approached quickly.

"Sir, here". Sascha beelines for an open cottage situated not far from the ice rink set up, which was a good 3 miles away from the main reception. The cottage was left open. Obviously, its occupants heard the siren and left without a second thought. The snow was fast on our strides. Sascha threw Ashleigh inside and waited for me to catch up. He had his arm outstretched. My pace was just enough as the snow caught up to us. I grabbed his arm, and he got me in, but before I could turn around to thank him, the door was shut and the snow hit the cottage. It became dark as all the windows were covered by the heavy snow. We were stuck. Sascha knew there would not be enough time, and he sacrificed himself to make sure I was safe. I peeked through the curtains and saw the snow was up to the roof. Great.

I looked around, my eyes adjusting to the change of light to dark. I heard utensils clattering as something fell. "Campbell". I called out. No response. I took a few steps towards where the noise came from. The dark added to the mystery of sudden jump scares, which would only be provided by Ashleigh herself. My steps stopped right by an island counter it seemed as I placed my hand on the edge, grabbing it. "Campbell". I called out again. Silence. This fucking woman.

As I turned around to search through the dark, she popped from behind the counter and jumped over it, holding a knife. "Are you fucking insane? Bloody su-ka *(bitch)*". I reached forward to grab her, but she quickly moved backwards. The light of her tracker was the only light we had. "Ashleigh, put the fucking knife down". I had my hands up to show her I meant no harm... yet.

She stood in silence for a few seconds before she launched herself at me with the knife. It took me a while to register before she had me down on the ground and I wrestled with her hands, which were clearly trying to lodge a knife into my eye sockets. We both grunted. I struggled. Struggled? Against someone so small? Fuck my life. "Give. Me. The. Knife". I managed to get out with the grunting in between. I barely had the knife away from my face until she pulled back, causing the knife to slash at my cheek and fall to my side. I did not react to the blood dripping down as I tried grabbing the knife, but she grabbed it first. I was quick to move as I rolled away when she attempted to impale me through the skull. She hit the hardwood floor under the furry mat. With that, I got up and looked around for some way to protect myself from this psychotic bitch. I saw her get up after swearing under her breath, and she grabbed the floor lamp next to the cabinet in front of her. I was quick to run into the closest room and close the door shut. I fumbled, looking for the latch to lock it. The door started banging, which was clear that Ashleigh was hitting it with that lamp she grabbed earlier. Once the door was secured, I moved away from it and slid down the wall to sit on the floor. I leaned my head against the wall, closing my eyes. The banging continued for what seemed like forever. This crazy girl had too much energy for her own good. She was quiet, except for that constant beeping of her tracker. It was faint, but it was still there, as if warning her what was already going to happen... if they can even reach us or if we survive. Her tracker's beeping became the only thing that filled the dark, cold, and quiet cottage.

Time was not overtly important right now. It was a risk, because I knew that Ashleigh's tracker had probably already alerted authorities of her whereabouts. With her parents nowhere to be accounted for, that possibility doubled. Somehow, our saving grace was that everyone at the ski lodge was either trapped or dead, which bought us time to escape when the opportunity presented itself. Eventually I remembered my phone and felt around my pockets until I found it. Clicking on the screen, I saw that it was already 6:08 pm, which meant that we'd been here for about four hours already. My battery life sat on a solid 62%, sufficient to get me through the night but useless without cell signal. I hated the mountains.

I turned my flashlight on, silently wishing I had thought about this when Ashleigh decided to attack and aimed it around the room. By the sparse furnishings and piles of blankets on the double bed, I figured that I was locked in one of the bedrooms while she had the rest of the cabin to herself. I hoped that I'd be able to find a key that would surely unlock the door, but with my luck today I guessed that she had the only key belonging to this room. I looked around, hoping to find anything of use before getting out and risking my life once again to a fucking death midget. I found a couple of women's bobby pins, probably left by the original residents. As I kneeled to work, as quietly as possible, I thought about how easily it was for me to overpower grown men, some twice my size, but not her, and the insanity of it ate away at my ego. I was supposed to kill her, and yet I was the one bleeding. I managed to loosen the lock just enough that it was almost silent as it clicked open. Still, I held my breath, listening to the other side of the door. I couldn't hear any movement besides the beeping of the ankle monitor, close enough to the door to suggest that she hadn't moved. Maybe she was asleep. I took one deep breath, for courage – because I obviously needed it with her, before turning the doorknob all the way and pulling it open. I scanned the room with the flashlight from my phone and found her staring up at me from the floor, exactly where I thought she'd be. Her eyes were ferocious, like a tiger's, always on the attack, always ready to spring – but she seemed tired, forlorn. I held my hands up in surrender as I bent down next to her.

I shouldn't be trying to placate her, I know. I have an opportunity, not the one I wanted, but I was staring at the object of my revenge thinking about every way I could make her pay for Annika's death and not acting on any of them. Instead, I was showing her I wouldn't hurt her and trying to reason with her. Something about seeing her face-to-face tampered with my ability to think clearly, and I was determined to find out what. For now, though, I simply said,

"We are stuck together for who knows how long. Could we perhaps try not to kill each other until we get out?" I handed her a blanket I found.

"That's a guest bedroom and I am pretty sure the door at the end is the main bedroom." I looked at her, trying to find some sort of acknowledgement.

"So, we stay civilized until we are out of this snow globe?" she asked, raising her brow at me, tilting her head and ignoring my suggestions about the bedrooms. "It's after six in the evening. They are most probably looking for survivors. This cottage's windows are jammed, but the roof is sticking out a bit, which means they will dig to find us". I assured in a civil manner, choosing not to comment on the little side remark she made.

"It could take a day or two, and I am sure there is food, so you can either sit around and decide whether to slit your wrists or you can help me prepare whatever this place has so we can get to bed and out of each other's hair."

That earned me an eye roll, and I did not have time to argue with someone with the maturity of a 14-year-old. I sighed at her before getting up to look for a kitchen. When I found it, I rummaged through the cupboards and drawers, found candles and a match box. I grabbed a few candles and set them in glasses that hung under the cupboards before moving them to where I needed light. I lit each one, before blowing out the match. As I turned back to the cupboards, I heard a shuffle and the beeping of the tracker. I looked over and saw Ashleigh, arms crossed as she leaned against the counter. I returned my focus to what I managed to find. There were cornflakes and milk, and that's what we'll be living on until we are out of here. Everything else needed electricity to either be opened or cooked. Ashleigh found two bowls and spoons while I was lost in thought over the fact we will be living off cereal in the cold.

I poured some into the bowls on the counter and added the milk before grabbing a bowl and spoon and moving to the side. The crunching of the cornflakes in our mouths and that bloody tracker beeping filled the room while we stood there in silence. It did not take long before the bowls were deserted, and we went our separate ways. The beeping made me aware of exactly where she was.

There was no use changing clothes with the cold. I took some of the candles to the guest bedroom. After that, I took a seat on the edge of the bed, closing my eyes, praying for some miracle, not that I have been a saint to deserve one. What bothered me is the lingering question that plays through my mind ever since I got that phone call about Annika's murder. My hands squeezed the sheets of the bed, clenched so hard my knuckles turned white. Annika's murder... Ashleigh being the killer - and me being stuck with her for fuck knows how long.

I didn't trust either of us to not try and kill the other in our sleep. I opened my eyes and grabbed my phone to check the time. It was only 7:04pm. I set the phone on the table next to the bed. Just as I laid down, I heard the soft beeping of Ashleigh's tracker approach. I looked over at the door and saw her stop in her tracks, staring at me. I cleared my throat.

"We need to talk."

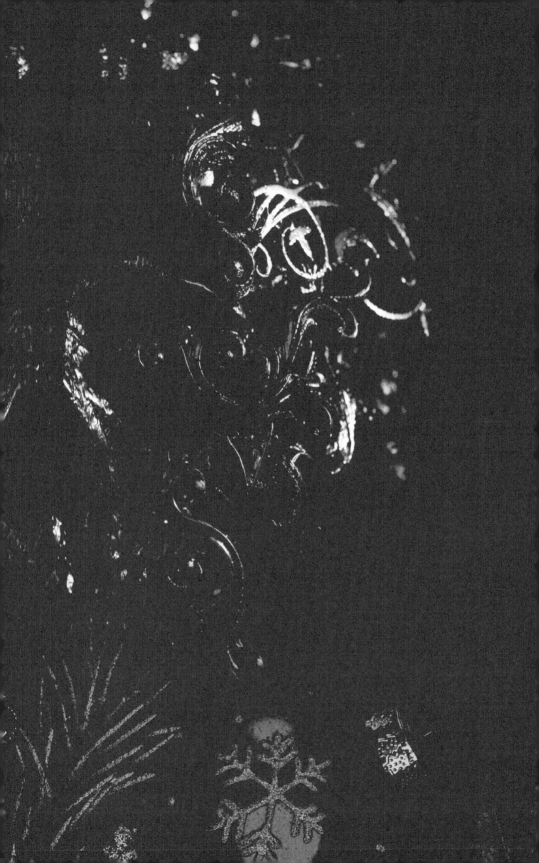

FIVE

ASHLEIGH

"WE NEED TO TALK."

"I was going to kill you, the same way you killed my sister." He started; the way the candlelight lit the room made him look dark, evil. The grim reaper in the shadows, waiting to lead me to the underworld. I tilted my head slightly. "What's stopping you?" I asked. He gave me a deadpanned look of 'you got to be fucking kidding me' which I was familiar with because I always used that same face with people who clearly were not on the same level of intelligence as I was.

"I'm tired, and I don't really have the patience to humor your silly little questions at the moment, not after the stunt you pulled earlier." I grinned at him.

"It's instinct. You tried kidnapping me - my adrenaline was high, and plus, I would have done you a favor. Girls love the whole pirate look, you know... the eye patch." I couldn't help but smirk at my own words. "Especially with your height. Just grow a beard; or try to because no one likes a baby face." He sighed in frustration. "Can you be serious for once?"

"Can you shut up and leave me alone forever?" He got up from where he sat and I watched his body react to me, saw his muscles tighten and the veins stick out from his neck. My question was more on the rhetorical side since I knew the answer. "Why did you do it?" The hint of his Russian accent was thick when he spoke now. He was tall, yes, and built well, and had tattoos and those piercing blue eyes, and those...

"Ashleigh". He cut my thoughts before they could get anywhere we did not need them to be. "Tell me why you put a bullet between my sister's eyes without remorse or thinking of consequences." I went silent. I had my reasons, and I didn't think it was wise to share them with a Volkov. I could see his impatience stretch into his hands, where they were now balled up into fists. "Answer me."

"Your father and my mother had a thing in the late 90s. I confronted my mother and, of course, she denied everything, but I saw evidence, evidence in which Annika was going to use to split the ties between our two families. I spoke to my father about what needed to happen and suggested that we get rid of the problem. Your sister was the problem." His gaze darkened. He was out of his bed and over to me in a flash, and before I could blink, I felt his hand around my neck, forcing my eyes up to meet his as he squeezed – not hard enough to inflict pain, not yet, but hard enough that I felt a tremor of fear move through my body. I continued. "It's more complicated than you think. I don't regret it because she was selfish. The two families have been cooperating for years and she wanted to ruin it with something that should stay in the past." His grip around my neck tightened.

I licked my lips; my breathing came in short, quick bursts. His hold on my throat and the pure fury in his stormy blue eyes should make me want to cower, run for the hills, spend the rest of my life in hiding instead of just making me slightly, so subtly afraid. It didn't. His face was so close to mine I could smell the fragrant sweetness of his mouth, see the stubble where it was forming on his sharp cheekbones. If I reached up on my toes, we'd be close enough to kiss...

And so, without another word, I launched my knee into his groin, causing him to let me go. I shoved him back, making him fall onto the bed. "Ye-bat!*(Fuck)* What is wrong with you, you crazy bitch?" He groaned in anger and pain.

"You should know, choking me gets me aroused." I stalked towards him, my slow, measured steps the only sound as they echoed off the wood floors. He didn't speak as I reached for his face, yanking on his ear so I could lick the dried blood from the gash I gave him. He winced and fisted his hands in my hair, forcing me to look at him. I opened my mouth to speak, but he cut me off, capturing my open mouth with his lips.

We collided, fighting for dominance in a tangle of tongues and teeth. He lifted me up, sliding his hands under my ass so that my legs wrapped around his waist. I bit down on his lip, causing the sweetest whimper to escape his lips. I swallowed the sound as my tongue moved against his. He pinned me against the wall, his hands gripping and squeezing my ass. My fingers ran through his thick locks of hair as sucked the blood from his bleeding lip. He pulled away, catching his breath while I watched the blood drip from between his swollen lips. I couldn't help but laugh.

"You're fucking crazy". He said in between breaths. "Shut up and either fuck me or put me down so I can go back and ride my fingers to finish off the job that you couldn't do." In one swift motion, he took me from the wall to the bed. His fingers worked fast to undo his belt. He slid the leather away from his pants and used it to bind my hands above my head.

I narrowed my eyes at him as he tied my hands together. "This isn't what I had in mind." I said, breathless. He let out a grunt of frustration and hand his mouth on mine again. "You need to shut the fuck up, Lisichka".

We parted only for him to remove my shirt and jeans, leaving me in my underwear. He stood there in silence, chest heaving as he licked his lips before grabbing my thighs and opening them wide. I needed relief right now, and it did not help that my hands were tied. "Needy?" He smirked as he knelt in front of my aching core. His hands still firmly gripped my thighs, keeping them apart. I could feel his breath against my heat. He gripped my panties in between his teeth and pulled them aside, exposing me for his amusement and plea-sure. I shivered as the cold nipped at me, teasing my folds. He replaced the iciness with the heat of his mouth. His tongue traced my bud in circles. I gasped at the contact, the feeling of his tongue trailing up and down in a rhythmic pattern making my core to pulse. "Oh, fuck yes!" My breathing matched his tongue as he ate me out in the candlelit room. He squeezed my thighs tentatively and removed one hand insert a finger into my soaked pussy. My moans were soft but needy as he slowly played with me. His fingers were slower than that gold medal-worthy tongue of his.

"If I could document this moment I would, you're putty in my hands, Lisichka". His voice was commanding and *oh,* so sexy. "You like it, huh? Want me to add another finger?"

I nodded my head, my walls clenched, needing more. "What was that? I didn't hear you?"

"Yes! Fuck!" He chuckled darkly. "So much profanity from that mouth of yours." He said as he added another finger and my eyes rolled back. His movement increased as he fucked me with his fingers. My back arched and I pushed myself into his fingers. As I was reaching my first orgasm in months, he stopped and removed his fingers, which had me growling like a wild animal. "What the fuck? What the fuck!" I struggled to catch my breath.

"Relax, you think it will be that easy?" My core ached for some relief as I stared at him darkly. He licked off my juices from his fingers as his free hand removed his pants and freed his pulsating length. "You are not the only one, Lisichka." He flipped me over to lift my ass in the air. My breasts fell out of the bra I was still wearing.

He positioned himself near my wet heat and gave my ass a

squeeze with both his hands. "Is this going to take long, becau-"

Before I could finish my question, he thrusted into me, causing my words to slur into a moan. "Fuck." We both said in unison. His hold on my ass was blissfully painful as he started his thrusts in and out. Our bodies clashed loudly each time, almost drowning out the sound of my moans. "Your pussy feels way too good." He gave my ass a spank as he picked up his pace, breathing at the same pace as me. My breasts swung with each movement, forward and backward. "Yes! Yes! Right- oh!" I pushed my ass towards him each time he thrusted forward, and my walls clenched around him.

"Gahh. Fuck!" I could feel him swell inside me while my orgasm began to peak. He grabbed my hair from behind and pulled. My moans became incoherent as his thrusted harder, faster.

My orgasm hit and I screamed out, legs shaking. He pulled harder on my hair, and I felt him explode inside me swearing, his own orgasm taking over. With my ass in the air and his dick inside me, I moved with him with each thrust that slowed. We stayed like this for a few seconds, his length throbbing inside me while we recovered. He pulled out and undid the belt around my hands. I turned to face him and his still hardened cock. He grabbed it in his hands and started stroking it gently. My core started pulsing again. I reached over and stopped his hand. I replaced his hand with my mouth. His cock filled my mouth, causing me to gag. He groaned, grabbing a fistful of my hair as I started sucking him off.

"Ashleigh, fuck you're amazing." He said in between his moans as I worked him, moving his cock in and out of my mouth. I hummed against his length, which made him twitch in my mouth as he shot his cum down my throat. I swallowed all of him. He removed himself from my mouth, letting some of his cum drip onto my lips and thighs. I looked up at him as he grabbed my chin. "You're mine now". He gently stroked me with his thumb, tracing my lip, wiping his leftovers from my lips. "All mine."

I said nothing, still coming down from my high.

Six

Avgust

I woke up to the sound of my phone vibrating. Groggily, I found that it was an alarm I always had set for 5:00 in the morning. I silenced it and lay back down. I looked to my side, seeing Ashleigh balled up, facing away from me. We had gone another three rounds before we both passed out. That mouth worked wonders, and the feeling of being inside of her already had me painfully hard. I sighed at myself. Yes, I fucked my sister's murderer not once and not twice, but four times, and I claimed her as my own every fucking time. It was a miracle Annika's ghost hadn't strangled me in my sleep yet, but it was still early to be thankful. It was the 21st of December, and officially 4 months since my sister's murder. Something about Ashleigh was intoxicating - and not just her magical pussy and her wonderous mouth. That attitude, her fearlessness. It was all intoxicating to me.

She moved around in her sleep; she faced me now and her face was so relaxed. Is this how all criminals sleep? Peacefully? I have never seen anyone who understood our family matters and killed the way we did, sleep. The women I have been with were no murderers, or thieves, maybe prostitutes, yes, but not criminally insane like us. I should choke her right now for sleeping so soundly while my sister spends eons in the dirt. What was stopping me? No fucking clue.

LATER

MY EYES SHOT open as I heard glass breaking and a chorus of cusses followed. I noticed the bed was empty next to me and knew immediately that Ashleigh was behind the noise. I ran a hand over my face and sat up, looking over at my phone, double tapping to activate the screen. It was 10:07am. I stood up and groggily slipped on my pants and shirt before going to where the noise came from.

"Take another step, and you will spend the rest of our stay picking glass out of your foot." She warned. It was still dark because of the snow surrounding the cottage. The dim light from the candles shone against the pieces of glass. "What did you do?" I could almost feel her roll her eyes. "I am fine, thanks." I heard her gather some of the glass. "I tried breaking open the window. It's fucking unbreakable by the way." She huffed, scooping up the broken pieces. "I got annoyed and frustrated and threw things at said window. Now the floor is decorated with plates, wine glasses, mugs, the lot." I closed my eyes, shaking my head. "What are you picking up the glass with?" She didn't answer me.

"You know what, enjoy. I'm going to find a way to find a signal for my phone before the battery runs out." I shrugged at her and returned to the room to gather my phone and put on my shoes to avoid any lost glass pieces stabbing my feet. I moved along the small corridor with my phone held up, trying to pick up some sort of signal which was no use. Service was still unreachable. The roof wasn't covered in snow when we got hit, so I needed to find a way up onto the roof.

I heard more profanity from the main room and kitchen, which I ignored and investigated for some way up to the roof. All the windows that I could see were still covered with snow. I walked up and down, checking for some sort of exit, until I looked up in the small hallway and saw a thatch door. An attic. There had to be some windows in there too. I grinned to myself and then thought of how I was going to get up there. I rubbed a hand over my face and sighed.

The constant beeping of Ashleigh's ankle monitor blended into the atmosphere now and was barely audible unless I was listening for it. She stood in the hallway and tilted her head up to look at the space in the ceiling where the thatch was. "What are you staring at?" I looked down at her. Her head stopped just above my shoulder, so she wasn't that small. "That's the opening to the attic."

"And how do we get up there?" I noticed the small cuts on her hand from gathering and picking up the broken glass with her bare hands. I kept quiet, trying to debate on the suggestion I wanted to make, which only got her impatient. "Fine, don't tell me, asshole." She turned on her heel to leave, and I pulled her back by her shoulder. "I am going to hoist you up, then you are going to take my phone and try to find some signal, but we need to work together." She looked at me with no expression. Honestly, I didn't know if she was listening, or she was staring into space. I noticed she could be easily distracted. "So, you trust me?"

"No."

"Then why give me your phone?"

"Do you want to get out of here?"

She rolled her eyes. "Fine, manhandle me and I look for a signal, then what?" I looked up at the thatch again. "Then you will look for a window or something, since the roof is not under the snow, I think. If you find anything, you will dial 911."

"Nah." I looked back at her incredulously.

"Now is not the time to get cocky and crazy, Lisichka. You want to get out here as much as I do, you can dial, and I'll talk." She looked at me with her narrowed green eyes. "And how will you get up?" I shrugged. "Spiderman style."

She scoffed. "Clearly a child." I took my phone from my pocket and looked back at her. "I am a year older than you. If anything, you are the child, now zip those plumpy lips and let's do this...just don't drop me. Actually-" She wanted to change her mind and plead to be dropped on her head, but I placed my phone in her bra and before she could react, I grabbed her by her waist and hoisted her. "Warn a girl." She muttered under her breath and pushed the thatch aside, coughing at the dust that fell from the movement. She grabbed my phone and woke the screen. "Password?" I sighed in annoyance, forgetting about that. "Give it to me."

"No, password."

"Ashleigh, I am not playing, hand it over and I'll put it in." I could see her attempt to crack the code herself. "Password. You can always change it." I bit down on my tongue, careful about my next move. I took a deep breath. "Fine, it's 1704." My birthday. The 17th of April. She unlocked the screen and set the phone in the attic as she pushed both her hands onto either side and hoisted herself into it. I watched to see if she was doing anything. It was quiet and honestly, maybe this was a bad idea. "Ashleigh?" I called out but heard nothing, not even the beeping of that tracker on her ankle. "Ashleigh." I called out again. Silence. I squinted my eyes trying to see inside, but it was just black. I sighed to myself and looked around for a chair in the dim candle lit cottage. I went to the guest room where I slept, remembering there was a stool in front of the vanity. I grabbed it and put it down underneath the open thatch. "Ashleigh". I called out again and heard shuffling accompanied by the sound of her ankle tracker beeping again. I pushed myself up onto the stool to grab the edges of the opening with my forearms. As I tried pulling myself up, I heard a crash of glass. What is it with her and broken glass?

SEVEN

ASHLEIGH

"Fuck." I muttered as I stared at the now broken portal window of the attic. "Ashleigh, answer me for fuck sakes." Avgust was grumpy and you could hear it in his voice. I rolled my eyes and picked at the little glass pieces that stuck into my arm. "Yeah, sorry I was occupied." I heard some movement and a grunt, then cursing. I turned around to see him pull himself up.

"You weren't kidding about Spiderman, huh?"

"Shut up. What did you do?"

"I climbed in, saw the window tried opening it but it was locked so I went to the other side of the attic to find something to smash it open." I explained with a shrug as I dusted myself off and handed him back his phone. "Two bars, it's something." He moved towards the window and pushed out the rest of the broken glass as he typed something into his phone.

Now that I think of it, he couldn't dial 911 if he wanted to because his family is connected to my trial, and everyone knows about the families' history of crime. "Who are you going to call?" I asked as I looked around. The attic was lit by the natural light coming from outside the window. I moved to stand next to him. The snow was just a foot or so away, but I'm sure we'd sink right through or something like that.

"Trying to get hold of my mother." He said as he looked at his screen before dialing the number. "Zdravstvuy *(Hello)*, mamma." His accent was probably one of his most attractive features, that and his eyes, his jawline, those muscles and those bloody tattoos. Men with tattoos do it for me. I snapped out of my thoughts and tried listening to the conversation.

"Yes, mamma. We, it doesn't matter who." Interesting. He continued and mentioned where we were stuck and that we needed help as soon as possible. After a few more sentences and words were shared in Russian, he ended the call. "My battery is at 31 percent. So, no flashlight." He looked around in the attic.

I leaned out the window to check and estimate how far deep the snow was and if we could make it. "Say... You think we'll sink?"

"What?"

"Do you think we will sink into the snow if we jump out?" I could hear his sigh of irritation. "I'm not sure. Probably depends how thick the snow is, but we can't stand too long in one place. It'll become like quicksand." He explained with a shrug and ran a hand through his hair. "Let's try."

"No, stop being insane for once." I narrowed my eyes at the comment. "So, what? We wait for your mother and the minions to come save us like some pathetic versions of Lois Lane and her gay best friend?"

"Firstly, shut the fuck up. Secondly, we don't have any other choice." He shook his head at my words. "And who are you calling the gay best friend?" I smirked and shrugged. "If the shoe fits." He stalked towards me. "There is not a bone in my body that is not straight. I like women. Let me put it in an easier language for you to understand. I like boobs and pussy, not dick Lisichka." I couldn't help but laugh, and he grabbed my chin with his fingers. "Easy enough to understand?"

My eyes locked with his, and I nodded. "My apologies, it would have been very confusing if you were." He tilted his head slightly to the side. "You mean because I fucked you four times and every time, I made you scream my name and had you begging for more?"

"Well, I don't know. It would have been confusing but if you put it that way, I take back my comment." He grinned slightly as he looked down at me. "Good girl." My insides twirled like a ballerina. This man was bringing out kinks I never knew I had. He moved his hand and looked out the window. "We will just have to wait up here."

I looked between him and the window, grinning slightly. My mind wandered around like a hamster on its wheel. Do I run? Do I make a break for it?

Or,

Do I trust the man who is the brother of his sister I killed in cold blood? Yes, he was attractive, but that won't save my ass or my family's name. Trust needed to be earned. I know for a fact he doesn't trust me at all because he had this fear I was going to bolt as soon as he gave me his unlocked phone. What is stopping him from killing me? Taking revenge for his sister? Can't be the mind-blowing sex, and it can't be that he cared at all. His goal was to kidnap me and put a bullet between my eyes the same way I executed his sister in that park. I look back, seeing him stare at me. It was now or never. I jumped out the window, taking the chance of sinking into the snow.

EIGHT
AVGUST

I WATCHED HER HOP OUT THE PORTAL WINDOW without any hesitation. Fucking psycho. I ran quickly to see if the snow had engulfed her, unfortunately it hadn't. She looked over at me and laughed as she stood in the snow.

"Don't stay too long in one place, you could sink." I warned, but of course she had to plonk her pretty ass on the snow and lay back. She was making a snow angel and honestly, this started to piss me off. "Can you listen for once?"

"What was that? Sorry I can't hear you over the arrogant manly aura you're projecting." She said as she sat up. She heard me. She is just trying to get me to join her. "Arrogant manly aura? What in all things holy is that?" I raised a brow slightly. Sometimes her dialect is one of an 8-year-old girl because she is speaking in ways no one could understand. "You have this aura; it radiates off you. You assume I should follow your lead because you're the big strong man." I started laughing. "You don't make sense. Okay enough playtime. Out of the snow." I wave my hand inward as a command for her to come in. She stayed seated.

"Ashleigh, seriously." My voice showed how annoyed I was getting. She fell back into the snow, and I saw her body slowly get sucked in. I blinked to see if I was actually seeing this. I thought quick snow was a made-up thing.

I was too busy talking in my head that when I snapped out of it, Ashleigh was gone, and her outline of her body is what was left. I swore under my breath and hopped out the window, landing in the snow. I moved over to where she was and there she was, sinking further. Her eyes were closed. I tried reaching for her while I had to extend my arm. I grabbed her arm and pulled her up, which had caused her to open her eyes and glare at me. "Not even a thank you for saving you? I could've let you die from hypothermia."

"Yeah, you should've." She rolled her eyes. This girl welcomed death with open arms. I see now why she is defined as scary by my little sister. Having not a second thought, she was ready to let the snow consume her whole. "Do you have a death wish?". She looked over at me. "We all do, don't we? In our lineage, we are supposed to be ready for anything. I don't know what is going to happen to me because my father is too slow to actually do something and I know as soon as we are rescued, you and your family will have my head on a silver platter decorated with fruit and vodka". She looked up at the sky. Some snow still fell, it glittered her pale face, got stuck in her dark thick eyelashes.

"Might as well die now. It would be very embarrassing for my family and myself to end up in a dirty, cold jail cell and rot." I looked over at her. She spoke as if she didn't deserve it, yet she was a cold-blooded killer. "You're right, my family and I will get our revenge, especially when your motive is null and void. You refuse to tell me, which only means it was just a heartless act, and if the judge doesn't give my sister justice, I will." I got up.

"I told you my reason".

"No, you said it was something that would destroy our families' names and so on, you blabbered on about not giving me what that something really was". I snapped and held my fists to my side, trying to control myself.

"Because I can't tell you. I don't trust you." Her voice was equally annoyed as mine. "And I'm supposed to trust you? Protect you from your actions?". My voice raised towards the end and I stalked towards her as I spoke. "I didn't say protect me, did I?". I scoffed as I looked down at her. "No, but you want me to sit back and watch as you try every attempt to kill yourself and escape your consequences?" She shook her head in response. "This is the first time".

"First time? You think I'm stupid, Lisichka? The 'attempt to break the windows' was a bullshit story you spun because you tried to slice your wrists but you were too much of a coward to actually go through with it, so you covered it up". She looked at me with this glare in her forest green eyes. Such beautiful eyes. "So?". I clenched my jaw and grabbed her chin. "I will not let you take the easy route; you will pay one way or another for Annika's death". I held her gaze and darkened mine. "Unless you spit out the information you are withholding, that is your fate".

I could see her thoughts spiraling as she debated in her head whether to speak. Her lips parted slightly now and then as if trying to say something, but something held her back. I let her go and stood up. "Very well then". I turned on my heels and made my way back to the open portal window of the cottage's roof. "Wait-". She called out and when I looked over my shoulder, she stood up with her hands behind her back. The red light and beeping of that tracker continued. She took a few steps and stood behind me.

"Annika found out that our mothers were pregnant around the same time. She then found out that your father was having a fling with my mother at the same time, too. My mother was pregnant with me and she put two and two together. She confronted your father, who was quick to deny, and she went to my mother. Marisol is easy to crack. She does not do well under pressure and she confessed. Annika demanded there be DNA tests done between your father, my mother, my father and myself".

I blinked and took in every word she said. "You're telling me you are my half-sister?". I wanted to throw up on the spot. We fucked and I crave her touch, but she's, my half-sister?! Fuck me.

"No, the DNA results came back. I am a legitimate

Campbell, but that information was not enough for Annika. Because of my fair skin and dark hair, she did not buy it, saying it was rigged. She wanted to cut ties between our family and yours and the rest of the mafia gangs. She was determined to destroy us, so I spoke to my father and he was against it. I went along with it, anyway. She became a threat to all of us, including her own family." My mind was trying to make sense of this. How did I not know about this? Why would Annika not talk to me? I may have been to another country but this...

"So, you decided to execute her? No second thoughts, no remorse, just a bullet between her eyes". There was silence between us before I looked over at her and as I did, all I saw was the crazy look in her eye and she lifted her arm up with a glass piece she had jagged from the window and hid behind her back. I dodged her and tried getting the sharp object away from her. We grunted from the struggle of each other's strength. She was small, but fuck, she was strong with determination. As I tried grabbing the shard of glass, it sliced my palm open and she tried aiming for my eye. Again, with the eye.

I could feel blood drip from the open flesh wound in my palm. I still fought against her, trying to unarm her. She managed to break free from my hold and pushed me down. She held the shard by my face and I gripped her wrists, pushing them away from my face and struggling. That look in her eyes is what scared me. Not that she was trying to kill me or remove my eyes from their sockets. It's like she became something different, like a split personality. I pushed her hands back by her wrists and, while doing so, the glass shard sliced at her cheek. The blood dripped on me and my hand painted the snow red with my blood.

"Ashleigh". I tried talking to her. "Ashleigh, stop this". She glared down at me with the glass piece still in her hand. "I understand, you did it for everyone". Hell, I'm trying to buy some time, really. I can't die at the hands of such a small woman. That is an embarrassment. "Annika was a bit off her head. She had the heir title in her head and that's it. That's why I always traveled. She was controlling". I spoke, trying to get to her head, trying to tell her that this was not the answer right now. Ashleigh looked down, her green eyes meeting mine. She took in the information and slowly brought her hands down and threw the glass shard aside. I sighed with relief before she leaned down and pressed her lips against mine.

NINE
ASHLEIGH

I KISSED HIM, AND I DON'T KNOW WHY. HIS MOUTH moved against mine and I slipped his tongue into my mouth. The kiss was a hungry one. I had him pinned down, his hands held my waist tightly. He dug his fingers into my fair skin. I moved my hips in a circular motion, grinding on him and feeling his arousal grow hard. I continued and he moaned into my mouth. The cold snow surrounded us and small snowflakes fell onto us. I grinned and pulled away from his mouth as I continued swaying my hips in rotation. "Oh Lisichka, fuck". He watched me with an aching voice, holding my gaze and my hips. He guided my hips while I caused him to moan with every movement. Rubbing against his hardened length with my wet aroused and clothed heat. I bit down on my lower lip as I had let out a small moan filled with need. "Yes, I'm so close". I moaned out.

The cold was not a bother in my mind right now as we dry humped each other. The movement and moans warmed me up, actually making me feel hot and sticky. My orgasm was on the edge and I could feel him twitch under me. "Ah! Yes!". Our breath became short as I rubbed against him, and came in my panties. "Fuck".His orgasm followed not so long after, I felt him twitch against me and we both panted trying to catch our breaths.

I laid my body on top of his as we waited to regain oxygen and energy. He had a strand of my dark hair in between his fingers. I looked at him, studied his features and honestly... He is so breathtakingly and painfully gorgeous. "What does that mean?". I asked as I had rested my chin on my arms, which rested on his rising chest looking at him. "Hm?".

"Lisichka... What does it mean?". I asked again with a soft tone, mostly because I was tired. "Little fox". He replied with his husky voice and Russian accent. "Why call me that?". He chuckled and twirled my strand with his finger. "You can't trust a fox, no matter how beautiful they are". I grinned slightly, "You calling me beautiful?". He rolled his eyes and I laughed. He laughed a bit as well and sighed a bit. We stayed silent as the snow fell upon us. I closed my eyes. He moved his fingers to remove the snow from my eyelashes and hair, dusting it off.

"It's getting cold, we need to get up and back inside". I opened my eyes and shifted to push myself up and get off. He sat up and dusted the snow off his shoulders. I looked over at him as I stood up. "Do you really believe my words? About my reason to kill your sister". His blue eyes met mine and he stood up. "If you're lying to me-". He started and I lifted my hand up to silence him. "I'm not, you can do a lie detector test on me if we are ever rescued". I assured and he closed his mouth for a few seconds. "I do believe you, my sister was obsessed with the title 'Heir to the Volkov Mafia Family'. She needed power and that's why I stayed out of her way for most days, if I'm lucky, months as well. Will you share this information back in court?". I furrowed my brows slightly. "I don't think I will be making my welcome back appearance there. I cannot be placed in jail serving time, that would ruin my family's reputation". The other mafia families will see us as a laughing stock that we couldn't even keep ourselves off the radar.

"Although your mother is dead set on having me there, she was not impressed with Annika's findings, she wants my whole family locked up or dead". Avgust widened his eyes a bit as he looked over my shoulder. I could hear some footprints forming with each step in the snow. "I'd rather have you dead". A thick Russian accent spoke from not far behind me. "So good news, we might survive the snow. Bad news, my mother is going to hunt you like a deer now". I had a worried expression on my face and turned to look at her. Natasja Volkov was a fierce and brutal woman. When she learnt of her husband, Igor Volkov, possibly having a child in the Campbell family, she insisted a full massacre to her daughter. Jealous, naive and an alcoholic. Natasja could never think straight, the vodka ran in her veins and she always had this resting bitch face.

She had a rifle in her hands, a few men stood on each side of her. "Come Avgust". She called out as she readied her rifle aiming towards me. I looked over at Avgust. "Hunt me like an animal? You can't let her do this". He barely sighed. "Mamma". He started walking forward slowly. "We can't do this". His mother aimed the rifle at him, his hands fell quickly into a surrender position. "This will tarnish our family name". He added. He took another step, this time between me and her, right in the middle. "I don't care about names; I want her dead". Natasja spat forward. "She will pay, with her life". She pressed the trigger, Avgust ducked and so did I, nothing came out. It seemed the trigger was stuck and she swore in her native language trying to loosen it. "Mamma! You'd really kill me?". Avgust had a pissed off tone in his voice. "Put the bloody thing away and let me talk to you". Natasja grinned as she managed to fix the trigger. "No talk. No excuse. You protect her, you are no son of mine. You are no Volkov". As she finished, she pulled the trigger and the bullet headed my way. Everything went in slow motion. All I saw was Avgust shoving me aside and ducking, he hissed as the bullet grazed his arm.

"Mamma! You are insane! Enough!". He spoke as he got up looking at the graze, some blood dripped from the small wound and he approached her, still keeping her aim out of sight from me. Her aim moved to her son as he stalked towards her. The irritation and frustration radiated off his body. "Stop! Right there, boy!". The command of her voice was loud enough to be heard by someone a few feet away from me. Avgust did not stop. He obviously did not take his mother seriously, and the fact she shot at him probably ticked him off. "Avgust!". She fixed her hold on the rifle. "I will shoot you". I watched this unfold. I never had a great bond with my mother, but you'd think a son is his mother's pride and joy. Natasja clearly did not feel like being a mother right now. I could somehow understand her anger, just didn't care about her opinion and anger towards me. What's done is done and she needs to get a rude awakening to realize her daughter was the snake in the grass. I watched as Avgust stood right in front of his mother, the rifle's end hitting his chest. "Do it. Shoot me". He spoke down to his mother who swallowed back down a gulp. Her eyes never changed, they kept narrowed and glaring towards him. You could see her bite down on her teeth through her wrinkled cheeks. "You'd take a bullet for her? A murderer? Your sister's murderer?". She asked, her voice was hoarse which was signs of a nicotine addicted chain smoker and alcoholic. Avgust went silent but I saw his shoulders rise and fall as he breathed hard. His mother clicked her tongue and took the rifle in a swift move knocking the end towards his face, hitting his chin. He stumbled backwards and swore loudly. Natasja said something I couldn't hear properly before she aimed the rifle at me and fired. I closed my eyes and waited for the bullet to pierce me, the way it pierced my victim.

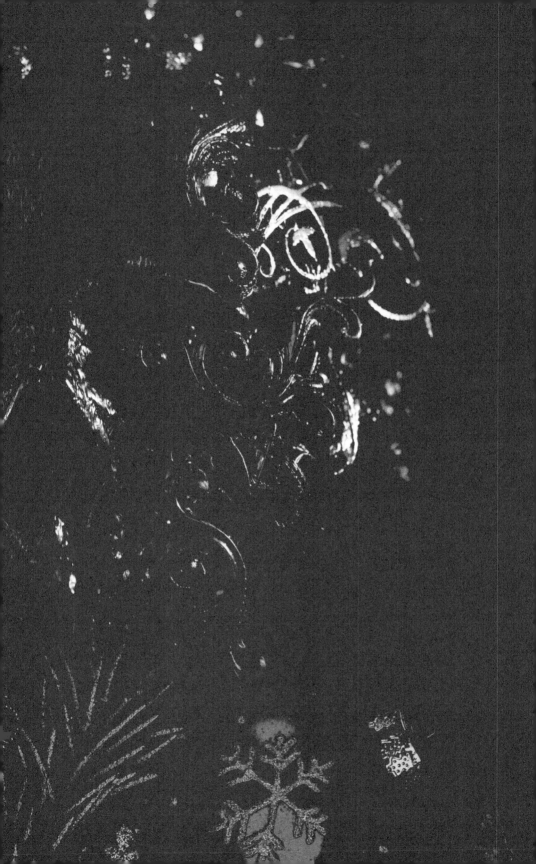

TEN
AVGUST

I RUBBED MY CHIN AND WATCHED THE BULLET FLY towards Ashleigh. Before I could register how to act, I saw it pierce her right through her shoulder. She fumbled backwards crying out and holding her wounded shoulder. I looked over at my mother who readied her rifle to fire again. I balled my fists and moved fast towards my mother grabbing the rifle, and she pulled back trying to regain control.

We fought for control, pushing and pulling. I looked over at Ashleigh as I continued with my mother. "Go!". Without another thought, she ran through the snow holding onto her bleeding shoulder. The blood left a trail of red in the snow. I shoved my mother back into the snow, grabbing the rifle and throwing it aside. "Enough, mamma. Listen carefully". She glared at me as she fixed her hair, removing the snow from her dark clothes and dyed hair. "Have respect for the woman who carried you for 9 and a half months and pushed you out in the back of a strip club". She spat out; the Russian accent was strong. Her English was better than what it was when I was still in middle school. "Mamma, you need to respect me. You should be glad I don't kill you right here and now". I crouched down to look in her eyes. "She will not be touched, not by you and not by anyone else. We both know how Annika was. You are just upset and in denial over your husband who couldn't keep his dick in one place".

My mother kept silent; her eyes narrowed as I spoke. Maybe I did believe Ashleigh, or maybe she was a really good actress. "We need to fix this. Our families need to be fixed. We don't have to forgive her, but the Campbells have a bigger influence in this town than we do. They have more access to the ports, which we need. Think about this before you let your drunkard-self make life changing decisions that will not only ruin you". I tilted my head slowly to the side. "But ruin our family too, you know. The one you claim to love?". She spat at me and I stood up wiping off her saliva. My eyes searched the area, the men that came with her were gone. I furrowed my brows slightly and took a few steps to look for any sign of them. The snow held secrets and created a beautiful trail. The red stood out. I blinked back, as I was taken back at the small trail of blood merging with a big puddle surrounding one of the men.

He was breathing still. Ashleigh stood beside him; her arm now bloodied from the wound that leaked it out. She held a gun in her one hand as she pressed a material into her wound, the bleeding man's tie to be exact. She had shot him in the leg and in the shoulder, clearly to disable him. The other men were near and away from her sight. I shook my head at the sight and looked over at my mother who now stood up and behind me. "Still want to keep her?".

"Our families mean more than a few spilled blood". I said as I heard my mother click her lighter. She lit a cigarette in the cold. The snow stopped. "We need to get out of here now, I'm sick of the snow". I mentioned and moved towards Ashleigh. I unarmed her gently trying not to scare her into a fight mode again. I looked down at her leg, the ankle tracker was still on but I think the speaker, making the blaring sound, got snow which melted over the body heat she produced.

Ashleigh did not move, she stood there with her eyes on the bleeding man beside her. She had no sort of emotion expressed on her face, not even a wince of pain. I gently placed a hand on her healthy shoulder to get her attention. "Let's get out of here, Lisichka". I pressed a kiss to her head and made my way, following the footprints my mother and her men left. My mother followed and eventually so did Ashleigh. We reached the black van with tinted windows; the other men appeared after a while and helped my mother and Ashleigh into the van. Ashleigh sat in the passenger seat; my mother sat behind with me. One of the men climbed into the driver's seat and started the engine.

The drive was long, silent and filled with tension. My mother had almost finished a box of cigarettes by the time we came to a stop. She was the first to hop out and made her way into the family mansion. I looked over at Ashleigh. "Let's get you fixed up; I'll call your father". She didn't speak but she opened the door and got out. I guess that was an answer on its own. I got out, closing the door, and followed her up the stairs towards the Volkov mansion. I led her to the ground level kitchen and checked through the cupboards where the first aid kit was supposed to be. She stood aside, the blood was sticky and halted on her bare arm. It left a rainy pattern.

I moved towards the island counter after finding the first aid kit. She didn't look up at me, that cocky personality of hers dulled out. I kind of missed it. Missed that sharp tongue she presented back at the cottage. I gently lifted her in one motion onto the counter and set the kit on the left to her. I took her arm gently, no reaction.

With a small sigh I lifted her shirt and arm out of the shirt so I have access to assist the wound and stitch it up. I looked at her face to see if there was any sort of painful expression but there was nothing. She looked numb. This side of her was... worrying. I just wanted to hold her and protect her from the demons that are haunting her thoughts right now.

I used an alcohol swab to clean off the dry and sticky blood from her arm and shoulder, being careful not to cause any pain or discomfort for her. Gently, I cleaned up the wound and disposed of the blood-stained swabs. The search began with what to use to close the wound and how to remove the bullet lodged in her shoulder. She shifted a bit and stayed silent after I got the right gear to remove the bullet.

Lucky enough it had lodged between her flesh and not

pierced through her shoulder blade. "This may hurt". I softly spoke and tried as quickly as possible to remove the bullet with a tweezer and scalpel. The scalpel was used to make the wound slightly bigger so it was easier to access the lodged bullet. Blood covered my fingers and ran down her bare arm once again. After a few struggles and attempts to not hurt Ashleigh further, I eventually got the bullet out and quickly tried to clean up the excess blood on her arm and covered the wound with a gauze. Either she had a high pain tolerance or she has yet to register what just happened.

ELEVEN

AVGUST

IT TOOK ME A FEW MINUTES TO STITCH THE WOUND up after applying a salve to ease the irritation. I started placing the things I used back in their place in the kit, and looked over here and there to check if Ashleigh had snapped out of that trance. She moved a bit, checking the work of her stitched-up wound and her now clean arm. Her eyes wandered to where I was busy zipping up the two kits. I placed my hands on the counter and gripped it to hold my stance. "Thank you". Her voice was hoarse and soft. Our eyes met and I nodded in response. Her facial expression had changed a bit, a faint smile upon her lips.

"I'm no doctor, you should probably get it checked by a professional". She nodded and tried getting off the counter, I helped her down. She looked up at me and swallowed back her words. My brows furrowed before I could say anything I heard someone behind her clear their throat. "This is how we justify your sister's murder? By welcoming her killer into the home, she grew up in?". My father's accent was faint, but stern. He guided his electrical wheelchair to stand right by us. "Otetz*(Father)*". I acknowledged my father but, in a manner, where he knows I am the authority in the household and family. My father's gaze was on Ashleigh who had not moved.

My father looked between the both of us awaiting one of us to speak. I cleared my throat. "You know, we wouldn't be in this situation if you didn't whore around with Marisol Campbell". My voice had irritation in it, and what I said was the truth. My father opened his mouth to speak but I stopped him. "Also, regarding Annika's death, yes, I agree it's very unfortunate. But in my eyes, it was deemed necessary for our family. She found out about your sleeping patterns and wanted to cut ties with the Campbells, expose them and have the others' cut their ties too, causing a major disruption in the chain and giving us a bad name". I explained while my hands shoved their way into my jeans' pockets.

"She is a psychopath for fuck's sake!". My father held his chest after he shouted out those words and took deep breaths. His heart wasn't in the best conditions and he refused a transplant. "So are you, so is this family, we are not saints". I darkened my gaze looking down at him. "No one will touch her, not you, not the government and not her family". I warned, a protective side emerged only because I am more aware of her vulnerable side now than I ever was, and I understood the type of person my sister was. "What? Are you out of your mind, boy? You are speaking as if you are in love!". He spat out still with a hand on his chest. Not in love, not yet. I felt I needed to keep her safe. If my sister could see me now, I'd be the one in that coffin. "Enough". I warned in a small growl.

My father scoffed and shook his head in disapproval. "I don't need your or anyone else's permission to make my decisions". Before he could respond we heard cars moving on the gravel outside. I walked over to the window to peek, seeing 5 black SUVs parking around the fountain piece in the middle. I waited to see if anyone was going to climb out, and as true as fuck, Denis Campbell got out and couple of men followed close out the SUVs behind. Marisol got out as well and stood beside her husband. The snow had cleared up, but the gravel was covered and so were the plants. I watched them approach the entrance; their men had a hand on their guns that were tucked in their sides. "Fuck". I cussed and put a finger to my lips towards my father.

I looked to Ashleigh, who still stayed expressionless but met my eyes. The look was all I needed as I nodded towards her and reached for her hand. She took it and I led us to the entrance. I could hear some bickering amongst themselves before I opened the massive door. "Campbells".

"Volkov".

"Ashleigh! You're alright! Oh, my baby girl". Marisol reached for her daughter who stood by me. I watched as Ashleigh looked between her parents. Denis kept his gaze on me. "Let's go home, Ashleigh". He announced and looked over at his wife who nodded in response. Ashleigh stayed silent. "You broke my baby". Marisol looked at her daughter with worry and narrowed her eyes at me. "Denis had an envelope that he had removed from inside his suit jacket and handed it over to me. I took it and opened it to find some documents. "What is this?".

"Confirmation that Ashleigh is 100% my daughter, so your mother can calm down and your father can leave my wife alone". Denis explained as his nose twitched slightly, which made his graying mustache move from side to side. "My parents won't be an issue; I can assure you that. I have the authority to pull back the charges against her and use the connections to cover it all up". I spoke with assurance and sincerity. I placed a hand gently on Ashleigh's good shoulder. "Your daughter did what needed to be done to protect our families, and the rest of the mafia world". Denis watched my movements carefully. His men stood around him with their guns nearby. "She is safe, from us at least, so look after her, will you? It's the least you could do after causing everyone such hell over your little love affair". I spoke towards Marisol who had turned and left halfway, clearly not in any mood to discuss how this could have all been prevented. I look over at Denis. "Thank you, Volkov. My family is in your debt". His words were sincere indeed and yet Ashleigh has yet to join her family.

"Clearly there was some sort of trauma you both endured, when she is ready to come home, you know where we live". The old man grinned slightly and shook my hand. His Irish accent was thickly laced in his voice. I nodded and watched him turn around and get back into the SUVs they came in. His men joined after a few seconds. They drove on the gravel and out of the gates. I closed the doors and looked over at Ashleigh. She seemed more at ease right now, my arm gently wrapped around her shoulders. "You're okay, Lisichka. You're with me, remember?". Her eyes met mine. "You're mine". I smirked slightly and took her face in my free hand lifting it and pressed my lips against hers. Her lips were intoxicating, her body, her pussy... Fuck. This may not just be a physical attraction, but a fatal one. One that may be the death of me. I pulled away from her lips for a bit. "No one will touch you; no one will harm you my little psycho". She grinned at the last part and brought me back into a deep kiss with our tongues colliding.

My Lisichka. If Annika saw me now, she'd slice my throat and use my blood to bathe in. Ashleigh may have some screws loose but Annika was a different breed, one that could not be trusted.

The kiss halted as we heard a massive explosion coming from outside. My men scrambled around us to find out where it came from. I held Ashleigh close amongst the chaos.

I could feel her grin against my neck as she nuzzled into me. What the fuck just happened?

The door flung open. One of my men rushed in, ushering Ashleigh and I aside.

"What happened?" I demanded. He looked pale as he said, "Sir, the explosion was the result of one of the Campbell cars going up in flames, done deliberately. It was Marisol's, she and the men that accompanied her are all dead by the looks of it."

My stomach dropped, now just an empty pit in my abdomen. I looked over at Ashleigh, expecting her to be in just as much disbelief as I was. She wasn't.

"Did you?" I asked carefully, both ashamed of my own assumption and concerned that it might be true.

"No, but that was genius, really. 50 bucks says it was Natasja." I was caught off-guard at the heartless composure of her tone, but something in the back of my mind told me that she might be right. There was only one other person I knew that had the balls to sabotage another Mafia family in this way, and only one that was also a jealous alcoholic with no sense of self-preservation. Regardless of who it was, though, an act of this magnitude meant the same thing for all of us. Me, Ashleigh, our families and titles. This meant war.

Конец/ Deireadh
(The end)

ABOUT ALISON MACKENZIE

Born and raised in KwaZulu Natal, South Africa Allison is a dreamer at heart. Although her overthinking gets the best of her she always overcomes it. She is a dog mom and devours books in her spare time. Her favorite characters are Love Quinn, Daenerys Targaryen, and Toothless the dragon. She loves anime and she's currently watching Attack on Titan, but Jujutsu Kaisen has her heart. May look innocent but we all know she ain't.

a BB g

Covert Desires

M KAY NOIR

CWs, TWs & Kinks.

(*Warning: Contains Spoilers)
This book contains mature themes and is intended for adult
readers. Specific content warnings include, but are not limited to:

ON-PAGE MENTIONS

Dubcon
Violence & Murder
Child Abuse
Neglect & Abandonment
Death/Murder of Loved
Ones
Captivity
Unethical Kink
Unprotected Sex
Forced Chastity
Pregnancy Loss
Organized Crime
Graphic Medical
Procedures (including
needles)
Scarification
Domestic Violence

OFF-PAGE MENTIONS

Rape (not between MCs/
mentioned)

KINKS

Femdom
Age Gap (F44 | M28)
CNC (clear consent)
Collaring
Goddess/Teacher-Brat
dynamic
Humiliation
Public Sex
Exhibitionism
Male Chastity
Orgasm Control
Brat Taming
Primal Kink
Praise Kink
Bondage
Impact Play
Pegging
CBT
Orgasm Denial &
Control
Overstimulation
Pierced Peen
Ass play
Nursing BJs

STORY WRITTEN IN
US ENGLISH

THE KNOCK

KIAH

NOBODY KNOCKS AT 2 AM.

Not at this time of the year.

And definitely not during a tropical storm.

Only a lunatic would venture out in this weather.

Yet there it is again—the frantic pounding forcing me to put down the paintbrush.

Every instinct shouts at me to ignore the commotion outside. To continue painting black flowers onto the large canvas until my mind calms.

The inn's closed. I'm not expecting anyone for another two months.

But curiosity nags, whispering of long-forgotten excitement. When was the last time anything unpredictable happened on this island?

An old restlessness stirs in my bones as the voice outside

grows more frantic, barely audible over the rain but impossible to ignore.

Fuck-it.

I wipe my paint-stained hands on my apron and move towards the door I hadn't planned on opening for days.

"Hold on!" I call to the unknown guest, bracing myself for the ferocious weather as I unlatch the inn's front door.

On the other side, a drenched six-foot-something stranger with raven black hair clutches a duffel bag for dear life in one hand, the other ready to knock again.

"About fucking time," he snarls, his broad shoulders already trying to push past me with almost as much force as the gale at his back.

"What do you want?" I ask sharply, blocking his entry.

When you've lived the life I've had, you don't simply let unannounced men into your home in the middle of the night.

"Room for one. This is an inn, isn't it?" His eyes, a piercing shade of blue that could rival the coldest winter sky, meet mine briefly, and a shiver runs down my spine despite the oppressive humidity around us.

Leaning back to create some distance between us, I study the man closely, trying to discern any useful clues. It's one of those work habits that hasn't died out despite my early retirement.

Know your enemy; know your target. This drenched man could be either. Except I have no idea who he is.

He doesn't fit the profile of the island-adventure guests

who usually stay at my inn. Even if he did, this is not the time for island adventuring.

Physically, he seems to be in his late twenties, way younger than my 44 years. He's got that immature bravado about him that men of that age often waltz around with.

As far as I can tell, he's not carrying a weapon.

In the dim yellow glow of the porch light, the unannounced guest looks like an unsettling mix of serial killer and heartthrob with those brooding eyes and a strong, chiseled jaw shadowed in light stubble.

He's handsome by any standard, but I'm way past the age of letting dangerous men with haunted looks upset my entire world. *Fuck that.*

Soaked from the storm, the man's dark suit might have been expensive before the rain ruined it. The torn white shirt, however, suggests his troubles are far more severe than bad weather.

But that's not the part that concerns me the most.

It's the blood dripping down his forehead from a nasty-looking cut on his temple. I only notice it when he turns his face to scowl at me.

Immediately, my senses switch to high alert.

Something is off.

I cross my arms over my chest, standing firm. "We're closed. The inn doesn't open until December."

"Hmm. Doesn't matter," the bulky man declares as he pushes past me, forcefully shoving me out of the way before I can stop him. I didn't think he'd be so bold.

"What part of we're closed was unclear?" I shout after him as I watch the dripping stranger beeline for the closest seat.

The fucker is going to ruin my couches—not that the tacky set in Reception is fancy or anything. Still, I prefer my furniture dry, just like my floor. I don't want future guests complaining about a moldy smell.

My jaw clenches. "Go somewhere else."

"No. It has to be here," he insists, tattooed fingers tightening on the armrest.

"Why?"

"Please," he forces the word through gritted teeth like it hurts him to be polite, "You can't send me back out there."

"I can do what I want, thank you very much. Especially in my own place," I tell him as I calculate my next move.

The unannounced guest is a bit taller than me and more muscular, but I could probably take him out; I've crushed men far bigger than him.

Calm down, Kiah, I try to talk myself down, fighting my natural instincts to remove any threat—forcefully, if needed.

He's just *some guy.*

There's no need to jump into combat mode.

But he shouldn't be here.

I don't owe this asshole anything.

In the five years I've been hiding out on this island, nobody has ever bothered me during the off-season.

The stormy months are for solitude and introspection, hobbies, working on my strength training...stuff like that.

I'm not about to start changing my routine now.

But the dark-haired stranger refuses to take *no* for an answer. "Just tonight. I have nowhere else to go," he insists. His eyes don't change as he speaks—they remain dead, unmoving.

"Touching story, but you haven't explained how you ended up here in the first place. There are no ferries now, no planes. Everyone knows the island is closed this time of year."

"It was a private service. Our plane crashed," the stranger says simply as he looks around the space. As he turns, the light follows the black ink wrapped around his neck like a tattooed scarf. The complex, intricate design makes him look like a man who's etched his sins directly onto his skin.

I arch a brow, "*Our?*"

"The pilot didn't make it." He turns away, his face unreadable.

"But you did?" I can't help but be skeptical. Who in their right mind would fly in a storm like this? And even if they did, the rest of the story doesn't make much sense either. Surviving plane crashes aren't as common as people think.

Plus, it's 2 AM!

"What can I say? I got lucky?" The stranger grins, making his face look even creepier—like a deranged criminal. The grin doesn't reach his eyes; it just sticks to his cheeks like a cold mask.

For the first time, I notice the small scar under his right eye, a thin line that makes him look like even more of a threat.

There is something so unsettling about this man's presence.

I can't empathize with his situation—maybe because I don't believe him.

The urge to get rid of him is overwhelming.

Still, I can't exactly chuck him out in the rain again. All the other hotels and inns are closed. The only people on the island are the locals peacefully asleep in their beds.

I couldn't care less about what happened to this asshole, but I don't want to wake up to find half the island decimated by some maniac. These people have been nothing but kind to me; they don't deserve it.

Plus, any action would undoubtedly attract outsider attention to the island—which would be problematic, considering I'm trying to keep a low profile.

Goddamnit. I wish the phone lines were working, that I could just call someone to take care of this man, but alas, the storm has cut us off completely.

The bleeding stranger either stays here where I can keep an eye on him, or he takes his chaos elsewhere.

At least I have the training to deal with dangerous men.

With a heavy sigh, I reluctantly give in, going against my better judgment. *What's the worst he can do?*

My voice is stern and assertive as I tell him, "You can stay, but only until the storm clears. Understood?"

"Thank you, Ma'am," the bloody stranger says with no sign of genuine gratitude.

"Don't call me Ma'am."

He cocks his head to the side. "What should I call you then?"

"Kiah is fine. And you are?"

He rubs his finger like he's twisting an imaginary ring. "Kiah? Hmm...Nico."

"And you came from?" I try again, unsettled by the lack of explanation.

He doesn't answer; he just stares me down with a curious look.

"Fair enough," I concede, grabbing a room key from behind the reception desk. The faster I get him out of my sight, the better.

The drenched stranger stares wordlessly at the large wooden keychain shaped like a dolphin that I shove in his hands. He's lucky I don't shove it in his rude mouth.

"House rules," I explain, gesturing to the door on the left, "My private space is off-limits, but you can use the common areas."

Nico grabs the key without acknowledging my boundary.

"This is the part where you thank me."

"Hmm. Where is the room?" he asks instead, heading toward the hall without waiting for an answer.

I trot along to keep up with him. "Second door on your right. I need to put on fresh sheets—"

He suddenly halts, and I crash into him, almost losing my footing.

"I can take it from here." Nico snaps his head around to

glare at me with a snarl that could make the dead shiver, and I gladly part ways with a single nod.

He's clearly not worried about fresh sheets, so why should I be? There are blankets in the cupboards, he'll manage.

The unwanted guest heads down the dark hall to his room as I retreat to my personal haven, locking the door behind me.

It's not much, but it's mine—just a small open-plan space with a double bed, some armchairs, a rust-colored futon that doubles as a couch, and a mostly-for-show kitchen. To the side, an en suite bathroom with a shower completes the cabin-like refuge decorated with mismatched furniture and strings of seashells dangling from the roof like mobiles.

It's a relief to pick up my paintbrush again and return to the midnight roses crawling over the canvas in acrylic.

Usually, the strokes spreading over the white soothe the chaos in my mind.

But there is no calm for me now; my mind keeps returning to the strange visitor down the hall.

This storm better clear up soon so I can get rid of him. I don't want to get caught up in whatever he is running from.

My life is all about peace and tranquility now, not harboring strangers bleeding in a storm—no matter how curious I am about who they are, why they're here.

Boring is good.

Boring is what we want.

That little familiar pulse of excitement in my veins felt good, though.

Forget it, Kiah.

With a sigh, I dip my brush back into the black, forcing my focus back to my canvas.

But I don't get far.

The next moment, my peace shatters like crystal on stone.

I barely register Nico's presence before I feel the cold, unforgiving metal of a knife digging into my throat.

Pressing harder, he flicks his tongue over my earlobe, licking me as he whispers, "I've changed my mind...I prefer *this* room."

Fuck.

Psycho

Kiah

THE PAINTBRUSH SLIPS FROM MY FINGERS, clattering to the floor in what feels like slow motion.

Nico's threat ghosts across my neck, his warm breath a stark contrast to the cold steel digging into my skin. "I wouldn't make any sudden moves if I were you."

My body stiffens, every muscle coiling like a spring ready to unleash.

The bastard caught me off-guard.

How long has it been since anyone managed that?

You're losing your touch, Kiah.

I knew I should've replaced that weak door lock. Nico overpowered me before I even had time to turn around, his stealth moves masked by the thundering storm.

He's clearly not just some average guy. It takes skill to sneak up on me.

I should've trusted my instincts and never let him in.

But what's done is done. I've never been one to get hung up on regrets. I have too many of those. They'd drown me if I let them.

I exhale slowly, letting Nico think it's a shaky breath of fear. In reality, I'm centering myself. I need to stay calm, focused.

Yet, a part of me—a part I thought I'd buried deep—sings with a perverse excitement. This is living!

"What do you want from me?" I ask, my voice low and steady despite the adrenaline surging through my veins, "I don't have any money."

"Money is not my problem," Nico replies, his tone dripping with menace. He wraps his free arm around my waist, pulling me even closer to his still-sodden frame behind me, his grip rough and bruising.

"What then?"

He thinks about it for a second. "For starters, some duct tape."

"I don't have any," I lie.

"Well, let's see what you do have."

With a violent yank, Nico drags me to the kitchen.

I should do something, fight back, but it's hard to argue with a knife against your throat.

If this was five years ago, maybe I could risk a sudden move, but I don't trust my skills anymore. Despite keeping in shape, I know my reflexes are not as sharp as they used to be.

This island was supposed to be a *temporary* escape while I

figured out what to do next. But half a decade flies by quickly when you're avoiding the world.

But I don't have time to ponder my past.

Nico is tearing through my drawers like a madman.

When he reaches the cupboard underneath the kitchen sink, my heart plummets. I was hoping he wouldn't find it.

"Well, well, well," my assailant exclaims triumphantly, his voice chillingly calm, "Open it," he demands, the blade indenting my skin as he increases the pressure, holding me firm.

Reluctantly, I do what he asks, unlatching the simple grey plastic box that used to be the previous owner's fishing box but now serves as my fix-everything toolbox.

Nico's face twists into a smirk when he sees what's inside.

He shoves me into a nearby wooden chair, and I topple over the antique piece of furniture that is too worn to be valuable any longer—much like all my stuff.

Moving quickly, he pulls some zip-ties from the box and secures my wrists behind the chair.

The plastic bites into my skin, almost cutting off circulation.

Don't panic, just breathe.

I've been in way worse situations than this, and I've always survived. I just need to remain calm and wait for the right opportunity.

But as Nico pulls out the spool of fishing line, I know things are about to get a whole lot more complicated.

This life is supposed to be in my past, *damnit*.

I'm all about island vibes and self-healing now.

But the psycho with the fishing line doesn't give a fuck about the lies I keep telling myself to justify why I'm wasting my prime away.

He wraps the sheer string around me—around and around—as he ties me to the chair like I'm some powerless damsel in distress.

The fishing line is surprisingly strong, and my skin bulges between the gaps.

When I try to move, it only cuts the line deeper into my skin.

From experience, I know there is no way to break through this—not with my hands alone, at least.

"Now stay," Nico tells me as he returns to his search, rummaging through my stuff and throwing my perfectly organized things on the floor like they don't matter.

This man is deranged, I think for the umpteenth time as I watch him touching things—*my* things—he shouldn't be touching.

I try to wiggle my arms behind my back, but the zip ties have no give; they only cut into my wrists as I struggle to free myself.

It's no use.

"What are you looking for?" I ask, my voice strained.

"Quiet. I'm trying to think," Nico replies, pacing the small space with heavy steps.

"Please, I—" I start, but I never get to finish my sentence.

His backhanded slap cuts me off mid-sentence, my head

snapping to the side. Instantly, a searing pain starts to blossom across my cheek.

That's going to bruise for sure.

Nico rubs his temples. "I told you to be quiet."

Before I can protest, he grabs one of the nearby dish-cloths, shoving it in my mouth like a makeshift gag before securing it with a second cloth tied around my head.

The cloth tastes faintly like bleach and spilled tea. I used it earlier to wipe a spill from the floor. Just the thought of it makes me nauseous, but I push it from my mind.

"That's better. Now I can focus," Nico continues, speaking like I can respond. But he doesn't seem to care (or mind) that the conversation is one-sided. I have a feeling a man like that doesn't care about much.

He grabs a bottle of whiskey from my liquor cabinet and pours it straight down his throat, not even flinching as he swallows down nearly a quarter of the bottle neat.

The alcohol seems to relax him a bit, and he puts the knife down on the counter—out of reach, sadly.

"Now..." is all he says. He doesn't have to narrate what he's up to next; it's clear as day.

Without so much as an inch of modesty, the psycho with the dead blue eyes starts stripping out of his wet clothes, drop-ping them right here in the kitchen.

I can't help but stare as more of Nico's muscular tattooed flesh is exposed before me. He's built like a Viking—young, strong, toned.

It's unfortunate that such a dick of a man should be blessed with such an incredible body...

In another life, under different circumstances, he could've been my type. (At least for one night.)

When he turns around to face me, a gasp traps against the dirty dishcloth stuffed in my mouth.

He has a raging hard-on.

Does this turn him on?

As Nico walks closer, I can't tear my eyes from his size-able erection, especially not once I notice the piercings through the tip of his dick—two barbells form a cross through the inside with four beads poking out at opposite ends.

I've never seen anything like it, and I can't help but wonder what those four bells would feel like scraping the insides of your pussy.

It's been a long time since I saw a naked male body up close, and an unwanted shiver of lust snakes down my spine to my cunt.

Jesus, Kiah. Get it together. This asshole is going to kill me, and I'm here lusting over his muscular ass.

Danger has always made me horny, though. Maybe that's why I made so many questionable decisions in the past.

But now's not the time to get lost down memory lane.

"Enjoying the view?" Nico sneers, making him look even more deranged.

Forcing my gaze to his, I shake my head—no.

He laughs out loud, a jarring sound, and then heads for

the bathroom without saying anything else, leaving his wet clothes strewn across the kitchen floor.

The moment Nico vanishes, my mind snaps into survival mode.

This is my chance. I need to escape.

Looking around the apartment, I catalog every object, weighing up my options.

Nico's knife is still on the kitchen counter—that seems to be my best bet.

But I will need to move quickly, before he finishes his shower.

Despite the chair strapped to me like a tortoise shell, I struggle to my feet. But my movements are agonizingly slow, each inch a battle against the restraints. I can't get enough leverage to move one leg ahead of the other.

Come on, come on!

Hurry!

The shower's rhythm taunts me as I shuffle towards freedom, one excruciating baby step at a time.

Just like that.

Careful.

Finally at the counter, a new challenge emerges: how to grasp the knife with bound hands?

Determination fuels me as I contort, angling for the blade.

Sweat beads on my brow. Victory is within reach—

Suddenly, a solid impact from behind sends me crashing.

The knife skitters away, hope scattering with it.

"Such a naughty girl. Tsk, tsk."

Nico's voice, dripping with dark amusement, freezes my blood.

I howl loudly, frustrated.

So close. I almost had it.

The naked intruder grabs me by the ankle and drags me away from the kitchen, the worn wooden floor burning my skin with friction.

I expect Nico to pick the chair up again, to put me right side up, but he leaves me on the floor, flat on my back, with my knees bent up like I've just tipped backward and stayed there.

"This would be much easier if you just complied." He sighs, staring down at me with his hands on his slender hips.

With everything I have, I tug at the ties, desperately trying to free myself as Nico just laughs, almost absentmindedly reaching down to his cock.

"Struggle all you want, lady; you're not going anywhere," he states the obvious, trapping my gaze in his own as he continues to palm his erection.

Fucking pervert! I want to shout, but only an indecipherable mumble passes the dirty dishcloth.

How can he be touching himself right here? *What the fuck is wrong with him?*

Those sick eyes remain lifeless as he jerks himself off, towering over me like a nefarious god while the shower goes in the background, all the hot water running into the drain.

Nico doesn't make any sound. His face doesn't change.

There is no visible indication that he's enjoying any of this. But he keeps stroking, those haunted eyes pinned on mine.

Desperate for a reprieve from this nightmare, I close my eyes. I don't want to see this.

"Oh-no, you don't."

I gasp as a large hand wraps around my throat, pressing the air from my lungs.

My eyes shoot open to find Nico bent over me, choking me as he continues to pleasure himself.

"Keep them open, or this will be the *least* fucked-up thing you see tonight," he threatens, and I believe him.

Despite wanting to throw up, I force myself to watch, swallowing down the bile that pushes up in my throat.

Nico's pierced tip looks ripe and ready up close, but there is nothing erotic about the scene. It's a violation.

"Hmm, how about some *inspiration*." He finally loosens his grip, and I desperately suck in some air.

My skin shudders as Nico's rough hand suddenly dips into my bra. Like he has the right to do so, he rolls the hard tip of my nipple between his fingers, and I bite down an involuntary moan.

My mind is screaming at me, but my body is painfully aware of the fact that nobody has touched my breasts in years, and definitely not with such possessiveness, such urgency.

"Now, hold still," Nico says, returning his palm to his cock.

I watch in horror as the unannounced stranger jerks

himself to completion with a single grunt, spilling his thick cum on my cheek.

It's warm and gross, and the worst part is that there's nothing I can do to wipe it from my skin.

"Much better," the fucker proclaims with a creepy grin before returning to the shower, leaving me there to stew.

Shouting into my gag, I struggle against my restraints as rage burns through me.

Who does Nico think he is?

He'll pay for this!

Brute

Nico

The island doesn't look how I remembered it.

But then again, it's been 15 years since my father brought me here as an impressionable 13-year-old.

It's probably the only good memory I have of that asshole.

The last time we stayed at this inn, there wasn't some crazy storm. Nor a stubborn innkeeper with an explosive temper and magnetic body.

That woman should be grateful she's still breathing. I've ended people for much less than trying to stab me with my own knife.

But I don't feel like being trapped inside this shithole with a rotting body. I'm here to hide out, not create more problems.

Besides, she could be useful.

Muscle Mommy's clearly got more skills than I thought.

Plus, she's got nice tits for an older woman—if Amazonian blondes are your thing.

She's still wearing too much clothing for my liking. But that will be a fun present to unwrap later.

My cock thickens again at the mere thought as the hot water rains down on me in the shower.

Kiah is such a distraction.

I can't say I usually go around jerking off on my captives.

But seeing those brown eyes flare in fury was worth it. She's even hotter when she gets all flustered.

The image of her disgust is burnt onto my mind, filed for future indulgence.

But I have bigger problems to deal with than the feisty innkeeper.

Involuntarily, my mind wanders back to the scene I've just escaped.

Try as I might, I can't put the jumbled pieces together in a way that makes sense.

I've run through it all so many times, but I still don't know what happened.

Who the fuck killed my father?

It wasn't me.

Sure, I was planning on killing him.

That cunt deserved it for what he did.

But not like that.

I had a plan.

And my plan definitely didn't involve waking up in my car with no memory of how I got there, covered in blood, murder weapon in hand...and my dead father beside me in the passenger seat.

Playing Nancy Drew and solving his murder wasn't really on the cards. I had to get out of there quickly.

Before the shit hit the fan.

Before they blamed me for it.

Driving like a maniac, I kept looking back at my father's lifeless body beside me, his dead eyes staring at the roof.

But I felt nothing.

Nothing but the urgency to get the fuck away from him.

In hindsight, I could probably have kicked his body out of the car first or drove the whole thing into the water somewhere.

But at that moment, I was acting out of pure instinct. There was no time to be strategic.

I had to leave the city ASAP.

That pilot sure didn't want to fly in this chaotic weather, but I suppose he had little choice with a gun to his head.

Pity he didn't survive either way.

I couldn't risk anyone knowing where I am. He had to go.

After a bumpy landing, I shot him right there on the runway before chucking the gun into the ocean on the way to the inn. I wasn't going to keep my father's murder weapon on me.

I have to be super careful.

Until I know who is behind this whole thing, I can't trust anyone. Not that the list of people I trust is very long to begin with.

I should be safe here, though.

For now.

The water goes cold, pulling me back to the present.

I turn off the shower and grab the still-damp white towel off the rack. It must be Kiah's. I'm sure she'll *love* me using it, rubbing my scent all over it. The thought amuses me, bringing a grin to my lips.

Not bothering to dry my legs, I slip into the fluffy white bathrobe hanging behind the door. It smells like coconut and something else I cannot name, a woody smell, almost musky.

I like it.

My prisoner looks up immediately as I enter, her eyes widening at the sight of me in her robe that stretches over my chest.

Although Kiah's tall for a woman, I'm definitely bulkier than her, and the robe doesn't reach all the way around, leaving a strip of skin in front.

Not that I give a fuck. If it were up to me, I'd spend my life naked. Clothes always feel weird on my skin. The robe is just to rile up the innkeeper.

She's still lying on the floor where I left her, my cum drying on her cheek. I would take a picture if I didn't break my phone before we even left the city. I'm not taking any chances.

"Look who decided to be a good girl for once." I push Kiah over to her side with my foot, just because I can.

She makes an awful lot of noise, wiggling about.

"What do you want?" I ask.

Her eyes are wild, frantic almost. But the only sounds that escape her mouth are incoherent mumbles.

I sigh, lifting her chin with my foot. "I'm going to take out your gag, but if you scream, 1) nobody will hear you, and 2) I will fucking rip your vocal cords out with my bare hands, understood?"

Kiah nods furiously, and I reach down to untie the dishcloths.

"Jesus," she gasps, making gagging sounds as soon as her mouth is free.

"So dramatic." I leave her there and pick up the whiskey bottle again, pouring another shot or two down my throat. It's probably not going to help the headache but *Aspirin is for weaklings*, my mother always said.

"I need to pee," Kiah says, her voice surprisingly measured for someone in her position. She wasn't even crying yet or begging for her life like they usually did when my father sent me to collect debts.

I like her. She's spicy.

My laughter rings through the house, but Kiah doesn't join me. Instead, she stares daggers into my skin like it could actually affect the outcome of this situation.

"What's so funny?" the innkeeper demands with those plump lips, her brow knitting with little wrinkles that make her even hotter.

She looks a bit like that actress Charlize Theron, I decide, as I watch the woman squirm around on the floor, the chair still strapped to her like an inescapable burden.

"You thinking I'm going to let you loose," I answer.

"Are you deaf? I said I need to pee," she spits, her entire face straining with tension.

"Doesn't sound like my problem." I take another gulp of whiskey as I plunge down into one of the brown armchairs that seem more for comfort than style. Everything in this place seems that way.

It's a far cry from the luxury I'm used to back at the Ricci mansion I usually call home. Our servants' quarters are more equipped than this sad excuse of a home. It's so...*basic*.

But it will have to do, for now at least.

At least it's clean.

"I can't hold it anymore." Her voice is growing desperate, much to my amusement.

"Then don't."

The horror spreads on her face as she realizes I'm serious.

"You animal. Untie me!" Kiah's measured tone is a thing of the past now.

"If you're just going to complain, I'll put the gag back in. Do you want that?" I ask, waving my finger at her like she's a naughty child.

She doesn't answer, just glares at me.

"Please," Kiah tries again, softer this time.

"You're pretty when you beg. But it won't work," I tell her, pushing myself out of my seat again to hover over her.

"Here, let me start you off." Tipping the bottle, I pour the remaining whiskey onto her crotch, watching as the liquid spreads over her grey linen pants like she's already wet herself.

She gasps loudly.

I wonder if it burns.

I hope so.

But at least it keeps her quiet.

The innkeeper doesn't bring up needing to pee again.

Whether she pisses herself or not, who knows.

I'm not interested.

It doesn't help me fix my current predicament.

Cracking my knuckles as I speak, I stare out into the darkness beyond the window that keeps rattling in the wind. It's irritating me. "Tomorrow, you're going to help me get the fuck out of here. Ideally, to Mexico for now."

I have to keep moving. Sooner or later, they'll find me here. This was supposed to be the first stop only, just for the night.

"You can't," Kiah says simply.

"Wrong answer. Try again."

The innkeeper sighs. "Trust me, I would love you gone. But nobody is getting in or out until that storm passes."

"You better not be lying; I don't tolerate lies." There are enough lies in the world. Few things make my blood boil like people who aren't truthful.

"I'm not lying."

"Call someone."

"The lines are dead."

"There has to be a way." As anger floods through me, my jaw tightens, the bones creaking under the strain—an old habit that I can't seem to shake.

"It's off-season. The place is deserted. There are no ferries for another month. And no plane can fly in this." Her voice is surprisingly calm. It pisses me off even more.

"No!" Uncontrollable rage rips through me as I smash the whiskey bottle against the wall. It shatters onto the ground, followed by the unfinished canvas I pull from its easel to break over the table.

Perfectly stacked plates.

Glasses.

Fuck 'em all.

"Stop it!" Kiah calls as I destroy her things.

But what is she going to do?

"Shut up!" I rip the abstract painting from the wall, bright colors that mean nothing to me, and hold it over her, my chest heaving with rapid breaths.

"Don't—" She doesn't get to finish her sentence before I break the painting over her knees, and she cries out in shock.

But the innkeeper's the least of my worries.

I can't stick around; they'll find me.

And I don't even have my gun to defend myself with.

Cazzo!

ESCAPE

KIAH

FOR FIVE HOURS, I LIE IN A PUDDLE OF MY OWN filth and whiskey, every muscle in my body screaming with aches.

But I refuse to let him break me.

I've met a lot of bad men in my life but Nico definitely makes it into the top ten of that list.

That's if *Nico* is even his real name.

Whatever his name is, he has no idea who he's dealing with. I'm done playing nice.

It's way past daybreak before the asshole finishes enough of my liquor to knock him out.

He's snoring loudly in my bed, passed out on his back with his arm hanging off the side, another half-drunk bottle of whiskey spilling out on the floor. I was saving those for Christmas. *Prick*.

Passed out, Nico almost looks peaceful...serene. But there is nothing peaceful about the brute who forced me to wet myself with his sticky cum still drying on my face.

I'll have to burn that bathrobe—it's touched that animal's body. He's probably stretched it too.

Who does he think he is coming into *my* house, tying me up, and breaking my shit?

My eyes burn with disgusted tears, but I force them back. They won't help me now. I've learned a long time ago that tears won't save you. Nobody will save you if you can't save yourself.

This is my chance.

I need to do something before he wakes up.

It's been a few years since I've had to use my survival skills, but one doesn't simply unlearn one's training—especially not if one's background includes more than a decade in the military.

You sure don't make it into the Special Forces by simply rolling over and playing dead whenever someone ties you up.

This is *not* how I die.

The storm howls outside, a fitting backdrop to my silent struggle.

I take one final, steadying breath, my chest tight with anticipation, and then I throw my body weight sideways.

The world spins, then settles as I find myself curled in a fetal position, the hardwood floor cool against my cheek.

My ears strain for any reaction from the bed.

Nothing.

Nico's rhythmic snores continue uninterrupted.

Relief washes over me, but I can't relax.

Not yet.

I clench my jaw, focusing all my energy on pressing my shins into the chair's legs.

Sweat beads on my forehead as I push, push, push.

The wood creaks in protest but holds firm.

Frustration bubbles in my chest. I need more leverage.

Tilting my feet forward, I take aim. My muscles coil, then release as I slam my heels back into the chair. Once. Twice. Three times.

Each impact sends shockwaves up my legs, but I bite back the pain.

On the fourth try, a satisfying crack echoes through the room as the chair's legs start to splinter.

My head whips around, heart in my throat. But the passed-out brute on my bed hasn't stirred.

The tempest outside masks my efforts as I continue my assault on the chair. Kick after kick, I chip away at its integrity.

Sweat stings my eyes by the time the chair's front legs splinter and give way.

It's a small victory, but I'm far from free.

At least I can move my legs now.

As I struggle, the zip ties bite into my wrists, a constant, throbbing reminder of my captivity. But I push the pain aside.

Focus, Kiah.

Maneuvering onto my knees, I survey the destruction

around me. My once-peaceful cottage is now a battlefield of broken pottery and shattered art.

The knife from before is nowhere in sight. Nico must have hidden it.

It doesn't help that my own kitchen knives are blunt as shit; completely useless. I usually do most of my cooking in the big kitchen at the back of the inn.

Plan B? My eyes lock on the shards of my mismatched plates broken on the floor: porcelain—sharp and deadly. That will have to do.

With my hands still bound behind my back, grasping a shard is a Herculean task. I twist and contort, desperation fueling each attempt.

At last, my fingers close around a triangular piece. Its edge bites deep, and I feel warm blood trickle down my palm. But I welcome the pain. It's proof I'm alive, still fighting.

Gripping the makeshift blade, I saw frantically at the zip tie. The plastic resists, mocking my efforts.

Soon, my hands become slick with blood, making each movement treacherous. But I persist, driven by a primal need for freedom.

When the tie finally snaps, I allow myself a moment of silent triumph.

With grim determination, I attack the fishing line next.

Each strand gives way relunctantly, loosening my bonds bit by excruciating bit.

At last, I wriggle free from the chair's embrace, my tortoiseshell prison.

For a moment, I just remain on the floor, trying to catch my breath as it races through my body, chasing my pounding heartbeat.

The whole plan was way easier in my head.

When I imagined freeing myself with a broken shard, I didn't factor in the bleeding hands that now leave scarlet prints wherever they land.

But freedom is freedom.

Phase one—complete.

Standing up, I stretch my legs, wincing as the pins and needles fade. They ache like hell, but the feeling slowly returns.

It's time to move.

I tuck the shard into my back pocket and head to the bed.

Nico is still sleeping, though the whiskey bottle has dropped to the floor.

This should be the part where I gather my essentials and get away as quickly as I can.

But there is nowhere to run in this storm.

So, I have no choice but to deal with the passed-out asshole in my bed.

Moving swiftly but silently, I dig out the duct tape underneath my other art supplies. It's nestled among the glues and palette knives—hidden in plain sight.

Of course, I have duct tape.

Who doesn't?

But I wasn't going to tell Nico that.

Considering the alternative he came up with, I almost wish I did.

Holding my breath, I approach the bed, the sleeping beast's snores cutting through the rhythmic tapping of the rain on the roof.

Carefully, I wrap the tape around his right wrist, stretching it to the nearest corner of the poster bed and securing it tightly.

The shard comes in handy as a makeshift pair of scissors, sawing off the stretches of silver tape with much less damage to my hands now that I have control over them both.

Nico mumbles something incoherent in his sleep but doesn't wake.

Adrenaline courses through my veins as I work to repeat the process with his left wrist, making sure he can't break free.

But I get as far as wrapping the tape around his wrist when Nico wakes with a groan, stormy blue eyes fluttering open with a start.

He blinks groggily, probably still drunk, and it takes a few seconds for him to react.

"What the fuck?" he exclaims as he pulls free and shoves his hand in my face, trying to force his fingers into my mouth.

I jerk my head back instinctively, reaching for my pocket.

Before Nico can react, I jab the porcelain shard into his shoulder with as much force as I can muster.

Immediately, blood starts gushing from the wound— more than I expected. The fucker is still drunk; it's making his blood thin.

"Ah! What the fuck?"

Nico starts thrashing, his movements frantic and wild. But I refuse to budge, pressing my body weight onto him to keep him still.

Working quickly, I wrap more tape around his left wrist, pulling it toward the opposite corner of the bed to secure it firmly.

His shouts grow louder, more frantic, as he fights against his restraints. But he stands no chance.

My military training is one thing, but the subsequent nine years I spent as a mercenary are way more useful to me right now. Fewer rules, greater rewards. I was unstoppable...until I wasn't.

Focus, Kiah.

I move on to his ankles and narrowly avoid being kicked in the face. But I'm not letting him bruise me any more than he already has.

The duct tape stretches taut as I secure his ankles, fixing him in a spread-eagle position.

"You fucking whore!" The fury in Nico's voice is unmistakable.

His body twists and turns as he continues to curse at me, but the duct tape holds firm.

"Just shut up!" I demand.

But he doesn't listen.

So, I tape his mouth too.

Finally, I step back, surveying my work.

Nico's face is twisted in rage as he tugs at his restraints. But his attempts are futile.

"Two can play this game, little boy," I whisper to my prisoner as I stroke a tousle of dark hair from his sweaty forehead. "You messed with the wrong woman."

Satisfied that he isn't going anywhere, I quietly collapse in the armchair beside the bed, exhaling loudly as I wipe the sweat from my brow.

All tied up, Nico doesn't look so scary. He looks quite vulnerable, in fact. I must say I prefer him this way—bound and spread.

I should probably deal with that shard in his shoulder, but the cut doesn't look too deep; he'll be fine.

If I have to play nurse right now, I might end up jamming that shard in deeper on purpose just because his face pisses me off.

I pick up what remains of the whiskey and take a long swig that burns through my throat to my belly. It's a welcome sensation, though.

"Fucking hell."

Sitting back, I study my bound captive as his muffled moans fill the air, his stormy eyes wild.

Desperation is a good look on him. Who knew?

We could have a lot of fun like this...

An unexpected flicker of lust sparks through my spine, and I bite down on my bottom lip, looking away, out the window, to the storm.

What the fuck?

How am I turned on by this psycho?

But I have a feeling it's not so much the tattooed devil tied to my bed but the danger, the excitement of it all, that's soaking my already wet panties with desire.

The adrenaline rush is undeniable.

I feel alive!

Jesus, Kiah. Stop it.

Trying to force the desire from my mind, I take another swig of the liquor.

Time to plan my revenge.

I have just the thing in mind...

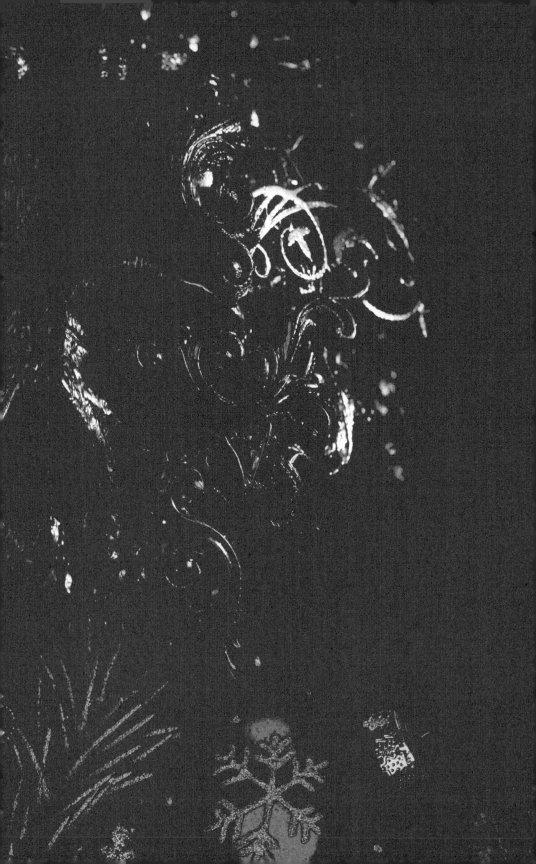

CAGED
NICO

PAIN EXPLODES IN MY SHOULDER WHEN THAT BITCH stabs me.

It burns through my insides, white-hot and searing.

I gasp, the air catching in my throat as I see the jagged piece of porcelain jutting out from my flesh.

A mixture of shock and rage surges through me as blood wells up around the shard, warm and thin, soaking the gown.

I can't believe the innkeeper stabbed me.

They don't usually fight back...

I clench my jaw, the taste of copper on my tongue as I bite down on the inside of my cheek.

The pain in my shoulder is blinding, but I force myself to stay conscious as my vision blurs at the edges.

Every breath sends a jolt of agony through my body, but I push it aside, focusing on Kiah.

I won't show weakness, not now, not ever.

That harlot will regret the day she was born.

You don't fuck with Domenico Ricci and get away with it. My father is Don Ricci himself, head of one of the most ruthless crime families on the East Coast.

Was.

My father *was* Don Ricci.

Manipulative cunt.

He got what he had coming to him.

Even if things didn't go according to plan.

My family history doesn't change shit about my current predicament, though.

I'm still spread out on this bed with my shoulder throbbing like a motherfucker, clouding my thoughts, making it hard to think straight.

Kiah studies me from the foot of the bed, her posture defiant, her eyes blazing with determination. It's a look I know well—the look of someone who believes they have the upper hand.

My mind races, calculating, assessing. There's a part of me that almost admires her nerve.

It takes guts to turn the tables on me.

But that admiration is fleeting, quickly smothered by a surge of anger and betrayal.

How dare she?

A cold fury coats my veins—a deep, simmering rage.

I feel the familiar tightness creeping into my jaw, my teeth grinding together as the rage builds inside me.

As Kiah disappears out the door, I test the duct tape again, wincing as the shard of porcelain cuts deeper into my shoulder.

Fucking bitch was lying about the duct tape.

I *detest* lying.

She'll pay for this.

She thinks she has control now, but control is an illusion.

Kiah suddenly drops a large black crate on the bed beside me, forcing me out of my revenge loop.

What is this crafty whore up to now?

Is this the part where she tortures me?

The thought is amusing, and I laugh, a sound only partially muffled by the gag.

I doubt it. What does a silly old innkeeper know about my world of torture and terror?

Ignoring me completely, Kiah carries on with her business, unlocking the padlock on the crate.

She doesn't narrate her actions or even address me; her full attention is on the crate and sifting through its contents.

"Aha!" is the first thing she says as she pulls a shiny metal object from the crate.

I can't see what it is—not from this angle. Cranking my neck that far out only hurts my wounded shoulder.

"I wouldn't move if I were you," she tells me as she opens my bathrobe fully, reaching for my cock.

My, my, Miss Kiah. Why didn't you say you wanted some of this sweet dick?

Roughly tugging at my flesh, she lathers cold lube on my shaft.

I gasp.

Her touch sends a shockwave of need through my body.

My cock instantly perks awake.

Hmm, of course, she wants my body.

I should've known.

Women always throw themselves at me.

How basic, I—

My thoughts dry up instantly as I feel the cold metal ring slide over my cock.

What the actual fuck?

With clinical movements, Kiah tugs at my balls, pulling them through the ring as well. I'm sure there's no way they're going through that small space, but she somehow manages.

Fucking hell, it's so uncomfortable.

I squirm under her, but I have nowhere to go.

What is she up to?

"This next part would be much easier if you weren't hard," the innkeeper tells me with no discernable emotion in her voice. Her face is impossible to read as she disappears into the kitchen.

I may not know how to *feel* most emotions, but I know what they *look* like in others. People are so easy, so open; they let their true feelings show for the world to see—to use and abuse.

When you spend your whole life studying people so you

know how to act, so nobody gets suspicious that there's nothing but words running behind your eyelids—no pictures, just words —it becomes almost too easy to read other people's emotions.

But not this woman. She's hiding something. Something I can't figure out yet.

I don't have time to ponder Kiah's secrets, though. The cold ring around my dick is impossible to ignore.

Stupid bitch.

She doesn't know who she's messing with.

When I get free, she's going to regret this. I will slice her open and fuck her in a pool of her own blood until she's nothing but a bad memory.

The innkeeper returns from the kitchen with a large bucket.

Before I even have time to wonder what she's up to, I choke on my own breath as the icy water hits my erection.

Fuck!

It's painfully cold, instantly deflating my hard-on.

Like a wild animal, I moan into my gag, trying to express my displeasure.

But Kiah seems to enjoy my torment.

"Perfect," the smug bitch declares, dropping the bucket on the floor with a clatter while I miserably wriggle around in the wet bed.

Her eyes narrow in concentration as she takes my now-limp dick in her hand. It looks small and pathetic—all shriveled up.

Biting her lip, she picks a little metal device that looks like a miniature birdcage if birdcages were banana-shaped.

Oh no! The realization of what she's doing suddenly hits me.

I've seen one of those before—in porn, sure, not in real life—but I've seen them.

Fuck no!

I squirm under her, but her grip on my dick is firm.

"This little guy has done enough bad deeds for one day. He's not needed anymore," she says simply, bundling my sad cock into the metal.

The cage is small, smaller than my cock, but she somehow gets my pecker inside, thanks to its shriveled-up state.

My piercings were not made to be caged, and they press uncomfortably against the top—metal against metal—but it doesn't seem to make any difference to Kiah.

With a grin, she locks it with a little gold lock and hangs the key around her neck.

It dangles down between her tits, taunting me.

I scream and shout into my shitty gag, the cold metal uncomfortable around my junk.

It even detracts from the pain in my shoulder, forcing my mind on my needy dick.

But there's no use.

Laughing manically, the innkeeper sits back in the chair and admires her handiwork.

My face flushes with embarrassment—I can feel it

creeping up my neck, warm, unstoppable. *This is fucking humiliating!*

Instantly, I feel myself getting hard again.

What the fuck?

There is nowhere to grow though, and my dick presses uncomfortably against the sides of the cage, trying to spread through the thin spaces between the bars.

My tormentor picks up the bottle of half-drunk liquor from the floor and takes a big swig, eyes locked on mine defiantly, as she crosses her legs like she means business.

Kiah grins, speaking slowly. "What did you say earlier? Oh yeah...Much better."

That bitch!

NURSE

KIAH

WHEN I WAKE UP FROM MY MUCH-NEEDED POWER nap on the futon, I almost expect to find Nico hovering over me with a knife. But the fucker is thankfully still tied and caged on my bed.

Relief soaks into my tired limbs as I drag myself off the floor.

I should probably move him and burn those sheets, but right now, I'm too drained for that kind of physical labor.

Coffee. I need coffee.

Glancing at the kettle-shaped clock above the stove, I do the math: I only got about four hours of sleep. Not ideal, but it will have to do.

After finally restraining the asshole, my victory drink turned into a victory binge, and I finished an entire bottle of red wine as well, trying to calm my mind enough to sleep.

It's a good thing I kept that chastity cage. The things people leave behind at their holiday destinations…It's been in the lost-and-found box since two seasons ago.

I don't even know what made me think of it now, but once the idea took root in my mind, there was no turning back.

Probably not the *right* thing to do. But who gives a fuck? That brat deserved much worse for his bullshit behavior.

I wish I could just snap my fingers and make Nico disappear.

A bit of back-up would've been great right about now.

But as usual, I'll have to deal with this alone.

What's new?

I've never had anyone but myself.

I didn't know they still left babies outside churches?, my classmates would whisper behind cupped hands as I walked by, giggling like I couldn't hear them. *Shame, her parents didn't want her, did you hear?*

My foster parents always told me to pay the gossips no mind, that I was special, meant for great things.

They were lovely people, kind people, but they were old—they died a few months apart when I was 12, leaving me with nothing except a single suitcase of clothes and the instruction to move in with Aunt Martha down South.

Aunt Martha was not my actual aunt, but she was okay; she liked to bake square carrot cupcakes and watch birds through her oversized binoculars. Her taste in men was atrocious, though. She probably could've had a good life if Uncle William wasn't around.

Uncle William had a scruffy mustache and always smelled like rum. He liked to *rearrange* things with his fist—mostly Aunt Martha's face, sometimes mine. I was too weak to do anything, to fight back.

Once, when I was 16, he spat on the black eye he himself had given me, laughing maniacally as he told me how I'd never amount to anything more than a cum dumpster for low-life men.

Fucking asshole.

I joined the Marines as soon as I legally could. And when I went back, Uncle William wasn't the one laughing, I was. His head made a hollow crack as I smashed his skull against the doorway—I'll never forget that sound. I felt nothing but relief as I watched him bleed out on that stained gray carpet in the lounge.

My only regret was that Aunt Martha was no longer alive to see him pay his dues. It was never proven, but I know he was the one who pushed her down the stairs that day. She didn't deserve any of it.

So much for family.

I never bothered tracking my biological parents—if I was dead to them, they were dead to me.

With a sigh, I stare out the window, willing the storm to slow down so I can think, but the weather is as insubordinate as my unexpected guest.

It's dark and chaotic out there. Rain still hammers on the roof relentlessly as the wind tugs at my shutters like the big bad wolf is trying to blow my house down.

I'm overly aware of the extra body in my space, but I try my best to ignore him as I force myself through my normal routine.

After putting the kettle on the stove, I add an extra spoon of coffee to the plunger, hoping for a miracle from the additional caffeine.

Nico doesn't make any sound as I sip my black coffee at the kitchen counter...or when I lock myself in the bathroom to scrub myself under the scalding water that is finally heated again.

No matter how hot I make the water, it's not hot enough. I can still feel that creep's warm sticky cum dripping on my face despite having washed it off before bed already.

The mere thought of that scene makes my stomach churn with disgust...and something else—a tinge of need that shouldn't be there.

Why can't I stop thinking about those dick piercings?

For fuck's sake, Kiah.

I force the thought from my mind.

Fresh out of the shower, I throw on some denim shorts and a black tank top, gathering my wet hair in a messy bun on top of my head without bothering with a bra.

With a deep breath, I brace myself as I head to the bed I've been avoiding.

As much as I want to ignore Nico all day, I know I need to get that shard out of his shoulder. He may be a creep, but I don't want him to die.

I don't exactly have a clean-up team anymore; I'd have to dispose of the body myself.

When I get closer, I notice that something is clearly wrong. Nico's skin has turned pale and clammy, his brow slick with sweat. His eyes are half-closed and glazed over.

The sight of the wound is even more alarming.

Oh, shit.

The area around the porcelain shard is angry and inflamed, a red, swollen mess that looks painfully tight.

The piece must have gotten lodged in deeper as he moved about.

Fuck.

I lean down, removing his gag, "Nico, can you hear me?"

The restrained man offers only a low grunt, his eyes drifting, unable to focus.

"Nico?"

The heat radiating off his body is unmistakable.

Fever.

This is bad.

I should've known.

Damnit.

I've dealt with so many messy wounds during my years in the Marines; I know this is not the kind of thing you leave in.

But, in my defense, last night (this morning) didn't exactly go according to plan.

Nevertheless, this asshole is not dying in my inn. I don't need that kind of heat. Not when I'm supposed to be dead. The police will definitely come looking if a body washes ashore, and I can't risk blowing my cover.

Just the thought of finding a new hideout is exhausting.

"Hang in there," I mutter, trying to reassure both of us as I use Nico's knife to free his arms from the duct tape.

Gathering supplies, I grab a clean towel, a bottle of water, and some antiseptic from the bathroom cabinet.

What I'm about to do could either help him or make things worse, but I have to do *something*.

Gritting my teeth, I soak the towel with water and kneel beside the bed to get a closer look at the wound.

"This is going to hurt," I say more to myself than to Nico, who seems beyond hearing.

The towel turns pink with diluted blood as I gently press the wet towel around the shard, trying to clean the area as best as possible without disturbing it.

I swallow hard, focusing on the task as I pour some antiseptic onto a clean part of the towel and dab it around the wound, praying it will do something to stave off the infection.

"Here goes," I whisper, wiping my sweaty hands on my shorts before gripping the shard. Forcing my breath past my lips in a steady flow, I slowly, carefully, begin to pull out the foreign object.

Nico jerks slightly, a strangled cry escaping his throat as the shard finally lodges free, coated in blood and something thicker—pus.

The sight makes my hungover body gag, but I force the bile down back into my stomach; I can't afford to lose it now.

With the shard out, I get a clearer look at the wound. It's bad—deep, with ragged edges and signs of serious infection. The skin around it is an alarming shade of red, and there's a thin coating of yellow I wish wasn't there.

I press the towel against the wound, trying to stem the flow of fresh blood and clean it as best as I can. "Come on, come on," I mutter, feeling the tension claw at my chest.

Nico's breathing is shallow and fast, and he's starting to shiver uncontrollably.

This isn't good.

I grab the antiseptic again and pour it directly into the wound, watching as it foams and bubbles.

Nico moans in pain, but I have to keep going.

Using the remaining clean water, I flush the wound as thoroughly as possible, trying to remove any debris and pus— just like they taught me in the army.

This man needs proper medical attention, but there's none on this island right now. I'm his best bet.

Thank fuck I always keep a well-stocked first-aid kit. An old contact ensures I have all the meds I need, including some pretty strong antibiotics I'm going to have to force-feed this man.

But for now, that wound needs to be closed. So, I rummage through my art supplies for the sewing kit, grabbing a few other things I will need.

My mind is calm and focused as I sterilize the needle and tweezers over a candle flame, dousing them in antiseptic afterward.

It takes some effort, but I manage to get Nico to swallow a couple of painkillers and an aspirin. For what it's worth.

Like I'm about to mend a sock rather than a man, I thread the needle with the cleanest, strongest thread I have, sterilizing the sharp metal again before use.

Oh god. This isn't ideal. But there is no other option.

I take a deep breath, reminding myself of my training.

You can do this, Kiah.

Climbing on the bed, I position myself over Nico's waist with a leg on either side to get the best angle on the wound, straddling him. "This is going to hurt like a motherfucker," I whisper without expecting a response. There is none.

Working carefully but quickly, I begin suturing, stitching the edges of the wound together.

The cut is deep but not deep enough to reach muscle. He should be okay with external stitches only—I hope.

As the storm continues raging outside, the needle moves in and out of the bruised skin, my hands steady despite the situation.

One stitch, then another, until I've closed the entire length of the wound with about twelve more stitches.

Each pass of the needle through Nico's skin makes him twitch and groan, but he doesn't fully wake up.

When the jagged line of tiny stitches reaches the end of

the nasty cut, I tie the thread off with secure knots, hoping it's tight but not too tight to fuck with his circulation.

Finally, I smear a generous amount of antibiotic ointment over the sutures before wrapping up the wound as best I can with gauze and bandages from my medicine drawer.

That's when I notice it—the familiar tattoo hidden among the other artworks on Nico's fully-inked arm.

No, it can't be.

But it is.

Staring back at me is the Ricci family crest, clear as day, permanently etched onto Nico's skin, just like every other member of that fucked-up family.

It was my job to know everything there was to know about the crime families. It's what kept me alive, out of their way.

Surely, he can't be a Ricci?

Not here.

Why is he here?

Holy fuck. This is worse than I thought.

If the mafia comes looking for him, it won't end well for me.

I'm supposed to be dead, a ghost.

You never know what connections these assholes have. If they start pulling on the thread that is Kiah McClane's identity, who knows how much they'll unravel?

A bit of blonde hair dye only goes so far.

What if someone figures it out?

What if they realize that Jenna Cade didn't die that night at the docks?

That Jenna and Kiah look suspiciously identical, down to the dragon tattoo on their backs?

I put my hand on the feverish man's head, silently begging for his recovery.

Please don't die.

Delerium

Nico

Like a madman, I'm running through the forest, the darkness wrapping around me like a suffocating mantel.

The ground beneath my feet is uneven, roots and rocks conspiring to trip me up.

But I push on, running, running.

I don't know what's chasing me, but I hear it—heavy foot-steps crashing through the underbrush, a low growl that makes the hair on the back of my neck stand on end.

I don't dare look back.

The growls are closer now, almost at my heels.

Panic rises in my throat.

I try to scream, but no sound comes out.

The silence is deafening, oppressive.

I'm not going to make it, I—

I wake up before the beast catches me.

Cold sweat clings to me like a second skin. My breath is rapid and unsteady; it burns my throat.

Cazzo!

It was just a nightmare.

The damn forest one again.

I hate that one.

That place is so creepy, so dark.

But as my real surroundings blur into focus in the warm orange light of the cabin, I remember that my nightmare isn't contained to my dreamworld.

My waking life is a scene straight from Stephen King's *Misery*, and my own personal Kathy Bates still has my dick in a cage and my legs tied to the bed on this secluded island like I'm not the heir to the Ricci dynasty. Like I'm some common low-life.

I don't know how long I've been here.

My world has been reduced to running through a dark forest and waking up in pain, my shoulder throbbing angrily.

The sound of the rain crashing on the roof seems endless, drowning out reality.

I try to move, even just my hand, but my body isn't my own; it no longer obeys me.

All I feel is pain, a hazy torment that stains my reality with its black liquid, threatening to drown me for good.

The innkeeper is usually there whenever I wake up, but she doesn't speak much.

That worried look in her eyes tells me all I need to know

as I tether on the edge of reality, ready to plummet into the abyss at any moment.

She wipes my face with a cold cloth sometimes, but perhaps that's also part of my dreams. I can't imagine her giving enough of a fuck to do something like that.

All I know is that I don't want to die.

Not like this.

Not without clearing my name, claiming my throne.

But I'm not strong enough to fight yet. I'll have to bide my time.

My dreams aren't all about running through the forest.

Sometimes, real memories haunt me, muddying my shitty present with my shitty past.

Faces come back to me, conversations. Things could have been so different. But with parents like mine, every possible reality would've been fucked up either way—that much I'm certain of.

When I was younger, I let myself believe it could be different, that I had some control over my own life.

But what I wanted never mattered.

I was but a pawn in my parents' little game.

When I met Annika, I thought I could have a normal life.

It's been three years since her death, but every little detail of our tragic love story will forever be burned into my memory.

The happy memories hurt as much as the reminder of her painful demise.

Annika didn't care about my violent tendencies; she

didn't need my empathy. Born into the Russian mob, my dark-haired princess was well-accustomed to our nefarious life and its dangers. A Bonnie to my Clyde, we were going to set the world on fire, to have it all.

Despite my displeased parents, we were married within a month.

Too young, everyone said, but I was done letting them control my life like they did my childhood.

However, Mommy Dearest already had my match all set up for me. *Don't be silly, Dom. You can't marry into the Russian mob.*

She laughed when I told her I was engaged. They had Don Greco's niece lined up for me, *a harmonious merger of families*, my father called it.

I always blamed myself for Annika's death.

We had two happy years of beautiful chaos that set my skin on fire and left me in a permanent state of arousal.

Once, I fucked her right there in a pool of someone's blood, someone she had just stabbed. It was everything I ever wanted.

And then it was over. I found her body dangling from the ceiling beam in our bedroom, a suicide note neatly stashed in an envelope.

The guilt tore me apart.

It was all my fault.

Until the day I learned that it wasn't...

It wasn't my fault at all.

My life is divided into two distinct periods: Before Annika and After Annika.

The latter era became a cruel joke of pointless days and painful nightmares.

The only thing that took the edge off was breaking someone open until their blood streaked the concrete in dark red.

That and a boatload of alcohol.

I knew I was toxic; I couldn't get close to anyone again. They would inevitably end up dead.

No, it was better I focused on work—much to my parents' relief.

And then that heartless cunt that called himself my father got a bit too liberal with his words one drunken evening, a bit too free. He let something slip that I couldn't let go.

I tugged and tugged on the thread until the entire nasty mess untangled before me.

The part where my father raped my bride and had her killed shouldn't have been a surprise to me.

But the part where he boasted about Annika accepting the generous cash bribe to leave me, that part stung.

The betrayal was unbearable...on all sides.

It didn't matter that she changed her mind and wanted to give the cash back—the whole reason my father took care of her and wiped her off the face of the planet.

The fact that she could even *consider* his offer was too painful to bear.

The day he told me, rage ripped through my body as I

stared at my inappropriately cheerful father. The asshole was proud of his sins.

My hands had clenched and unclenched with such might that I could hear every knuckle crack individually.

But I didn't kill him then.

No, I bided my time.

I wanted him to have a slow and painful death—poison. It was already planned, ready. I had the perfect alibi lined up.

But things didn't work out that way.

It all went wrong.

Someone beat me to it.

Someone who wanted me to take the fall for the crime.

]\When I woke up next to my father's lifeless body, I knew I had to get out of there before my brother buried me next to our father without giving me a second to explain.

Who could I trust? Nobody on the payroll could help me.

So, I grabbed the duffel full of cash I kept stashed where my car's spare wheel should be and found the closest private airstrip.

Always have an exit strategy.

Always.

Some nights, I wake up from these nightmarish memories convinced that I'm back at home instead of the island, stuck in the world my parents have created for me.

No friends, no real school, *no leaving the house without your guards, Domenico*. I was a prisoner in my own home.

The future Don needs to be safe at all times—the tune my mother recited ad nauseam until her dying day.

But I was never safe.

Not then.

And definitely not now.

I've simply traded one hell for another. One where the busty inn-keeper with muscle arms like Madonna feeds me lukewarm thin soup like I'm a baby, feeling my forehead with the back of her hand repeatedly.

The delirium refuses to leave me as my present, past, and dream worlds conspire to keep me caged in painful misery.

The loop keeps repeating.

More soup.

More pills.

More running through the dark forest with the faceless beast in pursuit.

I don't know why Kiah doesn't just finish what she started and just kill me, but she seems to be taking care of me.

She must have some ulterior motive...

At some point, the haze starts to lift slightly.

I'm almost convinced I hear birds chirping outside, but I know it can't be—the storm is endless.

Except it isn't...

One day, I wake up to the welcoming warmth of the sun on my face, stray rays sneaking in through the window.

After this, the fuzziness starts to dissipate slowly.

I'm fully present as the innkeeper with the soft hands and concerned eyes washes my body with a cloth, trailing it over my skin, my caged cock, like a real nurse.

I keep my eyes closed, pretending to be asleep. But it's

difficult not to moan, especially when she lifts my balls and strokes the cloth over them.

There is nothing sensual about her movements; they are clinical, precise...but my dick doesn't know the difference.

Only when she turns the lights off and the warm glow switches to darkness do I open my eyes.

The moon is but a slither outside, offering no illumination. The only light in the room comes from the microwave's number dials, a neon green glow that casts more shadows than light.

If I keep absolutely still, I can hear Kiah's hurried breaths in the darkness, the soft hum of electricity radiating from the futon by the window—a vibrator.

Eyes glued to the scene, I try to imagine the innkeeper's face as she masturbates, trying to muffle those cries of pleasure she thinks nobody can hear.

Such pretty little sounds. I'm sure she'd sound amazing at full volume.

My dick is uncomfortably hard in the confines of its metal cage that feels cold against my sensitive skin.

With my good arm, I reach down, trying to slip one of my fat fingers into the space between the metal bars, but it's no use.

My balls are so sensitive, though, just like the flesh protruding from the cage. Wherever I touch, need burns my skin with its familiar urgency.

In no time, my orgasm builds to the edge, pent up for too long.

Who knows how long I've been here, how long I've been in this cage without a release?

But it's no use.

As a muffled howl of pleasure floats from the futon, I have to content myself with the ruined orgasm that drips from the top of my inescapable chastity cage. Unsatisfied.

For fuck's sake! I feel no relief, just frustration, and it takes every ounce of self-control I have not to express my displeasure out loud.

It's in my best interest that Kiah doesn't know I'm getting stronger yet.

If I move too soon, I'll ruin my only chance of escaping.

Fucking whore!

Why does she get to have a climax, but I don't?

Just wait until I get out of this cage. She's going to pay.

Just wait...

INFORMANT

KIAH

MY DAYS PASS NOT TOO DISSIMILAR THAN THEY would've had the little Ricci brat not shown up on my doorstep.

My daily jogs around the island are back in full swing—the only remedy for the tempestuous thoughts that plague me.

I still get my reading done, my painting, laying in jams and pickles for the festive season. With one small change—caring for Nico.

There is something almost therapeutic about washing his body, tending to the wound, watching it slowly heal. My days have purpose again. A purpose beyond the mundane.

His complexion is looking much better than it did three weeks ago when I sewed the cut shut that morning after our fucked up first encounter.

The longer he's here, the more disheveled his beard gets, his perfectly trimmed dark hair turning slightly curly as it lengthens. This completely changes his look, making him even more handsome—in a rugged way.

But it can never be enough to erase the memory of how he treated me before I managed to turn the tables and restrain him.

I should probably feel bad about how I retaliated, but I don't.

Putting Nico in a chastity cage without consent goes against every rule in the book, but we threw out that book when he tied me up in my own house and violated *my* consent.

Fuck choosing the moral high ground. Why should it be on me?

My mind still flashes back to him towering over me, dick in hand, as he jerked off onto my face.

But it's hard to marry the image of that rain-soaked brute with the delirious shadow of a man who's been occupying my bed for weeks, still fully caged.

Nico should live—that's the good *and* the bad news.

But now that I know who he is, there is one thing I know for certain—I can't have him around here; he's a liability.

With a sigh, I turn on my mobile. There's probably been cellphone reception for a while now. But I've been putting off checking.

The stormy season is pretty much over, and life is slowly

returning to the island. Pretty soon, guests will start arriving for the festive period.

I've procrastinated long enough, delaying the inevitable. But I need to know what's happening out there in the real world.

I want to know and at the same time—I don't; I'm scared of the answer. An answer means I have to do something.

One bar, then two...the signal triangle lights up in the right corner of my phone as I step outside.

With a steady hand, I type the familiar number into the phone that doesn't have a single contact saved. I know the digits off by heart.

It rings only once before the voice of the only person I trust in the world answers.

"Kiah," she breathes, no discernable emotion in her voice.

"Hey J. How are things?"

"Is this a social call?" the voice on the other line asks, to the point as always. In the two decades I've known J., she's never been known to beat around the bush.

"I need information." I know my secrets are safe with her. We spent four years together in the Special Forces, and J. proved herself through and through. I'd take a bullet for that woman (and I have before).

"Anything."

"What's going on with the Riccis? I've been hearing rumors..." I try to keep my voice steady, but it's hard to sound casual when asking such a serious question.

"It's no secret. The Don is dead."

My heart skips a beat, my breath catching in my throat. It's worse than I thought.

"Oh?" I try to sound nonplussed, even though J. definitely knows me better than that.

But she doesn't challenge me.

"Fucker had it coming," J. adds simply.

"You can say that again. I assume it wasn't natural causes?"

"It hardly ever is. Nope, he got murdered."

"Any idea who did it?"

"No, the family is tightlipped about that part. But word on the street is that it was an inside job."

"And now? Who's taking over?"

"That's the strange thing, the new Don is missing. It's been weeks, and nobody knows where Domenico is."

Domenico?

Fuck.

The math slowly adds up in my head.

I had my suspicions, but I didn't want to know.

Nico could've been anyone in the Ricci lineage—a lowlife prince, a cousin maybe. Why did he have to be the heir to the throne?

This is bad.

This is really fucking bad.

"How strange," I say like it's really strange and I don't have the very Don-to-be in question tied to my bed right now.

"Quite. All the families are on edge. His brother has taken

the reigns for now. But between you and me, Ricardo Ricci is even worse than his dad."

"How is that even possible?" I snort. Don Enzo Ricci was the worst of the worst. I've seen the reports of the carnage he's caused. And for every story that's public, ten more are usually hidden.

"Beats me. I don't think anyone would be upset if the entire Ricci family tree was wiped from the earth. Scum, all of them."

"Can't say I disagree," I say, eyeing the beautiful villain in my bed.

"It will only be a matter of time before they find him, though, the missing Ricci. The family has a massive bounty on his head, wanted dead or alive."

Dead *or* alive.

Fucking savages.

"Thanks, J. Everything else okay there?"

"Yeah. And you? Ready to stop hermitting and return to the real world yet?"

"I'm happy here," I reply, but we both know I'm lying.

J. sighs. "Look after yourself, Kiah."

She puts down the phone before I can say anything else.

Keep the calls under 60 seconds, always, that's the rule.

But 60 seconds was enough for me to get all the information I needed.

The remaining questions I have aren't ones J. can help me with.

This is worse than I thought.

I can't be harboring a fugitive.

Especially not a Ricci.

Closing the door behind me again, I pace around the kitchen.

But it does little to alleviate the tension. It's just stressing me out more.

So, I grab another canvas and sit down behind my easel, hoping to distract myself from the chaos in my mind.

As I go through the soothing routine of setting up my paints, I can't help but steal glances at the bed where the caged man lies groaning and squirming.

Almost absentmindedly, I start painting, finding relief in the soft strokes of the brush as it stains the acrylic onto the white surface.

I already have his torso done before I realize what (or rather, *who*) I'm painting. It's Nico.

It's been so oppressively hot in this weather that I've left him with only a sheet that he's since discarded to lie before me fully uncovered, except for the chastity cage.

Over the past weeks, I've become familiar with every inch of his skin as I cared for him—washing him, wiping him down, cleaning up his shit without so much as batting an eyelash.

There is something so stunning about his slightly tanned complexion that gets lighter around the areas normally hidden from the sun. I've had to stop myself numerous times from crossing the line, resisting the impulse to kiss that small clover-shaped birthmark on his collarbone.

Studying Nico's face, I let my paintbrush dance around the canvas in rushed strokes, capturing the depraved enigma spread with his ankles tied to the corners of my bed.

If I wanted to, I could kill him right now, and there's nothing he could do.

But I don't want to.

Even after everything he's done.

I will never admit that I've gotten attached over these past few weeks, that it's been nice to have a distraction from myself, my memories.

And I will definitely never admit that it's the thought of Nico's naked skin pressed against mine that I've been masturbating to—every day.

My sex drive has been virtually non-existent these past few years...since that night at the docks, since they took my baby.

Since that dark day, nothing has excited me.

Nothing but that young, chiseled demon in my bed.

Even with his cock all sad and locked up in its cage, he sparks uncontrollable lust between my thighs, drawing the wetness from my insides...

The more I paint, the more aroused I get—a frustrating realization.

Jesus, Kiah, pull yourself together. He's in the fucking mafia. No good can come from this.

Reasonably, logically, I know that.

But there is no logic involved in my desires, only primal, urgent need. How fucked up is that?

As I paint the sleeping man, I can't help but drop my other hand into my shorts, seeking out my sensitive clit.

It's already sticky down there when I tease the hardness between my fingers. I nearly press my head into the wet paint on the easel for support as my knees grow weak with the building pleasure.

I stop painting; it's impossible to concentrate as my orgasm quickly takes over my system's entire CPU, like a computer overheating.

It's broad daylight; I'm right here in the middle of the open room, but does any of that stop me from working myself into a climax? Oh no.

With my eyes glued on the sweaty body on the bed, I pinch and twist and rub until a little moan catches in my throat, threatening to turn into a roar of pleasure if I don't bite down on my lip so hard I taste blood.

All I can think about is my recurring fantasy of unlocking that cock and burying it inside me without him waking up; of riding him, impaling myself on his hardness—again and again —as he lies motionless but warm, tied up and hard, beneath me like a flesh dildo made just for me.

For the millionth time, I wonder what those piercings would feel like *inside*. Would I feel them scraping me?

The thought instantly sends me over the edge, toppling over into ecstasy as the orgasm vibrates through my body from the center out.

The pleasure takes over, dotting my skin in shivers as I try to tame my rapid breaths.

Relief washes over me as the peak slowly ebbs, and in vain, I try to turn my thoughts away from the future Don Ricci as I ride out the feeling.

This is a recipe for disaster.

But I would order it from the menu again and again. Just to feel something, anything—it's been so fucking long.

With a sigh, I regard the half-painted figure on my canvas.

What the fuck am I going to do with you, boy?

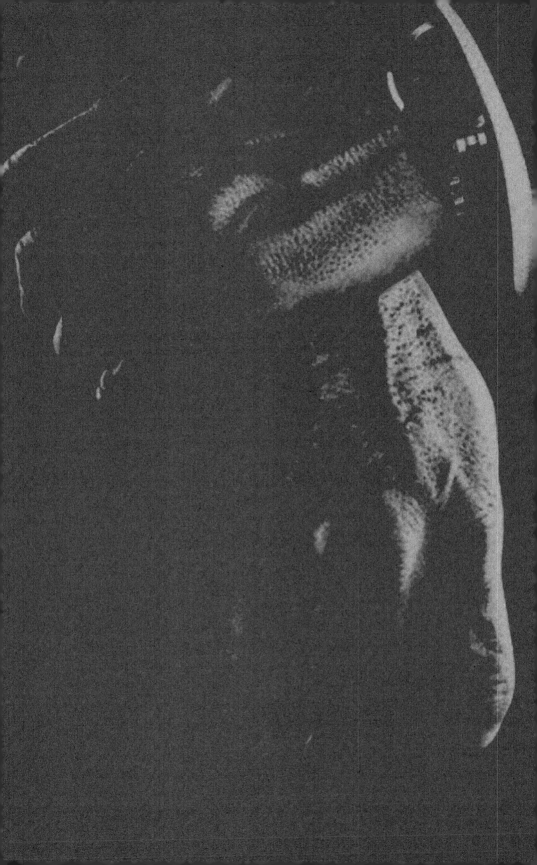

REAWAKEN

NICO

I HAVE NO IDEA HOW LONG I'VE BEEN HERE, HOW many ruined orgasms have dripped from my sad dick in silence as the innkeeper went about her day, painting and stretching, and whatever other shit she does.

She doesn't even know I've been watching her, studying her routine.

My delirium has become an act; I see *everything*—especially the way Kiah looks at my naked body like she wants to do more than just feed me soup.

Nobody has come for me yet. Which is good. But I know my luck won't last forever.

If my mother were alive, she would've found me ages ago already. That bitch was far cleverer than any of them, especially my slimy brother.

But it's been more than a year since we found her lifeless

body floating face-down in the pool, the water stained a pretty shade of red with her blood.

Death was a good look on her.

Nobody shed a tear for that whore except my brother.

I felt no loss; she was never a mother to me.

Nannies raised us. My mother was always *busy* with something else.

I was 11 when she told me she never wanted us, never even wanted my father.

An arranged marriage *to bring peace and power* to the two rival crime families. We were merely for show. She pushed out an heir and a backup for the Don as per her contractual duty, and that was that.

That woman didn't have a maternal instinct in her body. Her only response to her young children crying was to threaten to give us something to cry about.

The scar under my eye is a testament to her idea of *motherhood*. It reminds me that love is a currency and everyone has an agenda.

I was only seven when she gave me that scar.

In a fit of unprovoked rage, my mother hit me across the face with her half-drunk wine glass, shattering it to pieces against my soft skin.

The cruel bitch just laughed at my hysteric crying and forced me to clean my blood off the floor myself.

She didn't even bother to look whether the profusely bleeding cut under my eye was serious. She didn't care.

The criss-crossing scars on my back were from the belt

buckle, but that was my dad's doing. He was hardly any better than her.

But none of that matters now.

What matters is my throne and taking back what's *mine*. I've put up with their cruel ways my whole life, holding onto the thought that the empire would be mine one day. Only to have it stolen from me at the last minute.

How did it all go wrong?

I had it all planned out. The poison would've given me the perfect alibi. I would act *so* shocked when they phoned me with the news that my father *suddenly* died. I'd step up like the loyal son, swearing to avenge my father as I took my rightful seat at the head of the table.

It was supposed to be a smooth transition.

But that's not how it went down.

Not at all.

What a fucking mess.

My skin itches with impatience.

My future beckons; I can't stay here.

But my body is too weak to beat the restraints. All this time in bed has drained the power from my muscles.

At least my shoulder healed somewhat. It no longer aches in the night.

However, Kiah has restrained my wrists again, making my life much harder. They are secured in front, over my stomach, with more duct tape than I could ever break.

Her cautious ways are annoying the shit out of me.

It's painfully obvious that I'm not getting out of here by force. I'll have to catch some flies with honey...

Charm it is.

The fog encapsulating my brain has finally lifted enough for me to start scheming.

I wait until the innkeeper sits down to wash me before I stutter a dramatic breath, fluttering my eyes open like I'm just coming to—dazed, lost...*vulnerable.*

It takes what little energy I have to channel my most non-threatening side, acting so docile it makes me want to puke.

But I know it's the only way.

If I want any chance of being cut loose, Kiah needs to trust me first.

"Where am I?" I ask in a raspy voice, looking at her with innocent eyes like I'm a little boy instead of a monster.

"Nico." She smiles but quickly wipes it from her face again, locking a stern expression in place.

This bitch is good. What is her story? Innkeepers are not supposed to know skills like sewing people up or overpowering crime lords. Her moves were calculated as much as they were desperate.

"You tried to kill me," I say in an accusatory tone, hoping to pull on some guilt strings.

"You weren't exactly an exemplary house guest," Kiah replies simply, putting down the washcloth, her hardened face unchanged.

"I'm sorry." I hate those words. *Never apologize.* But I

know that's what she wants to hear. People always want you to beg, to grovel. It makes them feel powerful.

Kiah doesn't reply, just gets up and heads to the kitchen to stir some shit on the stove—lunch, I presume.

I have to be careful; I can't rush this.

If I move too soon, I'll blow my chance.

Patience, Domenico.

THE NEXT DAY, Kiah brings me solid food. A fucking relief after all those damn soups. I never thought I'd be so happy for a simple toasted cheese sandwich. She even buttered the corners, how thorough.

I say nothing other than *thank you*, watching her intently as she heads out, leaving me alone in the cabin.

She's been going out more and more.

Judging from the increasingly festive bustle outside, I guess the tourists are finally returning to the island.

There should be flights out of here by now.

That's good.

I just need to figure out how to fucking get to them. That and where Kiah's hidden my duffel bag with the money. I don't exactly have a gun anymore to force a pilot to take me, but I doubt anyone would argue with that amount of cash. It has to be here somewhere...

"Where are you going?" I ask on the third day after my *miraculous recovery.*

"I need to get ready for the guests," Kiah says simply like I know what day it is, what month even.

It must be November by now.

But who can be sure?

"Do you need help?" I ask like I give a fuck.

She scoffs, pausing with her hand on the open door. "From you? No thanks. You don't look like the helping kind."

"I think we got off on the wrong foot." I put all my effort into giving her an uncharacteristic toothy smile, one packed with all my sweetest charm.

"Oh? You don't normally violate people's personal boundaries in the most fucked up way?" Her voice is dripping with poison; it reaches all the way to her fiery eyes.

"Normally, no," I lie. She wouldn't be able to handle what my life was like *normally*. I bet Miss Kiah had a nice cushy upbringing, retiring early to this lovely slice of paradise. What could she possibly know about the darkness of my world?

The first time I slit someone's throat, I was fourteen. Father said it would make me a man. All it did was make me numb.

It was Ronny. Our guard since before I was born. The man who taught me to ride a bike when Father was *too busy*. Who tended my wounds after my parents' *lessons*.

I still don't know what he did wrong. I begged Father to let him go. Pleaded. Ronny was more family than blood ever was.

But mercy wasn't in Father's vocabulary.

Ronny's eyes, wide with betrayal, still haunt me. The

gurgle of blood. The fading light as he bled out on the cold pavement, discarded like trash.

You always remember your first kill.

After that, they blur together.

The innkeeper has no idea who she's dealing with...

"I don't trust you," she says simply, still in the doorway.

Kiah trails her gaze over my bound naked body, and my dick instantly jumps to attention—well, as far as he has to grow in this stupid cage. He likes the way she looks at him.

She bites her lip like it doesn't give away her intentions, like her lust isn't written on her rosy cheeks in capital letters.

But I know what wanting looks like, *real* wanting. It's one of the few emotions I understand.

"Let me help. Make it up to you."

"Abso-fucking-lutely not." Kiah crosses her arms over her chest.

"You can't keep me locked up like this forever!" I can't help it, I snap, my voice rising to dangerously aggressive levels.

Kiah closes the door behind her and walks over to the bed. Towering over me with her hands on her hips, her scowl is as menacing as her posture.

"That is the last thing I plan on doing. My happily ever after doesn't include spoiled brats who can't keep their dicks in their pants," Kiah scolds, smacking my caged cock with her backhand.

I winch in pain, swearing under my breath in Italian.

My body fucking betrays me, though. Her mere touch makes my dick needy, pressing against the edges of its confines, desperate for more—a reaction that doesn't escape Kiah's notice.

The innkeeper arches an eyebrow, an amused smirk falling over her pretty face.

Up close, the little lines around her eyes are more noticeable, the grey streaking her hair in highlights. But it only makes her look even more attractive. She reminds me of the Spanish tutor I had as a kid.

Though my Spanish tutor never put my dick in a chastity cage.

And she definitely didn't keep me tied to her bed in the middle of nowhere as she poked her slender fingers into my chastity cage, burning my skin with even the slightest contact.

I gasp involuntarily, every sense, every nerve-ending focused on the hand wrapping around my dick, tugging at the cage ever so slightly, just enough to be painfully pleasurable.

"Let me go, you bitch," I spit before I can stop myself.

"I think you misunderstand who has control here." Kiah's voice is but a seductive whisper, a contrast to the cruel sneer on her face.

Fire builds in my loins as the innkeeper traces the outline of the metal cage like she's following a map, barely touching me at all but it's enough to drive me insane.

Why does this woman have this effect on me?

I'm not even fucking her, yet I'm more turned on than I've ever been.

A grunt escapes my lips before I can swallow it back, and I feel even less in control.

She has me right where she wants me, a little desperate bird in her hand. But I don't even care. I'd do anything for her to keep touching me, to make me come.

But she has no intention of giving me what I want.

Kiah drops my cock and walks away without another word, leaving me desperate, on the edge, and so needy to finish.

This time, I can't do anything about it. My hands are tied—literally and figuratively.

An anguished cry erupts from deep inside my belly, forcing my tormentor to look back on more time before leaving me to my misery.

"I'm in charge now, you little brat. It would serve you well to remember that."

"I need to come. Please. Just finish it. You can't leave me like this." I sound desperate, but I don't even care. Who can be calm and calculated when your dick is burning with uncomfortable need?

"Watch me," Kiah retorts, slamming the door in my face.

I shout curses after her in all the languages I know, but the door remains closed, my dick painfully ripe.

Squirming, I try to find some relief, some friction, but there's none.

"You'll pay for this!" I vow to the empty room. But it changes nothing about my situation.

I should never have come to this stupid island.

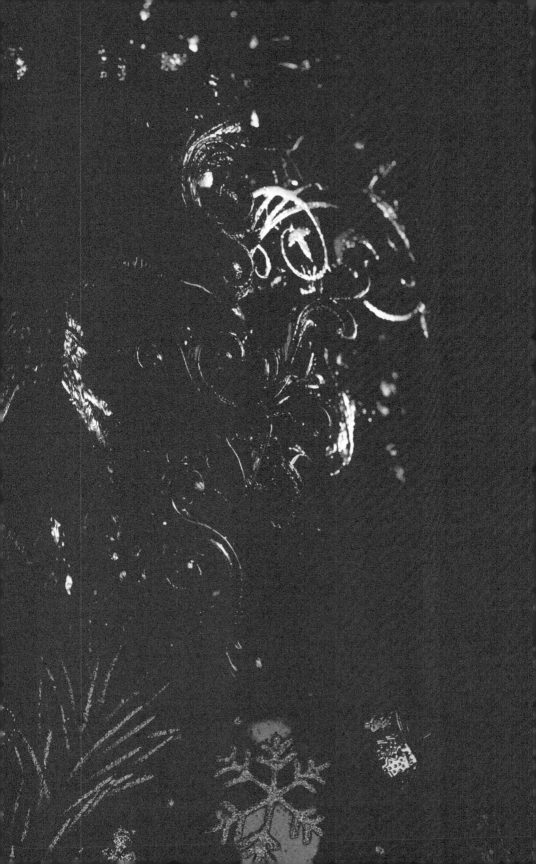

COLLAR

KIAH

In only a few weeks, the first guests will start arriving at the inn. Where has the time gone? *Fuck.*

Usually, I start getting everything ready for the festive season way earlier. But my unexpected visitor-slash-prisoner has kept me otherwise occupied, the list of chores piling up.

My seasonal staff don't arrive for another three weeks. I usually take care of the initial set-up of the inn myself.

There is something almost therapeutic about putting everything in its right place. The routine of it all—dusting off decorations, hanging lights, arranging rooms—usually gives me a purpose after the stormy months.

But this year, I've been a bit *distracted*.

I haven't even started planning the annual Christmas party yet. It's usually quite an event, and people come from all over the island to attend.

It's one of those things I inherited when I bought the inn.

The first year, I tried to cancel the event, but people showed up anyway, and I had to scramble to feed them all.

Over the years, I've accepted the Christmas party as inevitable, even looking forward to it—or perhaps only looking forward to it being over. The setup is always more enjoyable than actually dealing with the guests.

If you told me ten years ago that I'd be happy to run an inn tucked away on a tiny island, I would've laughed at you.

But a lot can change in a decade.

Where once I moved in shadows and violence, now I fuss over fresh linens and breakfast menus.

This place has become my sanctuary.

I'm not sure I could ever leave.

The isolation is...comforting. Miles of ocean between me and my past, yet I'm not entirely cut off from the world. Guests come and go, never staying long enough to see beneath my carefully crafted exterior.

It's connection without the risk of intimacy—perfect for someone like me who's been burned too many times.

On good days, I can almost forget the blood on my hands, the scars on my body. Almost.

There's a certain irony in me, of all people, creating a home for others. I never had one growing up, bouncing from one foster family to another. Even in the military, home was wherever they sent me.

But now I get to build my own home, or at least try to.

I won't lie—there are days when the tranquility of

this place suffocates me. When the sound of waves lapping at the shore sounds too much like blood rushing in my ears.

But what's the alternative?

I can never go back.

No, the only option is to get back on track and prepare the inn in time for the guests so I can continue living the life I had planned.

Easier said than done when you've got a 28-year-old naked mafia prince tied to your bed.

Why is he still here?

What the fuck am I even doing?

I should get rid of him—I know I should.

Yet...I don't want to.

There's something so addictive about that desperate look on Nico's face when those blue eyes go from cold to needy. It changes him; humanizes him in a way.

Is it ethical? Fuck no.

Is it normal? Also no.

Does it make me want it less? I hate to admit it, but no.

That's why it's damn near impossible to figure out what to do next.

I am reluctant to accept Nico's offer for help—as much as I could use the extra muscle to catch up.

What stops him from just tying me up again? Given half a chance, I'm sure he'll correct his first mistake of letting me live.

But, at the same time, I'm also getting tired of swapping

out the waterproof bedsheets and cleaning up his shit (literally). I can't keep him tied to that bed indefinitely.

Option C is ratting him out and letting him face the music. If he killed the Don, there is no way they'll let him live.

I don't know if he did, but he sure as hell seems capable. It would explain why he's hiding out here.

But that option puts me at risk. Dealing with one mafia asshole is one thing. Dealing with a whole lot of mafia assholes is another.

I didn't work this hard to build myself a new life, a new identity, to just blow it all up because I can't handle a little brat.

None of these options are ideal, no matter how many times I repeat them in my head.

It takes four days of listening to Nico's bitching and whining before I come up with Option D while I'm enjoying my sunrise coffee on the porch, the air already thick with an oppressive heat that will only get hotter, stickier.

Swallowing the last of my now-cold coffee back in a single gulp, I head to the inn's storeroom.

In the left corner, there's a false wall only I know about, safe from any workers who might let their curiosity get the better of them.

I place my finger on the hidden scanner, unlocking the secret closet space where I keep what little I've decided to horde from my years as a private military contractor.

I was the fucking best mercenary money could buy. For nearly a decade I lived like I was unstoppable, a god.

When I gave it all up, I couldn't resist keeping a few items. You never know when enemies could come knocking again.

Sure, after five years of peace, I'd grown complacent. But I never got rid of the box. *Just in case.*

The particular item I'm looking for today is a one-of-a-kind beauty I designed myself, my pride and joy.

It's a bit unorthodox, sure, but it's proven helpful many times before.

Nico's eyes widen with suspicion when I return with my new gadget.

I'm sure the calculating bastard is trying to figure out what this contraption is, but he'll realize soon enough.

The explosive collar feels heavier in my hands than I remember.

I designed it for situations exactly like this—when a simple threat isn't enough, when I need absolute control.

The collar itself is a sleek band of reinforced metal—deceptively thin yet impossibly strong. On the inside, an intricate circuit with a small explosive charge is carefully embedded between the layers, designed to deliver a deadly message with the push of a button. I've checked all the wires again, and everything seems as it should be.

Walking slowly, I approach my uninvited guest cautiously, every muscle in my body tense as those blue eyes track my moves.

"What is that?" Nico asks, eyes narrowing as he pulls against the restraints that show little sign of giving in.

"Hold still," I command, my voice cold and steady, not bothering to answer his question.

There is no room for error.

No room for hesitation.

With swift, practiced movements, I secure the collar around his neck. It clicks into place with a finality that even he can't ignore.

Nico's pulse thrums beneath my fingers as I adjust the fit, ensuring the device sits snugly against his skin.

When I press it, the small LED indicator on the side blinks to life, a sinister red light that mirrors the one on my detonator remote.

Smiling, I step back, holding up the remote for him to see. It's a small, nondescript device resembling a typical car key fob, but the power it wields is far from ordinary. A single red button sits at the center, encircled by a safety switch that needs to be flipped up before activation.

"Fancy tech for an innkeeper," Nico remarks with a tightlipped smirk.

"You have no idea, little boy. You don't want to fuck with me." My voice is low and dripping with animosity; there is nothing empty about my threat.

"I guess this explains how you got me in this position." He laughs inappropriately, a sound that echoes through the room like unwelcome thunder.

"You think this is funny?"

Nico continues laughing, undermining my authority,

even now with a literal bomb strapped to his throat. "A little. Of all the people who could've taken over this inn..."

I don't entertain his what-ifs. I'm not letting him distract me.

Tugging the metal loop at the front of the collar towards me with force, I bring Nico's eyes level with mine as I deliver my final warning. "You try anything—anything at all—and I press this button. No second chances."

He stops laughing as he glares at me, eyes unreadable.

"You're bluffing. If a bomb goes off, we both die."

I grin as I add the button to the chain around my neck. "Nice try, but no. The charge is small enough only to be a danger to you, not anyone around you."

"Does that mean you're going to untie me finally?" Nico says in a cool tone, despite his jaw visibly clenching.

"Hmm...I've decided it's time you start to earn your keep around here."

He sneers. "Do you accept cash?"

"No," I say simply, walking to the kitchen.

"Isn't this the part where you untie me?" Nico calls after me.

I pour another cup of coffee and wave him off dismissively. "Maybe tomorrow."

Am I having second thoughts? One hundred percent.

But fuck it, what's he going to do?

That boy is way out of his league, even for a mobster. I used to literally hunt men like him for a living—men way scarier than him.

I thought joining the Marines would satisfy my need for power, for control, but the bureaucracy was bullshit. Even after they promoted me to the Special Forces, I only lasted a few years before the dark side of private contracting lured me in. They had fewer rules, better pay, and way more exciting targets.

Those were the good years; before it all caught up with me like it inevitably would.

I was ready to retire, to get out.

Not a day goes by that I don't regret how it ended.

But I will not let my guard down again like I did back then.

I won't make the same mistake.

This is just for now, until I figure out what to do with this psycho. A temporary measure, if you will.

But deep down, I know I'm lying to myself.

There is something that draws me to this man. All these years later, something is finally giving me that rush of excitement again; that rush that used to be my reason for living. Before....

No, focus Kiah. I push the thought out of my head and take my coffee outside to let the waves calm me as they always do.

But there's no calm for me today.

The ocean is as chaotic as my thoughts.

I know I haven't solved my problem. Merely kicked the can down the road.

In three weeks, I'll have staff around, and then what?

How do I explain the murderous man with the explosive collar?

I take a sip of my coffee, counting my breaths.

One problem at a time.

SPANKING
NICO

THIS WOMAN IS A COMPLETE WHACKJOB, I think for the umpteenth time as I continue my struggle with the fitted sheet.

Three days into *helping*, and I'm already over it.

I need to get out of here ASAP.

Not exactly an easy mission with this fucking bomb collar around my neck. How does she even have such a thing?

The worst part is that I'm starting to *like* my collar. I've only had it for a few days but I'm so hyperaware of it at all times. It makes my pulse race and my dick press uncomfortably against its cage.

The metal around my neck feels like someone has their hands wrapped firmly around my throat, just holding me, ready to choke me.

I don't think Kiah would press that button, but I also

didn't think she was anything other than a helpless woman. So, who knows what she's really capable of?

Miss Kiah seems to like hiding things from me. She clearly can't be trusted.

Then why the fuck am I so turned on by her?

Sure, she's beautiful if you're into older women with a nice rack (which, I just found out, I am).

But it's been a long time since I let a woman distract me...

This whole situation is just weird.

And the insane heat isn't helping me clear my thoughts.

Wearing clothes has become unbearable, so I've just given up altogether. It's not like this woman hasn't seen (and touched) every part of my body already—repeatedly, often when I wasn't even awake. Not that I mind that part. I wish she'd spent *more* time feeling me up.

Kiah's so damn hard to read, though; it drives me mad. The innkeeper didn't even fight me on the no clothes thing; she just shrugged when I defiantly declared I wouldn't put anything on. It made me furious, but I refused to let her see it.

Urgh, the lack of clothes is worsening my constant state of unfulfilled arousal.

If only she'd let me out of this fucking cage. It's changing me. I don't know how, but it's making my mind think about things I wouldn't usually think about, leaving less and less space for the demons that usually live rent-free in my head.

Focus, Domenico.

I don't exactly have time to get sidetracked here. My father is dead, and everyone thinks I did it. I need to get off this fucking island and find a way to clear my name and take my throne as the rightful heir. Not play house with some deranged blonde having a midlife crisis.

Yet here I am, trying to figure out which side goes where with this stupid sheet, and I'm oh-so tempted just to set the whole lot on fire.

The piercing sound of laughter sounds behind me, and I snap my head around to find Kiah regarding me with what looks like amusement.

She arches a brow. "Lemme guess, nobody ever taught you how to make a bed?"

My only answer is a glare.

She's right, though. Domestic chores were for domestic helpers, not fucking mafia royalty.

I expect a mockery, but instead, her face softens as she takes one corner of the sheet. "Here, let me help you."

The stupid bottom sheet finally snaps into place, all four corners firmly secured. But when she tries to show me how to fold those fancy corners on the top sheet, I give up and walk off with an exasperated huff.

"Come back here," Kiah calls without raising her voice. But something in her tone changes...

I've become like a dog, obeying that assertive voice's every command. Because that voice holds the key to both my dick and my life at this stage.

But that's not the only reason...

I suspect I would go to that voice even if she weren't holding my keys.

Clenching my fists at my side, I stomp back in, my jaw locked in a seething rage that's becoming difficult to control.

Taking orders is not exactly my thing. The only man whose orders I ever took is rotting underground by now.

"Watch carefully. See how I tuck this one in here?" Kiah starts patiently.

It looks simple enough, but when I try those dumb things she calls *hotel corners,* it doesn't look anything like her example.

After my third failed attempt, I let out a frustrated grunt. "This stupid fucking thing!"

I pull the sheet with all my might until a loud tear shreds through the room.

"Nico!" Kiah's voice is loud and commanding, and I freeze, half-ripped sheet in hand.

"Useless," I hiss.

"Put the sheet down," she says slowly as she sits down on the bed.

With an exasperated grunt, I throw the sheet on the floor, my eyes glaring daggers into her calm gaze.

Kiah puts her right hand out, palm facing up, and looks at me expectantly. "Come here."

We both know what that move means. She's been *training* me—her words, not mine.

Crossing my arms over my chest, I remain firm, defiant. *Fuck that*; who does she think she is telling me what to do?

This is the part where my mother would've lost her shit

and beat me within an inch of my life in a blind fury. I have the fucking scars to prove it.

But Kiah's punishments are not rash or impulsive. She's composed, firm, and consistent.

"Nico," she says in that sultry tone that makes my insides churn and my dick press uncomfortably against its cage.

"I-I don't. St-st-stop...Fuck!" My frustration turns to rage as humiliation burns into my skin. Why am I fucking stammering? I haven't stammered since I was a kid when my stupid cousins teased me relentlessly for my inability to string together simple sentences.

What is she doing to me?

Pull it together, Domenico.

Kiah doesn't move, doesn't say anything, just holds out her hand until my fit passes, and I reluctantly shuffle over to her, lifting my pathetic dick and putting the cage in her hand.

When she closes her hand around my cock, a mix of relief and primal need rushes through my veins. Her touch is firm yet soft at the same time.

"Nico..." It's the same tone my mother would use when she was extremely disappointed in us, which was often.

Kiah tugs lightly on my dick, and I gasp, completely at her mercy. With a single finger, she traces S-shapes over my balls until I'm leaking pre-cum through my cage, whimpering like a little boy.

But she doesn't let me come, she never gives me the satisfaction of finishing.

Not that there's any satisfaction to be had in this cage. It's been weeks since I've had a decent orgasm, and it's all this bitch's fault.

It's making me so desperate, so needy. I'm usually a twice-a-day kind of guy when it comes to jerking off...

"What did I say about violence?" Kiah asks patiently, stroking the cage I wish wasn't between our skin.

"Not necessary," I give her the answer she wants, despite wanting to be a brat.

She smiles. "Exactly. Look at you being such a good boy." The words of praise sink into my gut like a sharp knife, cutting deeper than the shard she jammed into my shoulder before. It makes my insides burn.

How can I be so affected by those simple words? Who the fuck would be so naive as to call Domenico a "good" boy? I'm not good. She clearly doesn't know who she's dealing with.

I don't have time to ponder the psychological effect of her praise because Kiah bends me over her lap with a single command I follow like a hypnotized puppet.

The bed is low, and my bulky 6'1" figure bows over her like a bridge, the tips of my extremities touching the faded floorboards.

Trapping my cock between her thighs, she clamps her knees down around the cage, holding me in place.

"It seems you will need to learn this lesson again," the innkeeper says simply, without rage, as she runs her hand over my bum in a move that covers my skin in goosebumps like a freshly plucked chicken.

Is she about to spank me?

What the fuck?

I'm a grown-ass man.

Fresh humiliation creeps up around my neck, flushing my cheeks, and I'm grateful to have my eyes glued on the floor, my face hidden from her.

"I want you to count with me. Just until ten. Okay?"

I nod, not trusting my voice.

"Words, boy," Kiah insists, and I respond affirmatively in a voice that sounds ridiculous—small.

How can she have this effect on me?

I'm Domenico Ricci, for fuck's sake. I'd break someone's fucking neck for trying a move like this. I once fed a man's eyeballs to his own dog for accidentally knocking into me on the street.

Yet I lie perfectly still as the first smack lands loudly on my ass, stinging me with pain as much as embarrassment.

My lack of control is painfully obvious—a feeling I'm still trying to get used to.

"Count, Nico."

I bite my lip and press out a strained "One."

Why do I feel like crying?

This is crazy.

I could just get up. Even with the collar on, I know she wouldn't kill me for refusing her punishments.

But I don't want to get up.

I want this.

More than I've ever wanted anything from another person.

Because I *deserve* this.

"Count!" Kiah insists as the second and third smacks burn my skin.

I'm so fucking turned on right now, my dick feels like it's going to break through its steel cage simply with the power of its hardness. There is nowhere left to grow, but it's still growing.

Blows *four* and *five* fall in quick succession, and by the time *eight* rings out, my ass is on fire, stinging like a mother-fucker. I can't believe she's doing all this damage with her bare hand.

When the final smack lands on my soft flesh with a loud whack, I can't hold it any longer, I just let go, uncontrollable sobs ripping through my body.

I don't know why, or what this unhinged wench has done to me, but I can't stop the tears from coming.

I didn't even cry at my own mother's funeral. What the fuck is this?

Kiah helps me up onto the bed and then just holds me as I stain her shirt with my tears. Like I'm a baby, she puts her arms around me, rocking gently.

All I can think is that she smells nice. Like suntan lotion and fresh linen.

"Hey, shh. It's okay. All over now," she coos in a soothing voice, the total opposite of her assertive one.

She strokes my hair softly in a move so tender it hurts more than her spanking.

Why is she being nice to me?

Why does she care?

I don't deserve this.

I deserve the spanking, all the punishment, being locked up, but I don't deserve her stroking my hair.

The familiar self-loathing curdles in my gut. *A waste of space just like your father*, my mother's cruel words come back to me.

Kiah holds me through all of it, asking no questions and demanding no explanations, just enveloping me with her warmth.

I'm crying for everything and nothing at all—all the tears I've kept inside for so long.

"It's okay. Let it all out," Kiah whispers, and I know I'll never be able to look at her the same again, not after she's seen me like this.

What is happening to me?

BEACH

KIAH

NICO HAS BEEN DIFFERENT SINCE HIS SPANKING. He's more docile, more present. When he's not being an infuriating brat, he's actually quite intelligent, amusing me with weird, useless facts about everything and nothing.

That haunted look never leaves his eyes, though. Considering his familial background, I can't say I'm surprised. Who knows what demons he hides?

Demons like killing his own father, I remind myself.

Don't get too attached, Kiah.

You know how this ends.

Men like Nico are the reason I got out of the business in the first place. They're narcissistic cunts with no moral compass who treat women like objects at best.

He can't be trusted.

That's why I have to keep my guard up.

But with every passing day, that gets harder to do.

The fucker is actually quite helpful and, sometimes, outright sweet—which is unexpected.

But I'm not fooled; I know Nico is a terrible person like the rest of them.

I'm playing with fire, but I'm not ready to stop—not when I finally feel something other than the crushing weight of life's banality.

For half a decade, I've been hiding on this island, trying to convince myself that this is the life I've always wanted. Calm, peaceful, away from the excitement—*this* is where I will grow old.

But deep down, I know that I'm bored as fuck.

I miss the danger, the challenge; I miss being good at something—being the *best*.

My old life was equal parts danger and delectable luxury.

As much as I try to tell myself that I was born for the simple life, I know it's just an excuse.

I'm hiding. Just like Nico.

Something inside me dies with every Christmas party that rolls around. The same decor, the same entitled guests with different faces, the same loneliness when they leave; it's all the same.

But this year is different...

My eyes return to the naked mafia prince in the lobby, concentration knitting his brow.

"Motherfucker!" Nico curses loudly, ripping the red tinsel from the tree and chucking it on the ground.

He's cute when he's frustrated with his chest all puffed up, nostrils flaring.

"Everything okay there?" I ask my naked helper as he wrestles with the Christmas decorations.

"The stupid thing doesn't want to sit right," he complains, baring his teeth as he throws his hands up dramatically.

Such a little spoiled brat. Who knew chores would be his undoing?

"It doesn't have to be perfect. It's decorations; they just need to be up," I reassure him, picking up another piece of tinsel and draping it around the reception desk.

"Why can't I do anything right?" Nico's grinding his teeth as he does when he gets upset with himself—which is almost as often as he gets upset with me.

"This is supposed to be *fun*," I tell him, hanging an ornament on the large tree we've dragged from the storage. It's the same tree I use every year—synthetic and tacky. But that's what people expect around here.

"Your idea of fun is fucked," Nico says simply, picking up the discarded tinsel and trying again.

I can't help but feel proud. He actually picked it up instead of storming off or ripping it to shreds. That has to be some kind of *progress*.

For the next hour, we work in silence, covering the common spaces in disgustingly festive decorations until my cotton shirt is soaked through with sweat.

The suffocating tropical air clings to my skin, even with

the ceiling fans lazily circling above us.

It's not raining but the air is thick with moisture. My hair sticks to my forehead as I try to brush it away.

Nico doesn't look any less sweaty either, despite his usual lack of clothes. We'll have to do something about that habit when the staff arrive next week.

I'm trying very hard not to think about the future. I know I'm running out of time to make a decision.

But that's next week's problem.

"Enough for now; I need a swim," I declare, the ocean calling me.

"Yeah, right," Nico scoffs, gesturing at his collar. "I doubt your technology is waterproof."

"You make a good point. I guess you can just watch me swim then. The *keys* are 100% waterproof."

Nico whines for dramatic effect but follows me outside, nevertheless.

I chuck a towel at him, and he wraps it around his waist to cover himself.

The collar, I'm not worried about. It looks like any collar a sub would wear.

Sure, it will probably be embarrassing for him should anyone see us, but that's his problem, not mine.

Besides, if I've learned anything about this psycho, it's that he seems to get off on humiliation.

Which is great for me because I find humiliating him cathartic.

It's nice having the power, for once, to not be the victim but rather the one dolling out the flushed cheeks.

The beach should be mostly deserted either way. Unlike the buzzing main beach that's lit up like a carnival at night, this little slice of paradise is a private one, shared by only three of the inns.

It's just us and the soft lull of the waves out there.

I've taken Nico outside a few times. The poor boy can't stay inside forever. But he seemed indifferent to nature.

Even the nearly full moon blossoming in the sky doesn't impress him, and he just grunts something unintelligible as he follows me to the beach.

It's a beautifully clear night, the first one in ages, and it revitalizes me despite the sticky heat plugging up my pores.

In silence, we follow the wooden walkway to the sand, where I spread out one of the towels for us.

"Sit," I command, and Nico does so without resistance.

I give him the usual speech, just to make sure he doesn't take any chances. "You can run all you want, boy. But you'll always be within range of the detonator. So, I wouldn't risk it if I were you."

"I'm not going to run, Kiah." Nico sighs, running his hand through his sweaty hair.

He doesn't often use my name. But every time he does, I freeze. There is something in the way he says it, something that makes my heart skip out of its usual pattern.

Usually, I cringe when men say my name, but not Nico. I'm overly aware of this seemingly useless fact.

"Good," I say, just to say something.

I turn my back on Nico, my hand hovering at the hem of my shorts. A familiar wave of shame washes over me. The scar on my stomach feels like a brand, a constant reminder of my past failures.

But then I catch a glimpse of the moonlit waves, and the pull is too hard to ignore.

I used to love skinny-dipping, the feel of the ocean on my bare skin.

How long has it been since I allowed myself that freedom?

I take a deep breath.

Fuck-it.

With a surge of defiance, I wiggle out of my sticky shorts.

The relief is instant, both physical and emotional.

I haven't felt this alive in years.

I pause, my heart racing. Nico's presence behind me is palpable, but strangely, it doesn't feel judgmental. Like I could turn around right now, battle scars and all, and he'd still look at me the same way.

The realization is both unsettling and liberating.

Before the old doubts can creep in, I pull off the rest of my clothes too.

As the cool night air caresses my bare skin, a flicker of my old confidence ignites.

Without looking back, I sprint towards the water.

The sand shifts beneath my feet, and I plunge into the waves without hesitation, letting the ocean wash away my troubles.

I lose myself in the rhythm of the swim.

Dive. Glide. Surface. Breathe.

Invigorating doesn't begin to describe it.

Each time I break the surface, my eyes seek out Nico. He's a dark silhouette against the moonlit sky, motionless on the blanket. Still there. Still waiting.

Much to my relief.

Despite my threats, I don't actually want to be forced to blow up the pretty brat with the moody eyes. I've gotten used to having him around, to who I am when he's around. I like this version of myself.

Salt clings to my skin as I make my way back to shore with slow, deliberate strokes.

I can't see Nico's eyes in the dark as I approach, but I know they are glued to me, to my naked body, my muscular legs, my wide hips...probably my breasts.

But I feel no shame, no insecurity as I imagine his eyes on me. Instead, I straighten out my shoulders and walk proudly, decked out in nothing but salty water and semi-darkness.

Nico says nothing when I reach him; he just hands me the extra towel to dry myself.

"Thank you." I smile, flopping down beside him with the towel around my hair.

Nico's eyes are glued to my chest, just as I've predicted. He doesn't even notice my scars, and if he does, he doesn't let it show.

The poor man is virtually drooling. His hands are

clenching and unclenching at his sides, his knees clamped firmly shut. I'm pretty sure he's hard as fuck again.

Like a dormant volcano awakening, I feel power stirring deep within me with every second of Nico's attention. Each reaction from him sends the magma rising, heating my core and fueling my confidence.

"You didn't run," I remark, daringly seeking his gaze as I bask in the moonlight, digging my toes into the damp sand.

"I said I wouldn't," Nico says simply, not meeting my eyes.

"Well, good behavior needs to be rewarded too." Much to both our surprise, I take the chain off my neck and push Nico's knees apart slowly, his flimsily-tied towel flailing open.

His sharp intake of breath is loud as his skin instantly dots in shivers under my touch.

What are you doing, Kiah?

He's my captive, I shouldn't be seducing him.

This is highly unethical and incredibly stupid.

But I do it anyway.

Because I want to.

I want *him*.

So badly.

And out here, in the dark, with us both already virtually-naked, that need seems less insurmountable than inside the controlled environment of the inn.

"You're unlocking me?" Nico asks in disbelief as I do just that, slipping the little key into the lock to wriggle the cage apart.

As I work, I don't spare a single thought for us being in public. It's the kind of island where people fuck in the dunes all the time, so who cares who sees what.

Nico's cock instantly springs free, thick and hard, as his entire body slumps into a relieved sigh.

He's way too hard for me to bother trying to get the ring part of the cage off too, so I leave it.

"Oh, *fanculo*," he swears under his breath as I take his cock in my palm, finally uncaged.

When I run my fingers over the bells of his piercing, I swear both of us shiver.

Lust coats my veins and I know I'm wet—not just from the swim.

I've thought about this for over a month, wondering what his dick would feel like without its cage.

"Someone feeling a bit sensitive?" I tease, enjoying the way Nico squirms in my hand. Even the slightest movement makes his entire body dance to my touch, and it's the most addictive power.

The brat's usually neutral face is an open book as he moans softly, bucking his hips into my hand, desperate to be touched.

"Y-you have n-no idea," he stutters, pre-cum leaking over my fingers already. His eyes are still glued to my chest, raking over my hard nipples.

"Do you want to suck on them?" I ask, a surge of need stronger than the ocean current tugging at my insides.

"*Dio mio,*" is all Nico says like a god has anything to do with his good fortune.

As he closes his eager lips around my sensitive nipple, pleasure erupts over my skin.

It's my turn to moan softly as he suckles, reaching out to hold my other breast, needily squeezing my flesh between his fingers.

It's been more than five years since I've let anyone touch me, and the wanting flares up like an uncontrolled wildfire.

The bearded chin feels incredible against my body, scratching me just enough to feel something.

Nico whines against my skin, his breath warm, ragged.

"What is it?" I pant.

"I-I'm close."

"Do it," I whisper, speeding up my movements, "Come for me, baby."

Release

Nico

As soon as those words leave her mouth, my dick explodes in the innkeeper's hands, spilling cum over both of us. *Jesus, so much cum.*

It's the first complete orgasm I've had since the night I arrived, when I came on Kiah's angry face.

All I can do is keep on sucking, holding onto her incredible breasts as the most intense climax of my life rips through my body, threatening to tear me apart.

The satisfaction is instant, overwhelming, and I swear I forget how to function for a second.

It's never been this intense.

Fucking hell.

I'm so sensitive.

But those thoughts are fleeting. My mind is reduced to insular thoughts as Kiah keeps milking my spent dick.

Dio mio.

Gasping, I spit out her breast, desperately trying to regain my breath. "N-no more," I stutter like I'm a child again, over-stimulation burning my skin to the point of tears.

After two more tugs, Kiah mercifully stops torturing me, dropping my sticky, sensitive dick.

Exhaling slowly, deeply, I keep my eyes closed for a moment longer as I try to summon my senses.

Until the innkeeper whispers "Look at me" in that commanding tone, and I force them open again.

I'm rewarded by a radiant grin on Kiah's face, and I can't help but smile like an idiot, a satisfied idiot.

She pushes her sticky fingers between my lips, and I suck my cum off her digits, never breaking eye contact.

"Look how pretty you came for me," she praises as she twirls her fingers inside my mouth, and my stupid spent dick perks up again.

What is this woman doing to me?

I don't trust my voice to speak, so I focus on sucking her fingers. The taste is salty, surprisingly so, but not as unpleasant as I thought it would be. I've never tasted my own cum before.

"Such a beautiful cock. It's such a waste keeping it locked up."

I nod, incapable of a more elaborate response.

Kiah pulls her fingers from my mouth and uses both hands to push me down on the towel.

Climbing over me, she pins me between her muscular

thighs, one on either side of my waist as she straddles me. Her body is cold and wet from the ocean, exploding shivers all over my skin.

But my mind has a single focus—those perfect tits of hers. From down here, those round mounds look even more glorious. Hypnotized, I reach for them again with both hands.

But Kiah smacks my hands away. "Not without permission. Ask first."

"Please. Please!" I plead shamelessly.

"Words. What do you want?" she torments me, shaking her torso ever-so-slightly so those delectable breasts dangle before me like a prize I simply have to win.

"Please m-may I t-t-touch?" I murmur, begging, like this is how I speak now.

My threatening voice has reduced weaker people to tears with its menacing tone, but the only one close to tears today is me.

Why is this so fucking hard?

But I don't have time to berate myself or my regression into stuttering. My feral desires are in the driving seat, and they want only one thing—Kiah. *All* of her.

"Not yet. Hold still," she instructs, and I whine like a little puppy.

For a hellishly long moment, Kiah just sits on top of me, studying my face as she makes up her mind about how to proceed.

The indecision is clear on her features. I know what a

woman looks like when she's about to do something she really wants but knows she shouldn't.

I don't dare move, as difficult as it is. If she leaves now, I'll go insane, I know that. I *need* her.

The primal urges tearing through my insides burn brighter with every second that passes, threatening to make me come undone at the very seams.

I want her so fucking badly. To feel her warmth, her fire. I want her to consume me, destroy me, *anything* to dull this incessant yearning that flows through my veins like poisoned blood.

Please!

With a single "fuck-it," the Devil on her shoulder wins, and Kiah repositions herself, wrapping her hand around my dick and lining it up with her entrance.

Oh god, she's so wet! The realization hits me as soon as my flesh touches hers. She wants this too.

"This is the part where you lie completely still, little boy," Kiah whispers, and my cock twitches defiantly, out of my control.

"I said still!" her voice raises, and then she does something that short-circuits my entire world—she smacks my cock.

An unimaginable pain surges through my skin as a loud groan rips from my insides.

My skin is on fire.

It hurts so fucking much!

Fuck.

I can't think of anything but the pain.

Until Kiah suddenly thrusts her hips down and impales herself on my cock, dousing my pain in an incredible amount of pleasure.

My mind empties except for those two all-encompassing feelings—pain and pleasure—rippling through my body, mixing, dancing, as I float into bliss.

For the first time, everything in my head is quiet, calm. Nothing exists except this moment, right here, right now. There is no ocean, no beach, no moon, no stars—there is only the naked Queen above me, using *her* cock as she pleases.

Kiah moans loudly as she pushes out again, slowly, only to plunge back down on my dick seconds later.

I am reduced to an inanimate object as she brings herself to pleasure, and it's the most freeing experience.

I don't have to do anything, be anything. I can't fuck this up; I can't do it wrong. I just have to lie here, be still, and it's enough.

The most beautiful symphony of sounds builds around us as my brutish grunts mix with Kiah's increasing moans.

The innkeeper's face looks exquisite contorted in pleasure like this. Even better than when I've secretly watched her masturbate late at night. But those nights pale in comparison to the ecstasy of actively being involved in pleasing her.

"Now you may touch," she tells me, and I vaguely remember my earlier request, my hands reaching for her breasts like magnets drawn to steel.

When the innkeeper drops a hand to rub her clit, a loud

groan tears from her lips so unrestrained, the sound damn near sends me toppling over the edge again.

She looks so stunning like this, like a real Goddess, towering over me with her eyes closed and the moon glistening on her skin. Her wet hair falls around her face in tousles, framing her mature beauty.

Struggling to keep my eyes open, I surrender complete control as Kiah rides me, my only job holding her breasts up as they bounce in my hands.

"C-close," I mutter, hoping she knows what I mean because fuck knows I can't do sentences right now. I can barely hold onto my grasp of reality as the delirium of another intense orgasm approaches.

"No," Kiah says, and my entire body tenses.

No?

What?!

Her eyes flutter open, and she traps my gaze in hers. "Not until I come," the innkeeper says, and I don't know what to do with that information.

I *need* to come, like now, it's all I can think of.

But somehow, it doesn't feel right to do it without her blessing.

"P-please!" I cry, desperate.

I'm going to lose my mind like this.

I can't hold it; I need to explode.

"Not without permission," Kiah tells me, and I know it's the truth. My pleasure is no longer mine to release when I feel like it; it's *hers*. She owns it. She has since she first slipped that cage over my cock. Since then, it's always been hers. And I gladly surrender control.

The thought doesn't ease the agony at all, it intensifies it.

My desperation takes over every corner of my mind.

Nothing is real outside my primal need to come, outside the effort it takes not to.

I'm on the verge of crying.

I can't do this; I can't.

And then, the most beautiful sound I've ever heard fills the night sky. Kiah cries out in climax, her body shaking above mine.

I lose it.

Nothing can stop me from coming inside her right there and then, filling her with my cum as our orgasms mingle into one.

Dio mio!

My head spins.

It feels so damn good.

Better than sex has ever felt before.

And I didn't even do anything; I just lay here.

My climax subsides long before Kiah's, and I'm treated to the most enigmatic show—her riding out the waves of her ecstasy, her bottom lip trapped between her teeth, eyes firmly closed.

Eons pass before the moonlit Goddess finally collapses on top of me with a soft gasp, my sticky dick still inside her.

Instinctively, I put my arms around, pulling her close until her head rests against my pounding heart.

I don't ever want to let her go.

What the fuck just happened?

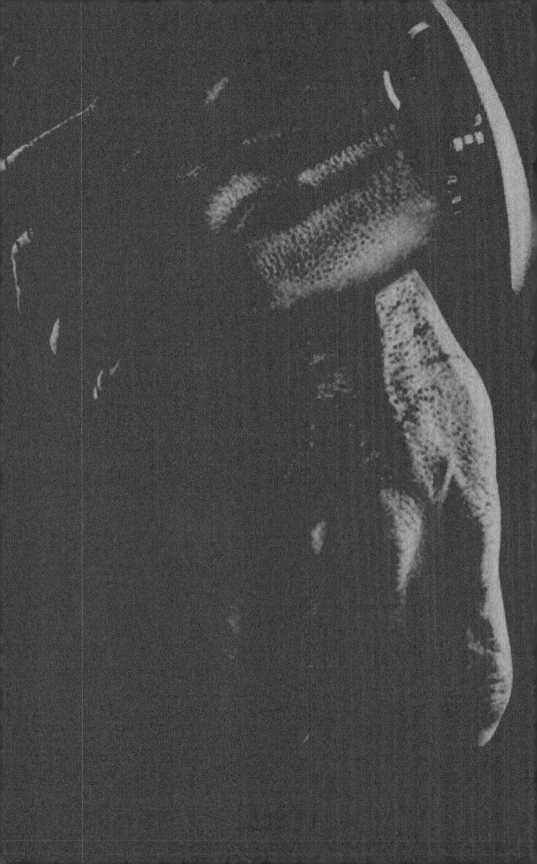

Regression

Kiah

Like clockwork, my body wakes with the sun.

But that's the only thing that's normal.

For the first time in more than a month, I wake up in my own bed instead of the futon.

Fuck!

Panic surges through me as I detangle myself from Nico's naked body, draped around mine like a weighted blanket made of muscle and tattoos.

He grunts but doesn't wake up, snoring lightly, sprawled out on his stomach.

Throwing a t-shirt over my nakedness, I drop into the armchair beside the bed, my racing mind running loops around my brain as I try to figure out what now.

How could I be so stupid?

Letting him out of his cage is one thing but fucking him

without a condom is the kind of mistake I should know better than to make.

I'm not worried about getting pregnant; I know that's not possible anymore, not after what they did to me.

But who knows what diseases Nico could have? He doesn't exactly seem like the responsible kind. No, he's a reckless brute at best.

The first man I fuck in five years, and I'm stupid enough to do so without protection. *Jesus, Kiah.*

But deep down, I know condom isn't the only problem with what happened...

I should never have fucked Domenico Ricci—period.

He's a dead man walking. And the last thing I need is to be in the splash zone of whatever chaos is coming his way.

Scrubbing my hand over my face, I regard the beautiful body passed out on my bed.

It wasn't just on the beach...We came back and hooked up again (and again) in the bed, the sheets now a sticky mess of sweat and cum.

Oh god, I swear that dick piercing of his scraped my insides raw in the most incredible way.

I've been thinking about it for weeks, wondering what it would feel like from the inside, but dear god, I could never imagine such mind-numbing pleasure.

I just got caught up in the moment; I can't explain it.

He seemed so different yesterday, more *human* almost.

But it's no excuse for my lapse in judgment.

I moved to this island to get away from men like Nico, not

to fuck them on the beach like we're just normal people on a normal holiday.

But there's nothing normal about fucking a mafia prince with a bounty on his head.

The chaos in my mind shows no signs of slowing as I drag myself into a shower, scrubbing my body under the steaming water.

I have no idea what to do next.

Coffee, I need coffee.

Let's start there.

Bit by bit, I compartmentalize my life, breaking it into tasks.

By the time I turn the shower off, I feel better, more centered. It's a farce built on shaky willpower at best but it's all I have.

I throw on a dirty dress from the washing basket without bothering with underwear, tying my hair up into a messy bun.

I know what I need to do next: I need to put on the kettle.

However, as soon as I leave the steamed-up mirrors in the bathroom for the open plan, all my carefully laid plans dissipate like mist.

Nico is no longer passed out face first; no, he's staring at me with those icy, haunted eyes, devoid of yesterday's unexpected warmth.

"Hey," I say, trying to hide the awkwardness from my voice as I head for the kitchen.

Why am I being weird? It's not like I haven't had countless one-night stands before...They're all I've had.

But this is different.

If I'm honest with myself, I don't actually regret fucking Nico.

It felt incredible!

For the first time in half a decade, I felt alive; in control of my own life.

I actually came! I never come, not when there's another person involved. The only time I ever reach the peak of climax is by my own hand and perhaps a little help from a toy.

But Nico, *Jesus*, he didn't even do anything, and my body exploded into a million little stars as he pumped my body full of his cum.

I know no good can come from this.

Getting mixed up in the mob is a sure way to lose your life.

I don't need that kind of action.

What I need is to stay right here, live my quiet life, and be the wise old innkeeper with lots of hobbies.

Turning my back on Nico, I turn on the kettle. *Stick to the plan, keep it simple*, I try to get myself back on track.

"You want some?" I ask, counting the scoops of coffee into the plunger.

Nico doesn't reply, just gets up and stretches, his semi-erect cock hanging free.

The chastity cage's ring eventually came off last night, now discarded with the other silver pieces I didn't bother locking back in place.

Pretending to busy myself with the coffee, I watch Nico from the corner of my eye as he opens the window.

What is he doing?

Without warning, the fucker grabs his dick and pisses onto the porch like the bathroom isn't right there.

The dipshit is taunting me.

"What the fuck, Nico?" I call, but he shows no signs of hearing me, just continues relieving himself out the window like some hooligan.

When he finishes, he turns to me, walking over without saying anything as he palms his dick defiantly, keeping eye contact.

"Whatcha gonna do, bitch?" he asks, snarling at me as he masturbates.

I see—Mister Macho appears to be having masculinity issues. Clearly, having his dick freed and his needs met has erased all submissive tendencies.

There is no correct answer to his taunt, so I focus on the coffee, pouring myself a cup as Nico jerks himself off onto the kitchen counter like it's not unsanitary as shit.

I should've put him back in the cage when I had the chance. Sure, he still has his dangerous collar, but he seems to have lost faith in my threats.

"Where's mine?" he asks rudely.

"You didn't answer when I asked if you wanted any," I reply simply, taking a sip of coffee.

Fuck this asshole if he thinks he can get under my skin. He doesn't know who he's dealing with.

Nico reaches for my cup, trying to rip it from my hands like a naughty two-year-old, but I pull away, smacking him across the face with my free hand.

"Stop acting like a brat, Nico. I thought we were past this."

He laughs cruelly. "You don't know shit."

"Why are you being like this?"

He stretches his arms out like Da Vinci's Vitruvian Man, his body naked, tattooed, and perfect. "This is who I am. Deal with it."

I don't say anything, just turn to leave.

If he's going to be like this, I'm taking my coffee on the porch.

This is ridiculous.

If I had any doubts that I shouldn't have fucked this guy, they're all gone now.

Nico grabs my arm, halting me in my tracks. "Where do you think you're going, *bitch*?"

Before I can reign in my emotions, I throw my scalding coffee at his crotch, watching with a neutral face as he drops to the floor, screaming.

"You whore!" Nico howls, rolling around the floor in agony.

"Please refrain from calling me a whore." My tone is cold, devoid of any emotion; not like last night. If he wants to regress to his caveman bullshit, then why should I be the bigger person?

"Make me," he hisses, getting up from the floor, hand still

protectively cupped over his junk.

"If you want a brat tamer, look somewhere else. I'm not applying for the position."

I head for the door, but Nico moves quickly, throwing his body at me to send us both tumbling to the floor, the coffee cup shattering beside us.

Before he can overpower me, I reach for his balls and tug as hard as I can, completely incapacitating him.

"Asshole!"

He howls loudly, frozen on the floor.

It seems we're back to square one. Nico has made it clear that he can't be trusted with this much freedom.

This time, I don't bother getting him to the bed to tie him up. I duct tape his naked, defiant body to the wooden column in the kitchen, right there and then.

It takes an entire roll of tape, of which I luckily always keep plenty—because is there anything more useful than duct tape?

Nico tries to resist, but nothing like a kick to the balls to turn a grown man into a baby, and he's no different.

Whining and cursing, he spits at me.

"Stop that." I whack him across the cheek again with my backhand. Usually, I have more restraint than that, but *usually*, I'm not this emotionally invested in the people I'm tying up.

"I should've known you'd be as fucked as the rest of your family," I say, panting from the struggle as I pour myself another cup of coffee.

Blind rage courses through my veins, and it takes every bit of self-control not to pour the entire plunger of coffee onto the naked brute on the floor.

"You don't know shit," Nico spits.

"Really? The Riccis aren't the biggest assholes of all the families?" I raise my eyebrow for effect, staring him down.

The weight of my words hits him like a ton of bricks, and for a second, Nico's armor slips, letting the darkness cloud his face. "How long have you known?"

I shrug, my voice bitter, "Since the start."

"And you didn't rat me out?"

"Foolish, I know, right?"

It's his one chance to repent, to beg, but he chooses the wrong path. "I always knew you were a stupid bitch," Nico says as the meanest snarl contorts his face into something twisted.

I don't bother justifying his remark with a verbal response. Instead, I cut off a strip of duct tape and shut him up.

Grabbing my phone and my cup, I head out before Nico can push any more of my buttons.

The porch smells like piss, so I take my coffee to the beach, desperate for space, for air—I need to *think*.

Dropping your guard only gets you hurt—how many fucking times do I need to learn this lesson the hard way?

The fucker played me, and I was stupid enough to fall for his charm. I should've known he was up to something or another. This was never about a connection.

I sigh heavily.

This isn't going to work.

I can't have that delinquent running rampant when the guests come.

I should've done this a long time ago, I think, as I punch in J.'s number, my heart beating in my chest.

She answers after the second ring. "Kiah?"

"Hey, so that little Ricci cunt? I know where he is..."

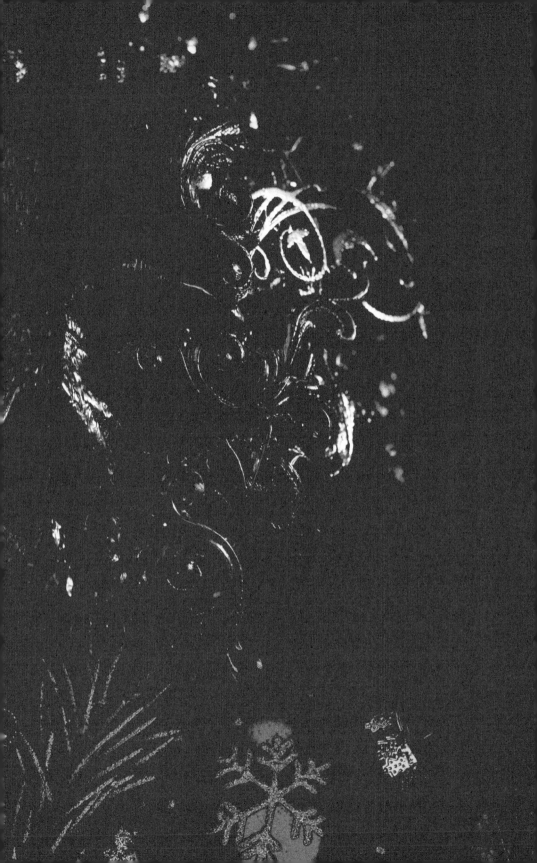

Betrayal
Nico

Shouting muffled profanities at the empty room, I continue my fight against the duct tape.

But it doesn't budge.

It just hurts my healing shoulder with every futile move.

I can't believe that bitch tied me up again. I haven't even recovered from the last time. Fucking *de ja vu*.

Kiah better return soon. She's been gone for over an hour already. Where did she go?

I fight until I have no energy left, groaning like a wild beast with little result. It's no use.

Exhausted, I slump against the column, dropping my head to my chest in defeat.

Outside, the sun claws its way higher.

Gradually, my fury ebbs, seeping from my body like blood from a wound.

As the familiar rage retreats, it leaves behind a hollowness I can't quite name. Regret floods in to fill the void, bitter and choking. But even this remorse is fleeting, a mere ripple on the surface of a much deeper, darker pool.

What remains is the bedrock of my existence: self-loathing. It's always there, a cancer eating away at my core. Every thought, every action, every breath is filtered through its toxic lens.

I clench my fists, feeling my nails bite into my palms. Pain —sharp, immediate—offers a moment's respite from the relentless chorus of self-hatred.

But it's temporary.

It always is.

You're a fucking idiot, Domenico.

I know I've fucked up.

And not just because my balls ache and I'm tied up again.

Things just...escalated so quickly.

Everything was fine when I woke up this morning. I actually felt good.

Until my brain caught up with my body, exploding in chaos before I even had time to wipe the sleep from my eyes.

The more I thought about last night, the more I freaked out.

I let Kiah walk all over me; I let her use me as she saw fit... and thanked her for it too.

This isn't me.

I'm Domenico fucking Ricci—the boss, a *real* man.

And real men sure don't ask for permission to come.

Who in their right mind would ever dare to challenge my masculinity?

No, she must have done something to me, bewitched me, made me want this.

But it felt so fucking good, though...

Shut up! Shut up!

The same panic from this morning starts clawing at my throat again, but I push it down with force. Instead, I focus on reigniting the anger—the only emotion that feels comfortable.

This isn't about what my dick wants.

The fact of the matter remains that she *knew*. She knew who I was all along. *Lying cunt!*

It was probably her plan all along to emasculate me, to humiliate me.

I've been fucking played.

None of it was real.

The sound of approaching footsteps pulls me back to the present just as the front door swings open.

Kiah walks in without looking at me.

I make as much noise as possible to get her attention, but she's on her own mission.

The innkeeper busies herself with cleaning up, restlessly pacing the room as she moves things to a new place only to move them back to where they were before.

Finally, when the bed sheets are clean and the art supplies packed up, she drags one of those shitty wooden chairs over and sits down front to back like a 90s rapper.

She inhales slowly, closing her eyes briefly.

"I think I've made a mistake..." she says, leaning down on the chair, her fingers tightening around the wood. "Your brother won't kill you if he rocks up here, right?"

My eyes widen as the weight of her words sink in.

The last person I want to see right now is my brother. Fucking Ricardo, that absolute dick stain of a human. I'm pretty sure he's the one who's framing me in the first place. He hasn't exactly been subtle about his desire for the throne despite me being the eldest.

"Please don't scream," Kiah tells me as she pulls the tape off my mouth.

I glare at her with all my might, wishing I could shoot lasers from my eyes, but my voice is calm. "You ratted me out."

"I did."

"Why? For the bounty?"

This is what I get for letting myself be vulnerable—betrayal, backstabbing...*Fuck her.*

The innkeeper lowers her head. "I didn't do it for the money."

That somehow makes me feel worse. "Then why did you do it? *Why?*"

"I'm sorry, Nico. I thought I was doing the right thing."

"What changed?"

"Can we not do this now? We need to make a plan." Her voice is urgent, "They'll be here in a few hours."

I shake my head. "No, Kiah. Now. Or you can leave me

right here because I'm not going anywhere with you. And last I checked, you may be strong, but you're not strong enough to chuck me over your shoulder."

She sighs heavily, twisting her fingers over the edge of the chair until her knuckles go white.

"Well, you were being an absolute cunt this morning—I'm sure we can both agree on that..."

My eyes narrow. "You're doing a terrible job of explaining."

"Just let me finish. I was furious when I left this morning. Furious at you as much as myself for what happened last night."

I feel like I've been punched in the chest. "I knew you regretted it." Of course, she did.

Kiah shakes her head. "I don't. That's the problem. I don't regret it. I know who you are, what you've done, and I still want you."

"Then why?"

"No good can come from this, Nico, from this chaos you stir in me. The world you come from brings nothing but death and destruction. I can't get mixed up in all that again."

I scoff at her stupid speech but don't say anything.

Kiah takes a deep breath before continuing, measuring her words carefully. "Mostly, if I'm honest, I did it because I was angry, hurt, rejected...I reacted on impulse, without thinking. Nico, I'm sorry," her voice wavers, heavy with regret.

"Why are you telling me? Why not just let them take me?" I spit out, anger and confusion warring inside me.

Kiah takes a deep breath. "After I made the call, I didn't know what to do, so I ran. I ran until my lungs burned and my legs gave out. Somehow, I ended up at the old lighthouse on the north point."

She pauses, her gaze distant. "I've always gone there to think, to escape. But this time, it didn't work. I climbed to the top, looked out at the endless ocean, and felt nothing but your absence."

"How sweet." The sarcasm drips from my voice like venom, but she continues as if she hasn't heard me.

"The more I thought about it, the more I realized that this island, this life I've built—it's my refuge as much as my prison. I've been hiding from who I really am, from feeling anything real." She returns her gaze to mine, her voice dropping. "But with you, I feel alive. Angry, frustrated, excited—but alive."

"What are you saying?" I narrow my eyes, regarding her with suspicion as I try to unravel the meaning behind her words.

"I'm saying that I've spent years running from my past, from connection. But now, the thought of you leaving—it terrifies me more than you staying."

Her vulnerability is palpable, and it shakes something loose inside me. The innkeeper doesn't usually let her defenses down.

I sigh, clenching my jaw. "What do you want from me, Kiah?"

"I want to be the only one who gets to hurt you, Nico. I can't explain it, and it doesn't make sense, but I can't let them kill you. Even if you did take out your father."

"Ah, jeez, thanks." I roll my eyes at her. "It's a little bit too late now, isn't it?"

She shakes her head. "It's not. We can take them. If we work together."

"Oh, so *now* you want to protect me," I scoff.

Her voice cracks, pleading almost. "Nico, please. Let me fix this."

"What does an innkeeper know about fighting the mob?"

"You'd be surprised." She sighs, wiping a stray strand of blonde from her sticky brow.

"What does that mean? And no more lies. I despise lies. Who the fuck are you, and where did you learn to fight?"

She doesn't hesitate. "The Marines. The Special Forces. My life as a mercenary. Take your pick."

"Christ. Then why the fuck are you running an inn?"

"I'm hiding."

"What are you hiding from?"

"It's a long story..."

"Well, you better give me the quick version because, apparently, we don't have much time."

Kiah shrugs. "The world. Myself. I don't know. I ran away to get out, start fresh, and heal from what happened. It was only supposed to be temporary. But now it's five years later, and I still haven't figured out what next..."

She sounds sincere, but how can I be sure?

I don't want to care.

The bitch betrayed me.

Still, I can't help myself from asking what happened.

Kiah gets up from the chair and slowly lifts her shirt to reveal the nasty scar running over her belly from hip to hip. I've noticed it before but never seen it in the full light of day.

The tissue is raised and slightly puckered, forming a ridge. In some places, it's smooth and shiny; in others, it's slightly indented or rough.

"Five years ago, I was at the height of my career. I only took high-profile cases and made a shit ton of money. Think James Bond but female. I whored my way around every city, living fast on temporary identities and perfect lies..."

"What changed?" I ask despite wanting to give her the silent treatment.

"I was careless one night. We didn't have a condom. Long story short, I got pregnant. At first, I was certain I'd get rid of the baby and carry on with my life. But the more I thought about it, the more I wanted to keep it, to start my own family. To finally have someone in my corner who would love me unconditionally."

I have many follow-up questions, but I don't interject.

"But, similar to your line of work, one cannot simply *get out*. Especially not if the father of the child is an illegal arms dealer. A married one at that. I was stupid. I should've just taken my baby and left. But I wanted him to know, to have the option of being part of the kid's life. Needless to say, he didn't take too kindly to the news."

My blood runs cold. *That bastard...*I can barely contain the fresh rage boiling inside me, my jaw clicking loudly. How dare anyone lay a hand on her, let alone try to rip her open like some animal?

"He cut you like that?" I ask, the words thick in my throat.

Her gaze is far away as she speaks, drifting. "No, his wife did. The crazy bitch sent a message from her husband's phone to meet at the docks to *make future plans*. And I was stupid enough to fall for it. Driven mad by years of infidelity that had nothing to do with me, I was just the scapegoat for her anger. She had four guards with her, and they just stood by as she gutted me like a fish and left me for dead right there, bleeding out on the concrete."

"Jesus." That's fucked up, even for me, and I've seen too many fucked up things in my life.

Despite wanting to stay mad at her, I can't. Not when she's being this honest.

"I almost didn't make it. Some stranger took pity on me and dropped me outside the hospital, on the sidewalk. They managed to save me, but it was touch-and-go there for a while. Queue the long and painful rehab years and skip to the part where I hid out on a remote island to figure out what to do next. Give or take a few years, and now we're here." She shrugs, finally meeting my eyes.

I want to say something, anything, but there are no words that would be useful. *Those fuckers.*

She saves me from an awkward silence by changing the topic, covering up her vulnerability as quickly as she flashed it.

"My turn, *Domenico.*" It feels strange to hear my full name on her lips.

"Do people even call you Nico in real life?" she asks, forcing her face to neutral as she so often does.

"Not really. Most call me by my full name. The rest call me Dom."

She cracks a faint smile that cuts through the tension of the moment. "So one day, you'll be Don Dom?"

"I never thought about that." I can't help but smile.

"Domenico is a beautiful name," she says almost absent-mindedly.

My only response is a grunt.

"But I'll stick to Nico if you don't mind."

I shrug, forcing myself to be nonchalant. "Whatever, doesn't mean I trust you now."

Kiah touches my cheek affectionately, her eyes softening with warmth. "I know. But let me earn it..."

And then she cuts me loose from my restraints—again.

Escape
Kiah

The silence stretches between us as Nico's gaze bores into me, a tempest of emotion raging behind his eyes. They remind me of the ocean during hurricane season—dark, turbulent, and hiding depths I can only imagine.

The weight of my betrayal hangs heavy in the air, an unspoken accusation. I resist the urge to look away, to shield myself from the intensity of his scrutiny.

I don't expect forgiveness for ratting him out. Hell, I'm not sure I deserve it. But I have to do something—and quickly. We don't have time for this.

"Come here," I call Nico over as I fish his collar key from my cleavage.

He doesn't budge, just narrows his eyes suspiciously. "You're not helping your case, woman."

"Just come here. I want to take it off," I say with a sigh. Jesus, he's infuriating.

Still hesitant, Nico leans in to let me unlock his collar.

As soon as I twist the key, it pops open with a satisfying click, and I carefully remove it, placing it on the counter between us.

Finally free, Nico stretches out his neck, touching his fingers to the space where the collar rested before. It looks almost strange now, so empty. I've gotten used to the collar; it suited him.

"Do you think I can also have a turn to ask some questions?" I ask, stepping back.

Nico's jaw clenches. "Why?"

"I'm going to ruin my life for a mob killer, I want to know what I'm dealing with."

He sighs, sinking into the armchair beside the bed. I don't know if that's a yes or a no, but I hope we've moved beyond keeping secrets.

Despite the clock running out, I fetch a couple of the beers from the fridge, reaching one out to him like we're sitting down to a quiet night in, not counting the hours until his death sentence.

Nico opens his beer with a loud crack, downing half of it in one go before speaking, "I am many things, Kiah, but I'm not a *mob killer*, as you call it."

My eyes widen in surprise. "You didn't kill your father?"

I never even considered the possibility. J. said it was an

open and shut case. She used her connections at the police to get the case file.

All signs pointed to Nico's guilt. Body in his car, a solid motive, no alibi, a missing murder weapon, and him fleeing the scene...what more proof did they need?

J. sent a copy of the case files to my phone last week, but I didn't see them until today when I finally turned the phone on again to make the call I shouldn't have made.

The photos of the crime scene were so brutal. Especially the close-up of Don Ricci with his face all busted. The report said he took quite a pummeling before finally being put out of his misery with a single bullet.

Those photos were the reason I didn't immediately regret my traitorous call. They validated my actions. Domenico Ricci was simply an evil man who needed to pay for his actions. I was just doing what was necessary to protect myself, protect my slice of paradise.

But paradise doesn't exist. But the more I thought about it, the more I realized I was just lying to myself. I didn't want to spend the rest of my life wondering *what if* my soul shriveled up and died.

Besides, it's not like suddenly taking the moral high road would erase my own list of sins, my own murders. I've done some fucked up things in my life...

The guilt sits heavy in my stomach now; I shouldn't have thrown Nico under the bus like that.

J. was surprised that the missing mobster had *suddenly*

just *appeared* on the island, but I spun some vague story about how I saw him on the beach one day, how he was staying somewhere else.

As soon as I put the phone down, a tinge of regret started tugging at my insides, a little thread that unraveled faster and faster the further I ran.

By the time I got to the lighthouse, my regret had grown unbearably heavy, threatening to strangle me, suffocate me.

I called J. back, trying to revoke my treachery. But it was too late, she'd already passed the message along to the Ricci's.

As my heart plummeted, I hung up without any further explanation and ran home, throwing myself into domestic activities while I racked my brain for a solution, a way out of this mess.

I wish I could go back and undo it all.

But what's done is done.

The only real question is, *what now?*

"I don't think I killed him," Nico answers, rubbing his temples, "I was going to. He would've deserved it too, but not like that..."

Taking a sip of my beer, I keep quiet, waiting for him to continue. I'm too restless to sit down, so I pace around the kitchen as he speaks.

Nico's shoulders slump as he begins, his voice hollow. "The last thing I remember, we were driving to some ware-house to pick up a package." His hand unconsciously rubs the back of his neck, tension evident in every movement. "The next moment, I woke up with a knock on my forehead, zero memories, and my father's dead body in my car."

He pauses, finishing his beer. "So, I bailed, just ran as fast as I could."

I stop for a second, my brow furrowing. "You know running makes you look guilty?"

A bitter laugh escapes his lips. "I know. But if I stayed, they would've shot me first and asked questions later." His jaw tightens, a muscle jumping beneath the skin. "You don't just kill the Don, no matter who you are."

I watch him closely, noting his hands clenching into fists at his sides. "And then you came here of all places?"

Nico nods, his posture softening slightly as a faraway look crosses his face. "I had good memories of this place." His fingers trace absent patterns on the arm of his chair. "My father once brought me to this very inn when I was younger. Some or other business trip."

A ghost of a smile touches his lips, gone as quickly as it appeared. "He bought me a peanut butter milkshake. Figured it was obscure enough, they wouldn't look for me here."

I take a deep breath, steeling myself for what I'm about to ask.

My heart races, but I keep my voice steady.

It's not relevant to our case, but I need to know.

"*Why* did you want to kill your father?"

Nico takes a long time to answer, and I almost give up on a response.

Then he slowly starts digging the broken pieces from his

treasure trove of trauma, his gaze far away, drifting in vastness like a castaway lost at sea.

My heart breaks into a million pieces as the broody-stranger-who-isn't-a-stranger-anymore tells me about his oppressive childhood, his fucked-up parents, about what they did to his wife, to Annika.

What the fuck is wrong with people?

It sounds unreal, like the plot of some movie on Netflix, but the way his face contorts in pain, like someone is ripping out his organs with their bare hands, makes it crystal clear that this is not fiction; this is his history.

"Nico..." I whisper when the last word has dissipated, his painful story stretching between us like an unbridgeable abyss.

Closing the distance between us, I reach out to the scar under his eye, gently tracing its path with my fingertips. He flinches at the contact but doesn't pull away.

"I'm so sorry, Nico," I whisper, seeking his distant gaze.

"Why? It's not your fault." His words are icy cold and hard, just like his face.

"Nobody deserves a childhood like that."

"That's where you're wrong. You don't know me. I deserved it. I deserve all of this."

I take his face in both my hands. "Look at me."

But he refuses to meet my eyes.

"Nico."

His blue eyes flash toward me, raging, intense.

"No, you don't. You don't deserve any of it."

He sighs, and I press my forehead against his, pulling him closer, into my arms. I wish I could erase his painful memories, stop them from ever happening.

How could any parent be so cruel?

This poor man, the things he's endured.

"I'm sorry," I repeat.

His gaze finally softens as he studies my face, reading the emotions I don't know how to voice.

Gently, I caress his cheek, keeping my eyes locked on his.

In this moment, I'm overly aware of his proximity, of his naked body, his warmth.

My body moves like it belongs to someone else, slipping an arm around his neck to pull us closer.

He doesn't resist, just lets me brush my lips against his like I've dreamt of so many times.

Oh god.

My breath catches as our lips meet for the first time. It's soft at first, almost hesitant, as if he's afraid I might break. But then something ignites between us, and the kiss deepens.

I feel the heat of his body as he grabs me closer, onto his lap, his hand resting on the small of my back.

There's an urgency in the way he kisses me, a desperation that matches the pounding of my heart. It's as if he's trying to erase all the pain of our pasts with this single act. And for a moment, I let myself believe he can.

The thought of losing him is fueling the intensity of the moment.

Our movements become more hurried, more intense as

the endless kiss picks up speed, enveloping my entire universe in Nico's scent, his taste.

Biting his bottom lip between my teeth, I finally pull away, my breath ragged and uneven—panting.

I lean my head against his chest, trying to catch my breath.

When he wraps his strong arms around me, I let him, closing my eyes to enjoy the intimate moment amidst the pending doom.

There is so much to say, but I say nothing at all.

Oh god, this won't end well.

But I no longer care.

Because for the first time in too long, maybe even forever, I feel *something*, something real. And I'm not letting anyone take that away from me—least of all myself.

"How long do we have?" Nico asks when we finally part.

"A couple of hours. Three tops. Nothing but clear skies today, sadly."

He goes quiet, calculating, before he speaks. "This airstrip can't handle the jet, so my brother will take the smaller plane. There will be six of them, max, excluding the pilots."

"Your shoulder will probably slow you down..."

"It's feeling a lot better. But you're right. We'll have to be smart."

"They don't know about my background. That's our one big advantage. We can draw them out, and I can surprise them."

"You don't have to do this for me," Nico says.

I run my fingers through his messy hair, rearranging it, "I know. But I want to."

Nico cocks his head to the side as he asks his usual, "Why?"

I smile, kissing his forehead. "Because...you may be an infuriating brat, but you're *my* brat."

ACTION

NICO

WHEN THEY KICK DOWN THE DOOR, SHAKING IT ON its hinges, I'm ready.

There is no fear, no anxiety, no hesitation—only a focused resolve.

This ends today, one way or another.

Just as we planned, Kiah hides in the closet, waiting, while I remain seemingly tied to the wooden chair. Hands behind my back, facing the door, they can't see that the ropes Kiah dragged from her secret room are not fully knotted at the back.

She even made me put on my clothes for this part, the ones I arrived in that first night. Freshly washed and ironed, the materials feel uncomfortable against my skin; foreign.

Almost as weird as the empty space around my neck. For

some reason, I miss the comforting grip of that collar. There was something grounding about its constant deadly threat.

But there is no time to ponder its loss for long.

As if almost on cue, five goons dressed in all black barge in with their weapons drawn. Correction: five goons *plus* my short-shit brother in one of his flamboyant blue suits.

"Well, well, if it isn't my cowardly brother. Hey, Dom," Ricardo says in his high-pitched voice as he waltzes in last, twisting his ring (my ring) like he owns the place. I knew he stole it. *Fucker.*

He walks right up to me, cocking his gun, as his entourage surrounds me like a rent-a-crowd. Some of them are my father's men, but there are some new faces too—Ricardo's men.

"Domenico," Stefano, my father's right hand, says with a curt bow of the head as the men encroach on my space. He doesn't look too pleased to be following orders from Ricardo.

I respectfully nod to Stefano before returning my attention to my brother.

"Took you long enough," I taunt, smirking at him.

Ricardo snarls, his cruel smile twisting his face as he cracks his knuckles. "Such a fool, Dom. You were never going to be king," he says simply, waving his gun around carelessly as he speaks.

"Do you really think you'll get away with it?" I ask.

Darkness flashes in his eyes. "Shut up, or I'll make you."

Until that moment, I wasn't 100% sure it was him, but

now I know without a doubt—this fucker killed our father and then framed me for it.

Stupid twat. He's always had more muscle than brains.

"Why did you do it? Did you want the throne that badly?"

"I'd stop talking if I were you, Dom. You're wanted *dead* or alive..."

"Then why not kill me right now?"

"Hmm, I thought about it. But it would be more fun to torture you slowly." He laughs, his voice screeching like nails on a chalkboard. Always our mother's favorite, no wonder he turned out such a vile cunt just like her.

"This isn't over," I threaten.

"Oh, but it is. Get him!" Ricardo orders and the others tighten the circle around me.

"Pity about that," I say calmly, "We could've used some *dolphins.*"

"What?" Confusion clouds my brother's face, but he doesn't have time to ponder the weird sentence choice.

When we planned our attack, Kiah did say *dolphins* was a dumb code word, and I'd *never work it into conversation naturally,* but fuck that, it worked.

Quick as lightning, Kiah throws open the cupboard door, my knife raised.

It's show time!

It's my cue and I jump to my feet, shrugging off the loose ropes, adrenaline surging through my veins.

The room explodes into a frenzy of shouts and gunshots.

"What the f—" Ricardo's curse is cut short as Kiah's fist connects with his jaw. The sickening crunch is music to my ears. *Atta girl.*

I duck under a wild swing from one of the goons, driving my elbow into his solar plexus. He doubles over, gasping.

There's no time to savor it, though.

"Domenico, you treacherous bastard!" One of Ricardo's men, Marco, I think, lunges at me with a knife.

I sidestep, grabbing his wrist and twisting.

The blade clatters to the floor.

I slam my forehead into his nose, feeling cartilage give way.

With his own blade, I slice his throat open, watching as it bleeds onto the washed wooden floor.

Through the chaos, I catch glimpses of Kiah. She faces two attackers simultaneously, her movements fluid and unstoppable. One asshole swings a baton, but she ducks under it effortlessly. As he overextends, she drives her palm up into his chin. His head snaps back, and he staggers.

Without missing a beat, Kiah pivots, using his body as a shield against the second man's wild punch. She grabs the asshole's arm, twisting it behind his back in a painful lock. A quick strike to the back of his knee sends him to the ground where she steps on his throat until his eyes roll over in the back of his head.

Watching her fight is the most mesmerizing thing, but now is not the time to get distracted.

Too late.

Before I can pull my gaze away, a meaty hand closes around my throat from behind.

I struggle, vision blurring as oxygen is cut off.

Then, a sickening crack and the pressure releases.

I gulp air desperately, turning to see Kiah standing over my attacker, her eyes blazing, newly acquired gun raised.

"Thanks," I gasp.

"Eyes on the fight, Nico," she says, already turning to face the next threat.

Forcing myself to focus, we work in tandem now, covering each other's blind spots.

I spin, barely avoiding a bullet that whistles past my ear.

Suddenly, a scream pierces the air.

My blood runs cold as I see Ricardo's chokehold on Kiah, a knife pressed to her ribs. A trickle of blood stains her shirt where it has already nicked her.

"Stop, or I'll end this bitch right now," the fucker snarls.

Something primal snaps inside me.

The world narrows to a pinpoint, everything tinged red.

Not Kiah.

With a roar that doesn't sound human, I launch myself at my brother.

My hands find skin, breaking, ripping.

I'm barely aware of my actions, only the feral need to destroy the asshole who dared harm the innkeeper, even if he's my brother—*especially* because he is.

"Don't. You. Ever. Touch. Her." Each word is punctuated by another vicious blow. I'm dimly aware of my brother's

M KAY NOIR

screams, of the warm blood on my hands. But none of that matters.

The mere thought of anything happening to Kiah, of losing her, tears through me, unleashing chaos in its wake.

"Nico! Stop!" Kiah's voice cuts through the haze. Her hand on my arm is gentle but firm. "You'll kill him."

"Let me!"

"Nico! No!" her voice is authoritative, commanding. It snaps me out of it.

"Nico..." she says, softer this time, as she tugs at my arm. "Remember the plan."

I blink, the red fog slowly clearing as I find my way back to her voice.

Ricardo's limp body drops to the floor, still alive, but barely.

Around us, the other attackers are sprawled on the floor, either dead or unconscious.

My brother laughs like a maniac, blood splattering from his missing teeth.

I pull him up by his ripped collar, "What's so funny?"

"This won't change shit. You'll just be the guy who killed two Dons," he spits, getting his dirty blood on my shoes.

"I don't think so. You're coming with me. So you can tell them what you did," I say with conviction.

"Oh? Doubtful. Why would I confess?"

I don't answer, just stand aside to let Kiah click the explosive collar that used to be mine around the battered asshole's neck.

666

"We have ways," she answers, kicking him in the gut for good measure before turning to me.

Kiah's wild eyes meet mine, a mix of concern and something else I can't quite name. "You okay?" she asks softly, wiping the blood from my cheek.

I nod, my hands shaking as the adrenaline begins to slow.

"You were amazing," I murmur.

She shrugs, but I catch a hint of pride in her eyes. "You didn't do so bad yourself, little brat. Good job."

The praise sinks into my skin, warming me from the inside, and I grin, letting some of the tension seep from my veins.

It's far from over, but phase one is complete.

Throwing caution to the wind, I reach for Kiah.

My hands cup her face gently, a stark contrast to the violence of moments ago.

I pull her close, my lips crashing against hers in a passionate, desperate kiss.

The world falls away, and there's only Kiah—the softness of her lips, the warmth of her body pressed against mine, the faint taste of blood and sweat.

It's messy and urgent, born from the chaos we've just survived and the realization of how close I came to losing her.

My fingers tangle in her hair as I deepen the kiss, leaving streaks of red highlights in the blonde.

But she doesn't stop me as I pour everything into the kiss —my gratitude, my admiration, the storm of emotions I can't put into words.

She responds with equal fervor, her hands gripping my sticky shirt, pulling me closer.

When we finally break apart, both breathless, our eyes meet, and I see my own tumultuous emotions mirrored in her gaze.

"I..." I start, but words fail me.

Kiah's lips quirk into a small smile. "I know," she says softly. "Me too. But first things first, you need to get out of here."

She chucks my duffle bag at me. There's nothing in there but money, but I suppose it will be useful for the next phase —the one where I steal the plane, force them to take me back to the city, and swoop in to clear my name.

It's everything I've wanted since I set foot on this island.

Then why does it no longer feel enough?

The realization hits me like a punch to the gut. The thought of leaving this island, leaving Kiah, feels wrong. Empty.

The innkeeper grabs my hand and starts heading out, but I pull her back.

"What is it? We need to hurry, we—"

"Kiah. Wait." My voice sounds strange, even to my own ears.

"There's no time; you have to go."

"No." The word comes out before I can stop it, surprising us both.

Her nose wrinkles as she looks at me with confusion. "What do you mean *no*?"

I take a deep breath, trying to organize the chaos in my mind. How do I explain this feeling? This need?

"I can't do it alone, Kiah; I don't want to."

She cocks her head to the side, "You don't need me, Nico."

But I do. God, I do. The thought of facing my old life, the accusations—it all seems insurmountable without her by my side. She's become my anchor, my compass in this storm.

"You're wrong. I do need you. With you by my side, I feel unstoppable. The mere thought of being away from you, even for an hour, grips my throat like a tightening noose."

I watch her face, searching for a sign, any sign, that she feels this too.

The innkeeper sighs, her eyes sad but smiling. "Nico..."

"No, Kiah. I'm not going without you." I've never been more certain of anything in my life. Whatever comes next, I need her with me. "Come with me. Please."

IMPULSIVE
KIAH

ADRENALINE SURGES THROUGH ME AS I SURVEY THE carnage.

Incapacitated attackers lie scattered among the wreckage of my once-peaceful sanctuary. Around them, broken furniture and shattered art bear witness to the violence that just unfolded.

Yet, I don't feel anger or loss.

I feel...*alive*. Powerful. Like my old myself.

And the rush is intoxicating!

I had almost forgotten how natural combat felt, how exhilarating it was to push my body to its limits, to wield it as a finely-tuned weapon.

My limbs had moved with a fluid grace that surprised even me, muscle memory kicking in as if no time had passed.

For the first time in ages, my muscles had sung with purpose beyond mere exercise. That visceral dance of survival —it was what they'd been yearning for all along.

But that wasn't the only reason my heart rate shot through the roof.

Fighting alongside Nico was...unexpected, incredible.

He held his own—I'm quite proud.

Who knew we'd make such a formidable team?

For once, everything is going according to plan...

Well, *almost* everything.

I stare at Nico, my brain short-circuiting. "What do you *mean* you're not going without me?"

This wasn't part of the plan.

Get the guys, get the plane, get Nico home. Return to my solitary existence. The end.

That's what my brain has locked onto, eyes on the mission. But Nico...

He takes my hands in his.

"Exactly that," he says, his voice low and earnest. His eyes, stormy as ever, hold a softness that wasn't there before, "Come with me, Kiah."

The simple request shatters my carefully constructed world, leaving me uncertain.

"Nico...I can't. The guests will be here next week. I have a whole life here. Responsibilities. I can't just pack up and go. I —" There are a million reasons why not.

"Then, I'll stay."

I shake my head. "That's ridiculous. You can't stay. They'll come for you, one way or another. You need to take your rightful place on the throne. Wrong the rights. Get justice."

"Then come with me," he insists, returning to his original request.

"I can't just *go*."

Panic pushes up in my throat as the introduction of a choice throws my perfectly planned future into chaos.

"You said it yourself, you miss the excitement, the city. You can't hide out here forever."

I lower my gaze. "You're using my words against me."

"Were they true?"

Nico tilts my chin toward him, forcing my eyes back to his. "Were they true?" he repeats, and I nod slowly. For all his faults, I know Nico values the truth above all else.

"Yes. But I can't just leave..."

"Why not?"

"Because it's absolutely crazy? How do you think this next part is going to go? Anything could happen..."

As many times as I try to run every imaginable scenario through my head, I can't cover all the possibilities—there are too many variables.

My heart screams yes, my body does too, but my rational mind knows it's the most ridiculous idea I've ever heard.

How can I just leave everything I've built and run after some young brat with a death wish?

At the same time, how can I let him leave? After everything we've been through...

"I don't know what's going to happen next," Nico admits, "But I know that I will protect you with my life, come what may. That has to count for something?"

I want to roll my eyes at the cliche, but I've literally just watched him do that exact thing, nearly killing his own brother with his bare hands for threatening me. Nobody has ever cared that much. In this whole miserable existence of mine, nobody has ever wanted to *protect* me.

But is it enough?

What if his Stockholm Syndrome wears off as soon as we enter civilization again? What if he gets bored?

"You have a whole world waiting for you back home, Nico. You're either ending up in the ground, in prison, or on a throne—where does that leave me?"

"On the throne, right beside me, as my Queen," he says without missing a beat, smiling like a fool.

"I'm no Queen, Nico. I'm an unwanted child turned assassin nearly twice your age." I sigh, shaking my shirt to try and force a breeze onto my sweaty skin.

"Despite your terrible math, you're perfect. You know you're only 16 years older than me, right?"

I laugh, shaking my head. "I've literally nearly stabbed you to death, held you hostage for weeks, caged your cock against your will, put a bomb collar around your neck...and you think I'm *perfect*?"

Nico nods, that stupid grin not going anywhere. "Yup. Perfect...for me."

"But why?"

Nico takes a deep breath, figuring out the words in his head first before finally laying his soul bare, "Because you see me, Kiah, the real me, and you still care. You could've just let me die, but you nursed me back to health when I didn't deserve it. You trained me and punished me and calmed the chaos in my mind in a way that made the world feel okay for the first time in a very, very long time. Through it all, you somehow manage to channel all my fucked-up energy into something useful—all while looking like a fucking Goddess. A bad-ass Goddess who fights like the Devil." He takes a step closer, the space between us disappearing, "I don't want you by my side, Kiah, I *need* you by my side. I meant what I said— I can't do this without you."

I stare at him in silence, letting the words sink in.

Surely, confessions like these are meant for other people only, not for me.

I'm hardly the girl next door—quite the opposite. I usually get death threats, not declarations of affection.

Yet, despite my instinctive skepticism, I know he's being sincere.

Nico's eyes do not lie, and right now, his entire expression is that of a star-crossed lover serenading his sweetheart.

That look of utter devotion on his face is my entire undoing. It's a primal need, etched onto his forehead like a permanent marker—undeniable, raw. Nobody has ever looked at me like that, like I'm their entire world.

That look is the only thing I trust in this fucked up world.

It's stirred a part of me that's been dormant too long, a part of me I've been too stubborn to admit I miss.

"Oh, Nico," I finally say, unable to find the words to adequately respond to a confession so grand.

Words have never been my strong suit.

But I don't need words to know how much his declaration has affected me, how badly I want Nico to be mine.

If he leaves, I know I'll lose this version of me—who I am when I'm with him—forever.

"Come with me and rule by my side, Kiah. We'll be unstoppable." He takes my hands and brings them to his lips in a soft kiss.

He's certain enough for both of us, and it's hard to doubt.

"You drive a hard bargain, kid." I smile.

"It's because I'm not taking no for an answer."

"What about all my stuff, the inn?" I feel my resolve slowly melt under Nico's imploring gaze.

"My family has more money than anyone knows what to do with. Sorting out those things will simply be a matter of logistics. We can ship whatever you want over. I'm sure we can find someone to run the inn if you want to keep it, or sell it, if you don't."

"It will be cold in the city," I say, quickly running out of rational answers.

Nico smiles, like actually smiles, not just that sneer of his.

"Don't you miss the cold? It's weird being so sweaty over Christmas."

"Nico...I'm broken." My final excuse...the sharpest arrow in my chest, the one that's really holding me back.

"So am I. But you didn't mind, why should I mind?"

I look around nervously. "We're running out of time; you have to go."

"I know," Nico's voice is urgent, almost pleading, "So can you stop making dumb excuses and come with me already? If you hate it, you can come back to the island, I promise. But don't make me go alone now, please, Kiah."

His vulnerability, so raw and unexpected, pierces through my defenses.

I know that I'm about to do something incredibly stupid.

"Fine," I concede, my voice barely above a whisper. "But only because I don't want you to die."

"I'll take it," Nico declares victoriously, pulling me in for a kiss that doesn't end until I forget how to breathe, panting in his arms, my knees weak like I'm a teenager with a crush.

As we part, I murmur against his chest, "This is a terrible idea."

"Oh yes," Nico agrees, lips brushing my hair. "The absolute worst."

Our laughter, tinged with exhilaration and a hint of fear, fills the room.

"Give me a second," I say, darting to grab my emergency bag—always packed, always ready. Old habits die hard.

I navigate the carnage in my kitchen as if it's an everyday

occurrence, shoving a jacket, phone charger, and Kindle into the bag.

At the door, I pause for a final look at the space that's been my sanctuary for five years. The finality of the moment isn't lost on me. But I don't feel sad about it. I'm excited.

Nico is already waiting outside, his bloodied and barely conscious brother draped over his shoulder like a sack of potatoes.

"After you, my Queen."

I smile, taking his hand. "I could get used to that."

As I lead the way to the airstrip, I don't spare a single look back at the life I thought I wanted but was, in actual fact, just an excuse to hide.

Fuck it. I'm too young to retire.

Besides, as Nico said, I could just come back if I wanted to.

I don't want another lifetime of what-ifs and regrets.

What I want is a home, a real home.

And it's not here.

Nico's woken up a slumbering part of me, a part I can't lull back to sleep again. It wants excitement, risk, danger. It craves the high stakes, the smell of expensive cars, the sheer opulence of hedonism.

What is there to stay for anyway?

This island may be peaceful, but it's been suffocating my growth. Trapped in amber, I've been stuck in between worlds, not daring to breathe. Nico's given me a reason to exhale again.

I guess this is what they mean when they say home is not a place but a person.

And it turns out my person is the future Don Ricci—of all people.

Fucking hell, Kiah, only you.

As we mission over the sandy paths, I realize I'm not running away. For the first time in years, I'm running *towards* something.

And I'm ready.

EPILOGUE

CHRISTMAS

KIAH

THE PAST SIX WEEKS HAVE BEEN A CRAZY BLUR. How did we get to Christmas already?

For the first time in five years, I don't have to worry about getting up early to start getting everything ready to feed a bunch of people I don't give a single fuck about.

In fact, there is nothing on my to-do list today—nothing except the newly-crowned Don Ricci, who's currently lying passed out beside me in our giant four-poster bed.

Just like when we were on the island, there's not a stitch of clothing on his perfectly sculpted body.

Every day, as soon as he locks that bedroom door behind him, the clothes are discarded into a messy pile on the floor. I've given up on trying to make him fold it neatly—one battle at a time.

Getting back to the city had been easier than I thought it

would be. The pilot was very cooperative once he understood his lack of a choice in the matter.

Nobody stopped us when we drove into the family compound. The staff and the guards were actually happy to have Nico back. Turns out nobody liked his asshole brother.

That little fucker Ricardo squealed like the pig he was as soon as I waved that explosive collar's key in front of his face. One of the easiest confessions I've ever gotten.

With J.'s help, Ricardo was swiftly charged with the murder of his father, and Nico's name was cleared.

If it were up to my little brat, he would've sunk his brother to the bottom of the ocean, but I couldn't let him. It was the only family he had left...

So, we had the little shit Ricardo locked up. In his own private, cushy cell, but a cell, nonetheless. He'd be safe there. And out of our way. That's the only part I cared about. That and not adding more trauma to Nico's long list of fucked up family memories.

Dealing with the inn was even easier. True to his word, as always, Nico had sent for my stuff when the clean-up crew returned to deal with the carnage we left behind. I don't know what happened to the others we left alive, but only Stefano was allowed to return.

I also don't know if they found someone to take over the inn in time or if they canceled the bookings for this season, but I don't particularly care. When I'm ready, I'll put it back on the market. It won't be hard to sell, not in that location.

For now, I want to revel in the fact that we're free to make new Christmas traditions this year.

I told Nico to clear the schedule for the next three days for our special scene.

He's trying so hard to be good. It makes me immensely proud. Even when he fucks up, he always owns up to it; tries to be better—in work and in our relationship.

He's had a shitload of Don stuff to do since we got back, catching up on everything and making some changes. I can tell how stressful it has been. The doubt never leaves his mind.

But I know he'll be the best Don.

I patiently tell him so every night as he falls asleep with his face buried in my chest, usually suckling on a nipple.

Some days, we don't even hook up or do anything traditionally sexual—we just hold each other, naked body pressed to naked body, soothing my skin with his.

Things feel different now, more real.

Our dynamic couldn't continue as it did on the island—I made Nico sign a contract properly outlining his limits and needs.

I don't want to force his submission; I want him to surrender it freely like the gift it is. It's a beautiful exchange. One where he holds all the power. With a single word, he could stop it all if he wanted to.

As much as he insisted he didn't need a safe word, I would not budge on this one. Our exploration of his submissive side could only continue under more consensual conditions. He was no longer my prisoner, after all.

As for me, I haven't just gone from one holiday to the next. I finally have purpose, something to do. Nico made me the head of his security. I get to recruit the new guards, train them, set up new systems and protocols to keep us safe.

The family has so many businesses; keeping everyone alive is a full-time job, one that I'm happy to do. Give me another couple of months, and the Ricci army will be impenetrable.

It feels amazing to finally receive the respect and recognition I deserve. Nico has full confidence in me, and it's not a job I take lightly.

It does mean that we've spent most of our days apart. As painful as that is, I actually don't mind. Because when Nico closes that bedroom door behind him at night and takes off his clothes, I know I have his full attention, he's mine...and he's *needy*.

Especially on the days I don't give him permission to come. He's so cute when he gets frustrated and desperate.

Sometimes, the brat defies me, but it's nothing a little well-meaning punishment can't correct.

I've sent him off to work many a morning with his ass burning bright red beneath his fancy suit.

But nobody knows except us; it's our little secret.

Nico grunts in his sleep, pulling me back to the present.

Snoring lightly against my breasts, legs draped over mine like he's afraid I'll leave while he's asleep, he stirs only slightly when I run my fingers over his semi-erect dick.

Sometimes his dick gets caged—when he's been really

bad, or when we go away for a trip—but he's currently out on good behavior.

It doesn't take much to tease his cock to full hardness; it responds to my most gentle touch like a ravenous animal.

When I reach over and flick my tongue over the sensitive cock head, Nico jerks awake.

"Good morning, baby." I smile, kissing his sleepy face.

His only response is a snoozy grumble.

"It's Christmas morning. You know what that means, don't you?" I whisper in his ear, and Nico's eyes pop open fully.

I chuckle, slowly palming his cock. "I thought that would get your attention."

"That, and your hand on my dick," he says, looking down at his hardness.

"Is that a complaint?" I kiss his lips, and he nips at my bottom lip, biting it briefly before letting go.

"Uh-uh. No complaints."

"You ready for today, Don Ricci?"

Nico pulls me into his arms, "I've thought of nothing else all week."

"Sames." Since we first discussed this scene, planning out the details and setting up the boundaries of play, my imagination has run wild, lust pooling between my thighs at the mere thought of what we have planned for Christmas this year.

"The staff are gone?" Nico asks, fighting through the grogginess.

"Yup, everyone's been sent home except the gate guards. It's just you and I, baby."

"Hmm, I like it when you call me baby," he says, nestling his head between my breasts and inhaling deeply.

"Well, *baby*, if you can detangle yourself for a second, I need to use the bathroom."

Despite grunting his objection, Nico rolls over and lets me go.

When I return, he's wide awake, watching my every move as I dig through my bedside drawer.

"I got you something, by the way," I tell him as I hold up the simple, flat black box topped with a gold bow.

"You said no presents!" he whines.

"Well, you've bought me so many damn things since I got here. It's the least I could do."

"Kiah," he protests, getting up.

"Nico, you literally set up an entire art studio for me. And a library. *And* a weightlifting gym."

"I'd set up Dexter's laboratory for you if you wanted it," he replies, wrapping his arms around me from behind. His unmistakable erection presses into my back, and I smile.

"Dexter the scientist or Dexter the serial killer?"

He kisses the side of my neck. "Either."

"Look at you being all romantic."

"I have my moments. But I'd venture a bet and say it's all your fault."

The naked Don spins me around and kisses me deeply, lifting me onto my tippy toes.

"Well, I can't say I'm sorry."

"So what's in the box?" he asks, taking it from my hand and shaking it.

"Well, you said you missed the old one. I figured it didn't have to be a life-or-death situation...Open it."

My heart swells to overflow as I study Nico's face, the sheer wonder in his eyes, as he opens the box.

"Is it what I think it is?" he asks despite the obvious contents.

With a wide smile, I nod. "It's yours—if you want it."

I take the elegant metal collar from the box. It's made of solid steel with a metal hoop in the front, not dissimilar to the one he wore on the island (except for the lack of explosives). I had it custom-made to his exact measurements, engraved with three words on the inside—*Property of Kiah*.

"I want it," he says with conviction.

"Will you be mine, Don Ricci?" I ask, and Nico nods enthusiastically.

"I've always been yours...*Goddess*."

"Mine," I repeat, leading him to the mirror so he can watch as I snap the cold metal around his throat. It fits snuggly without hindering his breathing.

Nico inhales sharply, eyes glued to the mirror. "It's perfect," he whispers, his cock twitching in response too.

And my god, if he doesn't look like the most beautiful thing I've seen in my whole damn life...

Lust instantly flares up inside my belly, tugging at my organs with need. I don't even try to contain it.

Kissing him wildly, I push the newly-collared Nico out the door without bothering to get dressed.

Like it's a giant playground, we have the house all to ourselves, and there is no need for clothes; we can roam freely through the old mansion.

We damn near fall down the stairs as I lure him to the lounge, unable to keep my hands (or my mouth) from his body.

"Stay," I gasp into Nico's ear, leaving him by the massive Christmas tree, nearly double his size. We decorated it ourselves, this time with minimal tinsel frustration on the brat's side.

Nico whines when my warmth leaves him but stays put as he's told.

He eyes me with confusion when I return with a pair of handcuffs in one hand and a tube of blood-red paint in the other.

"Call it foreplay for later," I reply to his arched brow, pressing his naked body into the hard bristles of the tree behind him.

"I'm yours," Nico consents, letting me manhandle him.

It takes some maneuvering, but I manage to get my way, cuffing the naked Don around the tree with his hands behind his back.

I know the branches are probably scratching him; I'm counting on it.

He's not going anywhere, though—these are real handcuffs, not play-play ones.

And like old times, I dangle the key before him, taunting him.

Nico's still dumbstruck when I squeeze some (non-toxic) paint into my hand, rubbing them together before painting his chest in broad, messy letters: *MINE*.

"One day, I'll carve you up nicely, properly," I vow, imagining the letters in blood on his chest, permanent, forever.

"Please," Nico moans, cock virtually leaking at the mere thought. Only a psycho like Domenico Ricci would get turned on by blood, but he's my little psycho.

Grabbing his cock with both hands, it's impossible not to stain his flesh with red as I move him where I need him.

Nico gasps, his whole body tensing as he watches me use his piercings to get off, guiding his tip to my clit.

A loud moan rips from my lips without reservation as I rub the little metal bulbs against my sensitive skin, teasing my clit into climax in virtually no time.

I'm so wet already, it doesn't take much until I'm shivering and shaking, my toes curling as the pleasure burns through my skin like wildfire.

Crashing my body into Nico's, smearing the paint, I hold onto him as I ride the wave of my orgasm until I can trust my knees again.

"This is the best Christmas ever," Nico gasps between rapid breaths, kissing my temple.

Devilishly, I smile up at him, "Oh, but the fun has just begun, baby-boy..."

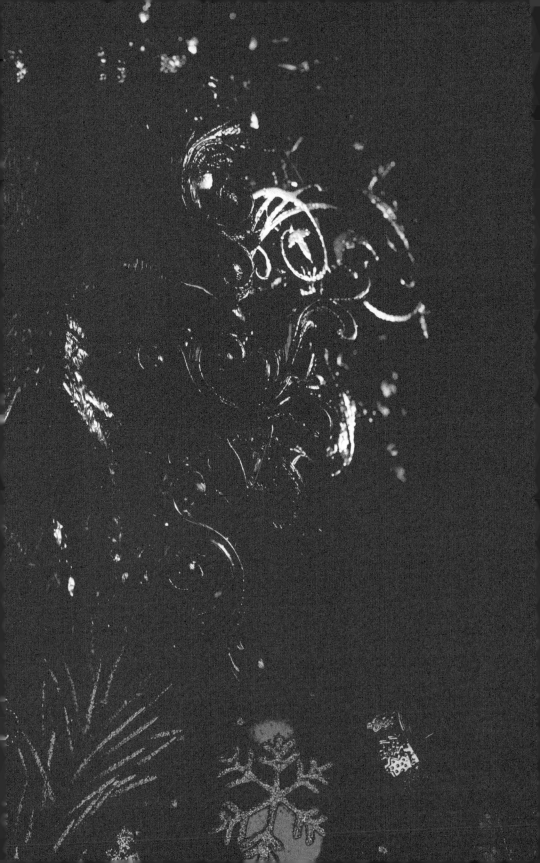

HUNTED

NICO

PERCHED ON A HILL, THE RICCI COMPOUND stretches out into a dark forest that seems to swallow the night itself.

The dense canopy of ancient oaks and towering pines creates an impenetrable wall of shadows, their gnarled branches reaching out like grasping fingers.

The untamed wilderness, spanning nearly a thousand acres, is a stark contrast to the estate's manicured lawns and pristine gardens.

As darkness falls, the forest comes alive with unseen creatures, their calls echoing through the trees in an eerie symphony.

Moonlight struggles to penetrate the thick foliage, creating pockets of silver amidst the inky blackness.

The air here is different—heavy with the scent of damp

earth and decaying leaves, carrying whispers of secrets (and bodies) long buried.

At least it's not snowing. It's cold enough for my fingers to go numb, but this year, Christmas is *mild,* according to the weather reports.

I've always been scared of the wilderness in our backyard. Ever since my mother tied me to a tree in the forest overnight as punishment for being a naughty six-year-old.

It was an accident. I didn't mean to break the cup; I just wanted to surprise her with tea in bed. But she didn't care about my intentions, just about the mess I made.

Grow up, Domenico, my mother said as she dragged me outside by my ear while my father wordlessly watched, *Stop crying. Boys don't cry.*

I begged and pleaded for mercy as she wrapped the rough rope around me, but she just walked away, leaving me tied in the darkness with the howling cayotes as my only companion.

It was the longest night of my life as I waited for the monsters to come for me. I was so certain I was going to die a painful death that moonless night.

The monsters never came, but it didn't matter.

When my mother finally sent Ronny to untie me the following day, I was shivering cold, terrified, and unable to form sentences without stuttering, my little red shorts soiled and clinging to me uncomfortably.

Monsters are not real, my mother insisted, dismissing my fears.

But tonight, the monster *is* real, not just a memory or a dream.

Faster, Domenico, faster!

I'm running as fast as I can.

But it's not fast enough.

Around me, the forest is a blur of black shadows pierced by only a slither of moonlight and the menacing beam of the flashlight in pursuit.

The night air is cool, but I'm burning up inside. Fear and exertion set my nerves on fire as branches whip across my face.

My chest is heaving, sweat mingling with the blood from a dozen minor cuts on my hands and face as the foliage resists my passage.

As my feet pound the uneven ground, my boots keep slipping on damp leaves and loose stones.

They're going to catch you, hurry.

Not unlike my recurring nightmare, I keep running despite knowing for sure that there's no escape.

The farther I run, the more desperate I get, the oxygen supply to my brain diminishing, along with my ability to feel anything but fear.

My lungs burn. I can't get enough air.

But I can't stop.

They're behind me.

Getting closer.

The flashlight beam suddenly illuminates the bushes to the side, and I dart in the opposite direction.

Behind me, I hear twigs snapping. Leaves rustling. Or is it just the pounding of my own heart, thundering in my ears?

I dodge around a massive oak, nearly losing my footing. My hand scrapes rough bark as I push off, propelling myself forward.

I can't see where I'm going, but I push at full speed.

A root catches my toe.

I stumble, arms windmilling.

For a heart-stopping moment, I'm sure I'll fall.

But I regain my balance, pushing myself to run faster.

They'll catch me if I fall. I can't afford to fall.

Thorny vines tear at my legs as I go. I ignore the pain, focusing only on the ground ahead, searching for obstacles in the dim light.

My breath comes in ragged gasps. Spots dance at the edges of my vision.

How long have I been running?

I've lost all sense of time.

A twig snaps behind me, closer than before, definitely real.

Terror surges through me, lending new strength to my tired muscles. But it's not enough.

My heart nearly stops as the flashlight's full glow falls on my body, blinding me.

The dark figure I've been running from suddenly looms before me, backlit and ominous.

I put my hands out, trying to fight them, but I can't see anything.

In an instant, they're upon me, overpowering me with a single knee to the nuts that takes what little breath I have right out of my lungs, doubling me over in pain.

Their flashlight drops to the floor, casting ominous shadows around me.

Grabbing me by my hair so roughly I swear the roots nearly pull loose, I'm forced upright again, pushed up against a tree.

My breath comes in short, desperate gasps that mist in the moonlight as I beg, my voice weak, "No, n-no...please, no."

Panic floods my system as the masked Hunter wraps their hands around my neck, pressing their body into mine, trapping me. Nothing, not even their eyes, is visible behind the all-black tactical mask.

Terror grips me, unlike anything I've ever known.

My mind races, searching frantically for a way out but finding none.

I feel utterly helpless, I feel...*afraid*.

Adrenaline surges through my body as I fight for a breath.

Every muscle is tense, trembling.

My senses are hyper-aware—the scent of pine and sweat, the cool night air on my skin, the sound of our ragged breathing.

Their hands move, releasing my throat, and I gulp at the air, desperately trying to fill my aching lungs.

But my relief is short-lived.

The sudden introduction of a cold blade against my

throat contradicts the warmth of the body pressing against mine.

"Hunt over, little rabbit. You've been caught," the whisper tickles my skin as every hair in my body rises to attention, an involuntary shiver slinking down my spine.

"Don't you dare move," the Hunter threatens, digging the knife deeper into my skin, deep enough to draw blood.

There is no more *fight* or *flight*—all that's left in my mind is *fawn*. I'm entirely at the mercy of my captor, and the thought is exhilarating and terrifying at the same time.

They yank my hair, hard, and I want to scream, but no sound escapes.

I remain entirely frozen as the Hunter wraps my body in rope they pull from a black backpack.

It's too tight, but I'm powerless to resist as they tie me up and force me to my knees.

As my heart races on, I can't think of anything but how hard my cock is. This shouldn't turn me on, this is fucked up. But I can't help it.

With a dirty boot right between the shoulder blades, the Hunter bends me over, pushing my face into the dirt. The gravel digs into my knees uncomfortably, adding to the mounting list of aches and pains blossoming over my skin.

It isn't real, I know it isn't, but it feels so fucking real.

With no weapons, no light...I am completely vulnerable, at the mercy of the merciless Hunter.

"P-please," I beg, digging my fingers into the dirt just to

hold onto something. I want to fight, but my limbs betray me —heavy and useless.

The Hunter bends down over me, tugging at my collar as they lick the back of my neck, biting down on my earlobe until I'm convinced they might bite it right off.

"I wouldn't recommend struggling. It will only hurt more," they whisper in my ear before smacking my ass loudly.

I gasp, digging my fingers deeper into the dirt as they rip my pants down without bothering to undo the belt. The cold air stings my exposed skin, but it's nothing compared to the discomfort of the gloved finger that suddenly pushes inside my ass, violating me without warning.

Oh god, it's so cold!

I cry out in surprise as the sudden pain mixes with the humiliation that burns through me.

"You're going to like this, whether you want to or not," they say, forcing a second finger inside, stretching me painfully.

When a third fills me to the brim, I can't help but buck my hips into their hand. I don't want to; I don't want *this*—but I do.

What's wrong with you, Domenico?

"Look how needy you are. You like this," the Hunter chuckles, reaching a gloved hand to my cock to run their fingers over my hardness. It feels foreign, plastic, so strange to have that latex hand on me.

I grunt despite myself, hating how aroused I am. My cock is virtually leaking into my assailant's hand.

When they suddenly pull their fingers out of my ass, I gasp loudly, feeling empty.

It's over.

But it's not over; it has just begun.

When I feel the cold, hard tip pressing against my entrance, I swear my heart stops for a second.

Oh, Dio mio!

"Have you had enough yet?" the Hunter asks.

I know it's a check-in, a rehearsed one, but it sounds like a threat, keeping me in the scene while throwing me a lifeline should I need it.

"No, n-no, please..." I whine. Despite everything, I don't want to stop.

"Hmm...Now be a good boy and let me in," the masked Hunter whispers as she shoves her cock into me—roughly, in one go, smashing into my ass like she's trying to rip me apart.

The pain is immense, immediate, muddled with discomfort, as she fucks me into the dirt, gloved hand palming my leaking cock until I'm delirious, circuits overloaded.

Again and again, she thrusts into me until I'm crying, unable to stop myself, shaking in the dirt.

All thought dissipates like mist until nothing but sensation remains, nothing but pain and pleasure. My mind is blank as I give into the moment, fully surrendering myself to the Hunter.

With a whining sound that sounds more animalistic than human, I spill my cum over the gloved hand as the Hunter fucks me into oblivion.

It's the most intense orgasm of my life that rips through my body, adrenaline adding to the rush as the world blurs away.

When there's not a single drop of liquid left in my body, I go limp. I want to collapse into the cold dirt, to let it swallow me whole, but the masked Hunter holds me up, refusing to release me, as she continues to milk my overstimulated cock.

Crying, I mutter words of nonsense, losing my mind as the discomfort burns through my mind.

Too much.

I can't.

No more.

Digging my fingers deeper into the earth as if it can find me strength, I find the single word I've stored in my mind.

"D-dolphins!" I mutter my safe word, and Kiah stops immediately, dropping my cock without hesitation.

Slowly, careful not to hurt me, she pulls her pegging dildo out.

Like a discarded rag doll, I collapse onto the forest floor, crying, my body ablaze with overstimulation.

Kiah removes her mask and sits on the cold ground beside me. Carefully, she unties the ropes and pulls my body against hers, onto her lap, with those strong arms of hers.

I can't stop crying, but for once, I don't feel ashamed about it. Kiah just tugs me closer, enveloping me with her warmth, her essence, as the flood of emotions takes over my entire being.

"It's all over now," the innkeeper says, her voice soft and

soothing as she strokes my hair. "You did so well, baby. So well," she praises, and I curl up in a little ball, still unable to open my eyes. Such simple words, yet I've come to crave them from her more than oxygen.

My Queen kisses my forehead, pressing her head to mine. "I've got you, Nico. You're safe."

I'm a dirty, broken, freezing mess, but none of that matters. All that matters is that Kiah is here, by my side, holding me.

She doesn't make me feel like I'm weird for wanting what I want; she lets me explore my desires, my curiosities, my needs. Within bounds, of course. But without shame.

The structure of our dynamic calms my mind. I know what's expected of me, how to be. I don't have to calculate a response. She's trained me in what she needs. I can just let go and be.

No matter how imperfect, I want her to have every part of me.

Everything I do is in service to her, the great Goddess who nursed me back to life when she could've left me for dead, who killed for me, sacrificed for me, took a gamble on me.

When Kiah's around, I don't feel lost. I'm not just darting my eyes around the room, trying to identify threats. Her scent, her warmth, it grounds me in the present.

She is as much mine as I am hers, and I will break anyone's neck if they even look at her funny.

But she doesn't need me to fight her battles. I've never met anyone Kiah can't take out. Maybe that's why I feel safe, in a literal sense too. I know she'd kick anyone's ass if they tried to fuck with me.

It's just us now.

Us against the world.

And I'm the luckiest fucking Don alive.

Somewhere, a coyote calls into the night, but I'm no longer scared.

I am *home*.

MINE
KIAH

I ONCE ASKED NICO WHERE THE DARKNESS IN HIS mind came from. He said it had always been there, that he'd spent his life trying to hide it, pretending to be normal.

I don't want him to pretend with me. I want to own all parts of him, even the dark parts, the ugly parts, the broken ones.

If I've learned anything about Nico, it's that sometimes he just needs a bit of punishment to feel okay. To rebalance. To soothe the chaos.

Who can blame him? Not when you hear the fucked-up tales of his past. Whenever I think this is it, it can't get any worse, he shares another twisted memory.

I wish his mother were alive just so I could kill her all over again.

That bitch.

It's her fault he has those nightmares; her fault the forest haunts him.

But nobody gets to fuck with his mind but me—never again. I have it in writing, in our contract, in black and white.

The contract also includes a long list of things my darling brat is curious about. Some were more of a surprise to me than others.

When Nico first approached me with the idea of a consensual non-consent scene, I was hesitant.

CNC is not something I've ever considered, and what little I've seen of it online looked abusive as fuck.

But the more we spoke about it and researched safe practices, the more I realized it could be cathartic for both of us.

Not only that, I found myself aroused by the idea, lying awake at night wondering what it would feel like to *hunt* Nico, to claim him in a way he would never allow anyone else to do.

But I didn't agree to the scene so I could overpower or hurt him. I did it because his mind craves it; because I want him to have peace from those restless nightmares that haunt his dreams.

It takes a lot of trust to do something like this with a partner, and the fact that Nico trusted me with it spoke volumes.

Letting himself be this vulnerable couldn't have been easy for a man who grew up in a world where toxic masculinity was celebrated.

But he did it; he let me chase him through the forest like a piece of game—just like we rehearsed.

I was worried about the weather, that it would be too cold, that we should wait until another time, but we got lucky with the exceptionally warm temperatures.

Well, *relatively* warm. It was still only 50 degrees out—killing Nico's dream of having me chase him naked through the forest.

Perhaps in summer, we can try a rematch...

Jesus fucking Christ. What a rush.

It felt good to take my power back, to be the hunter instead of the hunted.

As soon as that mask went on, I became a different person, a faceless hunter with a simple mission—to take what's mine.

It was exhilarating!

I haven't been that in touch with my primal instincts in a long time.

Even now, as I hold Nico's bruised body against mine on the cold ground, my heart is still pumping pure adrenaline.

"You okay, baby?" I ask, kissing the tears from Nico's dirty cheek.

"Yeah..." he manages his first word after nearly 10 minutes of silence. I was prepared to sit here for hours if he needed it, even if we both froze.

"Do you want space?"

He shakes his head; no.

I stroke his knotted hair. "Do you think you can walk?"

"I think so." Nico's voice is small and uncertain.

I help him up, leading us back to the mansion, away from the forest's shadows.

The walk to the house is silent and introspective but not uncomfortable. I'm super relieved that everyone has been sent home, that we have the place to ourselves. It would be hard to explain the state of us right now.

The harsh interior lights momentarily blind us as we enter. While my eyes adjust, Nico keeps his closed, clinging to my arm as I guide him upstairs to the bathroom.

I sit him on the toilet seat, assessing his injuries while the bath fills. He looks battle-worn, but it's mostly dirt and shallow cuts—nothing serious.

Holding his hand, I help Nico into the steaming water. He winces but doesn't say anything.

I start with his neck, washing him methodically with a red cloth, my hands tracing his skin from top to bottom.

It's good for me to care for him; it helps with the angsty feelings clawing at my insides.

I didn't expect the scene to affect me this emotionally.

But now, with the adrenaline emptied from my veins, anxiety is seeping in, tugging at my chest.

It's only hitting me now. I'd been so focused on Nico that I didn't make space for my own emotional comedown.

The scene was way rougher, more emotionally taxing than I thought it would be.

I've hunted down many assholes in a forest, but never an asshole I actually cared about.

As fun as the chase was, staying in character was so hard

when Nico cried and pleaded for me to stop. Even though I knew he had his safe word, it hurt me to see him like that.

Now, in the aftermath of it all, I am desperate to reconnect. I need to know that we're okay, that we're still us.

Nico remains perfectly still in the bath, lost in his own world, as I wash his body and hair, much like when he first arrived on the island, lost in delirium.

But it's different now.

He's different.

We both are.

I thought I was done with the dangerous life, but the dangerous life clearly wasn't done with me.

As soon as I had a taste of that old me, the excitement, the adrenaline, the addiction took over like an inkblot spreading in water, consuming me until I was all black.

I can't go back to being the docile innkeeper; I don't want to—I am finally *awake* again.

The Don murmurs softly as I reach the cloth down to wash his cock, trailing it over his balls too.

Instantly, his dick perks up, awakening from its slumber.

This man! Every time I touch him, he gets so hard.

I love it.

His mouth tells no lies, and neither does his body.

There is no confusion or mixed signals about his desperate desire for me.

"Do you want to come, baby?" I whisper, gently squeezing his cock, and Nico's eyes snap open.

He bites his lip and nods. "Please."

I can't help but laugh. "Dumb question. The answer is always yes, isn't it?"

Nico smiles, slowly coming back to me. "Can't help it. It's your fault."

"Yeah, yeah, such a smooth talker, hey, Don Ricci."

As I speak, I continue stroking his cock with the washcloth, stroking until his murmurs turn to little moans.

"I'm close," Nico gasps soon enough, his body tensing beneath me.

"Do it," I whisper as I milk him to completion, until his cum floats in the dirty bath around him.

He probably needs a shower too, but that's a later problem.

For now, I let my darling boy enjoy the moment before helping him out of the bath, drying him off, and applying ointment to his cuts.

Still butt naked, Nico collapses on the bed as I shimmy out of my hunter gear, dropping it onto the floor as unceremoniously as the young Don usually does. I'm filthy from the dirt and the lube, but I spare no thought to the clean sheets as I climb into bed beside him.

Nico wanted to do the scene without lube, but I told him *no fucking way.* I didn't want to really hurt him.

The bed feels so good after the roughness of the forest.

Nico opens his arms, and I snuggle up with my head on his chest, letting him hold me as tightly as a cuddly toy.

"This was the best Christmas ever," he says, fingers

absentmindedly playing over my nipples, hardening them to little pebbles.

"It's not over yet." I grin, reaching up for a slow, lingering kiss.

Nico presses his forehead against mine when we part. "Thank you, Kiah," he whispers, his voice low, sincere. "Just thank you."

"For what?"

"For everything. For letting me explore my fantasies and my fears, for letting me cry and break, for picking me up again and putting me back together."

"Careful now, Don Ricci, someone is turning into a poet."

Nico kisses my nose. "I'm serious, Kiah. You stabbing me with that fucking shard of porcelain was the best thing that's ever happened to me."

I smile. "Tad dramatic, but I'll take it."

He tilts my chin toward him, trapping my gaze in his. The haunted look has been replaced by something new—something I haven't seen before.

Nico grins. "I love you, Kiah McClane...Even if your surname is dumb."

My heartbeat escalates into a new rhythm as the words repeat in my head, in my heart.

Nobody has ever said those words to me and meant it.

I don't know why I am crying, but I am.

Laughing through the tears, I take his hand in mine, holding tightly, "I love you too, Nico."

My heart races as the loaded words hang in the air between us.

It's Nico who breaches the space between us, meeting my lips in a tender kiss filled with passion, filled with promise.

My fingers thread through his damp hair, pulling him closer as I breathe in his familiar scent, committing this moment to memory.

A soft sigh escapes me as we finally part, and I find myself smiling, unable to contain the warmth spreading inside me.

"I love you," I whisper again, savoring the freedom to say those words.

Nico responds by capturing my lips again, this kiss deeper and more urgent.

When I finally open my eyes again, I find Nico looking at me with such intensity, such adoration, that it nearly over-whelms me.

I'll never get tired of seeing that look.

He doesn't just want me. He *needs* me.

Oh god, I love being desired.

There is no greater feeling than having a powerful man worship every inch of your body, your existence.

I thought those years had passed.

But not in Nico's eyes.

In his gorgeous blue eyes, I am a Goddess.

And I never want to be anything less again.

For the first time in my entire life, I know what it means to be someone's world.

I never had family, long-term partners, friends...

But now I have all those things and more.

All wrapped in the body of a tattooed brat.

A tattooed brat who happens to be Don of the Ricci family.

THE Ricci family.

Yeah, I know. They're cunts.

But not Nico.

Nico is different.

Nico is *mine*.

And together, we're unstoppable.

Basking in the moment, I just hold Nico as we lie there, each drifting in our own thoughts.

"What's your beef with my surname?" I ask eventually.

"I think Kiah *Ricci* sounds better," Nico answers nonchalantly, a hint of mischief on his lips.

I burst out laughing, hitting him with a pillow. "Slow down, cowboy...I'm not taking anyone's surname."

Nico winks at me. "I know, I know. I'm just teasing."

"Isn't teasing supposed to be my job?" I cock my head to the side, getting lost in that stormy gaze I want to spend the rest of my life exploring.

"Yes, Ma'am," Nico says with a big grin.

"Don't you start with that," I threaten with mock sternness, "You know how that gets me worked up."

"Hmm. Yes...*Ma'am*."

Quick as lightning, I jump on top of him, pinning him between my thighs. "You little brat!"

"You mean, *your* brat?" My dark and broody boy tries to

pull his best innocent-looking face, failing so miserably that we both burst out laughing.

Straddling him, I shake my head as his unmistakable erection presses against my skin.

I tug at his collar, pulling his face toward me, "*My* brat. All mine. And don't you ever forget it, Don Ricci." I lean down to kiss the small clover-shaped birthmark on his collarbone. "Merry Christmas, baby."

About M Kay Noir

M Kay Noir is a queer romance author and journalist obsessed with moments of desire. Most of her stories are kinky, queer, polyamorous undertakings with neurotic characters who are often their own worst enemy. If you expect any regard for traditional gender roles or power dynamics, you will be disappointed.

Kay has been penning steamy moments for more than 15 years now, from fanfics to ghostwriting and now finally her own stories. Her day job also involves a lot of writing, albeit a different kind—mostly sustainability things. When she's not writing (or reading), she enjoys making her husband look at yet another sunset and listening to live music.

Creating safe spaces to explore desire is very important to Kay. Kinky and kind, that's the vibe. But don't be fooled into thinking the spice level is weak. Quite the opposite...

♪

Made in United States
Orlando, FL
03 November 2024

53412776R00436